FEAR AND COURAGE

Fourteen Writers Explore Sime~Gen

Sime~Gen Books by Jacqueline Lichtenberg and Jean Lorrah

House of Zeor, by Jacqueline Lichtenberg (#1)
Unto Zeor, Forever, by Jacqueline Lichtenberg (#2)
First Channel, by Jean Lorrah and Jacqueline Lichtenberg (#3)
Mahogany Trinrose, by Jacqueline Lichtenberg (#4)
Channel's Destiny, by Jean Lorrah and Jacqueline Lichtenberg (#5)
RenSime, by Jacqueline Lichtenberg (#6)
Ambrov Keon, by Jean Lorrah (#7)
Zelerod's Doom, by Jacqueline Lichtenberg and Jean Lorrah (#8)
Personal Recognizance, by Jacqueline Lichtenberg (#9)
The Story Untold and Other Stories, by Jean Lorrah (#10)
To Kiss or to Kill, by Jean Lorrah (#11)
The Farris Channel, by Jacqueline Lichtenberg (#12)

Other Jacqueline Lichtenberg Books from Wildside Press

Molt Brother
City of a Million Legends
Science Is Magic Spelled Backwards and other stories, Jacqueline Lichtenberg Collected Book One
Through The Moon Gate and other stories of vampirism, Jacqueline Lichtenberg Collected Book Two
Dreamspy
Those of My Blood

The Savage Empire Series by Jean Lorrah

Savage Empire
Dragon Lord of the Savage Empire
Captives of the Savage Empire

FEAR AND COURAGE

Fourteen Writers Explore Sime~Gen

EDITED BY

Zoe Farris and Karen L. MacLeod

WILDSIDE PRESS

My work on this book is dedicated to my family: those of the present and past, as well as the "family of my heart" — dear ones who are not biologically related, but are my family of choice.

In addition, I also dedicate this effort to Jacqueline Lichtenberg, Jean Lorrah and Sharon Jarvis, who taught me the craft of editing, and continue to support me in it.

—Karen L. MacLeod

I'd like to dedicate my work on this book to Eliza Leahy ambrov Halwyn, my Companion in the true Sime~Gen sense, who has been there for me during this project. I also dedicate this book to all those fans of Sime~Gen who have kept this universe alive during its long hiatus until the republishing of the old books and release of the new novels.

— Zoe Farris

Sime~Gen, Book 13

Cover Art by Eliza Leahy

Published by Wildside Press LLC.
www.wildsidebooks.com

ACKNOWLEDGMENTS

A big THANK YOU goes to Jacqueline Lichtenberg for creating the Sime~Gen Universe and encouraging her fans to play there. Jacqueline, along with co-author, Jean Lorrah, have been supportive and encouraging to all their fans over the years as we explore what life is like in the Sime~Gen Universe through art, role-play chats, and writing. I would also like to thank Karen MacLeod, who, along with Jacqueline, have guided and supported me during this project. To each of the authors in this book a big thanks for your contribution and willingness to tweak and review your stories. Without you this book would not exist. Last, but not least, I would like to thank Wildside for publishing this book.

—Zoe Farris

I'm in agreement in thanking these same people, as well as including Zoe, herself, and Eliza Leahy, whose "behind the scenes" assistance in this manuscript was invaluable, when software issues gave us strange characters and other oddities we just couldn't eliminate from various earlier incarnations of the manuscript before the submission draft was made.

We probably drove Eliza crazy with the difficulties we couldn't seem to get a handle on. Her unfailing patience, finding out what was incompatible, and offering solutions, kept Zoe and I on course, helping get this book into your hands in a timely manner.

—Karen L. MacLeod

CONTENTS

INTRODUCTION

Welcome to the first Sime~Gen Anthology written by the fans. This Anthology is a compilation of stories and poetry written by people who have been influenced by the published works of Jacqueline Lichtenberg and Jean Lorrah, in such a powerful way that they felt compelled to explore this universe in their own writing.

Since the early years of Sime~Gen there have been fanzines where people shared stories, poetry, art, and jokes; joining in on discussions about the lives, loves and fears of the people who inhabit this world. Of the three major fanzines one, A Companion in Zeor, edited by Karen MacLeod, has survived to the digital age. Some of these stories can be found in A Companion in Zeor on the Sime~Gen domain.

So what is Sime~Gen?

For those of you who are reading this book without previous experience of this expansive universe here is a brief introduction:

Sime~Gen is a series of novels written by Jacqueline Lichtenberg and Jean Lorrah. It is set in a future where humans have mutated into two subspecies. Simes, who go through a brief but dramatic change at puberty and Gens, whose change, while just as dramatic, is invisible to the naked eye.

The outward sign of the Simes' change is development of tentacles on their forearms, four strong and flexible "handling" tentacles and two smaller tentacles just for selyn transfer, called "laterals." Gens produce life energy called "selyn" which Simes require once a month to live. Unfortunately, the result in obtaining this energy is usually the death of the Gen.

This physical transformation happens just prior to puberty. There is no way of knowing, before that, if a person will be Sime or Gen.

At the chronological beginning of the published novels by Jacqueline, and Jean, a second mutation of Sime emerges. These "channels" are able to keep Simes from Killing Gens, thus saving mankind from self-annihilation. The stories that you find here, and the published books by Jacqueline Lichtenberg and Jean Lorrah, explore the role of these new Simes, and the Gens who live side by side with them as humankind struggles to become one again.

If these stories interest you, you will find more information about the culture in the novels listed above. As is common for fan fiction, much of the deeper explanation is excluded as the history and background is already known by the readers. For a more in-depth look at what Sime~Gen is, see

http://www.simegen.com/sgfandom/welcommittee/Exciting.html

The world of Sime~Gen fan fiction is special because the creator and author, Jacqueline Lichtenberg, has been supportive, encouraging and inclusive in the writings of her fans. Jacqueline's co-author in Sime~Gen, Jean Lorrah, wrote several fan stories for the Ambrov Zeor fanzine, and was also well known in Star Trek fan fiction, before publishing her first Sime~Gen novel, First Channel.

We hope that you enjoy reading these pieces as each author explores the varied aspects of living in a world where being a Sime or Gen could mean death, depending on where you lived, and how the human race might survive this dramatic split. These stories are about the human condition: love, hate, fear, courage, strength, loss and cooperation. All are put to life's test in the Sime~Gen Universe.

What is the A Companion in Zeor Fanzine
http://www.simegen.com/sgfandom/rimonslibrary/cz/

A fanzine is a non-professional publication of stories and artwork related to a theme. The word itself was a merger of fan and magazine, and dates back several decades.

'A Companion in Zeor' came into being in 1978, as the second of several publications tied to the Sime~Gen Universe. With the release of *House of Zeor* (1974), "The Channel's Exemption" (a short story found in 'Galileo Magazine,' July 1977), *Unto Zeor, Forever* (1978) and other titles, the fans of the series became prolific writers, meeting almost professional writing standards, drafting their stories, and re-writing them several times for both 'Ambrov Zeor,' the first Sime~Gen fanzine, and 'A Companion in Zeor' which we abbreviate as CZ. At one point the two zines alternated release dates so there would always be something new between professional novels. In addition to poems and stories you will also see some of the fans' artwork on the 'A Companion in Zeor' website.

A Companion in Zeor was originally produced by mimeograph machine, typewriter and stencils, with the mimeo relegated to Karen's parents' garage in Southern New Jersey, USA. Production took place in the heat of summer, when the ink ran profusely, or in the dead of winter, when at times, the ink was totally frozen. Later, we were able to utilize thermal stencils for illustrations; the rare affordability of a copy shop, or college housed offset machines also became available, courtesy of friend Jay Schiff, who had connections with an office supply store. The occasional use of offset and copying facilities improved the quality of the zine. A tribute to Jay appears in issue #22 (2005-2006) as his participation was quite vital in the early years.

Later, Karen moved the mimeograph to her apartment, replacing it with a photocopier. Correction fluid, carbon paper, white-out, glue stick, scissors and a heavy duty stapler were always at hand to create the print issues, often with the "help" of several cats.

When Sime~Gen fandom moved to the Internet, it was a whole new learning curve for Karen both in computer and HTML website building skills. Because of editing the fanzine, Karen gained skills and confidence to turn her abilities into a career. Her work on 'A Companion in Zeor' online was discovered by an e-publisher who hired Karen to edit for them based on her fanzine work. Other publishers also did the same.

The pieces in this book have now become e-book and electronic files. 'A Companion in Zeor' has come quite far in thirty-six years, and we hope to continue on this journey.

FOREWORD

JACQUELINE LICHTENBERG

When I was in seventh grade, my father bought a typewriter and taught me to touch type in 2 weeks. Then he insisted I practice every day.

Since the artwork in the science fiction magazines had annoyed me because it was inaccurate, I practiced by writing a letter to the editor lambasting the artists for not reading the stories. I was in seventh grade—what did I know of the business and trade of illustration? They published my letter with my snailmail address (it was a different era), and science fiction fans apparently agreed with me. I got dozens of letters inviting me to join "fandom." I joined the National Fantasy Fan Federation, the N3F.

Today, people don't understand that "fandom" was a web of social networks of organizations with constitutions, dues, by-laws, and internal publications, organizations of adults. Today people think "fan" means fanatic, childish, or not sane. Times change.

My first lessons in professional writing craft came to me via the N3F and a professional writer Alma Hill, who taught the N3F Writer's Workshop. So I have endeavored to teach the fans of Sime~Gen some of the tricks of the trade she taught me.

The stories in this compilation are written by fans of Sime~Gen. They are fans in the old school sense, people who delve deep and become expert in a fictional universe's quirks, then share their own creative variations on that universe using original characters they invent.

These stories were written by fans who then tediously re-wrote to more professional standards. Some have sold fiction or non-fiction professionally now.

These writers are "amateur" in the same way Olympic Team members are "amateur." Their skills are often greater than the skills of those who make a living at the craft of fiction.

FOREWORD

JEAN LORRAH

When I read a book or watch a film or a TV show, of course I expect to enjoy it while I am reading or watching. However, some works give me more than that—an added value in that they provide something to think about after consuming them the first time. They may spark conversations with others who have experienced them, and if that happens it is virtually certain that I will want to experience them again. A work that affects me that way gives me double or triple the value of a work that ends when I have seen the last scene or read the last page, for I have the added enjoyment of re-experiencing that work and discussing it with other people.

All of us who read or watch films or television regularly probably have this experience with a fair percentage of the works we consume—perhaps as much as half of them as we learn what kind of work and which authors, producers, or directors are most likely to produce the desired response. If the same works produce that effect in many people, they become classics. If the number of their consumers is smaller, but loyal and persistent, they are called cult classics.

But for some people there is another potential layer of added value: a work may inspire me so much that I cannot help but create something in that universe. I go beyond re-experiencing or discussing, and become a fan.

Fans create in many ways. Some produce traditional artwork. Some costume. Some make videos or write songs (called filksongs when the genre is science fiction). But the largest number of fans write stories that allow them to share adventures in the universe and often with the characters they have come to know and love.

This is not a new phenomenon! It is as old as storytelling, and one of the greatest sources of fan fiction—though nobody calls it that—is the work of the ancient poet Homer. Literally hundreds of writers through the ages have not been satisfied with only two works, *The Iliad* and *The*

Odyssey, in that fabulous universe, and have felt compelled to add their own. Aeschylus, Euripides, and Sophocles created plays about Homer's characters and events in classic Greek times. Vergil and Ovid followed with their own epics in ancient Rome. Boccaccio and Chaucer are only the best-known of the numerous Medieval poets who wrote in Homer's universe, as did Shakespeare. Modern books, plays, and films are too numerous to mention.

The same thing happened with the story of King Arthur and the Knights of the Round Table, first created by Geoffrey of Monmouth in his *Historia Regum Britanniae (History of the Kings of Britain).* From *Morte d'Arthur* through *Idylls of the King, Camelot,* and *The Mists of Avalon,* fanfic all, though none dare call the name.

We make no claim that Sime~Gen belongs in the company of these undisputed masterpieces. We can, though, demonstrate that it stands alongside Sherlock Holmes, *Lord of the Rings, Star Trek,* Harry Potter, and numerous other universes that have inspired the creation of fan fiction by a substantial number of their audience.

For me, and for others so inclined, the discovery of a universe so compelling that it practically forces me to create within it is an event that occurs only three or four times in a lifetime. Only *Star Trek, Blake's Seven, Alien Nation,* and Sime~Gen have so inspired me—and I have had the great good fortune of being admitted as a professional writer into two of the four.

Yes, professional writers write fanfic. What's good enough for Shakespeare or Tennyson is good enough for the rest of us! And fan writers often write at a professional level—some of them simply are not interested in writing other than in the universes they love. So don't be surprised at the quality of fiction you find in this volume.

But if nothing else, these stories should reassure you that the Sime~Gen universe offers readers all the levels of satisfaction: a rousing good story for those who never read anything more than once, books worth rereading, books worth discussing, and a universe that inspires those so inclined to create within it. This volume is the proof: we have inspired our readers to become more than just consumers. They have become fans.

MOONLIGHT SONATA

MARY LOU MENDUM

PRELUDE

"I'm ready, Daddy. Come and tuck me in!"

Tallin, First Companion in Dar, smiled at the imperious summons. "What, not already?" he called, pretending dismay. "No, you can't be in bed. I'll have to come and check."

He "tiptoed" towards his son's bedroom, making sure that each footstep was clearly audible, and was rewarded by a giggle and a muffled scrambling noise. However, by the time he poked his head through the door, Califf was on the bed and halfway under the covers, bouncing with excitement as he pointed at the clock.

"The big hand isn't straight up," Califf announced with the delight of a six-year-old who has trapped a parent. "Now you have to tell me a story."

"Oh, dear." Tallin made a show of inspecting the clock. "I do believe you're right." He sat down on the bed next to the child. "Well, then, what sort of story shall I tell you?"

"Tell me a 'venture story, with night raids, and bandits, and narrow escapes!"

"All of that? Well, let's see." Tallin considered how best to balance the demands of his audience, and of his audience's mother, who didn't appreciate having to deal with childish nightmares when she was in Need.

The thought of Nilba gave him the required inspiration. "Suppose I tell you about how I met your mother?"

Califf looked at his father suspiciously. "Don't want a mushy story."

"Well, I think there's enough adventure in the story, even for you. However, there are some mushy parts. I'll tell you what. If it gets too mushy, you can stop me. All right?"

The six-year-old considered the offer for a moment, then nodded, and settled back on his pillow to listen. "All right."

Tallin smiled, and smoothed the child's silky hair back from his face. "How I met your mother. Let's see, I was about fourteen natal years at the time, but still a child. Your Grandmother Japora, the locksmith, had been dead for almost two years. I was living in Sommerin with a pair of bandits who found my skill at opening locks very useful."

"Bandits!" Childish eyes opened with delight.

"Well, burglars, anyway. But Gloron and Kintha weren't always very good at choosing which locks I should open, and so money was tight. That meant hard times for everyone; and especially for your Daddy…"

ADAGIO SOSTENUTO

"Empty! Whadya mean, boy, the safe was empty?"

Gloron's face was saturnine at best. Now, taut with Need-tension and red with anger and an excess of porstan, it was something to give small children nightmares. He glared at Tallin, tentacles knotting.

"There were papers and stuff, but no gold or jewels."

Tallin ducked, but Gloron's fist found his ear anyway. With the hard-won knowledge of experience, he rolled with the blow, yelping loudly in hopes that his mentor would consider him sufficiently chastised. Sometimes, the tactic allowed him to escape a serious beating.

"Oh, leave the boy alone, Gloron," Kintha whined. "There's other Gens in the Pen; something'll come up before the taxes are due. 'Sides, he's noisy when you hit him, and I got a headache already."

Gloron growled, swearing under his breath, but did not threaten to hit Tallin again. "Outa my sight, boy," he ordered. "Don't come back until tomorrow. We'll see if you can do better, then."

Tallin was not surprised at being suddenly assigned complete responsibility for the fiasco, despite the fact that his part of the affair had gone flawlessly. If the safe had contained suitable valuables, he knew that Gloron would have taken all of the credit—and the proceeds—and for himself.

He started obediently for the door, but paused before he quite reached it. As often happened when the two Simes were in Need, regular meals had dwindled to occasional snacks. Gloron and Kintha didn't mind fasting, but Tallin had grown two inches since midsummer, and he was always hungry. The colder weather, as fall set in, was making it worse. The scrap of stale bread which he had been given the night before had long since been digested, and an all-too-familiar gnawing chasm in his stomach demanded to be filled. With the courage of desperation, he summoned his best imitation of an innocent child, and begged, "Might I have a bit of supper to take with me, please?"

He realized, immediately, that he had gone too far. Nothing enraged Gloron and Kintha faster than hearing him speak with the courtesy and educated accents his mother had taught him.

"Supper?" Kintha screeched in outrage. "We're scrapin' for Pen fees, and the boy thinks we got money ta feed him? After he messed up the heist?"

"Get out on the street, where we shoulda left you," Gloron demanded, throwing a scrap of firewood in his young apprentice's direction. Fortunately for the boy, his mentor had consumed enough porstan to affect coordination, and the projectile missed. As Tallin ducked through the door and scurried for the stairs, he heard, "And don't think you're gettin' any breakfast, either!"

INTERMEZZO

"They were mean bandits, to make you go without supper, Daddy," Califf said. "Were you very hungry?"

"Yes, I was," Tallin admitted, with the resignation gained over ten years of being teased for his Gen appetite.

"So what did you do, when they wouldn't give you any food?"

"I tried to find another way to get some, of course," his father answered. He paused a moment, remembering, until Califf's impatient wiggle brought him back to the present.

"Excuse me. I was telling you about the day Gloron and Kintha threw me out without supper…"

ALLEGRETTO

Being on the street was nothing new to Tallin. Since his mother's death, his memories of the safe and happy home of his early childhood had faded until they seemed like a dream. He could barely remember what it was like to live without worrying about his next meal. Still, it had been a long time since he had gone without food for over a day, and there had been less of him to be hungry back then.

I'm growing so fast, surely I'll go through changeover soon. Then I won't mind when there isn't food, any more than Gloron and Kintha do.

He refused to consider what would happen to his appetite if he failed to become Sime, on the grounds that in that unhappy event, he would be unlikely to live long enough for it to be an issue.

However, if he was still a growing child at the moment, with the embarrassingly large appetite that implied, he was also a resourceful boy.

Over time he had developed some alternative methods to supplement the meager offerings provided by Gloron and Kintha.

He had enough of his mother's pride left to want to earn his keep, so he settled into a suitable corner near the produce market and pulled out the silver flute she had given him shortly before her death. Putting it to his lips, he blew gently into the holes, coaxing an old melody out of the instrument. He didn't have the flare of a professional musician, yet, but he was good enough to earn the occasional coin from those who enjoyed encouraging youthful talent.

Unfortunately, the weather had turned cold and windy with the unpredictability of autumn, and the heavy clouds above threatened rain to come. The crowd was thinning rapidly, and the remaining customers were hurrying to complete their errands and reach shelter before the storm broke. They had no interest in dallying to listen to music. An adult musician might have caught their attention by manipulating the ambient, but Tallin's childish nager was far too weak.

And when I'm grown up at last, I'll set up as a locksmith, and I won't have to attract an audience in the market. It seemed a bit unfair that the ability would not be his while he still required it.

When the first raindrops began to fall, he put the flute carefully away and tried begging instead. He knew he looked ragged and forlorn, in his outgrown clothes, but he was also as large as most of the adults in the market. Without the extra appeal of a small child, all Tallin earned was a few cuffs for his impertinence.

As he made his way through the produce market, he edged close to some of the busier stalls, hoping to snatch something edible while the grocers were occupied with paying customers. He was too large and ragged to be a good shoplifter, though, and he had never really learned the tricks of that trade. A gaunt gang of full-time street children was also working the market, and the merchants were keeping watch on their goods whenever they zlinned hunger. The urchins were getting an occasional success, but Tallin was simply too conspicuous.

Just as he was beginning to despair, Tallin saw an apple fall from a crate that a dripping farmer was hastily loading into his wagon. With the speed of a pouncing cat, he ran after it as it bounced across the cobblestones. He let out a small cry of triumph as his hand grasped the lusciously red (if badly bruised and somewhat dirty) fruit.

He raised it to his lips to take a bite, and only then noticed that the street gang had surrounded him. The largest of them was a good foot shorter than him, but there were over a dozen of them, and they were all carrying sticks or rocks.

Their leader, a red-haired girl of about ten, was watching the apple in his hand in a very proprietary fashion. "This is our turf," she announced, hefting her improvised club, "an' all the pickins here belong to us. We don't like no compe-tition."

Her followers looked more than a little impressed by her vocabulary, and not impressed at all by Tallin's larger size. Or maybe they were too hungry to care that they might get hurt.

Tallin knew, with a sick fear, that while he would hurt many of them if it came to a fight, he could very easily end up dead. Under the circumstances, the wise move was to get away immediately. Mourning the necessity, he threw the apple as hard as he could. The leader grunted and doubled over as it hit her in the stomach, and when it bounced and rolled temptingly along the ground, several of the smaller children broke ranks to scramble after it.

Taking advantage of their momentary distraction, Tallin sprinted through the break in the circle and dashed down the nearest cross street. At their leader's panted command, a few of the older urchins chased him, but his longer legs allowed him to gain on them. He dodged right in front of a wagon to cross the street, and gained a bit of distance as his pursuers were forced to wait and cross behind it. Encouraged, he dodged down an alley, climbed onto a parked wagon and from there onto the roof of a building. He lay panting on the shingles as the urchins pounded into the alley after him and began to search.

Tallin was lucky: the children were too small to climb onto the roof from the wagon, and they failed to consider his greater height. After a minute or two, they gave up and headed back for the produce market.

Tallin went limp with relief, hugging the wet roof as his racing heartbeat gradually slowed to something near normal. When he recovered enough to feel the cold rain pounding on his already saturated clothing, he made his way carefully to the other side of the building. He found a place where a length of fence joined the wall, and started to lower himself down onto it.

He was cold and his fingers were stiff. It was perhaps not surprising when he lost his grip, missed the fence, and landed face down in a reeking pile of stable droppings.

INTERMEZZO

"You fell into a manure pile?" Califf giggled loudly. "Yuck!"

"I warned you there were mushy parts in this story," Tallin pointed out, with the full dignity becoming a Companion. "And those stable droppings were very mushy indeed. As well as smelly. But I've never been able to really regret that fall, because while I was washing the worst of the mess off in the water pouring off of the roof, I saw and heard something that changed my life forever. Not that I guessed it at the time."

"What did you see, Daddy?"

"Nothing particularly unusual, on the face of it. The building with the mushy manure pile was an inn. While I was washing, the inn's cook came out of the kitchen door to accept a crate of fruit from a farmer. I was a bit worried that they'd chase me off before I was done, but instead, their attention was caught by a group of riders going down the street."

"Were they bandits, like Gloron and Kintha?"

Tallin hoped that his son's mania for bandits was a passing phase. "No," he explained with a storyteller's prerogative to control the plot, "they were a team of Dar guards heading back home after a job. I envied them — they would soon be warm and dry, and even the horses and Gens were obviously well fed. The cook and the farmer looked at them and spat in the mud. The farmer muttered something about what he'd do if the 'perverts' should ever try to buy his produce. I remembered that I'd heard similar comments from other people. And then I knew where I was going to get some food."

"You decided to ask Dar if you could come to dinner?"

"Well, not exactly," Tallin admitted.

PRESTO

Like most good heists that Tallin had heard about, the basic idea was simple. If Dar could feed its livestock so well, and if people didn't like to sell them food, then they must grow their own. This, in turn, implied a stored supply locked away somewhere on the grounds, and there were very few locks which were more than a passing inconvenience to the son of Japora the locksmith. The thought cheered him immensely. When the rain slacked off, then stopped entirely, it seemed like an omen of good luck.

Unfortunately, like many plans, what was simple in theory, proved more difficult than anticipated in practice. When Tallin followed the team of guards to the Householding's main gate, he was dismayed to discover that there was an alert gatekeeper on watch, and that the gates were barred from the inside after the riders entered. Neither impediment seemed amenable to his lock picks. The high stone wall which surrounded the enclave was unclimbable due to the shards of glass embedded along the top.

He decided he required some perspective on the problem. After some exploration, he found a way up onto the roof of a building across the street. As the wind gusted, breaking up the clouds, he settled down to observe the situation more closely, shivering in his damp clothes.

By the time the sun had set, he had eliminated a frontal attack as impossible. However, the sight of the gardens and orchards beyond the main buildings only firmed his belief that there was food for the taking, if he only could get to it. His eyes lovingly traced the neat borders of the plots, and the well cared for road that wound between them…

…and out of sight through the woodlot. Tallin inspected the road again with a growing excitement that made his stomach growl loudly. He was no farmer, but he could see no reason that even perverts should so carefully maintain a road if it wasn't used regularly. That meant that the road must end up somewhere important, and the eyeway was not far beyond.

Which, in turn, implied the possibility of another entrance onto the Householding grounds—one that might not be guarded with live gate-keepers. Carefully, Tallin climbed down from his perch and started making his way through the outskirts of Sommerin, following the stone wall.

As the full moon rose, the houses gave way to fields, and the wall gave way to impenetrable thickets of blackberries, their razor-sharp thorns a deadly danger to any Sime who might attempt to break in. Tallin had no laterals to injure, but he was not quite desperate enough to brave the blackberries when there was still a possibility of finding a back gate.

He almost gave up many times before he found it: a discrete and un-labeled road winding toward the eyeway, just wide enough for a wagon. There was a gate across it as it left Dar's grounds, secured with a heavy chain and a padlock. Tallin stopped and listened, but there was no sound beside his own heartbeat, and no speck of light to imply that anyone was present. What he could see of the road in the moonlight showed no fresh footprints; human or horse.

Satisfied that he was alone, he made his way over to the gate and checked the padlock. It was slightly stiff from what Tallin assumed was a combination of infrequent use and damp weather, but in the end, it yielded to his efforts. He slipped through the gate, closed it behind himself, and wrapped the chain back around it so that any roving sentry who failed to make a close inspection would assume it was still locked. Then, stomach growling, he started down the road.

It was slow going, in the dark under the trees, and he stepped in more than one puddle, but eventually he found himself looking at Household-ing Dar from the opposite perspective of his earlier scouting session. The buildings were dark shapes with lighted squares denoting windows. There were occasional flashes of light as people moved around the com-pound, lighting their way with lanterns, but Tallin wasn't particularly concerned. His child's nager should not be zlinnable at this distance. The fields he had come so far to plunder were ahead of him, and the closest one held tall stalks of late corn, the plump ears silhouetted against the sky.

Tallin's knees were weak with hunger, and he was clumsy with cold, but he didn't care. He had just enough presence of mind to step a full two rows into the field, so that he would be hidden, before he tore the first ear off the stalk, ripped the leaves off, and filled his mouth with the largest bite he could manage.

It was feed corn, being dried on the stalks for winter silage. There was no sweetness left to the kernels, and they were tough and half dried, but they were the best thing Tallin could remember eating in years. He forgot all his hard-learned caution, and bolted down the rest of the ear as fast as he could swallow. When he had gnawed the last edible bit from the cob, he dropped it and reached for a new ear.

"Corn tastes much better when it's cooked, you know."

Tallin whirled. The light, childlike voice came from the road, not six feet away from his hiding spot. He peered through the stalks and made out the form of a girl—no, a woman, he corrected himself as he saw her tentacles. He rejected a half-formed idea of making a run for it. Instead, he drew himself up with what dignity he could, stepped out of the corn-field, and replied in his most educated tones.

"It didn't seem practical to stop and build a fire."

She chuckled, and then inspected him more closely. Tallin squirmed, aware of just how disreputable he appeared in his ragged, outgrown clothes, stained with mud and still smelling of manure despite his cold shower.

"You have had a time of it, haven't you?" she said, with more sympathy than Tallin had dared to hope. He began to wonder if he could talk his way out of anything more than a token punishment for his theft. Under the circumstances, it was a small price to pay for even one ear of corn.

"It hasn't been a pleasant day," he admitted. "I'm Tallin, son of Japora the locksmith." He didn't have a tentacle tip to offer in greeting, so he held out his fingers instead.

The woman looked faintly surprised at that, as if she had expected Tallin's manners to match his clothes, not his accent. However, she brushed his fingertips with the tips of two tentacles, and introduced herself. "Nilba, second channel in Dar."

"I hadn't expected to disturb anyone back here," Tallin apologized, overlooking for the moment the damage he had been doing to the corn crop.

"Most Simes wouldn't have noticed you," Nilba said. "Your field is still very low. Did your mother warn you?"

"….warn?"

"You mean you didn't know? You've Established."

Tallin's stomach unaccountably changed its mind, and threatened to reject the stolen corn. He could feel his entire future self-destructing as Nilba's light voice continued, "You're cold, wet, filthy and hungry. Why don't you come with me, and we'll see what we can do about that?"

Despite the polite phrasing, there was a Sime possessiveness about Nilba's manner which made it plain that she expected to be obeyed.

And why shouldn't she? Even perverts have the right to claim a stray Gen that's stupid enough to wander onto their land.

Glumly, Tallin turned towards the shadowy buildings and started walking.

CODA

"And that is how I met your mother," Tallin told his wide-eyed son. "It's a good thing she zlinned me raiding that corn patch, too. If I'd returned to Gloron and Kintha the next morning, the way I'd planned, they would have sold me for a Kill. Not that I appreciated what Nilba had done for me at the time."

"You didn't want to stay at Dar?"

"Not then. I wanted to be a junct locksmith like my mother, Japora. That wasn't possible, obviously, and I hated Nilba because she was the one who told me."

Califf's eyes were troubled. "Do you still hate Mother?"

"No, I grew to love her very much," Tallin hastened to reassure his son. "And we both love you even more."

The child considered for a moment, then nodded. "So you became a Companion because you couldn't be a locksmith?"

"Well, not exactly." Tallin tucked the covers closer around the small body. "But that is a story for another time. Good night, son."

"Good night, Daddy."

An earlier version of "A Mother's Choice" appeared in *A Companion in Zeor* #18 (2003) and can be found at: http://www.simegen.com/sgfandom/rimonslibrary/cz/cz18/choice.html

A MOTHER'S CHOICE

DONNA FERNSTROM

Annie watched her husband's anxious face appear in the doorway as she used a damp cloth to soothe her son's feverish face.

"Is it…" Cal choked on the last word and on his own fear. His hand trembled as he gripped the door frame.

"No. It's just a fever, Cal. Don't you worry none. I'll take him over to Doc's, if you get the wagon ready." She didn't look up at him.

"Are you sure? Are you sure, Annie?" Cal's voice was stretched wire-thin with stress.

"Of course I'm sure. Of all people, don't you think I'd know a change over when I saw one? I saw enough of 'em when I was growing up." Annie's voice was matter-of-fact and hard, reminding her husband of things he'd rather have forgotten.

Her husband sighed, a short, sharp exhalation, then walked away.

Annie continued to soothe her son's brow, pulling the blanket up higher as he shivered.

His fever-bright eyes focused on her, and she saw the fire of fear and hope in them. Between chattering teeth, he whispered "Is it true, mom? I'm not turning Sime? Is it true?"

She stroked his hair and smiled gently down at him. "Shush now. Momma's gonna take you over to Doc's. He'll be able to help you get well again, ok?"

Her son did not reply, but his breathing seemed a bit easier. Several moments later, her husband reappeared.

"The wagon's hitched, Annie. Maybe I better come with you."

"No, Cal, you got to stay here. Workman's comin' about that hole in the barn roof, remember? I'll take him over there, you know it ain't far." She continued to stroke her son's hair.

Cal's face twitched slightly. "But… Luke…" He closed his eyes. "All right, Annie. You take him on over there."

Gently, Annie wrapped the lovingly-stitched patchwork quilt around her son's frail body and lifted him up, then placed him in her husband's arms. "You go put him in the wagon, now, and I'll get some water for the trip, to keep him cool. Okay?"

Her husband nodded, then walked out, staring down at his son with a deeply troubled expression, the light weight in his arms only adding to his unspoken dread.

Annie quietly filled a jug with water from the basin and wrapped her warmest shawl around herself. Through the window, she watched her husband place Luke in the wagon, and paused slightly to take a deep breath. Then she stepped out the door.

Her husband stood by the wagon, looking older than he ever had, confusion and a hint of fear widening his eyes.

She set the jug in the wagon, then turned, giving him a quick hug and kiss. "Don't you worry Cal. It'll all be all right, ok?"

He nodded, a jerky motion, and reluctantly let her go. She climbed up onto the wagon and took the reins in hand. With a brisk clucking sound and a slap of the reins, she started the large draft horse on his way. As the wagon rattled down the worn dirt path, she did not look back.

Five minutes later she reached the crossroad. Hidden by the trees, she made her choice. One path was worn, rutted, and well-used. The other was eroded, overgrown....

Wagon wheels snapped branches from shrubs and small trees, and the cart swayed away down the abandoned trackway.

Annie's face was resolute and calm. She took in everything around her; trees, landscape, the wood of the cart, with a sort of reverent nostalgia. Occasionally, she would glance back at her son, her features would smooth further, and she would smile faintly.

A half an hour later, she stopped the wagon, as it seemed to her that Luke was losing consciousness. She climbed into the back with him, made sure he was well-covered, and waited. An hour passed before he woke again.

Clear eyes stared up at her. "Where are we, Momma? Are we at Doc's yet?"

"Not yet, sweetie. Don't you worry none about that. Momma's gonna take care of you, ok?" She stroked his hair gently and smiled down at him. "We're gonna move on now. I think you fell asleep for a bit there. Would you like a sip of water?"

Luke's face twisted in disgust. "No, momma. My tummy hurts, I don't want no water." He groaned, twisting slightly. The quilt fell away on one side, revealing his thin, light-boned arm. Red streaks described angry paths from elbow to wrist. Annie deftly replaced the quilt before her son's gaze wandered in that direction.

"You just hold tight now, you hear? We're heading out again. I know it's a rough ride, but you'll be all right."

She rose, climbed back onto the driver's bench, and set the horse off again at a quicker pace. The rough trail made the cart bounce and rattle violently with the increased speed and Luke groaned in pain behind her. Nothing to be done about that, though.

It seemed like hours before she broke through the trees at the top of a great hill. Meadow stretched out before her. Far off in the distance she could see buildings. A small town squatted on the plain, green pennant flapping lazily in the wind over one of the larger buildings...the town Pen, where Gens were kept until the townsfolk would come to collect their monthly Kills. This was a road she well remembered; a road she had traveled before in terror, shame, and desperation.

She halted the wagon. She heard her son's rapid breathing, and he called out.

"Momma?"

"Yes, Luke...Momma's comin'." She climbed out of the wagon and tied the horse's reins to a nearby tree, then returned to her son.

His face was full of fear, now, and he couldn't seem to catch his breath. "It's all right, son," she soothed. "Relax now."

"Momma, where are we? What's happening? You said we were goin' to Doc's place, that he'd make me better." His tone was tinged with anger. "We're not going to Doc's, are we? Where are we?"

"Shhhh... try and stay quiet, son. No, we're not going to Doc's. Momma's gonna tell you the truth, now." Luke gasped, his eyes widening to show the whites all the way around, but she stroked his hair gently. "Breathe slower, now, ok? You have to do that for me." She watched her son steel himself and slow his breathing by sheer force of will, despite the terror in his eyes.

Annie slowly lifted the edge of her blouse. Luke's expression was uncomprehending, then his eyes widened in horror. One side of her abdomen was discolored and bulged outward strangely. The skin around the perimeter was pinched and puckered. She lowered her blouse.

"Luke, honey, your momma's got the cancer. You remember old Donnie? He had a thing like that, and it ate him right up. It just kept gettin' bigger, and then he started feelin' the pain, and just wasted away. It was the most terrible thing I ever seen. When I first noticed this here on me, I knew that I didn't want to go through that kinda pain. That's the worst way to die, I think. So, I didn't tell no one. It was hard, keepin' it from your daddy, but I didn't let no one know."

She smiled at him with deep love. "Yeah, I thought mebbe you might changeover, become Sime. And if that was gonna happen, I figured it'd be a lot better for me to take you back home. If I gotta die, it might as well be for you and not for some evil cancer thing."

Luke's breathing was out of control again and tears rolled down his face. "No, momma, no" he gasped, "…you can't die. I don't wanna be a Sime, I don't wanna…" He began to cough violently.

"Shhhh… Luke. I'm gonna die anyhow, you hear? There's nothing anybody can do to stop that now. This here, this'll be quick, you understand? Not slow torture. Not like that…you gotta do this for me, 'cause I want you to live, you hear? You got family over here."

She gently reached out, pulling him to a sitting position.

He winced and his arms came free of the quilt again. His eyes flashed sheer terror as he caught sight of the long blisters there and he screamed.

"Hush, now, Luke!" She pulled his fever-hot body into her arms, hugging him tightly. Ignoring his feeble struggles she rocked him until he subsided again, sobbing. "You gotta calm down, ok? You gotta live, you hear?"

"Momma…" Luke's voice was anguished and muffled.

"Look over there." She pushed him away slightly and pointed out across the fields, toward the buildings. "You see that?" That's a Sime town. That's near where your momma grew up. There's people there, don't you believe otherwise. They's people, not demons. Yer momma's brothers and sisters are out there, and they maybe have kids too now. You go to them, and you tell them Annie Heathcombe sent ya, and they'll take care of you. Ok?"

"Momma, I don't wanna go, I don't wanna k…" His voice trailed off in panic.

"Hush!" She looked at him sternly. "You listen to yer momma now, there's no argument on this, hear? Yer all I got, you know that. You do as I say!"

He shook his head, eyes glazed, then suddenly doubled over with a loud grunt as the first of the breakout contractions hit him. It wasn't long before hot fluids spattered against the grey wood slats of the wagon. Tentacles lashed about her arms as his world dissolved into shifting fields and the bright, glowing beacon before him. She stared into her son's sightless eyes, and lovingly pressed her lips to his.

OBSESSION

ELIZA LEAHY

All my life I have seen Gens as objects. As a child I saw them as objects of fear, as something I might become one day if I was bad. As a child of two Simes, of course, I emulated my parents, and something as different, as alien, as a Gen was considered, by me, as someone who had been punished for some unspeakable, unknown crime.

As an adult, I saw Gens only as a source of selyn, even if it was through a channel. I'm afraid that this old fashioned attitude was deep seated, and didn't get me invited to many parties.

Recently, however, my attitude has been forced to go through a change.

It happened about three months ago. I was at work, doing the usual slog of filling out endless forms to requisition this and that, when a Gen walked up to my desk. I didn't bother to look up.

"What do you want?"

The Gen didn't answer and just stood there. I finished with the form I was on and looked up impatiently — into the most intense eyes I have ever seen. They were almost black; as were the long lashes that surrounded them. She smiled, but there was nothing friendly in her smile or her nager. Her field showed such contempt for me that I was taken aback.

She put some papers on my desk. "Mr. Feldman wants these replicated as soon as possible?"

Without another word she turned and walked off.

I must admit that I had never been treated that way by a Gen before. At first I was confused. Then I was angry. How dare she treat me that way? I dealt with my work, but for the rest of the day my mind kept coming back to the incident. I was interested in her and I had no idea why.

Over the next few days I saw her around the office. I learnt to recognise her by her field; which was growing stronger by the day. I had never in my life worried about what a Gen zlinned like — I got my transfers from a channel, I always had. I wasn't one of these back to nature freaks who wanted nothing but Gen transfer. I respected my laterals too much to want to lay them on Gen flesh. But this Gen kept getting into my thoughts and I found myself positioning myself in places where I knew we would meet.

Not that I ever said anything to her, or even looked at her directly. It was just — interesting — to zlin her. She was so cool, so detached! I think if a Sime went berserk right in front of her she wouldn't have flinched.

I began to get the strangest idea. She was somewhat ahead of me in my cycle, but if I augmented more than usual I could probably put myself in Need closer to her donation date. Then, if I went to the same Center as she did, I might get the same channel as she did, and maybe receive her selyn. The thought made me feel dirty, but at the same time intrigued me. Logically I knew that the chances were extreme, but I still couldn't keep from thinking about it. I didn't act on it though, not that first month.

During this time I found out her name and a few other things about her, like where she donated. It wasn't so far from my own home that it would look suspicious if I signed up there, so, soon after my transfer at my old Center I went to hers and put my name down. I told them I just wanted a change of venue, and they were happy with that. It's a nice new place, hasn't been around long, much nicer then my old place, so that was a plus as well.

At this time I was still high from my recent transfer and cocky about my change of venue and my plans. Once, in the staff room, I even deigned to talk to her. I asked her how she liked her job; she said she liked it fine. That was about it really. Beats me what you say to a Gen outside of normal work stuff. I mean, what do they think? Do they think like we do? They can't really, can they? They have so many fewer senses. Surely their world view is hampered by this?

As luck would have it we were thrown together in a more extreme manner, and it wasn't even at my instigation. The boss decided that we needed to hold a seminar to impress some new, and very wealthy, buyers, and he picked us to organise it.

We had two weeks during which we worked almost exclusively with each other. She is a dreadful conversationalist, not seeming to know how to make small talk with a Sime at all. At the same time she is still totally unflustered and doesn't seem to even realise that she is lacking. I certainly wasn't making it any easier for her. Towards the end of the two weeks I was approaching Need and was somewhat distracted by her. Several times I had to ask her to please control her nager, although, truth be told, she never lost control of it. That was the one time she came to even showing any emotion. She looked shocked, and yes that showed in her nager as well. She said, "Sorry, if I am disturbing you perhaps we should finish this later?" And then she left!

I could have gone after her, after all, she hadn't really been doing anything wrong. But why on earth would I follow a Gen anywhere? What would I say? I mean, she didn't expect me to apologise did she? I took an early afternoon and got some exercise. A little bit of augmentation made me feel better; probably helped settle my nerves. The next day we continued work as if nothing had happened.

The morning the seminar started was also my transfer day, so I wasn't at work until that afternoon. For that matter, I didn't have to go into work in the afternoon, either, but I had noticed that it was her habit to go to work after donating, so I was certainly going to go as well.

The big flaw in my plan was that I hadn't managed to find out what time she donated. I thought how interesting it would be to meet leaving the Center and finding out that we not only used the same Center but that we were due on the same day. That might even be better than getting the same channel she donated to. I'd have to give more thought to that for another time.

I waited for a while away from the Center, close enough to zlin, but not close enough to be seen by a Gen. I don't think I was there for more than an hour though, before a channel came up to me and asked if I was all right. Of course, I had to go with him then. He wanted to know what I had been waiting for, so I told him a story about how this was my first time to this Center (that part was true) and how I just wanted to get a feel for the area and enjoy the expectation of transfer.

And I couldn't zlin her anywhere. Needless to say, transfer was less than perfect.

I signed the forms, thanked the channel and rushed back to work. She hadn't returned yet. I raced around my office tidying up, and then I ate a huge lunch and regretted it almost instantly. I spent the rest of that afternoon trying not to be sick. She finally came into work late in the afternoon, which gave me the perfect opportunity.

"You are in late?" I said.

She looked at me up and down in that manner she has as if saying, "What is it to you?"

"I donated today, however it is my custom to return to work afterwards," she explained.

"Really? I had transfer today, what a coincidence!" For a full thirty seconds she just looked at me. I don't think she believed in coincidences.

"I hope your transfer was satisfactory?" Before I could reply she had turned her back and walked away! I mean, right, she knew I was at my least dangerous point, but it was still rude behaviour and I was shocked. If I hadn't been feeling so unwell I might even have gone after her.

I stayed home the next day. I was entitled to Post time, but in fact I actually felt unwell. I didn't seem to be able to relax. Being sick while being Post is the oddest feeling, and I don't recommend it to anyone!

During the next month I was more aware of her than ever. Whenever I saw her it seemed that she was looking at me, and I could zlin that she was interested in me as well. Instead of making me feel more interested in her it only served to worry me.

Things got worse after turnover. She seemed to always find reasons to be working near me, and I could zlin her concentration on me. I pretended not to notice and just enjoyed the attention. I must admit that I had never thought about the obvious advantages of having a Gen friend. It was almost worth putting up with the atrocious, self-centered attitude to be near that constant promise of selyn.

It was the last working day before my transfer day and her donation day. I still hadn't worked out what time she went to donate, and was working up the courage to ask her, maybe to suggest that we could travel together. I still hadn't managed to gather myself enough to ask her this rather personal question before it was time for me to leave, and I found, to my dismay, that she had already left.

I was in somewhat of a funk as I headed home. Home seemed rather lonely and without her field within zlinnable range the world seemed very cold. I warmed up a little soup, hardly wanting to eat but forcing myself for the sake of my health. I hoped that my transfer tomorrow would go more satisfactorily than the last one. Somehow I doubted it. All I could think about was the way she had zlinned that day, so calm, so full, so ready to be harvested!

I had only just taken my soup off the stove when I zlinned a Gen approaching through the badly insulated walls of my apartment. There was no doubting that field; I'd been obsessing about it every day for almost 3 months. I was at the door before she could signal.

All I could do was stare at her in shock.

"Am I invited in?" She looked at me with cool amusement in her eyes and nager.

"Why, yes, please come in. I'm sorry, you took me by surprise." I stood back and held the door open for her.

She entered and looked over my sparsely, but elegantly, furnished apartment. Then she turned and looked at me.

"I will come right to the point," she said. "I have noticed your attention on me during these last two months, and it has interested me. Recently I have been having some—thoughts—about my life, and I have decided that it is time to try something new. If you are interested, I would be willing to have transfer with you, directly, this month."

"WHAT?" I exclaimed. "Do you know what you are saying? I'm a law abiding citizen, I've NEVER even CONSIDERED having transfer from anyone except a channel! Are you mad?" I was trying to back away, but at the same time my body was letting me down, badly. I might not be interested in her proposal, but my laterals defiantly were!

She was so calm! That was the worst of it all. She stood there in front of me with that willing nager and radiated "calm" at me. I swayed towards her, despite myself. I tried to tell myself that I wasn't even in hard Need yet, but my body refused to listen. My physical attitude, so at odds with my words, must have encouraged her, for her nager brightened with "hopeful promise" and I was almost lost.

She put out both hands and I found myself staring at them in a mixture of horror and desire. I was switching from duo to hypo and desperately trying to keep some control. I had heard that Gens could control a Sime, but I had never put myself into such a perilous position before and had never really believed it.

She was enticing me to sin, to break the law. Didn't she see the danger? Didn't she know what she was risking? She was so calm—maybe she wouldn't fear. Maybe she knew what she was doing. Surely she knew what she was doing. I allowed myself to hope, and took a step closer to her. Her arms, with their promise of fulfillment, were so close.

I fell into her nager. She was there, I was there. Surely this is the way it was meant to be, Sime and Gen together? Suddenly I was afraid. She was there NOW, but maybe she would back out at the last moment? Would I be left in Need, far from any safe, trustworthy channel? In absolute panic I augmented towards her and grabbed her. Suddenly a burst of shock and pain fragmented that icy calm nager. I could feel the blood vessels on her arms break into bruises under my grip. I panicked and dropped her. It was both the hardest and the easiest thing I have ever done in my life. My body cried out for her selyn, but my fear of her was greater and I fled, not even knowing where I was going until I ended up at my old Center. Not one but three channels were there to grab me, and together they managed to get my intil down. They sent people after her, of course, but she was gone. I stayed at the Center, had transfer there, and stayed on a few days until they were sure, and I was sure, that I was all right once again.

She did not show up for work the next week, and the search for her continued for a month or two. Eventually the authorities decided that she must have left the area. I hope that she never comes back.

So you see, my attitude towards Gens has changed. I can no longer ignore the fact that they exist. They are all around me, every day, a constant threat. Gens aren't the ignorant sub-humans I had once thought. Gens are pure, malicious evil.

They don't deserve to live.

This poem first appeared in *A Companion in Zeor* #21 (2004) and can be found at:

http://simegen.com/sgfandom/rimonslibrary/cz/cz21/howfar.html

HOW FAR MUST I GO?
A Sime~Gen Free Verse Poem

WILLIAM LONG

How far must I go to see what is called Unity?
To the edge of the world as I know it?

How far must I go to see what is called Unity? Across the great waters to other places, where there may be those that can live not as two, but one.

How far must I go to see what is called Unity? Away from all people who hate and fear? Away from all those that seek to Kill and maim?

However, what can I do when I feel the urge to hurt and Kill?

How far must I go to see what is called Unity? Therefore, I do not act on how I feel when I see someone that is not like me.

How far must I go to see what is called Unity? To a place that is far away from where I am now.

I know that I must go a long way to reach what is called Unity, because I know that there is still fear in my heart.

A JOURNEY INTO DEMONLAND

MARY LOU MENDUM AND M. ALEXIS PAKULAK

COMPILED BY M. ALEXIS PAKULAK

For over a decade, twice a week, a group of writers has gathered online to create Borderlands, the longest Sime~Gen epic in existence. This is an excerpt from that saga, edited into standard story format. Set three decades after Unity, this is the tale of Nathan, a young Gen raised to be a caring, Godfearing young man, and his journey across the border. To see more of Borderlands, or to join the Borderlands team, go to www. Simegen.com. The actual "Cooperative Fiction" logs may be found here: http://simegen.com/sgfandom/fans/bev/boom

* * * *

Nathan came to his feet as the train slowed to a halt. He waited a few minutes, listening to the noises outside to make sure he was at a proper city or town, and not just a track signal. He worked his way out from his hiding place between several crates and over to the exit. He had sworn a vow before God's altar that before his eighteenth birthday he would rescue at least one of his fellow Gens from the Demon Lands. With that birthday only a few days away, he was ready to begin his mission for God. He cracked open the cargo door and looked around. There wasn't much to be seen, but a few cars up was a cluster of lights and movement along the passenger platform. From the other direction, in the dark, was the clanking and thumping of cargo hoists and the shouting of voices.

Nathan wasn't sure what town this was, but he knew it was several hours past the border, and as full of victimized Gens as any other place where Simes lived. That was all he needed to know. He shouldered his backpack more firmly, then dropped to the ground and started making his way across the train yard. He moved slowly and carefully, checking his footing with every step to avoid the many obstacles on the ground. He felt his way past another line of track and onwards into the pitch dark. He stubbed his toe, stifled a blasphemy, then continued forward.

A moment later, Nathan froze. Someone nearby was shouting, in the Demons' language. After a moment, when nothing further happened, he began edging away from the direction of the voice. Busy listening for the source of the voice, he tripped over a stack of old railroad ties and landed face-first on them. The air was driven from his lungs, and for a moment he couldn't breathe. Then something reached down, plucked Nathan off the ground with frightening ease and carried him off the tracks. A gruff voice lectured him in the Demon's tongue all the way.

As soon as Nathan got his breath back he began to struggle. He knew he was in the clutches of a Demon; nothing human could be so strong. "Let me go! Let me go!" he shouted in a rising panic.

"Not leggo. Not safe here," the gruff voice said in his ear.

Nathan struggled harder and began to shout, "Demon! God, help me!"

"Am helping you," the gruff voice answered in broken English. "Not safe for Gen on tracks in dark."

Hajene Khanna ambrov Zyax stood on the platform, having failed in her errand. She had been sent to meet the train and determine whether the Sime Center's new centrifuge had been delivered. She might be a First, but she was young enough to be the one sent out into the chilly evening damp. She hadn't minded. The lack of proper equipment had been causing everyone a headache for the past week and a half.

She had discovered that the centrifuge was not on this train after all, and was about to inform the Sime Center on her way home to Zyax when a disturbance caught her attention. She sought out the source, discovering to her curiosity what zlinned like a strange First, struggling in the grasp of a railroad worker and talking in Genlan.

She responded in the same language. "Is there a problem here?"

The uniformed railway worker addressed her in Simelan. "Hajene, can you help with this one? He was prowling around the tracks. I guess he came in on the freight train—Oh, thanks, Hajene."

Khanna had zlinned the man's distress, and moderated the impact of the strange First's uncontrolled nager. Her half-trained Sime perceptions told her this was a Donor with odd training. "Can I help?" she asked the guard.

"Doesn't seem to understand Simelan, Hajene. My name's Stallan, by the way," the guard said.

"Thank you, Tuib Stallan," Khanna said. "Would you like me to tell him something? I speak Genlan."

"Tell him he's an idiot and he's under arrest," Stallan grumbled. "No, what's the point? I just want him out of here before he breaks something, possibly his neck."

"All right, I'll tell him." Khanna turned to Nathan. "The guard is concerned that you might hurt yourself," she said in her excellent Genlan.

Nathan looked at the cute, petite young woman in a worn sweater. He felt a strong pull towards her. Perhaps this was the one God sent him to save. He stopped struggling, trying to get back some semblance of strength and dignity. He was aware of how ludicrous he looked as a rescue mission, tight in a Sime's clutches, but he had to try anyway.

"Miss, I was sent here for you," he told her. "My name is Nathan."

"What is he saying, Hajene?" Stallan asked.

"It seems he was looking for me," said Khanna. She turned back to Nathan, ignoring the guard's startlement. "I was over on the platform," she added in Genlan. "I'm Khanna."

"God bless you, Khanna," Nathan replied.

Khanna spoke again to Stallan. "You can let him go now, I think. Either one of us can catch him easily enough anyway, if he bolts."

"Sure." Stallan put the young Gen down on his feet.

Nathan made a show of dusting himself off and took a step closer to Khanna. His nager reached to mesh, tentatively, with her own. "I was sent to aid you," he said.

"You were sent?" she asked, visibly startled. She thought it was a bit early to have next month's Donor show up.

Nathan looked at her with holy adoration. This one innocent young woman, at least, would be slave to Demons no longer. "Yes, I was sent for you," he replied.

Stallan frowned. He understood only a few words of Genlan. "He's saying he was sent to you?" He'd caught that much, at least. "Who sent him?"

"I don't know," Khanna said. "We weren't expecting someone this early."

"Well, could you ask him? And what do you mean, expecting someone? Is he really a Donor? How can he be a Donor and not know any Simelan?"

Khanna turned to Nathan. "Were you sent by the authorities?" She addressed Stallan once more. "I don't know. His nager is strong, but very strange. And his control is a little weak."

Stallan observed, "Considering how he was kicking and screaming, I'd say he has no self-control at all."

Nathan figured this poor slave girl had been taught nothing of God, and here in front of a Sime was no place for a theology lesson. "Yes," he said simply. "By the One Who controls all."

Khanna kept her focus on Nathan. "Your Controller?"

"Yes. That's right."

To Stallan, Khanna said, "He says his Controller sent him." She switched languages again and asked Nathan, "Do you have paperwork? Nothing was received here, as far as I know."

Nathan had a Bible in his backpack so he replied, "Yes, I have the Word of the Controller, on paper." He wasn't surprised that the slave girl's English was so poor. He'd just have to simplify everything until she could learn.

Stallan saw a way out of this problem. "Well, look, Hajene. If he has a Controller, he must be Tecton, even if he's forgotten his Simelan somehow. Not to mention his uniform. Can you take charge of him, get him to a Sime Center or wherever? I can't leave here unless I call for backup, and that means an arrest. Nobody wants to arrest a Tecton Donor, especially if he has…problems."

"Yes, I'll get him to the Sime Center," Khanna replied.

"Thanks, Hajene." Stallan turned away and resumed his interrupted patrol.

Khanna turned her full attention to Nathan. "Please, Sosu Nathan, come with me."

Nathan stepped as close to Khanna as he dared. The closer he got, the stronger the pull was. He felt something odd swelling within him, and was more sure than ever of God's divine plan as he followed her down the platform.

"We weren't expecting you," said Khanna, "but I'm sure we can find you a meal and a place to sleep." She knew that both were priorities for most Gens. She noted that the Donor, however strange his nager, was at least doing a decent job of offering support, and leaned into it, just a bit.

Nathan involuntarily made a small contented noise, deep in his throat. "A meal would be good." He hadn't eaten since he got on the train, almost a full day ago.

"Tell me, where did you grow up? Your Genlan is perfect." Khanna asked.

"Porter's Ridge. It's a small town several hours west of New Washington City."

"Really?" she said. "My mother grew up not far from New Washington, but east. Hardesty."

"I know of Hardesty," he said, "though I've never been there. A schoolmate had some cousins there."

"What made you decide to cross the border?"

"The Controller had work for me here," he said

"Ah. Do you train on the other side of the border?"

Nathan puffed out his chest a bit. "Yes." He was the miller's apprentice in his town.

"That's difficult," she commented. "Weren't you afraid that your training would be insufficient?"

"I have a very good teacher. And he says that I am learning well." Nathan had, in fact, been told that if he kept it up, old Grisson Miller would feel free to retire in a couple more years.

"When did you start your training? Just after you Established?" she asked.

"The day after my adulthood."

"So you knew early?" she said. "What you wanted to do with your life, I mean. Many people take longer to realize their potential."

"I always knew what I wanted," he replied earnestly, "and was fortunate that it worked out for me. But my real work begins here, now, with you." Nathan saw his secular life as only the means by which he might work for God's purpose.

"So I am your first assignment?"

"Yes."

Khanna gave a charming smile. "I'm honored, then."

Nathan smiled back. "So am I. The Controller chose well for me, I think." He looked at the girl's face. She was thin—her masters had obviously starved her—and not conventionally pretty. But to him, she was beautiful.

* * * *

Nathan sat back in the rattletrap wagon, more tired than he'd expected to be. He realized now that he'd been naïve, thinking he could simply rescue someone by the tracks and hop onto a homeward train right away. There was only one train a day in each direction, after all, and it would take time to persuade this downtrodden young woman to trust and accompany a stranger such as himself. He figured a good night's sleep wasn't a bad way to start.

Khanna turned the wagon down a dirt road leading at right angles to the road. Nathan sat up as the quality of the road changed, and looked around. He couldn't see much in the dimness, but there seemed to be a cluster of lanterns up ahead. Khanna drove around a hill, then pointed ahead to a small collection of buildings clustered around a more solid, larger one.

"Is that where we're going?" Nathan asked.

"Yes. That's Zyax, such as it is. We've only got thirty or so families, and we're not wealthy, but we make up for it in independence."

"Independence?"

"The Tecton has a Sime Centre in town, but we're pretty much left to ourselves out here."

Nathan was glad to hear that there was no Devil Centre here.

"We've only existed for thirty years," she added. "We were founded by refugees from the Lost Houses that were wiped out by raiders from Norwest Territory."

"Ah."

"When they got here, there was nothing. The land had been picked clean, and there wasn't a living adult for a hundred miles."

Nathan was relieved to learn that there were no demons at all here. God was surely favouring him on this mission.

"The town was later settled by former soldiers," she continued. "When the railroad came through, things got easier."

A wave of sympathy, carried on Nathan's powerful nager, washed over her. "It must be a hard life," he said.

"All frontier lives are hard," she said. "But there are opportunities as well as hardships."

Nathan nodded, then realized that she couldn't see him in the dark. "True."

Khanna had no trouble zlinning the nod, of course. "Anyway, I hope you will accept our hospitality for the night. There's plenty of time to get to work tomorrow."

"Gladly. I'm quite tired," he said. "Thank you."

Khanna smiled fondly at such a Genlike admission.

Nathan sat up a little straighter as the wagon rolled to a halt near the big central building. The building was blocky and ugly, but at least it looked solid, made of sturdy stone. He saw a man approaching through the flickering torchlight. He nodded politely and waited for Khanna to introduce him.

Brenson smiled to zlin the First Order Donor's nager shining through the night like hundreds of torches together.

Khanna spoke. "Sectuib, this is Sosu Nathan, who came in on to-night's train instead of the centrifuge. I'll take the substitution, at least for now. Nathan, this is my father, and Zyax's Sectuib, Brenson."

Brenson was startled to hear English, but after all, he knew it perfectly well. "Howdy there, Sosu. We didn't expect you so soon!" He guffawed at his own pun. He took the horse's reins, just in case it decided to do something erratic.

"I'm very pleased to meet you, sir." Nathan smiled. Perhaps he'd be able to rescue the whole family?

Brenson saw how very young Nathan really was. "None of your sirs now. Call me Brenson." He extended his hand as a surreptitious way to do a little nageric leeching.

Khanna hopped off the wagon. "Don't mind Father," she said, giving him a hug. "He's never resigned himself to the dignity of his office."

Brenson gave as good as he got, and figured he'd get to shake the young Donor's hand another time.

Nathan stared at the man's exposed forearms as he seized the girl, and recoiled in horror. "God save me! I've fallen into a nest of demons!"

* * * *

Brenson grabbed control of the fields, though of course he couldn't do much for his daughter. "Now Sosu, that's not funny. Of course my daughter and I can handle it, but you don't know who else might be around. You're radiating real — Hey, what's going on here?" He turned to his daughter. "Khanna, I don't think this Gen is who you think he is. Not at all."

Khanna was a little slower on the uptake than her father, but her training finally kicked in and she took control with her own First Order nager. Brenson smoothly relinquished to her, a move they'd practiced quite a bit.

* * * *

Nathan realized, through his panic, that he couldn't hope to free the reins from the Sime's grip. He leapt from the wagon and started to run. Forget about rescuing the girl, he just wanted to get away.

"What the shen?" gasped Khanna

"Oh dear, he's panicked," said Brenson. "He's straight from Genland, kiddo, a natural Donor. Not Tecton at all."

"I'd better get him before he trips and hurts himself."

Khanna augmented after Nathan through the dark. She hunted the Gen down, grabbing him in her arms and tentacles from behind in order to restrain him without hurting him. "Hey, calm down!" she said. "You're going to hurt yourself!"

Nathan struggled briefly, then tried to calm himself. He'd never escape this way. He tried to remember what he'd learned in the week's training camp the church had sent him to. If he could just reach from this angle, he knew there was a pressure point near a Sime's shoulder that would render them immobile. He also reminded himself that he came here ready to battle Simes if necessary. God would not desert him in his faith.

Nathan slowly forced himself to calm. "God of my fathers, protect and strengthen me. Let not the Evil Ones defeat me. My faith is strong; be Thou my refuge."

Khanna spoke softly, slowly, as if to calm. "Nathan, what is the matter with you? There's no danger here."

Nathan spoke bitterly. "You wouldn't think so. Your own father is a demon." To himself he muttered, "I should have known it wouldn't be this easy."

Brenson had, by this time, passed the reins to someone else, and walked up to his daughter and the Wild Gen.

"My father's a channel," Khanna was saying. "So am I. And what isn't easy?" Her manner radiated hurt and confusion; she'd started to really like Nathan on their drive to Zyax.

Brenson said, "He zlins to me like someone trying to accomplish something. Besides getting away from being held by a Sime, of course." He might not have his daughter's field strength, but he'd had a lot more practice at reading people's intentions, Gen or Sime.

Nathan bowed his head, defeated. Not only was her father a demon; the very girl he'd thought he was here to rescue was one as well. He had clearly misunderstood God's guidance. "I thought I was here to save you from the demons. But you're one of them." Nathan still felt the pull to her, but now he understood that it was the work of the demon herself, and not any message from God. Had his error doomed him? "Lord God," he prayed, "forgive me. I have tried to serve you the best I knew how; please don't desert me now."

"Nathan, I don't understand your religion, but it's quite possible you can fill a purpose here." Khanna had developed a bad case of the drools over this particular Gen, and wished that he really was the Companion she desperately Needed.

Brenson boggled at what he zlinned. "Not a chance, girl. He is totally untrained. He could Kill you."

"Ignorance can be cured," she pointed out. "Lack of talent can't."

Brenson turned to Nathan. "Now, young fella. Are you going to run away if my daughter lets you go? Remember that Simes can tell if you are lying, so don't."

Nathan looked up, filled with fresh purpose. Yes, maybe that was why God pulled him to her. He was destined to kill her. For that, he had to stay. "I won't run."

Brenson zlinned truth. "Okay, let him go. He's exhausted anyway, and there's nowhere to run to around here. Let's start over."

"Good," said Khanna. To Nathan she added, "Because if you'd gotten beyond the potato field, you'd have been in the rocks." She released him. "Now, you're tired, we've both missed dinner, and the mosquitoes are out in force," said Khanna. "Why don't we go inside and discuss this like civilized people?"

Nathan stood, staring down the two channels, then nodded. Since they didn't seem inclined to Kill him immediately, he might as well let them feed and strengthen him.

Brenson said, "Just a minute, girl."

Khanna slapped a mosquito.

"Nathan," said Brenson formally, "I welcome you to Householding Zyax, and extend you the hospitality of the Householding. That means food, water, a place to sleep, provisions for your journey, defense against your enemies, and several other things you don't stand in need of just at present." After a pause he added, "Shake?" He offered the hand he'd tried to offer before.

Khanna let her father zlin her happiness at the offer of hospitality.

Nathan took a half step backwards, then reconsidered. If he was to fulfill his mission, or even survive, he'd have to roll with events for the moment. Reluctantly he shook the proffered hand. It didn't mean he'd given his parole, just that he would let them feed and shelter him for now.

"Okay then," said Brenson, "Let's eat. Should be easy enough with him around, eh, Khanna?"

"The mosquitoes seem to think so." Khanna reached out with her hand and squashed one on Nathan's shoulder.

Nathan stepped back, startled. The demon moved so fast.

"There. It was biting you," Khanna said.

"Losing a few drops of blood isn't hurting him. No reason to be so overprotective, even if he is your only match for hundreds of miles in any direction." Brenson laughed again.

Nathan shrugged. Mosquitoes weren't the danger here. The demons were.

"Oh, come on, Father. Do you want to feel him itching as well as you?" Khanna led the way. "Besides, I'm dying for some tea. It was thirsty work, waiting for the train. Which didn't bring the centrifuge, by the way." She sighed. "So I've got to go chase after it again tomorrow."

Nathan listened to this exchange. They were speaking in English, not the demon tongue, perhaps to reassure him. But he wasn't reassured. And he had no idea what a 'centrifuge' was anyway.

Khanna opened the door to the main building, and held it for her father and their 'guest.' "Welcome to our home, Nathan."

Brenson smiled at Nathan. "Not much, but it's ours."

Nathan hesitated in the doorway. By the thickness and solidity of the walls, this place felt more like a fortress, or a prison, than a home.

Brenson clarified, "That's a joke, son. Simes feel better when they can live behind stone walls."

"It cuts down on the random noise of other people's feelings," added Khanna.

Nathan remembered, belatedly, that everything he thought and felt could be read by the demons. He tried to swallow down his fear of this place and stepped inside.

"Attaboy," said Brenson. "Courage. Later, you'll need fearlessness, but courage will do for now."

Nathan looked around. Inside, there were a few homelike touches: cheery curtains, braided rugs, a jar of cut flowers on a small table. It looked almost like a residence for real people, lit by the bright candle-light.

"I've been in much grander places," said Khanna, "but none of them are home." She paused. "The evening meal is over, but I'm sure there is something I can scrounge for you."

"Sure there is," Brenson supplied. "No meat here, though, kiddo. But you'll get along. Our Gens do fine."

Nathan's stomach growled loudly at the thought of food, with or without meat.

Khanna smiled and slipped off to fetch dinner for them both.

"The dining room's that way, but I think we'll just sit over here." Brenson pointed toward a room with comfortable chairs and little tables. "All right with you?"

Nathan nodded.

Brenson led the way, and politely pulled back a chair for the guest, even though he was more than twice Nathan's age.

Nathan shrugged off his backpack and set it down beside his chair, then sat. "Your daughter said you came here as refugees, after the war." He figured he might as well learn everything he could about this place and its demons.

"Yeah. Y'know, the Unity Wars started when there got to be more Simes than Gens up in Norwest Territory. You know Simes used to Kill one Gen every month. What do you think happened then?"

"The de—, er, Simes starved?"

"No. They Killed all the Gens, and then set out to raid their neighbors. That would be us." Brenson waved his arm about. "Imagine a mob the size of a whole Territory. That's what came down on the towns and Householdings near the border. They were wiped out, all but a few survivors. When the Householdings further from the border took control of Nivet Territory, they gave us this land, what we could use of it. We formed new Householdings thirty years ago, and here we are. Our motto is 'Forgive, but never forget.'"

Nathan nodded and gestured for Brenson to continue.

"Eventually I suppose Simes and Gens will immigrate here, and we'll have neighbors again. For now, it's just the sixty-seven of us. Sixty-eight, if you decide to join us."

"Why would I wish to join you?"

"I know you've felt the call to serve my daughter." Brenson spoke firmly, but not intimidatingly.

Nathan squared his shoulders indignantly. "I serve none but God!"

"Of course. But there are ways and ways of serving him."

"I came here to rescue humans, not to consort with their oppressors."

Brenson chuckled. "Rescue us from what?"

"Not you. You are beyond God's salvation. The Gens, the humans."

Brenson sighed and looked at Nathan as if he were just being a young idiot. "Okay, rescue our Gens from what? Their parents, children, brothers and sisters, best friends?"

"Those who use them, who drink of their souls and enslave their bodies. You, and all others with tentacles."

"Nobody's body is enslaved here," argued Brenson patiently. "Everyone does exactly as they please, except on the rare occasions on which I find it necessary to give an order, in which case it gets obeyed. You, for example, are staying here of your own free will."

"Only because it became clear I could not escape," replied Nathan.

"That's true enough. But you got on that train freely, and followed my daughter here freely. Granted, you weren't well-informed at the time. But as she said, ignorance can be corrected."

Khanna returned with a bowl of soup for her, a larger bowl with a hearty stew and bread for Nathan, and tea all around.

"But now I know what I have fallen among," said Nathan bitterly.

"Yes. The bringers of soup, stew, bread, and tea," quipped Brenson.

"And Quarta's cooking," added Khanna, "which I assure you is well worth the trip."

Nathan reached hungrily for his tray. "Lord, I thank you for this food; given by Your grace for the nourishment of my body. Amen." He took two eager bites. Then he remembered his teachers' lesson: that food given by demons would likely be filled with the drugs that numb the will and dull the mind. He pushed the bowl away, and thrust the spoon down his throat, hoping to induce vomiting.

Nathan spewed stew all over the table.

"What the…?" Khanna stared at her father in distress. "An allergic reaction?"

"Nope, he's afraid of the food." Brenson clamped down on his own throat as the First Order nausea washed right past his showfield like it wasn't there.

* * * *

Khanna looked at her father in astonishment, then blocked Nathan's projection. "What's wrong with the food?" She was far too young to have ever seen a Pen Gen.

"Nothing, I'm sure," said Brenson. "I think he must think we're going to poison him, though whatever for, I can't imagine."

* * * *

"Drugs," muttered Nathan. "Demon drugs, from the Pens."

Khanna said, "This hasn't been a Pen for thirty years, Nathan."

Nathan flinched. "This? This building?" Nathan understood now why the building was so sturdy, the walls so thick. In a blind panic he rose to flee.

"Sure. Stone insulation, remember?" said Brenson. "And it's defensible, in case there are ever any more raids. We've learned our lesson there."

"Hey!" shouted Khanna.

Brenson winced. "Oh, not again. Grab him."

Khanna jumped to her feet and sprinted to circle Nathan, placing herself between him and the door. "Stop that. You're going to hurt someone if you continue bolting like that, and it might not be you."

Nathan wanted to hurt someone. He wanted to hurt every damned demon in this place. "Stand aside," he warned, "or pay the price!"

"The people here are my family and friends, Nathan," said Khanna. "They haven't done anything to deserve being attacked by you. Not all of them are Simes, either."

"Well done, Khanna," Brenson said. "Zlins like he thinks he can hurt you, though I don't see how or why. Anyway, as long as you hold the fields steady…"

Nathan remembered his lessons, the pressure point near the shoulders. He knew how to disable a Sime. He felt the fear and righteous anger drain out of him. The new calm left him clear-headed to act. "I have no quarrel with the humans. But you demons must die!" Nathan braced himself. The worst part was that to reach the shoulders, he must step within arms' reach of the demon. He lunged forward, ready to do God's will or die trying.

"In due course we shall," said Brenson calmly. "But not today." With lightning demon speed, he grabbed Nathan and pulled him back.

Khanna took a step back, keeping her vulnerable shoulders out of reach. Nathan's hands closed over thin air.

"Oh, stop it with the "demon" thing," she huffed. "I'm no more a demon than you are. And if you bothered to ask them, you'd find that our Gen members would consider your desire to murder us as having a very large quarrel with them."

Nathan struggled fiercely to escape, biting and kicking. Khanna restrained his flailing hands with her hands and tentacles, careful not to let them slide down toward her arms, which might let him reach for her shoulders.

"They have lived in ignorance," Nathan argued. "But I shall bring them God's truth."

"Father, I don't think we're getting through to him."

Brenson sighed deeply. "No, we aren't. Time for the Old Householding Trick."

"Which one?" she asked.

"You know. Lock him up and give him time to sleep it off. He's drunk on fanatical religion, so it'll take longer than if it were just porstan and shiltpron."

"Oh. The old quarantine cell we've been using for potatoes?"

"Just the place. No lock anymore, so you'll have to jam the door. Feel up to it?"

"I can do it." Khanna helped march Nathan out the door, down the hall, and down a narrow stairway to the basement.

Nathan continued struggling. The demons were taking him to their Pen in the basement; he was sure of it. They swiftly arrived in a clean but slightly potato-smelling, stone-walled room.

"In you go, now," said Khanna. "Maybe you'll be more sensible when you've had a chance to sleep on it."

Nathan couldn't see a thing in the unlit basement, but he heard the scrape of a heavy door. He struggled harder, but was suddenly thrust through the narrow doorway and into a cell.

Khanna slammed the door shut, then grunted. "I think that will hold."

Nathan pulled himself to his feet and flung himself towards the sound of their voices. He slammed against hard bars, which rattled but held.

"We'd better get him a lantern, Father, before he hurts himself stumbling around in the dark."

"Naah, he might use the lantern against himself if he despairs. 'A light in dark places, when all other lights go out.' We'll fetch him in the morning."

"All right." Khanna sounded reluctant. Perhaps she was eager to Kill him tonight?

"He'll be all right. He'll fall asleep soon enough, I think."

Nathan listened as the footsteps receded up the stairs. He then felt his way around the room, taking inventory by touch. There was nothing there, not even a chamber pot. He paced in the tiny space for over an hour, then gave up and lay down on the cold stone floor. Despair washed over him. "Dear Lord, have I misunderstood your plan? Have you utterly forsaken me? Or is this one more test of my faith?"

Finally, Nathan slept.

* * * *

Brenson was working on the selyn account books, one of his worst jobs as Sectuib. He swore softly under his breath, a constant litany as he worked. "Shen, shendi, shenoni, shenshay, shenshi, shenshid, and shidoni!"

Khanna signalled in front of her father's door.

"Come!"

She entered, zlinnably upset.

Brenson automatically damped the fields to contain the issue, whatever it was.

"Father, I've got to…. Oh, you're at the accounts. I probably should come back later."

"No, no." Brenson hastily closed the books and stuffed them away in a drawer. "What is it?"

"It's Nathan. I've been looking through his pack. He keeps a diary."

Brenson was outraged. "What right had you to do that? Even if he's not what we thought he was, he's still a human being and entitled to his privacy."

"He needs help, Father, or he's going to get himself Killed, and take somebody else with him. And how can we provide it if we don't understand what he's been through?"

"Still, that's no excuse for going behind his back. He's not going to do any harm locked up down there. You could question him when he becomes more tranquil."

"I know. I just…the thought of him, locked up in the basement, without even a blanket…it's cruel, Father. Like something out of junct times, when this was a real Pen."

"It's not that cold," Brenson reassured her. "In fact the temperature is pretty constant down there, which is why it makes a good potato storage bin."

"He won't get hypothermia, but it'll be chilly, uncomfortable, and in the dark…he'll be frightened, not knowing what's going to happen to him." Khanna was clearly stressed just thinking about what she already considered as 'her' Gen being abused.

Brenson sighed and wiped his face with his hand. "And he won't be frightened if we bring him out here, the captive of two 'demon Simes'?"

"At least that might challenge his assumptions. This…his church teaches that Simes are setting up the Pen system again: imprisoning Gens for the Kill. How do you think he's going to interpret being locked in a cage in the basement of what he's been told is a Pen?"

"Hmm," said Brenson. "That is a problem. Well, I won't say there's a good answer to this. Bring him out if you want. But shen and shid, make sure he doesn't know you were looking at his papers."

"Father…is what we've done even legal? Holding him prisoner, I mean?"

"Well, he certainly didn't cross the border legally, so I suppose that makes him a criminal of some sort. And a Sectuib has a lot of power in his own Householding, at least those of us who still have physical Householdings."

"The Tecton," Khanna said, "would probably say that we should have put him back on the train, express delivery to the peacekeepers in the big city."

"Well, perhaps they would. But I don't see any Tecton officials around here. Except you, of course."

"Shen, Father, I wish I wasn't. It's been so nice to be home, the past few weeks."

Brenson smiled. "It's been nice to have you home."

"But we can't afford to be in debt to the Tecton for a First Order Donor every month. It's bad enough as it is," said Khanna.

"Yes, well, that's why you have to work for them. But you'd have to anyhow, to pay our taxes. For sure we don't have any other way to pay them, way out here."

"How bad is it, Father? Haven't there been any Establishments among the children?"

"Not enough. And anyhow, the Tecton cares about net outward flow of selyn. It's not practical for them to send mules way out here. So we end up bartering your services instead of providing either selyn or money. And lucky to be able to do that, frankly."

"Father, that's the other reason I'm so concerned about Nathan. He's not only got a strong nager, but before he knew I was a Sime, he was giving me support. Good support, so that I thought he was my assigned Donor right up until he saw my tentacles."

Brenson nodded, idly twirling a pen in his tentacles.

"I think he's a Natural, Father. And he thinks it's his duty to murder me."

"Like Hugh Valleroy. But unfortunately without his flexible attitude," Brenson reminded.

"Maybe. We don't know that, yet." Khanna clearly hoped not, anyway. "I like him, Father. Despite everything."

"So I zlin." Brenson smiled again.

"Do you think…do you think he'd ever make a Companion? Or that at least we can convince him to stay?"

Brenson shrugged. "Technically? Certainly. With his current attitudes? Never. Can his attitudes change? I have no idea."

"Father, he's young. Barely an adult by out-Territory standards. Hugh Valleroy was a lot older when he Qualified."

"Valleroy's parents grew up in Sime Territory, as I remember. His mother, anyway. Anyhow, he wasn't a Church of the Purity fanatic, the furthest thing from it."

"I'm not saying it'll be easy, Father, but isn't it worth the time to get a Gen with First Order genetics, even if he can't work as a Companion?"

"I don't want to even have him around if his attitudes don't change drastically," Brenson grumbled. "Who knows what he could do to all the Seconds and Thirds, including me? And you certainly can't take him outside the Householding unless he's Qualified — or under arrest.

"I understand. In some ways, it might be easier for him to change because he's been taught such extreme beliefs. We can provide some solid evidence that what he's been taught is false," said Khanna. "If he's willing to be rational at all, that should poke some holes in his assumptions. And…" she added, "he responds to my nager. That should help."

"It could. Or he could decide that his selyur nager is a temptation from the Devil."

Khanna winced. "What a waste that would be."

"Life is full of disappointments."

"Father, I don't want to send Nathan off to spend the next five years in prison. Help me. I've never tried to work with an out-Territory Gen before. Not one as badly indoctrinated as this, anyway."

Brenson sighed deeply. "Okay, we'll try. But even though you're the First, I'm the Sectuib. That means I get to decide when to pull the plug."

"Yes. You're the one with experience. What's the best way to start getting Nathan to question what he knows about Simes?"

"I guess show him that he's wrong about us. But he'd systematically misinterpret everything he saw anyway." Brenson shrugged. "So we'll have to think of the second-best way."

"What's that?"

"I don't know. That's why we have to think of it."

"We're holding him caged like an animal in the dark. How can we get around that unpleasant truth?"

"I guess we could build a containment cell upstairs, where there's a window. Move all the bars up there with a little judicious augmentation," Brenson suggested. "How's that?"

Khanna considered. "Let's see how rational he is in the morning."

Brenson nodded slowly. "Let's."

* * * *

Nathan woke up, cold and stiff from sleeping on the stone floor of the basement. Still groggy, he took a few moments to remember where he was and why. He tried to leap to his feet, but his stiff muscles made him stumble and fall. A little more gingerly, he worked the muscles until he was able to stand in the disorienting dark. He stumbled around the cage, feeling out its boundaries once more, jiggling at the bars and the lock. He was still struggling at this futile task when overhead a door opened and a rectangle of bright light illuminated the staircase nearby. Nathan squinted, his eyes half shut, but redoubled his efforts at the bars. He stared in horror at the monstrous, shadow-lined form. As it came down the stairs, it resolved into the shape of the demon woman from last night. Behind her was her demon father.

"Good morning, Nathan." That was the Khanna-demon.

"God will defend me from you." Nathan was no longer quite so sure of this, after the past night. But he couldn't afford to abandon his trust in God, or he'd have nothing at all. He felt the demonic temptation once more as Khanna drew closer. He gritted his teeth.

"Zlin that?" said the father-demon Brenson. "Selyur nager, but he's upset and frightened by it."

Nathan ignored the meaningless demon-babble. He began singing, in a loud but untrained voice:

"Yes," said Khanna. "What a waste. And an opportunity."

Nathan sang, "Oh, God our refuge and our strength/Before whom demons flee…"

Brenson winced. "This fellow's no Ziggar, that's for sure."

"Through ages past you've guarded us…"

"Now come to set us free." Nathan finished the first verse.

Khanna interrupted, "You know, if you breathe in slowly like this..." She demonstrated. "...you can support properly, like this: Now come to set us free." Khanna's voice wasn't bad.

Nathan, who'd been about to start the second verse, stopped and stared. He'd thought a demon would burst into flame if it quoted scripture or hymns.

Khanna started in on the second verse, which was about the need for mastering one's bad impulses. She added a few flourishes and embellishments. Then she paused, apparently forgetting the lyrics. "What's the last line to that one, Father?"

Nathan's jaw dropped. His shock seemed to strike the demons like a blow. How did the demons know this song?

Brenson spoke the line in his rough demon-voice.

"Oh, of course." She turned to Nathan and beamed. "It was one of Mother's favorites. She was always singing."

Nathan clamped his jaw shut, taking a breath, speaking through clenched teeth. "The father-demon raped a Godfearing woman?"

Khanna blinked at him.

"Oh, God," Nathan groaned, "If you permit such things, what hope is there for me?"

"Why does that bother you, Nathan? Why shouldn't she be happy?" asked Khanna.

"Happy in a demon's clutches?"

Brenson grinned demonically. "Definitely."

Nathan scowled and looked away.

"'Not by any to be entered into unadvisedly or lightly; but reverently, discreetly, advisedly, soberly, and in the fear of God.' You know?" added Brenson.

Nathan recognized the quote from the Church's marriage ceremony. He staggered backwards in disbelief. "She...MARRIED you?"

"Well, not by a Church of the Purity ceremony, son. But yes."

"People do get married on this side of the border too, you know," added Khanna.

"But...a Godfearing, hymn-loving woman with a demon monster?"

"No. A loving mother with a loving father. Raising yours truly." The she-demon winked.

Nathan backed away from the bars. "If the next generation hopes to break me the way he broke her, you're mistaken."

"I sincerely hope not," she said.

Brenson said, "He still believes in Sime superiority over Gens, that's why we must be Evil, you see?"

"Well, sort of," she said. "Outside of the two glaring fallacies."

Brenson nodded agreement.

Khanna turned to Nathan. "You see, Simes don't have power over Gens. Pretty much the opposite, actually. And really, does Gen superiority mean Gens are Evil?"

"Our power is spiritual, not physical," Nathan replied. "There's no denying you're stronger than we are."

"Yes," Khanna agreed, "but how much time can one spend arm-wrestling, anyway? For dealing with most people and situations, it's rather useless, actually."

Nathan muttered bitterly, "It got me down here last night, didn't it?"

"Well, yes. But that wasn't all that productive, was it, now?"

"I'm locked up. You can Kill me any time you want." Nathan's shoulders slumped, defeated.

"Which would be very nice, I'm sure," said Khanna, "If anybody here had the slightest interest in doing so."

"Sell me, then. Or whatever it is you do. But God will save my soul." Nathan no longer had hope for his body.

"Actually," Brenson said with a smile, "what we really want is to hire you. You have very special talents."

Khanna zlinned surreptitiously, hoping for a positive response.

Nathan set his jaw, refusing to be tempted by whatever their offer might be. They had his body, but he wasn't going to sell them his soul.

"I would say we'd pay you a lot," continued Brenson, "but that would just insult you — and anyway, we wouldn't. This is a family, not a business.

"The work's important, though," Khanna put in. "And challenging. And there's lots of chances to help people. I'd gathered that was important to you."

Nathan snorted in disbelief.

"It's people like you," Brenson added, "that make it possible for Simes to live without Killing."

"What? Miller's apprentices? You're saying demons have learned to live on wheat instead of souls?"

"You know how to run a mill, too?" Khanna asked, excited. "You really will fit in well."

"Not people who do what you do," said Brenson. "People who have the skills you have. You are what's called a Natural Donor, someone who — among other things — can't be Killed by any Sime. Well, any you're ever likely to meet, at least.

"Once you learn how to use your skills, that is," Khanna clarified.

"I told you that God would protect me." Nathan felt a sudden swell of righteous confidence. He spat between the bars at the older demon. Or tried to — his mouth was too dry after a night of no food or drink.

"Ahh," approved Brenson, "now that's more like it."

"When you are confident like that," said Khanna, "and relaxed instead of hostile, you won't trigger aggression in Simes. In fact, you can calm most Simes down, whether they want to or not."

Nathan, armed with this information, felt even stronger. Perhaps even arrogantly so, some cautionary part of his mind warned. It could be a trap.

"If you were trained properly," Brenson added, "you could probably convince any Sime to let you out of any prison, however strong."

"I was trained by the best." Nathan was very proud of his church camp training.

"Well…I think that your teachers got a few things wrong," Khanna said gently.

Brenson said, "Whether or not, it's a different kind of training I'm talking about. You're never too old to learn new skills, right?"

Nathan refused to walk into whatever verbal trap was being set. He said nothing.

"Right." Brenson smiled. "So if you wanted to undertake the challenge of allowing millions of people to live long and healthy lives without Killing or being Killed, you've certainly come to the right place."

'If I can destroy just you two, I'll have done enough."

The father-demon cleared his throat. "Well now. Give the boy his breakfast, child."

Nathan bent down to the tray Khanna shoved under the bars. He had to have water, or he'd die. But he could hold out a bit longer without their drugged food. He picked up the bowl of oatmeal and flung it through the bars at the female demon, who plucked it neatly out of mid air without spilling a drop.

"You don't like cereal?" she asked blandly. "We have bread, if you'd prefer some toast."

'I'd rather starve," Nathan grunted.

Brenson laughed. "Try it and see, then. I notice you're making no attempt to die of thirst, which is fortunate. Come, my dear. Let him stew in his own juice, since he's too proud to eat Sime mush." He turned on his heels and headed out with the lantern. Khanna followed a little more slowly.

Nathan stared suspiciously at the glass of water until the door closed above. Then he turned and went to lie down, as far from the water's temptation as the tiny cell allowed.

* * * *

Nathan paced the confines of his cell in the dark. He'd finally given in and drunk the water; he figured it was more likely the food that was drugged anyway. It would be hard to hide the flavour of anything in plain water. He occupied himself with wondering what he'd choose if old man Miller offered him formal adoption at the end of his apprenticeship. To carry the Miller surname would be a rare honour for one of his trade. And it wasn't as if he felt any particular closeness with his own father. Father had been generous enough to buy him the apprenticeship, but Nathan suspected it was more to get rid of him than anything else. He tried not to think about the fact that he was unlikely to live long enough to go back home and have such a decision to worry about it.

He stopped pacing and looked up as the stairwell door swung open. His younger brother, Ryk, stumbled down the stairs ahead of his captor, a bit unsteady on his feet.

Nathan stared in horror. They'd captured Ryk! Was that how they thought to tame him, by threats to his wheezing, weak, defenseless little brother? Ryk was, at least, not wheezing much, yet.

"Ryk!"

"Nathan?" Ryk replied, joy and terror warring on his face.

"Oh, Ryk, I never meant for you to come. I thought you'd send some of the older men from the church."

"And turn this into even more of a fiasco than it already is? What were you trying to do, start a war?" Ryk looked at his brother indignantly.

Nathan hung his head. "Rescue some people. I thought I could do it."

Ryk's reply was deservedly sarcastic. "Well, that worked out well, didn't it?"

Nathan looked away but said nothing. His failure was self-evident. Out of the corner of his eye he noticed Brenson watching and listening intently as Ryk waited in silence for his brother to actually acknowledge his error.

Nathan looked back at Ryk, misery in his eyes. Half the fights he'd gotten into in school had been in defense of his sickly little brother; the kid wasn't supposed to sacrifice himself like this in return. "I haven't done too well at protecting you, have I?"

"You did fine at that," said Ryk. "What you've never mastered is behaving sensibly with regard to yourself."

"But now," said Nathan, defeated, "here you are." He looked past Ryk to Brenson. "All right, you've got me. I'll do whatever you want. Just spare Ryk."

Brenson snorted. "Ryk, does that sound like the way a man who thinks of himself as a willing partner talks? Bah. I should send the two of you back on the next freight, except I don't think I can trust Nathan to stay sent."

"Send Ryk back, at least. I'm begging you," Nathan pled.

"Ryk, would you go back without your brother?" asked Brenson.

Nathan silently begged Ryk to agree.

Ryk considered, then decided, "No."

Anguished, Nathan said, "Oh, Ryk."

Ryk glared at his brother. "He said he'd send both of us back if you'd give up this idiotic scheme of yours and stay on our side of the border."

Nathan considered this. Could he give up his promise to God, just because he'd failed once? Would God take the attempt for the deed? Or was he obligated to try again? "I made a promise to God, Ryk. I can't just shrug it off."

"Then I guess we're both stuck here until you change your mind." Ryk walked over to an empty potato crate and sat down.

Nathan thought some more. The demons were all liars; was it acceptable to lie to them, to save his brother's life? He turned to Brenson. "Let us go, and I'll take my brother home. You'll never have to deal with me again."

"You're lying, Nathan. If I let you go, you'll try again, and because you're a Natural Donor you could actually do serious harm."

Nathan muttered something unchurchly under his breath.

Brenson shook his head and made a "tsk tsk" noise.

Ryk shrugged. "He's got a point, Nathan."

Nathan scowled. "You're not helping, Ryk."

"Nothing but sincerity and truth is going to help here," said Brenson. "Simes can always tell when people lie, which is why we don't generally bother."

"That's a lie. Demons are the fathers of lies." Nathan reflected that even if the demon had promised to send Ryk home, he never would have known whether it had actually been done or not.

"I can't stop you from believing whatever you want to, Nathan," replied Brenson quietly. "but it's not actually what you yourself believe, it's what those 'wise elders' of yours have stuffed your mind full of."

"I told you they were idiots, Nathan," Ryk interjected. "but even so, do you see them crossing the border?"

"How would we know if they did?" Nathan argued. "People go missing all the time, especially kids."

Ryk rolled his eyes.

"Life is too full of actual dangers without making up new ones," said Brenson.

Nathan ignored the demon. "You've always been the thinker, Ryk. Think us a way out of this."

"Can you name even one of the elders who hasn't been present and accounted for at least twice a week for the six months since you joined that group?" Ryk persevered.

"Oh, you mean elders crossing the border. I thought you meant demons." Nathan considered. "Generals don't fight a war from the front lines, Ryk. They can't. They have to stand back and see the big picture."

"Yeah, but most successful generals have at least spent some time as a soldier. Those guys…not so much. In fact, I have to wonder if any of them have ever come face to face with a real Sime."

"We never saw them do it, because we were just kids. But how else would they know about things like the shoulder squeeze?"

"The one that works so well?" Ryk countered.

"I didn't get a chance for a proper grip," said Nathan.

Ryk looked at Brenson, who admitted, "The one that doesn't work at all."

"Of course you'd say that, so we wouldn't bother to try it."

"Actually," Brenson continued, "the grip that works is further down the arm, but you'll excuse me if I don't show you exactly where. Just yet."

Nathan snorted in dark amusement.

"Luckily for Ryk," said Brenson, "Killer Simes are almost unheard-of on this side of the border, as opposed to your side, where they happen all the time. But in your case," the demon added, "all you need to do is rapidly change your emotional state, and any Killer within a few hundred feet would drop dead on the spot."

"You're trying to say you don't Kill?"

"Never. Some Simes who come to us from Genland have Killed, but they either stop, or die within a year. Ryk knows about this already."

Ryk shrugged. "He told me that there simply haven't been enough Gens on this side of the border to support Killing since the Unity War."

"You're penning us for 'milk' instead of 'eat'?" accused Nathan. "But a Pen is still a Pen."

"Tell that to a cow," said Ryk.

"So what's this stone box I'm in," countered Nathan, "if it's not a plain old-fashioned Pen?"

"It's the house of my family, or extended family, the Zyaxes," Brenson said firmly.

"Which I guess means it's a new-fashioned Pen," Ryk added.

Brenson explained, "This building was built as a Pen, yes. But the people who live here now, Simes and Gens, are a family."

"So this basement," Ryk suggested, "is the equivalent of locking the crazy uncle in the attic?"

"Ryk," objected his brother, "Whose side are you on?"

"The side of common sense, I hope," Ryk said. "If I'm not happy to be here myself, why would I think it's great that you're here?"

"It's the equivalent of the potato storage bin," Brenson put in. "But it's suitable for confining a powerful and dangerous man who doesn't know his own strength, and is refusing to learn how to be responsible for its proper use."

Nathan was reassured that at least, the demons considered him powerful and dangerous. Unfortunately, it did mean they locked him up more carefully.

Ryk looked at his brother, who didn't strike him as any sort of superman. "He keeps saying that you have some sort of talent for something or other. Unlike your bookkeeping brother."

Nathan decided to make a joke of it before the Sime, and thus missed the sudden acquisitive gleam in Brenson's eyes. "I told you, little brother, that milling is a real skill."

Brenson deadpanned, "Yes, you have to learn how to hold your thumb down on the scales."

Nathan hadn't expected to hear that particular wisecrack on this side of the border. He stared at the demon. "Where did you learn that one?" He realized that knowing where the demons got their intelligence about his people would be valuable information, if he could just get it back home.

"From a story my granddad told me, actually," said Brenson. "We all have family on both sides of the border, whether we admit it or not. Stands to reason."

"Your grandfather was born among humans?" asked Nathan.

"If you mean was he born in a barn, the answer is no. If you mean was he born in New Washington Territory, the answer is yes. Close enough that he managed to make it here without Killing."

"That must have been well before the War," said Nathan. Ryk was visibly disturbed by this discussion of Killing. Nathan couldn't blame him, when there were real, honest-to-goodness tentacles only a few feet away.

Brenson said, "Yes. But we're upsetting Ryk. Let's change the subject."

"All right," said Nathan. "What will it take to get you to send us home?"

"A genuine commitment on your part to either stay on your own side of the border for good, or to stay here at least until you can be trained not to misuse your abilities. Nothing more, nothing less. Ryk, of course, can go home whenever he wants, though I surely could use a competent accountant. But that's not the deal I'm making now."

"And what exactly would this 'training' be like?" Nathan asked suspiciously.

"Hard. Hard work. The hardest you've ever done."

Nathan turned to Ryk. "Little brother, please say you'll go home, even if I have to stay here."

"Not without you."

Nathan tried to stare him down, then relented with a hopeless sigh. The kid had always been stubborn. He turned to Brenson. "Then, for my brother's sake, I agree to this 'training' of yours."

Brenson studied Nathan closely to make sure the younger man meant it. "Are you sure? There's no backing out half way through. You won't be injured here — but you will be changed, changed enough that you won't really be able to understand the way you used to be any more."

Nathan was confident that, with God's help, he could resist any brainwashing. "I'm sure."

Brenson smiled a secret smile. Nathan, at least, would be his now. It was only a matter of time. Khanna would be pleased and Zyax would prosper. And if the other brother, the accountant, could be acquired as well? No one would welcome his skills more than his Sectuib.

This legend originally appeared in *A Companion in Zeor* #13 (1998-2000) and can be found in Rimon's Library on the domain at:

http://www.simegen.com/sgfandom/rimonslibrary/cz/cz13/CNEED1.HTM

THE LEGEND OF THE CREEPING NEED

ZOE FARRIS

A TALE INSPIRED BY JEAN LORRAH

I wish to tell you a story. It is a true story. It is a story of a terror that has haunted Simes and Gens for centuries. This terror strikes without warning and without conscience. It even strikes fear into the heart of the toughest of Raiders. This terror from which there is no escape lurks in the darkest of corners, waiting. Waiting to feed on the unsuspecting. It is often zlinned but never seen, and leaves few alive to tell of its passing. Pray that you never meet this terror, because if you do you will never again forget its touch. If you survive at all.

My great grandfather survived one such meeting. He was never the same again. Living with the fear and guilt that it was he who unleashed this terror left him a sad and withdrawn man.

During the last years of his life he would talk of the ghastly fate that awaits anyone who tries to live in that empty town again. This town that was once a ghost town and is one again.

He was a middle aged Sime when it happened. He was a Pen owner who took over the business from his father. He was married and had two sons, one of which had changed over. The other son Established a year later and was taken to the border and left to make his own way across. They were a relatively happy family who enjoyed life as best as they could.

It was a night with a moonless sky, and strong gusty winds that whistled and bellowed strange melodic sounds through the trees and through any tiny crevice in the house and Pens. In the Pens the Gens were heard restlessly shuffling about their cells. Considering the Gens were drugged this was highly unusual. Old Jack, as great granddad was known, went to the cells to see what was upsetting the Gens so.

When he got to the door, he zlinned what he thought must have been a Sime inside trying to get a free Kill. Upon opening the door though Old Jack found no such Sime, yet he still zlinned the driving Need of a Sime that was close to Attrition. From the far cell came the sound of a muffled scream followed by the hard thud of something hitting the floor; and because Old Jack had been zlinning he felt the full brunt of the brutal and sadistic fear-induced Kill.

He quickly recovered, and enraged went to catch the culprit who had broken into his cells to steal his property, but when he reached the last cell there was no sign of the Sime responsible. He couldn't have gotten away; there were bars at the window that even a small child could not have climbed through. There was no back door, either. The only way out was through the front door and that meant that the culprit had to get past Old Jack, and no one had.

On closer inspection Old Jack was startled to find the cell door still locked. No one could have gotten in, yet he felt the Kill. Looking into the cell Old Jack saw a sight that was to haunt him for the rest of his life.

There had been ten Gens in the end cell and two of them were now dead. The others were huddled into the far corner quivering in shock as their gazes were fixed on the bodies of the two dead Gens. The one closest to the front bars was still standing, well not really standing but whatever force had thrown him against the bars had been so fierce that his shoulders had jammed into the spaces between the bars and left the Gen standing where he died.

The other dead Gen, who looked to be the one Old Jack zlinned being Killed, lay bent and broken up against the back wall. Sitting, slumped forward like a discarded child's doll, it stared with glassed eyes at the floor. The face was pale and drawn into some horrifying grin that had tried in vain to release a scream only to have it denied exit. Deep purple bruises covered both arms and the lips were bruised and bloodied from the pressure of the Killer's lips.

Old Jack zlinned both Gens and they had been drained completely, not a trace of selyn left in either of them. Every cell had been totally and violently wrenched of its life.

After removing the bodies Old Jack went back to the main house and filled in a report about the mysterious death of two of his Gens. He couldn't allow himself to believe what he suspected so he wrote, "Cause of death—Unknown." Not wanting to bother his wife and son—would they believe him anyway?—he didn't mention it and went to bed to an uneasy sleep.

During the early hours of the next morning Old Jack awoke to the presence of someone else in the room. His wife was asleep beside him yet he could zlin a third and unfamiliar energy in the room. As he became fully awake the energy source simply vanished. Old Jack didn't go back to sleep that morning, but lay there wondering if he had reawakened the figure from the town's horrifying past.

The next day was uneventful and Old Jack began to put the night before down to a nightmare brought on from whatever happened to the Gens. Falling asleep that night was easy as he was tired from the lack of sleep the night before and he was deeply asleep within seconds of hitting his pillow.

Suddenly Old Jack was woken by the same presence that had been in the room the night before. As he zlinned he realised that it was hovering over his wife and his wife was flaring extreme fear. The kind of fear that was usually zlinned in Wild Gens who have an awareness of their fate. He went duoconscious to see who was in the room but he saw nothing and no one with his eyes, yet he still zlinned the presence; and it was focused on his wife's fear.

He watched as his wife raised her arms skywards and her tentacles seemed to wrap around emptiness. Her laterals slowly emerged as if they were trying desperately not to. As his wife slowly opened her eyes and watched her own arms in disbelief she began to toss and struggle as if to free herself from some unseen grasp.

She let out a strangled moan and her eyes bulged as they glassed over and froze in openness to forever stare at that emptiness. Her dead arms fell back onto her now dead body. Tentacles limp around her own arms, laterals still extended, lifeless.

Old Jack sat up to wake his wife from what he thought was a dream triggered motion but it was over within the time it took him to sit up and reach for her. He started shaking her and calling her name. He began crying as he realised she was dead. He had known what it was but refused to believe that such a horror could be real, but now he had seen it, no not seen but zlinned. Fear began to rise in him. Fear for his wife, and fear for what he had released.

Old Jack was so focused on his wife that he didn't notice the presence still with him, and when he did notice it was too late. Suddenly his arms were pulled away from his body by some invisible force as he felt the steely grip of tentacles lash about his arms and his own tentacles forced from their sheaths to wrap around these unseen cords of death. Before he could make a sound his lips were sealed with an invisible kiss and his laterals were wrest from their sheaths and tightly bound. He could taste the blood in his mouth as his teeth bit into his own lips.

Shock turned to fear as he felt his system being wrenched inside out as his selyn was being stripped from him. On the verge of death he heard the bedroom door flung open and his son began screaming to him. He thought this would be the last sound he would hear before death carried him away. Instead this invisible Killer stopped and as Old Jack drifted into unconsciousness he felt sudden fear coming from the void above him. His body was released from the deadly clasp and he fell back onto the bed, barely alive.

The last thing he saw before he lost consciousness was the mask of sheer terror on the face of his wife. She too had been drained of her life, her system turned inside out to flow backwards. Killed like a Gen.

Old Jack finally came through after having to be forced to take a Kill after he regained consciousness. He refused at first, not wanting to live long enough to have to go through that again, but as his natural instinct for survival overrode his emotions he took the Kill and began his physical healing. As Old Jack lay on his bed he just kept muttering that they had to leave right away because "it" would come back. It would Kill everyone. He and his son, as well as the remaining Gens.

Old Jack told his son that he was sure he knew what it was, or who it had been. It had started several years earlier. One time there were only a few Gens in the cells. These few Gens were the last of a group of Wild Gens that had been caught just inside the border.

There had been a child, a pre-Gen, that had been kept in a cell by himself. Old Jack had made this child do menial jobs around the Pens and sometimes he would even allow him to work around the yard and in the barn. As the boy became less fearful he would often hide and occasionally he would attempt to escape, without success.

Old Jack let this pass for a while but when he caught the boy trying to pick the lock of the cell that held the remaining Gens he lost his temper. As he tried to return the boy to his cell the boy began to kick and claw at Old Jack's arms in an attempt to get loose. This sent Old Jack into a rage and he picked the boy up by the scruff and threw him violently back into his cell.

Old Jack realised that without fear this boy could be dangerous and from that moment on he treated the boy as if he were already Gen. No longer was the boy allowed out of the Pens, and Old Jack took his own Kill where the boy would witness it and know that Simes were to be feared. Whenever the boy showed any sign of defiance he would grab the boy as he would a Kill and terrorize him. The boy was also made to clean the Killroom after a Kill. The boy learned his lessons well. He became a pitiful, cowering child who shook and whimpered whenever a Sime came near.

Having to collect a new shipment of Gens, Old Jack and his son left early one morning so he could do some other business while in town. Sometime during that morning this boy went into changeover. When Old Jack returned he found his wife agitated and very upset. She had heard screams that afternoon and on investigation found the boy on the verge of death.

He had been so close to the Gens in the next cell, yet he was separated by the thick bars. Sitting, face pressed against the bars his desperation almost overwhelmed her. By the time she went to the house to get the spare keys and returned the boy had died of Attrition, arms stretched through the bars in a final frantic attempt to reach life.

After that, Old Jack would occasionally find several Gens drained of their selyn. Usually in that very same cell. Each time it happened there would be more Gens Killed and they would be Killed more brutally. It was as if whatever was Killing them could not be satisfied and each time its Need was greater. Old Jack always said it was that boy who Killed the Gens, and he was sure it was him that Killed his wife, and almost Killed him. He also believed that somehow this lurking non-entity still carried with it the fear that he had instilled in the boy, and when his son burst into the room it was that fear that drove it from the room.

His son, Marc, buried his mother and packed their wagon with as much as it could carry. Marc helped his father to the wagon and they headed for town. They stayed there the night at a friend's place and told them of what happened and the next day Old Jack and Marc drove out of town, never to go back.

Did it ever attack again? Well, some months later a good friend of Old Jack moved here and he told him that after Old Jack left several of the townsfolk went out to his place to get what Gens were left there. Although the cells were all still locked every Gen had been Killed, savagely. Completely drained.

Over the next couple of weeks the townspeople started to find their Gens dead in their Killrooms. Slowly people began to leave the town out of fear, and when another Sime was Killed in the same manner those who had remained did not take long to abandon the town.

Even today the town is dead. No one will even travel through it in case this invisible Killer attacks. Everything is still as it was then. And of those who do go there? It's said that they are never heard from again. There are many rumours as to what it is and whether it is still around, but one that I have heard is that once the town is empty and there is no one left to trigger it, it goes into some kind of stasis or hibernation until the utmost heart wrenching fear calls to it again.

Till the day he died, Old Jack never again slept at night, nor did he sleep alone. He only slept when someone else was awake. No one knows why it left when Old Jack's son entered the room. Maybe it thought Old Jack dead. Maybe it was frightened off by Marc's appearance. Who knows? I don't.

He never fully recovered from the guilt he felt at his wife's death and the fear that he might face this terror again someday. He always told the story, as a warning, to his son and his son's children of the terror that has no form. It was told to me and my sisters and to our cousins by my grandfather, Marc, and now I tell you.

This invisible death strikes in the still of night, covered in the blanket of darkness and camouflaged as dream. You will never see it, but if you're Sime you will zlin it. It will drain Gen and Sime alike of every drop of selyn and still NEED more. It cannot be satisfied. It cannot be fulfilled. It is an eternal hunter. It is the CREEPING NEED.

"Be Not Afraid" originally appeared in A Companion in Zeor #10, (1990) and can be found in Rimon's Library http://www.simegen.com/ sgfandom/householding/chanel/afraid.html

BE NOT AFRAID

MARJORIE ROBBINS

Kley's favorite time of day was early morning. The world was hushed and still in that quiet predawn moment before the sun would peek its rosy face above the horizon to begin its slow ascent into the daytime sky.

For just a moment Kley studied his reflection in the still-darkened windowpanes. His unruly red hair was, for once, under some semblance of control. His dark eyes glowed with pride as he fingered the Chanel crest stitched to the breast pocket of his new crimson uniform.

With a contented sigh he picked up his text on the psychology of disjunction and bent again to his studies.

A few moments later his door flew open with an alarming crash. Startled, Kley jumped to his feet. He'd been so absorbed in the text he'd failed to zlin the approach of three renSimes. Two wore the uniform of the Tecton police. They were dragging with them a young girl whose nager was defiant and hostile.

"Hajene Kley?" asked one of the officers. At the channel's nod of acknowledgment, he went on apologetically. "Sorry to disturb you, but the duty channel said to bring her to you."

"What's the problem?"

Kley had taken control of the rather discordant fields and was working to calm the youngster. She glared defiantly as his field engaged hers. "You shendi-flayed lorsh! Let me go!"

"We caught her trying to leave the grounds of the Center. Since we know she's a disjunction candidate, we brought her back. Your duty channel said the Controller is busy and asked that you deal with her. She was hunting Gens."

That wasn't surprising. Though he was not yet officially assigned to the disjunction ward of the Cedar City Sime Center, Kley had some training and did occasionally help out with counseling and routine transfers while he continued the study of psychology, his House's specialty that he had started while in First Year School.

"It's all right. She can stay with me." Smiling, he moved towards the girl. "Relax, honey. No one's going to hurt you."

She struggled futilely in the tight grasp of her captors. "Make those lorshes let go of me."

"Let her go. And you, young lady, stop augmenting. You're wasting selyn."

The girl struggled a moment longer then went limp, almost falling as the officers released her. "Her name's Arla," supplied one of the ren-Simes as they started for the door.

"Thanks." Kley dismissed the police with a wave then turned his full attention to the girl, who was regarding him defiantly. She was tiny, abnormally thin even for a Sime. She had very delicate features and extremely long jet-black hair that lay in a rumpled mess on her shoulders. Her legs were covered with tiny scratches.

Evidently she had come in contact with the many hedges on the Center's Grounds.

She was also very close to hard Need, so Kley raised his showfield to the pure Gen enticement of a working channel. Shutting the door he held out his hands to the girl.

"I don't want transfer," she muttered, staring at the floor.

The channel was surprised. He hadn't thought it possible for a ren-Sime that deep into Need to resist a channel's field. Strengthening his contact with the girl, he took a few steps in her direction. "Come to me, Arla," he crooned softly.

"You bloody-shen lorsh!" she screamed. "I can do what I want."

"Perhaps, but you may not go out and find a Gen. The Tecton won't allow it." Kley carefully kept his tone neutral, letting his nager speak for him. He knew that regardless of what Arla thought she wanted, her instincts would soon overrule her and she would attack him.

"I don't want a Gen!" screamed Arla, genuine revulsion in her field. "What do you think I am, a murderer? That man lied. I wasn't hunting."

This thoroughly confused the channel. "Well then, if you don't want to Kill, why run? There are plenty of channels to choose from here."

Arla sank into a seat, her nager taking on a frightening resignation. "I don't want a channel, either." She buried her face in her hands, surrendering to a cold despair that sent shivers coursing up and down the channel's spine as he zlinned her.

Unbidden, a well-known image swelled up in Kley's mind: the surface of a deep blue sea, moving restlessly, the long swells swiftly getting bigger as their color darkened ominously. *Oh, no! She's suicidal!* The channel was all too familiar with the anguish radiating from the youngster before him.

Something in him ached to reach out and comfort her. But the danger to his own peace of mind was too great. Keeping a firm grasp on his field, Kley willed the waters to calm, the darkness to return to placid blue. No way was he going to confront what lay under those waters.

Seeking to hide his turmoil from Arla, he said gruffly, "It's obvious something's bothering you. Talk to me. Perhaps I can help."

"I don't want your help. I don't require it. Nothing's wrong. Just leave me alone."

"I can't do that." Kley took a deep breath. He knew he was going about this all wrong. "All right," he admitted softly. "You don't have to talk to me. But I can't let you go until you've had transfer."

He shrugged as the girl shook her head in determined denial. "Very well. I'm not going to force you to take transfer. But I do have work to do. Let me know when you change your mind." Resuming his seat behind his desk, he opened the textbook and started to read, though his professional attention remained fixed on the girl. She was stunned and trying unsuccessfully to hide it from the channel.

The next half hour passed exceedingly slowly for Kley. Though he couldn't think of anything else to do short of grabbing her and forcing transfer on her, he wasn't at all sure that his tactics were going to work.

Fervently he wished that Sectuib Aran was available. But he could easily be tied up for hours. Not only was he Chanel's Sectuib, he had just taken over as Controller of the Sime Center across the street from Chanel headquarters.

Keeping his eyes firmly on the book in his hands, though he really wasn't reading much, Kley carefully monitored the girl. As he had expected, she remained resistant until the last possible moment, pacing restlessly up and down, fighting unsuccessfully to keep her agitated laterals in their sheaths.

Finally, however, she went hyperconscious, springing at the channel and knocking the book out of his hands.

Kley made no resistance as she roughly pulled him into transfer position. The girl had no will of her own now, but had surrendered to the Killer instinct, her tentacles whipping quickly into place on his arms. Kley deftly entwined tentacles with her, his laterals meeting hers, ready and willing to feed her voracious hunger.

She began her draw swiftly, but faltered after a bare moment. Before the channel could react, Arla had pulled away, reeling in flaming shen to lean weakly against the wall, arms held tightly to her chest, nager clenched in hopeless despair.

Moving swiftly, while she was still hyperconscious, Kley pried her arms free and again took her into position. She didn't resist as he entwined laterals. Doing his best to simulate the fear and panic a Gen feels in the Kill, Kley began to push selyn into her at a speed slightly less than her previous draw speed. At first she resisted and the channel thought sure he'd be shenned again. The waters rose in his mind, muddy-brown and moving restlessly, pouring fear and helpless into his thoughts, spilling over into his snowfield. Before he could suppress this, Arla's field changed. She was responding. Weakly, but she was responding.

Arla began a listless draw that only increased momentarily when Kley offered the feigned resistance that should have brought her satisfaction. It didn't.

Nearing repletion, Arla ceased even her token draw, leaving it to the channel to terminate the flow and break contact.

Immediately Arla began to cry hysterically. "Let me die! Oh, God, why didn't you just let me die!"

Kley waited a moment, then put a tender arm around her, crooning soft words of reassurance. At first she resisted, but after a few moments she let him lead her to a seat.

Still in tears, she cuddled against the channel and cried for a long time. Kley zlinned deeply and unobtrusively, discovering that her physical condition was very poor. Her selyn system was in knots. He also noted dark spots in her digestive tract that he suspected were ulcers. Considering the tremendous tension she was carrying, that wasn't surprising.

Kley debated deepening his contact with her to work on those dark spots, then decided against it. Undoubtedly she was already getting channel's therapy. And in any case, she was calming down, starting to draw away. To insist on therapy now might provoke more hostility.

Handing her his handkerchief, he asked softly, "Feeling better?"

Arla scrubbed the tears from her eyes. "Stupid question. I want to go back to my room now."

"Why not tell me what's bothering you?" asked Kley, hoping to take advantage of her momentary calm.

Instantly Arla's nager returned to its former hostile state. "Shut up! I told you I don't want to talk to you. You're a lorsh like all channels. Leave me alone." Rising, she retreated to the opposite corner, silently daring the channel to do anything further.

"Very well." Kley went to the door and ordered a passing renSime to go for a Donor to escort Arla back to her room. Picking up the book that had gotten tossed on the floor, he returned to his seat behind the desk. "If you decide you want to talk to me later, just tell one of the attendants. I'll come as soon as I can."

Nager radiating total rejection, Arla turned away without answering. Kley shrugged. So much for the idea that he might have been able to reach her.

They waited in uncomfortable silence for the arrival of Arla's escort. As the door opened the room filled with a dull grey nager dotted with silver-blue speckles.

The rolling waters quickly turned an angry black, huge waves crashing against the shores of Kley's mind. *This can't be,* he thought fighting down panic. *That nager, that voice... No! that was another time another place.* Rising, he forced the fierce waves back. "You're...?"

"Verlyn ambrov Alger at your service," the Gen said cheerfully. "Arla, what are you doing here? You missed language class." When the girl didn't answer he glanced over at the channel. His green eyes widened as he shifted into a standard working mode. "Is something wrong, Kley? Should I...?"

"No, thank you. I'm fine. Just take Arla back to her room."

The Donor shook his head. "No, Hajene. You're upset about something." Crossing the room, he took Kley's hands, closely studying the channel's face.

Kley took a deep breath, forcing himself to stand still to endure the Gen's uncomfortable touch. After all Verlyn was only doing his job. "Just put it down to turnover jitters," he said as calmly as he could. The waves were crashing wildly now, threatening to spill up onto the shore the dark things they were supposed to be covering.

"Take care of Arla. She's just had a rather rocky transfer." As he had hoped, the distraction worked. Though it was obvious that the Donor didn't completely accept his rationale, Kley had given a legitimate order.

"Yes, Hajene." Finally, Verlyn's professional attention turned towards Arla.

Though her nager radiated extreme fear, all of her belligerent hostility vanished, leaving in its place a sunny smile and outwardly submissive manner. Kley frowned slightly in puzzlement over the odd contradiction.

Verlyn held out his hand to the girl. "Come on, Arla, it's time for lunch. You must be hungry?"

"Yeah, I am." Arla took the Gen's hand, still smiling warmly. "I'm sorry I missed your class. I won't do it again, I promise."

The Gen grinned. "Don't worry about it. But you did miss some interesting..." He was still talking as the door closed behind them.

Kley sank back in his seat, burying his head in his hands. Stilling the dark waters took a lot of time and effort. As Kley regained his emotional equilibrium, his thoughts turned to the Gen. That name was very familiar.

Finally Kley placed it. "Oh, no! My next transfer. He's my Donor!" A fresh wave of despair swept over him.

True, he could probably ask Aran to make a change, but then he would have to explain to his Sectuib why that Donor was unacceptable. *I can't do that. I just can't tell Sectuib about the dark waters. If he saw what was under them, he wouldn't want me in Chanel anymore.* Feeling trapped, Kley finally got the restless waves under some semblance of control, then left the office to chart Arla's transfer.

* * * *

The next two weeks passed all too quickly for the young channel. By burying himself in his studies and volunteering for extra duty in the Collectorium and Dispensary, he was able to do a fairly good job of avoiding the Disjunction Ward and contact with Verlyn. But he couldn't avoid the inevitable meeting with his Donor for transfer.

Even though he was a few minutes early for the appointment, he found Verlyn waiting for him in the appointed place.

"Good morning, Kley!" the Donor said cheerfully. Rising from his seat by the window, he crossed the room to offer his hands to the channel.

Kley stiffened as the Gen made nageric contact. The waters stirred restlessly, the blue changing to a deep blue-black. *This is silly,* he told himself, *Verlyn's just a Donor. He won't hurt me.* But he couldn't keep himself from flinching or his hands from trembling as Verlyn's field engaged him.

"What's wrong?" asked Verlyn softly. "I seem to be frightening you. Am I doing something wrong?"

Shaking his head, the channel reached for Verlyn's hands, making an effort to relax. "No, I'm…" Kley stopped, unable to think of a good reason for his unusual reaction.

Verlyn grinned wryly. "Well, I haven't spent any time with you. I guess that was a mistake."

Kley seized the excuse gratefully. "I suppose that's it. Generally I get a Chanel Donor, someone I know."

The Gen chuckled. "That's what my channel said last month. Maybe coming here for specialized training wasn't such a good idea. I seem to be at a disadvantage. But I assure you I can do just as good a job as…" He hesitated, eying Kley speculatively. "You're not really ready for transfer, are you? Let me work a little."

Kley took a deep breath. "Yes, I guess that's a good idea." He let himself be led to the transfer couch, where the Gen started a gentle systematic massage of the channel's head, neck, and shoulders, gradually working his way down Kley's arms.

By cooperating fully with the Gen, Kley was able to relax somewhat. "Initiate trautholo. I'm as ready as I'll ever be."

But Verlyn wasn't satisfied. "My field isn't raising your intil as it should." He was genuinely worried. "Perhaps I should ask Sectuib Aran if another Donor…"

A wave of guilt washed over Kley at the faint hurt in the Gen's nager. "No," he said firmly. "You're doing just fine. I don't want another Donor." He wasn't sure he could take transfer from Verlyn, but he was sure that he didn't want to explain to Aran why he couldn't.

Verlyn wasn't satisfied, but he did as the channel requested; deepening his link to pre-transfer readiness.

Kley stiffened momentarily then relaxed. He slid into hyperconsciousness, zlinning only the selyn currents in the Gen's body. Though the angry waters were crashing wildly now, he ignored them, his Need blotting out everything but the promise of fulfillment in the warm glow of the selyn field before him.

Making lateral contact, he leaned forward, found the Gen's lips, and began his draw. For a few moments all was well. The warm selyn poured into his body in satisfying pulses of sparkling energy. The cold dark numbness and fear of Need receded, leaving behind the light and warmth of life renewed. But as he neared the terminus, the crashing waves began to get too big to ignore.

Images came out of the rolling waters. Images of a time long past that Kley tried hard not to think about. A face arose, features distorted with rage and loathing. "Evil child!" it wailed. "Devil's Spawn. Evil! Evil! Evil!" Memories of searing pain. Kley's arms began to ache, then burn with an intensity that made him start to draw back from the contact he was holding.

But even as he lost control of the selyn flow in the panic of withdrawal, the struggle to re-bury the dark face, the hated words, to overcome the searing pain that seemed to be tearing his laterals into shreds, he was aware of a warm compassion coming from the one who was holding him.

Verlyn had taken control of the selyn flow and was fighting the threatened abort with all the skill and compassion at his command. Realizing this and knowing that the "dark other" of his nightmares was not really present, though his nager seemed to be Kley was able to calm the crashing waves to a dull roar. The selyn flow resumed its speed, the abort was averted. But Kley was afraid to resume control, so he let the Donor bring the transfer to a barely acceptable conclusion.

He opened his eyes to see Verlyn's green ones staring at him in bewilderment and concern. "I'm sorry, Kley," the Gen whispered as the channel broke the contact between them and retracted his tentacles.

Kley sighed. Reaction was setting in and he felt very ashamed of himself. Low-field, Verlyn was no longer threatening and the agitated waters were slowly calming, the channel's automatic control mechanisms sliding into place. "For what? It wasn't your fault I lost control."

But the Donor was unsatisfied. "Something went wrong. What? Did I do something not up to Chanel's high standards?"

Kley shook his head. "You did just fine." He could sense that Verlyn was not satisfied, but he couldn't explain that Verlyn's nager reminded him all too vividly of his buried nightmares. That would just lead to other questions that he couldn't answer. "It's not your fault that I almost aborted," he repeated helplessly.

"Then what happened?" demanded the Gen.

"I, I..." Not wanting to confess the truth, Kley resorted to a subterfuge. "The flow became lopsided and I couldn't balance it."

He could see in the Gen's eyes and nager that Verlyn didn't believe him, but wasn't going to pry. "Sure, Hajene. If you say so. But it might not be a bad idea for you to see your Sectuib. Something IS wrong whether you want to admit it or not." He then left the room before the channel could reply.

Feeling miserable, Kley went outside for a short walk to clear his head before returning to his duties. On impulse he crossed the street and rounded Chanel's administration building. There was a small park behind it, where Chanel's children loved to play. This time of day, however, it should be empty. He was fairly sure he could be alone there for a few minutes.

However, that was not to be. As he rounded the corner, he could hear youthful voices laughing and shouting gleefully. A small ball bounded by him out of control. Automatically augmenting, he captured it.

"Thief!" roared a familiar voice in his head. "Give me the ball." All around him other voices were protesting.

"But he found it!"

"It was just lying there!"

Kley blinked. The park had disappeared. He was somewhere else being confronted by an angry face, features twisted with rage. "Devil's spawn, all of you! That ball is stolen. Give it to me."

"I found it," Kley protested.

"Liar!" Strong hands wrested the ball away from him, then slapped him across the mouth. "Evil child! Repent this instant or the devil will make you a filthy Sime. Repent!" roared the ugly voice.

"I can't," objected Kley. "I didn't do anything wrong."

He was hit again and again. "Repent! Repent!"

"I'm not evil," Kley protested helplessly. "Please don't hit me, please!"

"Hajene, what's wrong?" A small girl was facing him, a look of intense worry on her face. "We weren't trying to hit you, honest."

Kley took a deep breath. The waters were completely out of control now; the dark images refused to recede. Concentrating on the childish nager before him, he forced a smile. "Why aren't you kids in school?"

An older boy came up, "We have a long recess today. Several kids went into changeover and our teachers are busy."

The girl giggled. "So are the channels. Why aren't you working, Hajene Kley? Are you playing hooky?"

Gathering the remnants of his tattered dignity, Kley shook his head. "Channels don't play hooky. I was just taking a walk after my transfer."

The little girl shook her head vigorously. "If you had transfer, you wouldn't look so sick. Go see Sectuib. He'll make you feel better."

"Tasha, shut up," admonished her playmate.

Kley forced a smile. Tossing the ball to Tasha, he said, "I just might do that. Later. Now I do have to get back to work. So you kids go on and play."

Tasha grinned. "Yeah, or Sectuib will scold you, too. Bye, Hajene." She ran off, followed by her playmates.

Breathing a sigh of relief, Kley hastened to his office to take refuge in his studies. It was going to take a long time to still the angry waves this time.

But he didn't have that luxury. Less than an hour later a messenger told him that Aran wanted to see him as soon as possible. Wearily, Kley got to his feet and climbed the two flights of stairs to the Controller's office.

Aran looked up as Kley entered. "Oh, hi, Kley." The smile on his youthful face faded. "Wasn't your transfer satisfactory? You look like shen and zlin worse."

"You don't look so hot yourself," the younger channel retorted, hoping to distract his Sectuib. "You seem tired. Did you sleep at all last night?" Sliding into a chair, he ostentatiously began zlinning. "Shall I do some field work?"

"That won't work. The day you can zlin through my showfield is the day I'll resign as Sectuib," Aran teased. Making nageric contact with the other channel, he began working to gently iron out the kinks in Kley's systems left behind by the poor transfer.

"What happened? You and Verlyn should have been a good match."

"We are. It was nothing really. Sectuib, did you send for me to scold me?"

Aran raised innocent eyebrows. "I never do that." Then he sobered. "No. I haven't read the report on your transfer yet. But since you're in no condition to work right now, perhaps it's a good thing I did." He smiled as the younger channel relaxed in response to his therapy. "That's better. Are you sure you don't want to tell me about it?"

"I'd rather you told me why you sent for me." Kley forced an innocent smile. "There's really nothing to tell."

Aran's field reflected his disbelief, but he just nodded. "Very well, but the issue isn't closed. We'll take it up later."

He shuffled some papers on his messy desk. "Just now there's something we have to discuss."

"What?"

"You're supposed to be helping out at the Disjunction Center, yet in the past two weeks you haven't been near the place. Why?"

"Um..." Kley thought fast. "I've been working extra hours in the Collectorium and Dispensary."

"I know. All volunteer." Aran gazed quizzically at the other channel. "Is there some reason why you shouldn't be working with the disjunction candidates?"

"Of course not," replied Kley indignantly. "You know I've chosen that as my specialty."

"I'm beginning to wonder. Remember Arla Friet?"

"Arla, who?" In a hasty attempt to hide his sudden panic, Kley raised his showfield, which had weakened under Aran's therapy.

"Arla Friet. The disjunction candidate who tried to run away a couple of weeks ago. She asked for you this morning." Aran handed Kley a rather thick file and waited patiently while the other channel leafed through it.

"As you can see, she's very ill and approaching her crisis."

Kley was puzzled. "But surely ulcers are curable. You have her in the hospital under channel's therapy."

"She's not responding. Evidently she's lost her will to live." Aran ran his hands through his untidy reddish-brown hair.

"I was hoping you could tell me why."

Oh, shen! How much does he know? Kley had to work to fight down panic. The waves were crashing loudly now, images pounding away behind his eyes, interfering with his vision.

"She's the daughter of Reverend Gaylon Friet of Granite City. A rather prominent family, I gather. I thought maybe there was something...." Aran's voice became a dim whisper.

Kley's mother stood before him, a leather strap dangling from her hand. "I didn't do it, Mother. The ball was just lying there." Kley cringed, shrinking away. More than once he'd felt the bite of that strap.

"Liar! Reverend Friet saw you. Damn it, Kley, do you want to become a wicked Sime?" The strap flickered across his face...once...twice.

Kley stumbled and fell, tears falling from his eyes mingled with the blood that was welling up from deep cuts in his cheeks.

"Repent, you evil child! No son of mine is going to be Sime." The strap cracked again, this time cutting a deep welt across the arm he threw up to protect his eyes. "Mother, please," he sobbed. "I'm not evil. I swear. I didn't take that ball."

"If you're lying, you'll pay the price." His mother turned and walked away. Over her shoulder she snapped, "You're dripping blood on the carpet. Go wash your face then clean up your mess!"

"I'm not evil," sobbed the younger Kley. "I'm not. I'm not!"

"Kley, are you listening to me?" Aran's voice had an impatient ring to it.

Kley blinked. Sectuib was frowning at him.

"Have you heard a word I said?" Aran asked.

"Oh, um. Sorry, Sectuib. Yes, I've met Friet," he repressed a shudder. *If Arla was that man's daughter, then...*

"Well," prompted Aran. "Have you any idea why Arla wouldn't want to live?"

"No, I don't understand that." Kley took a deep breath. "I knew Reverend Friet. Everybody did. His church is the biggest in Granite City. But I have no idea why Arla would want to die." He squirmed uncomfortably, sure Aran didn't believe him.

"This is a serious matter. Arla isn't the only child from the Granite City area to feel this way. We've lost several children already. I don't want to lose any more. If you know something, you should tell me."

"Reverend Friet is a very devout man." Kley spoke slowly, trying to gather his thoughts. "Very strict. He believes that Simes are evil."

"What Gen doesn't?" Aran shook his head. "Anything else?"

What can I say? That wickedness causes changeover? That Arla and I are Sime because we weren't obedient enough; weren't good enough to please God and...

Kley shook himself, resolutely banishing that train of thought. He wasn't evil. *Friet was wrong, he had to be.* Holding to that thought in defiance of the painful feelings welling up inside of him, Kley said softly, "I'm sorry, Sectuib. I really didn't know the man, personally. I don't know what to tell you."

He stared at the floor, knowing that Aran didn't believe him, but he just couldn't tell the truth. However, there was nothing he could do about the shame and self-loathing that were flooding his nager.

He looked up at the answering tide of compassion coming from the other channel. "Kley, I hope you know you can tell me anything."

Yeah, except what I really am. Kley just nodded, unable to speak.

"Were you mistreated as a child? Were others…"

"No!" interrupted Kley. "My parents were good to me." Though he had put as much indignation into his voice and nager as he could, it obviously wasn't enough.

"What's the gist of our pledge?" Aran asked.

Kley blinked, caught off guard by the apparent unrelated question. "To give service to anyone who requires it."

"No matter what the price?"

"That's not in the pledge."

Aran steepled his fingers and just stared at the younger channel.

Kley dropped his eyes. "But you expect it of your channels," he admitted unwillingly.

"I expect it of anyone who claims the name ambrov Chanel." Aran rose, rounded his desk, and perched on a corner directly in front of Kley. "Arla requires your help now. She's dying and nobody has been able to reach her. She asked for you. It may be she's willing to talk to you. I know you haven't had much training and ordinarily I wouldn't think of making such an assignment, but if there's any chance you can reach the girl we have to take it."

Kley shook his head. "Sectuib, I can't do it."

"Why not?"

Kley was silent, unable to think of an answer that Aran would accept.

"Unless you have a good reason, you will take the assignment." He waited a minute, but shame and embarrassment kept Kley's tongue still.

Suddenly Aran dropped his showfield, revealing to Kley his deep and abiding love for the younger channel, his concern for Arla, and his sure conviction that Kley was not being truthful with him. Also present was a reluctance to take the course he was taking with the other channel. Overriding all was Aran's determination to help both Kley and Arla, no matter what.

Aran said softly. "In the last few minutes you've given me a lot of valid reasons for taking you off all your cases and putting you into therapy."

"But there's nothing wrong with me," Kley protested.

Aran raised a hand. "Please, don't make it worse by lying. I know something's troubling you. But I'm betting that you'll find the courage to tell me about it, without forcing me to take drastic action. So I want you to spend some time in the Memorial thinking about our pledge. I know you're deeply committed to Chanel. I want you to consider what that means. And consider this—you can't be an effective therapist unless you're willing to confront your own problems."

Feeling very unworthy of Aran's affection, Kley mumbled some quickly forgotten response and escaped to the privacy of his own office.

Running quickly through some relaxation drills, Kley was able to regain some control of the crashing waves. However, it was several hours before he could face obeying his Sectuib's orders. When he finally left his office in the Center's administration building to cross the quadrangle to the hospital, the sun was low in the sky. The tall oaks were casting eerie shadows that did little to improve the channel's wretched mood.

He found Arla in a private room on the critical care ward. Here the atmosphere was hushed, the lighting dim. Only the critically ill were housed here, patients requiring almost constant channel's attention.

When he entered Arla's room, she was lying on her side in a fetal ball, totally ignoring Hajene Tyrus, who was attending her. Inserting himself deftly into the room's ambient, Kley raised two tentacles, signaling to Tyrus that he would watch her for a while.

The other channel left the room, giving Kley an affectionate pat on the back as he passed by. Gently closing the door, Kley went towards the bed, zlinning.

He was stunned at the deterioration in Arla's condition in such a short time. Even without lateral contact he could feel the burning pain in her abdomen, her chronic nausea. Her blood pressure was low and her body extremely thin and wasted.

Kley noted and filed away the clinical details automatically as he moved towards the bed. Arla was at turnover, so he made his showfield a pleasant restful Genness.

Knowing that she was awake and fully aware of his presence, he sat on the bed and began to gently rub her back. He could feel each sharp bone of her spine under the thin fabric of her hospital gown.

"Go away, Kley" she mumbled after a few minutes. "I'm sleepy."

Kley chuckled. "You sent for me, remember? Sectuib Aran said that you wanted to talk to me, so I'm here."

"I...I changed my mind. Talking won't do any good." Abruptly sitting up, Arla shoved him away roughly. "Leave me alone."

Caught off guard, he almost fell off the bed. Retreating to a chair, he said "I can't do that. Not for a few minutes anyway." He studied her carefully. Her field was restless, changing colors rapidly as she tried suppressing feelings he couldn't quite identify, but which seemed quite familiar. *Shen, this kid should have been a channel. Her control is phenomenal for a renSime. Wish I could do that.* In a matter of seconds her nager was a cheery goldish-pink, sparkling like effervescent wine.

"Very good. Now tell me what's wrong."

She giggled. "Why should I? Your nager's yucky. You tell me what's wrong!"

Stunned by the surprising attempt at role reversal, Kley could only stammer, "I...I... I'm worried about you. They tell me you're very sick."

Her field dimmed. "So?" Hugging her knees, she rested her head on them. "It doesn't really matter. Not anymore."

Her loose gown fell off one shoulder, revealing an ugly scar that Kley hadn't noticed before. Reaching out, he touched the scar with a gentle tentacle. "Who did that to you?"

Pulling away, she yanked the gown back in place, glaring at him. "None of your business. That was an accident a long time ago."

"Your father?"

"Of course not. My father's a minister. He doesn't hurt people!"

"Not even filthy Simes?" Kley nearly choked on the words that had been screamed at him so many times. Maintaining a tight hold on his nager and an even firmer grip on the crashing waves, he waited.

Arla had turned her head and was fighting her own battle of suppression. "That's not fair," she finally whispered.

Kley touched her arm. "Arla, look at me."

She turned, met his eyes. "Get out of here," she said roughly. "You're a dumb channel and I hate you. You're just like all the others, wanting to tear my guts to shreds. Get out!"

"Arla, that's not true. I really do care about you. I want to help you."

"Then why is your nager so thick?" She shook her head as he started to speak. "No, I won't believe a word you say. You're hiding stuff. You probably hate me like everyone else does. Get out!" When he didn't respond, she threw a pillow at him, then reached for her water pitcher. "Get out!" she shrieked.

Giving up, Kley left the room. Pausing only long enough to send an attendant for Tyrus, he returned to his office and the omnipresent textbooks that were becoming his favorite refuge from an unpleasant reality.

* * * *

The next week or so was pure shen for Kley. Though he visited Arla every day, he made no progress in reaching her. He tried every avenue of approach he could think of, but got rebuffed at every turn. Either she would be defiant and hostile or she would do a very good job of pretending that nothing was wrong.

Making matters worse for Kley was the knowledge that Sectuib Aran was watching and waiting. Waiting for him to come in and confess the unconfessable; expecting him to accomplish a miracle with Arla. If the girl died, Kley was sure that Aran would hold him responsible. Yet he couldn't confide in Aran, for that, too, would bring Sectuib's wrath down on him. He disregarded the fact that other therapists were making no progress, either.

Arla's physical condition was deteriorating rapidly. As she got closer to her scheduled transfer, bleeding episodes became more and more frequent. On more than one such occasion it took two channels working in unison to stop the bleeding.

"Oh, bloody shen!" Kley leaned weakly against the wall outside Arla's room, dabbing ineffectually at the blood covering his arms and tentacles. Arla had vomited all over him and Tyrus while the channels had been trying to control her bleeding.

"Don't cuss," Tyrus admonished automatically. He tossed the other channel a towel. "That won't help. Besides she's stable now."

"For how long?" Kley was making more of a mess trying to clean Arla's blood off his uniform.

Tyrus shrugged, his expression grim. "Unless she regains her will to live, we're just wasting our time. She's going to die no matter what I do."

Kley glanced at the closed door. Perhaps if he tried talking to her again. Tyrus put out a restraining hand. "No, let her rest. Verlyn should have her asleep by now. And you're due on duty in a few minutes."

Kley knew that Tyrus was right. He had no choice but to report to the Dispensary as soon as he had taken a shower and changed his bloody clothes.

However, he was unable to concentrate fully on what he was doing. After hearing complaints from a couple of renSimes who were unhappy with the quality of their transfers with Kley, the duty channel told him, not unkindly, to take the rest of the day off and get himself under control. A trip to Sectuib's office was suggested.

But this Kley most emphatically didn't want to do. So he retreated to the Memorial where he could be alone. After all, Aran had ordered him to do just that.

At first he paced restlessly up and down the small confines of the room that held a replica of the larger memorial first built by Rimon Farris many generations ago.

After a while, he grew calmer and knelt by the edge of the reflecting pool to dabble his tentacles in the cool water. He stared in disgust at his reflection. *You lorsh,* he berated himself. *You don't deserve to be a channel, a Chanel therapist. You can't even reach one renSime in disjunction crisis.*

Violently he agitated the waters, destroying the image of his haunted eyes. "I wish I'd died in disjunction!" he cried in anguish. "Aran should just have let me die!" he screamed at the silent obelisk. "I'm not good! I'm no good!"

But the Memorial was silent, its flame steadily radiating a cheery yellow-orange glow that bathed the room in tranquility. In spite of himself, Kley calmed slightly, his thought turning backwards to the first time he'd ever been in Chanel's Memorial.

Aran had brought him there to talk after a rather rocky transfer during which he had aborted several times, begging the Sectuib to let him die.

At first they had just sat by the pool in silence, though Kley was painfully aware that Aran was doing his best, nagerically, to calm him down. But Kley hadn't wanted to be calmed.

"Why are we here, Sectuib Aran?" he had finally demanded.

"Why do you want to die?" Aran countered. "You've never given me a reason."

Kley hesitated. He couldn't tell Aran the truth: that just being Sime was proof that he was wicked and unworthy of life. "I'm a Killer," he said finally. "I have no right to happiness."

"Are you responsible for the Killing you've done?"

"What?" The question astonished Kley. He stared at Aran. "Of course I'm responsible. Two people are dead because I'm a Sime and I Killed." Tears rolled down his cheeks. He'd Killed his mother in First Need, then, after his capture by Reverend Friet, he had also Killed a Deacon in the church, one of his guards, during his escape from the small prison in the church basement.

He rubbed tears from his eyes and stared at Aran. "How can you even ask that question? I Killed two human beings."

Without answering, Aran rose and went to the monument. He took down a big book resting on a stand before it. Returning to his place by Kley's side, he handed the younger channel the book, now open to the first page. "Read this."

"Roll of martyrs to the cause of Unity. Billy Kell, Drust Fennell, Vee Lassiter, Jon Forester..." Kley read on for a while, the list of names unfamiliar to him. Finally he looked up at Aran. "Who are these people?"

Aran didn't answer directly. "There was once a time when all Simes Killed."

"I know that. They've been making me take a history class. Until Rimon Farris discovered he was a channel."

Aran grinned. "Right! But it hasn't been easy. A lot of people have given their lives in the quest for the precious knowledge we require to avoid the Kill."

Kley squirmed. The whole idea that Simes were willing to attempt to end the Kill didn't jibe with his sure knowledge that Simes are evil. "I don't see what this has got to do with me."

"Everything." Aran put his arm around the younger channel. "I think I know how you feel."

"But you've never Killed," Kley protested.

"True, but I've counseled many that have." Aran was silent a moment. "Let me ask you something. When you Killed, did you have a choice?"

"I don't understand."

"Did your parents make any effort to get you to a Sime Center or to summon a channel?"

Kley didn't answer. His parents had locked him up and sent for the Deacons. Because their child was wicked, they had had no choice. He should have died. Tears began to fall. Fervently he wished he was dead.

Aran's arm tightened around him, his voice gentle in Kley's ear. "I thought so. You weren't given a choice. You had to Kill to survive." For a moment, Aran's field radiated bitterness that such things could happen in a city where channels' help was readily available. Then the Sectuib quickly regained control of himself. "Nobody can hold you responsible for that."

"But, but, two people are dead because I was..." Kley abruptly bit his tongue. He had been about to confess his wickedness. "Two human beings are dead because of me," he finished weakly.

"Only because you had no choice. You have one now. It's up to you what you do in the future."

"Nothing I can do will bring them back."

"True. But you are a channel. That's a gift from God. You have the opportunity not only to forsake the Kill yourself, but to help others not to Kill. Won't that balance the scales?"

Kley raised his head to meet Aran's eyes. "Can I...? Can I really? I mean..." It had never occurred to him that the Tecton would be willing to use him as a working channel. Not an evil person like him. But Aran was smiling fondly.

"Kley, the day you come through disjunction, I'm going to offer you a place in Chanel. If you want it. As a working channel, you can save many lives by standing between other Simes and the Kill."

"But, but...what if I fail?"

"You won't." Aran's field was full of confidence and trust. "I know you can do anything you want to do. And I can use all the good channels I can get." He touched the book on Kley's lap. "The fight against the Kill began a long time ago with the sacrifices of these people. It continues even today. Will you help us?"

Kley hadn't given Aran an answer then, but he thought a long time about what the Sectuib had said. The opportunity to be a working channel seemed almost too good to be true. But if there was even a chance that he could be of some use, do some good to make up for his wicked past, he had to do it. He had to atone, somehow, not only for the Killing he'd done, but for his own evil nature.

The following month when his crisis had come, he chose not to Kill. Afterwards, he had knelt and offered his pledge to Aran, vowing never to betray the faith and trust his Sectuib had placed in him.

Sighing, Kley raised his eyes to the flame of the Memorial, still burning brightly. "Oh, Aran," he whispered. "I'm not the person you think I am. I'm wicked and evil. Chanel would be better off if I was dead. I haven't lived up to the promises I made to you and Chanel." Kley knew now that Friet was right. He was evil and useless. Becoming a channel had been a waste of Aran's time and an insult to Chanel.

"I can't help Arla. She's going to die and I can't do anything about it. I'm no good."

In his mind he could hear Friet's triumphant voice. "I told you, you are a wicked child. You're not even any good as a channel. Worthless son of Satan."

"No!" Kley seemed to hear Aran's rebuttal. "You can do anything you want to do, Kley. You can choose to help us in the fight. Will you join us? Will you join us? You can do it, Kley. I know you can do it."

"Evil child! Devil's spawn!"

"You are a good channel. You can do it!"

Back and forth the voices argued. Kley put his hands over his ears in a useless attempt to shut out the raging debate.

"Leave me alone!" he screamed in agony. "Both of you go away and leave me alone! Please!"

Suddenly the door flew open and Arla burst into the room. She was in terrible shape. Her nager was so dim as to be almost unzlinnable. She was very pale, while fresh blood spattered the front of her rumpled white gown.

Seeing Kley, she screamed "Make them leave me alone! Please make them leave me alone!"

"Make who leave you alone?" Kley struggled to his feet, his training coming to the fore. A Sime was in Need. He went into functional mode.

But this provoked fear and hysteria. Kley backed away a few steps, all the while zlinning. Arla was in disjunction crisis, near Attrition, yet rejecting his field. *How could she do that! And what's more, how can I get her to stop?*

At that moment, Tyrus and Verlyn came running into the room.

"Kley, get out of the way!" Tyrus ordered. "She's bleeding heavily. If we don't complete this now she'll die."

Kley changed his showfield to zlin like a renSime and retreated to a corner of the room. He knew he couldn't handle this. Not the disjunction crisis of a dying patient.

Tyrus approached Arla, strongly enticing her. Verlyn moved to form the third corner of the triangle, his field calm yet mildly tempting.

At first Arla seemed to be unaware of their presence, but then she went into hunting mode and began to stalk the Gen.

Tyrus responded by strengthening his showfield. But she ignored him, advancing rapidly and with deadly grace upon her intended victim. She grabbed Verlyn, her tentacles whipping rapidly around his arms. The laterals seated themselves and she leaned forward to make lip contact.

But that contact was never completed. Fear and revulsion showing in her nager, she thrust the Gen away and reeled backwards.

Her field was dimmer now, filled with self-hatred and a death wish so strong that it affected Kley's control. His showfield flickered in involuntary empathy, then again steadied under his determination not to interfere. He was out of his depth and he knew it. Arla turned to Tyrus, laterals seeking a safe selyn source.

For a moment Kley thought Tyrus was going to win, but she turned away from him, too, moving rapidly back towards Verlyn. Again she failed to make complete contact with the Donor. In Attrition, she retreated, her nager dimming rapidly.

She's dying. We're going to fail! I've got to do something. I can't let her die! In desperation Kley pushed his feelings of incompetence into the background and searched his mind for something he could do that Tyrus couldn't, that would make his field attractive to the dying girl.

Words that Aran had said to him earlier rang in his ears. 'You can't be an effective therapist unless you're willing to confront the problems in your own life.' *Oh, no!* Suddenly Kley knew what he had to do. He almost lost control as the angry waters crashed ominously, tearing free from his control, the hideous images bursting their bonds.

Black waves rose above him, their tops whipped into a churning froth by the violence of his emotions. Shame and fear flooded his entire being. This time he didn't fight. Perhaps if he showed Arla that they had a common bond, that she was not alone. Perhaps that would be enough to counter the all too familiar desire for death that was preventing her from taking transfer.

But can I do it? She wants to die as badly as I...

In desperation Kley glanced at the Chanel crest set into the side of the obelisk, just beneath the flickering flame.

'As long as this flame continues to burn,' Aran had said the day Kley had pledged. 'Our combined energies will serve as a beacon to all whom we serve.'

Suddenly the cresting waves were caught by a cooling breeze and dissipated as warm sunlight shone down upon his battered spirit.

A strength he didn't know he had filled him with renewed determination. Dropping what was left of his control on his nager, he let the feelings of shame and helplessness fill his field. If he could establish a rapport with Arla by admitting that he, too, had been a wicked child; perhaps he could save her life. At that moment nothing else mattered.

Shifting to functional mode, he moved forward, saying softly to the other channel, "Let me take it."

Tyrus was puzzled, but retreated, his field shifting to that of a neutral renSime.

Arla forced herself duoconscious, staring at Kley in disbelief. "You, too?" she gasped.

Unbidden tears were running down the channel's cheeks. "Come to me, Arla. You don't have to die."

"But Daddy said…"

Kley shook his head. "No, Arla. We're not evil. Your Father was wrong. Being Sime is not evil." He waited, soul bare to the world, hoping against hope that Arla would believe the words that he scarcely believed.

She zlinned him for what seemed like an eternity, then went hyperconscious and moved quickly, attacking him with a frightening desperation, beginning her draw even before their laterals were securely intertwined.

Kley carefully matched her draw with just the right amount of resistance, giving her the challenge and exultation she craved. As the transfer neared completion, Kley was filled with such a happy realization of success that in gratitude he fed Arla all his personal love and compassion.

As the transfer ended, he took her into a close embrace. Returning to an awareness of his surroundings, Kley discovered that Aran was standing just inside the door. *Oh, no!* he thought in dismay. *How much had Aran seen?* He started to put the blocks back into place in his mind, then realized it was far too late for that. Tyrus knew and he would tell. Sectuib would be disappointed, perhaps even want to kick him out of Chanel for being dishonest.

At least I saved Arla's life. That has to count for something. Fearfully, Kley met his Sectuib's eyes. To his surprise, he found no condemnation there, only the same warm affection and acceptance that Aran had always shown him. Tyrus, too, was smiling warmly, his nager touching Kley's affectionately.

"Congratulations, Kley." Moving forward swiftly, Aran embraced both Arla and Kley. "You, too, Arla. You'll be just fine now."

The girl smiled weakly. "Oh, Sectuib Aran, I…" Ashamed, she met the channel's eyes. "Are you mad at me?"

"Or me?" Wiping embarrassing tears from his eyes, Kley watched Aran closely, half expecting that both he and Arla would get reprimanded.

Aran shook his head. "No, Arla. I can't condemn you for something that isn't your fault. Either one of you." He had one arm around Arla. With his free hand he gently stroked Kley's arm.

A wave of profound relief washed over Kley, momentarily weakening his knees, but Aran's arm was there sustaining him, Aran's field engaging his in support.

Puzzled, Arla looked at Kley. "How much did you tell him?"

"Nothing," Kley reassured her. "It's up to you how much you want to tell him; or me for that matter."

"And that," said Aran firmly, "will come later. Right now, you're going to rest. And have some therapy for that bleeding." He gestured to Tyrus who gently took the girl from his Sectuib, immediately beginning healing therapy.

"Come with me," Tyrus said softly.

Arla's eyes remained fixed on the Sectuib's face. "Am I going to die?"

"Not if you cooperate with Hajene Tyrus. He's pretty good at healing ulcers."

"Can, can I talk to Hajene Kley?" she pleaded. "He understands. I know you're my therapist but…."

Aran grinned. "Of course, Honey. I think that might be a very good idea for both of you. He'll come see you in the morning." He patted her arm. "Go with Tyrus, now. He and Verlyn will stay with you for a while."

He smiled at Kley, who hugged the girl and reiterated the Sectuib's promise that he would be back.

Aran turned to Kley with a grin. "Do you know what you just did?"

The question confused Kley. "Served a successful disjunction transfer."

"And a bit more. That was a Chanel transfer. The extra dimension I encourage my channels to deliver whenever they can." Aran's smile faded. "What's wrong?"

Kley took a deep breath. He knew he had to finish what he'd started before he lost his nerve. There was no more hiding. "Sectuib, I...um, I haven't been totally honest with you."

Understanding flooded Aran's field. Encouraged, Kley went on. "Can we talk? There are some things I should have told you a long time ago."

RUNNING ON SELYN ALONE

D.H. AIRE

CHAPTER 1

"Run," Papa urged me, horror in his eyes, his tentacles stiff in their sheaths. In that moment my world changed forever. Childhood ended. I was a Gen. Never to be a Sime like my parents.

He grabbed the canteen he kept at the barn door and tossed it to me using the strap, afraid to come any closer. Tears in his eyes, he pleaded, "Run, Lena..."

I ran from the farm with only the clothes on my back. Mama was in the house and approaching Need. If she zlinned me, she could stalk and Kill me for the selyn I was now producing. She'd hate herself. Never forgiving herself. Oh, Mama, no goodbyes, just Papa turning away from me and zlinning to make sure Mama hadn't noticed yet.

I ran toward the woods, heading west, knowing I would never make it across the river. However, there was one place I might safely hide, which the Simes shunned. The Mizipi was the life blood of trade in the region, patrolled by a small Territorial Militia on this side of the border and larger Gen Army on the other.

My necklace, the Starred Cross that Mama had worn when she turned Sime and run for her life across the Gen border before I was born, felt like it was strangling me as I hung on to that canteen for dear life.

I could hardly breathe as I reached a stream. 'Trust the Starred Cross,' Mama had told me. 'If you turn Gen, it'll be your only hope... It certainly was mine.'

I gulped water from the canteen, closed it, then cupped the Starred Cross in my hands, willed myself to breathe deep, focused on it and wondered what it meant. The five pointed star could almost be me. The equal armed cross looked... I shook my head, feeling calmer, knowing what I had to do.

I ran through the stream and around one of the many strange hills that dotted this otherwise flat, but grassy, landscape. I looked out at the landscape, knowing the grass wouldn't hide me from a zlinning Sime. But the tallest mound might offer me a chance. I walked toward the large hill on the plain, not daring to run across, not without fear of tripping and broadcasting a flash of pain that no Sime could miss.

I paused, then climbed. At the top, catching my breath, I crouched, peering at the Mizipi in the distance. I couldn't cross it without a raft and I had no tools. I glanced around. The mound had another mound, taller than I was, protruding along the north face, offering a bit more conceal-ment for me. I blinked. There was a grass covered lean-to in its shadow. "So, I'm not the first person to seek sanctuary up here."

I raised the edge of the lean-to and my eyes widened. There was a wooden box with a Starred Cross etched across it. Opening it, I smiled, seeing dried fruits, nuts, and a net. "Well, Mama, you didn't Kill me and, at least, I'm not going to die from hunger."

Tonight I would see if I could master fishing. With so much grass around, I thought I should be able to make rope to lash together a raft. However, I had no idea how to make rope. I was soon chewing on dried fruit, wondering how hard it could possibly be to make rope. Not want-ing to think what else I might have to do, if that proved impossible. Papa had told me stories of Gens having drowned trying to cross it. That making a small raft was a Gen's only chance. I had never asked him why he had told me that, after all, I told myself, I was going to be Sime. I had to be… I shook my head.

I soon learned just how difficult it was to fish in the dead of night. Worse, how difficult it was to collect and keep the long grasses, which seemed so difficult to keep track of under the moonlight that might, just might, make good rope. It did not become easier as the moon ebbed over the course of the next month. Trying to twine the grass into rope, or even crafting twine, during the day proved fruitless. Though, I kept trying, sit-ting beside the lean-to, the breeze blowing, giving the illusion that I was safe here. But I knew the world was cruel. I was alone, producing selyn, something I could not even feel, yet more precious to a Sime than gold. So, I tried twinning the grasses, pulled on the twine, which came apart. I threw another clump down, knowing there had to be some trick to it as I kept thinking, Why, oh, why did I have to turn Gen?

* * * *

It was mid-morning as we rode the east bank of the Mizipi stretching for miles in the distance. "Reez, becoming a good Gen hunter is a real skill… could save your life, too. I know you respect them Householders, but the Choice Kills are great. "

"So, you keep telling me," I muttered, glancing back at my earnest mentor, Rale. He was thin, like a Raider, and clearly didn't have an "aunt" like mine, who said "a well fed Sime is a healthy Sime."

I didn't want to think about why I had taken this job. My aunt had put me in the Householding School, which taught us more than reading, writing, and arithmetic. They taught us about transfer and how to recognize the signs of approaching Breakout or Establishment. However, I had not recognized the signs and had been outside of town and alone when I found myself falling ill. First Need had led me to attack and Kill one of my former classmates, who had turned Gen several weeks before. My Disjunction was only recently achieved and everyone in town "knew" I had Killed.

Sectuib told me it was not my fault. I was too perceptive for a ren-Sime, something the touted Farrises might call being "delicate," if I understood the Sectuib right. Being too perceptive and the whole town looking at me as not being a Householder made me the Sectuib's choice for trying to help rescue those the local Gen hunter might not be able to so easily discern.

We rode in blissful silence for a time.

"Reez, you'll sees I'm right… out here when you're approaching Need, taking a new made Gen can be eerie-sistable."

"I really don't want… a Choice Kill."

"Well, I understan's that, I suppose, my young friend. That's likely why Scran thinks you'll do well bringing in the Choice Kills before they escape across the Border."

Well, that was true enough in more ways than he knew. I closed my eyes and zlinned for miles and… shit… a Gen was nearby, hiding, likely getting ready to find a way across the Mizipi. I looked at Rale, "You got anything?"

He zlinned toward the river, "Naw."

I nodded, trying to think about my best option.

He turned, still zlinning, "Shen and Shid."

Turning, I zlinned. "You can say that again."

* * * *

"Lena, once the world was different," Mama had told me when I awoke from that terrible nightmare night after night. She did not have to tell me much about the Eyeways, one of which ran across the land nearby. But in my nightmares I glimpsed them busy with carts that were not pulled by horses and saw metal birds that never flapped their wings flying across the sky high above them. Concentrate on those dreams, I told myself as I lay under the lean-to. Not the nightmare of feeling a bit fevered and sitting with my parents midway down the aisle of chairs as the steward called the captain asking that paramedics be waiting when we arrived.

In that nightmare, a teenage boy had fallen ill in what I knew was "first class" and suddenly screamed a half hour from landing, rising out of the seats, an odd fluid splattering everywhere, and howling in search of something. My heart skipped a beat. I heard people screaming. Saw the boy shoving people out of his way; saw smooth looking tentacles waving from his arms… a number of passengers threw themselves in his path, only to be flung away. Yet, he was slowed down, seemed desperate as he fought closer, growing weaker as people began hitting him from behind. He staggered as he got ever closer, his gaze meeting mine before he crumpled, writhing, and died minutes later.

Concentrate on the good dreams, I told myself, not a nightmare of some poor kid dying of Attrition without any Gens… could there ever have been such a time?

I focused on the Starred Cross, glancing at my sections of rope, made of what had been my skirt and blouse, leaving me half naked. My attempt at making a hemp rope was a dismal failure. I had been more successful at hiding a number of branches near the Mizipi's bank. My problem was that I didn't have nearly enough rags to make enough rope and I was waiting for a night without much moonlight to cross. The Mizipi was too large a river to cross, too strong for anyone not a Sime to swim this time of year, no matter how strong a swimmer I was. A good size raft under me might be my only chance to safely reach Gen Territory.

Shaking my head, I whispered, "Mama, sacrificing my clothes is the least of my worries."

I'll never forget the look in Mama's eyes, when she told me I was just having a Need Nightmare, reassuring me I would turn Sime, soon. Would that I had.

* * * *

Scratching his chin with a handling tentacle, Rale mused, "Reez, those Freeband Raiders must have taken out the Territorial crossing and raided Gen Territory."

"You need to get back to town and warn them," I said. "I'll stay and scout them."

"Kid, you should go…"

I shook my head, "I can hide in the Mounds."

"Reez, the Mounds? You crazy? They's haunted."

"Hopefully the Raiders know that, too."

"Don't count on it."

"Good luck," I said before spurring my horse onward.

Hiding my mount in the woods, I ran toward the mounds and source of selyn, who would be in just as much trouble from the Raiders as I was. As I reached the edge of the woods, I saw the Raiders riding toward the plain of Mounds, zlinned that they would reach the tallest Mound before I safely could.

* * * *

I heard a lot of horses nickering and knew I had failed. I would have tried to cross tonight or died trying. So close… I huddled under the lean-to, cupping the Starred Cross in my hands and did the only thing I could. I prayed, wondering what the Sime that Killed me was going to think of the half-naked young woman he found.

* * * *

I zlinned one of the Raiders pausing, more sensitive than the others, perhaps another Perceptive, zlinning the highest hill just south of them that towered like a small mountain on the plain studded by small version that were so incongruous. I could guess what he was thinking; no reason to let anyone else know about the Gen, now was there?

The Raider slowly rode away from the main ragtag group of Free-band Raiders as if he were just going off to take a dump behind one of the mounds.

I may not be a channel, but I could zlin a bit like one as I tried to project like another Raider in Need, and Raiders were constantly augmenting.

I knew I should turn back. That Gen was as good as dead… then realized I was augmenting slightly, fixing on the source of selyn like I was really a Raider. I blinked, knowing I was feeling my source of selyn was being threatened somehow. I never paused moving through the tall grass, hunched over, approaching the largest mound out of sight of the Raiders, who were on the other side. That is all save the Raider I was pursuing, who glanced back in my direction as he reached the base of the mound, which towered above all the rest.

The Gen was up there. The fear tightly controlled, but there, resigned to her fate.

* * * *

The breeze blew across my bare skin. I heard the Sime ascending and another close behind. I could hear a lot of voices and horses, knew I stood no chance.

"Mine," I heard, certain my life was over.

* * * *

He was more than half-way up the side of the steep mound. I augmented, struggling to catch up, knowing he was going to reach the top before me. That's when he pulled a leg bone from the side of the mound and stared in shock.

He took another grip and another bone spilled from the mound. He gaped down at me in horror.

That's when I laughed, "That's not a Gen up there."

The Raider shook his head, "Liar." He began climbing all the faster, pulling down bones, which rained down on me as I fought all the harder to climb. My handling tentacles gripped his foot and I drew him back just as he reached the top of the mound.

* * * *

I saw the Sime's hands reach the edge and I decided to die with some sort of dignity. I climbed out of the lean-to and half rose, partially dressed or not, I would meet my fate.

The Sime looked terribly thin, what clothing I could glimpse was ragged and filthy, long unwashed, a clear sign he was a Freeband Raider. His gaze bore at me, duoconscious. I knew he also saw me nagerically. I was just a glowing source of selyn to him, my standing there in my grass stained under-clothes meant nothing.

His lips twisted in feral hunger.

Eyes wide, I gaped as another Sime, much better dressed, leaped over him, and kicked him backward, sending him tumbling backward as the Sime landed right in front of me. "I'm Reez, don't be afraid. I'm here to, uh, help."

The other Sime fought back up over the edge, muttering, "She's mine."

* * * *

"Look out!" she rasped, crouching low as if this were some kind of running game as I turned to face the Raider.

"Mine!"

I tried to throw him back. He ducked, grabbed the young woman in Killmode and I pulled him off, only to have one of his laterals brush my arm. He recoiled and I grabbed, shifted, grabbed his neck in my arms and twisted.

There was a snap. The Raider slumped, dead. I sent his body tumbling back down the way we had come.

* * * *

Trembling, I knew I should have died. I was on my knees, the secondary outcropping behind me still screened us from view from the Freeband Raiders. However, shaking my head, I knew the Raider nearly had me. The tips of his laterals had touched my skin and his foul breath had made me want to gag. The two Simes struggled, then the Raider was dead. Reez swayed, not looking so steady himself as he stared at me. "Uh, mind my asking what happened to your clothes?"

Frowning, I pointed at my rope-making.

"Huh." That's when he zlinned and went a bit pale. "I'm sorry. They've noticed you're up here."

I chuckled. "Shidoni, then let's… at least try to scare them to death."

* * * *

"Are you sure about this?" I asked.

Lena replied, "No… you have a better idea?"

I swallowed, nodding as I removed my shirt and offered her my hand, "Well, then, we'd best climb to the top, quickly."

* * * *

Freeband Raiders raced from their horses, while others simply pointed at the mound and laughed. The lead Raiders began to climb as I peered down. Reez hunkered lower a bit, "You know how crazy this is?" he whispered.

"Zlinning us will, at least, confuse them," she replied.

"If I were a channel, we could do worse."

"Do what you can…" she said, seeing bones begin to rain from the Raiders' handholds. So many that the Raiders were shouting in consternation.

I blushed. "Uh, ready?"

"Shidoni, let's haunt them, forever."

* * * *

Her Gen arms wide, Lena shouted, "Come to me, Simes! Let us embrace death!"

They climbed all the harder, freeing an avalanche of human bones.

"Louder this time, Lena," I urged in a whisper, pressed up behind her, our selyn fields interacting.

"COME, SIMES! JOIN YOUR BRETHREN! ADD YOUR BONES TO MY MOUND!"

I waved my tentacled arms under hers, making us appear like a four-armed demon. Those zlinning below saw... they knew not what as they dislodged more and more bones.

"COME TO ME!" she screamed as I felt the pulse of selyn with every beat of Lena's heart. "DIE IN MY EMBRACE AS SO MANY SIMES HAVE ALREADY!"

"Wer-Gen!" they began to cry, no longer climbing. Soon they were fleeing back down the mound, bones tumbling after them, racing to their horses as their fellows scattered.

* * * *

"Um, Lena," I said, zlinning.

She took hold of my arms, drawing them close. "It worked. Shen and Shedoni, it worked."

"It did," I muttered as she turned in my arms and kissed me. We fell down, laughing.

She smiled, then kissed my cheek. "That was for saving my life."

Grinning, I raised my hand and several of my handling tentacles caressed her cheek. "Somehow, I think you ended up saving my life."

She shook her head, "In that case, I'd gladly accept the loan of your shirt."

"About that," I said, pointing at her shredded cloth lashings, dried grass strewn near them. "You would have had a lot better luck using the bark from the dead trees in the woods. There's strong fiber behind them."

Looking down at herself, she brought her hands to her mouth, "Oh."

* * * *

A little later, after I stopped laughing, I half-whispered, "Reez, I need to get across to the Mizipi. I've the makings of a raft, likely too small of one, which I hope with what lashings I have will carry me safely across to Gen Territory."

I stared, feeling suddenly bleak. "I'll never see you again."

She winced. "I don't know what else I can do."

I suddenly felt her selyn pulsing to the beat of my heart again. "I, uh, could take you to... Householding Muzu."

"The Householding?"

"Well, yes, I can't think of a safer place to defend against these Free-band Raiders and I need to make sure Colnzvil received warning about them."

She blinked, "Me... with you?"

I grinned, "If that's all right with you, Lena."

Nodding, she smiled back as I continued to feel every pulse of selyn coursing through our bodies, which was plain crazy. I nodded, remembering my old First Need nightmare, finding myself breaking out and the source of light, of selyn... that source was up the narrow aisle of what I oddly thought of as the "plane." Yet, I'd somehow been knocked back and with my dying gasp met the gaze of a weirdly dressed blue-eyed teenage girl.

I blinked. "Lena," I whispered, startled, recognizing those blue eyes from my Need Nightmare. Shaking my head, I knew it wasn't possible, but...

She leaned close and kissed me. "Mama and Papa never trusted the Householders... but if they trained you not to Kill that speaks well of them. Then again, I'd likely drown crossing the river or never even make it past all these Raiders without you."

I smiled at her. "Sime and Gen together, then. I swear, I'll get you safely to the Householding." Hoping against hope that we could be together. Even as I thought that, I knew Sectuib Ruit was going to want to strangle me because of this fool stunt, but somehow, just being with her, I didn't feel like, well, I was running on selyn alone.

CHAPTER 2 — PIGGYBACK GEN

In the rather austere office, Sectuib said, "And?"

I swallowed, glancing at Lena, who tightened her borrowed robe as I continued my report.

* * * *

"Reez, please tell me that you brought a horse."

I looked around at the line of trees where my horse should be, trying not to look at Lena, who was wearing my shirt. "Well, Lena, I did, but the Freeband Raiders apparently have scared it off when they fled."

We stood at the base of the southern face of the hundred-foot tall grass covered mound, which had lately been Lena's home. Bones were strewn down its base. Old human bones, legs, fingers, what were clearly ribs, covered in dirt. They had avalanched from the frenetic handholds of the Freeband Raider, who had sought to steal the prize: the young Gen woman besides me.

"So, exactly how are we supposed to get to your Householding?"

I thought about it, "Ever ride piggyback?"

"Piggyback?" Lena rasped. "I, uh, would rather run."

"You're only Gen, Lena, and the Raiders will zlin. You can't focus on that Starred Cross and run."

"I know I can't outrun a Sime, but carrying me piggyback?"

"Believe me, you won't be a problem."

"I'm not a child…"

My cheeks reddened. "Lena, I know you're a woman."

She swallowed. "I, uh, know. You sure about this? I mean…"

I swallowed hard. "Of course, I do."

"Somehow, I think it almost might be easier you carrying me over your shoulder," she hazarded.

"Lena, we've miles to go…"

"Oh, all right." She climbed up and I was glad she couldn't see me blush. "You won't tell anyone about this, will you?"

"Of course, not," I lied, my handling tentacles gripping her legs.

* * * *

"If I hadn't zlinned them coming in the back way — Sectuib, I wouldn't have believed it," the channel said as I tried not to squirm.

"I'm glad you two managed to get past the militia, I think," Sectuib Ruit said. "They have enough to worry about."

"Reez managed to get that right, at least," the channel chided.

"Well, leave us, then, and make sure the infirmary is fully stocked with Fosebine."

"Yes, Sectuib." That said, the channel left us with the Sectuib and his Companion in the windowless office.

"Reez, start at the beginning and tell me how you managed to find a half-naked Gen out there."

I told him, mostly. Lena looked chagrinned.

Sectuib and his Companion frowned. "Really, that's a fine tale, Reez," Sectuib said. "But I need to know more about these Freeband Raiders who, by now, have every farmer in the area fleeing to the safety of the town's walls."

"Sectuib, they aren't exactly the most organized bunch at the moment."

Sectuib Ruit said, "Which is apparently your doing with your fool Wer-Gen Goddess act. I have more questions than I think I want answers for at present. You, Miz Lena, perhaps, can best explain how you got here without a horse…"

* * * *

I held on for dear life as Reez augmented, giving me the weirdest piggyback ride I could remember. He ran back to Colnzvil, the town on a mountainy edge of the Mizipi bluffs across the flatlands on the Sime side of the Border. The place I'd called home all my life. These lowlands offered good crop land, if the spring floods weren't too bad, which made the farm life I'd lived difficult, but fulfilling.

That I had Established rather than changed over led to my fleeing my home, fearing Mama's Killing me as close to Need as she was. I never really expected to live to cross the river into Gen Territory, but I hadn't given up trying to build a raft. It was mastering making a rope to bind the best wood I could scavenge that presented me with my decision to use my shirt and pants to make enough rope for the raft I'd need. Then the Freeband Raiders appeared.

Reez had temporarily rescued me atop my hiding place, the largest of the mounds, even knowing the Freeband Raiders were certain to Kill me and murder him, made our, uh, practical joke, our only hope of survival. That it did led to our piggybacking it to Colnzil our next gamble.

I remember closing my eyes, arms across his chest, booted feet crossed at his midriff. Reez's shirt chafed, so I, well, unbuttoned it, causing it to flutter behind me as the wind blew through my hair. Everything that happened to me finally caught up with me. Exhausted, I drifted off to sleep, feeling safer than I could remember.

* * * *

"You augmented all the way back from the Mounds?" Sectuib asked, eyes hooded in thought. "After being attacked by a Freeband Raider?"

"Well, I didn't augment a lot, Hajene."

Sectuib glanced at his Companion, who shook his head in wonder. "I have to zlin you."

I rose and held out my arms, handling tentacles rising to meet Sectuib's arms.

* * * *

I had only run a few miles with Lena asleep against my back, understandably exhausted from her ordeal, when a group of five Raiders cut into view from behind a hill. They zlinned us as I slowed and stopped. I felt Lena stirring a bit; I prayed she would remain asleep. We should have made it, I remember thinking. After all she'd been through Lena shouldn't just die like this. I was so Shenned angry, which is when one of the Raiders zlinning us screamed, "The Wer-Gen has found us!"

I gaped as they turned and fled on their nearly spent horses.

Uncertain of what to make of that, realizing we must look quite the sight on the nageric level, I thought, well, we are still alive.

Re-balancing Lena on my back, I turned my head slightly and saw her sleeping soundly. I smiled, took a deep breath and, a moment later, off I ran, trying to stay clear of any more Freebanders heading east toward Colnzvil. I just hoped Rale had gotten warning to the town in time.

* * * *

"As soon as your Gen hunting friend rode in with the warning, we began ringing the warning bell," Sectuib Ruit said. "The Town Council sent warning to all the nearby farms."

His Companion shook his head, "There seem to be more and more Freebanders every year and their raiding is going to bring out the Gen Territorial Army at this rate."

"Mid-Crossing being burned out," I offered, "I might suggest that we weren't party to their incursion, either."

"Somehow, I don't think that will help," the Sectuib sighed. "Tell me again how the two of you managed to terrorize the Raiders."

"We didn't exactly," she began.

"We sort of did," I muttered as my Sectuib glanced at me in a mixture of curiosity and exasperation.

"Well, all the bones raining down on their heads scared them more than my theatrics," I said.

Sectuib Ruit glanced at our entwined fingers. "Bones? You didn't mention anything about bones."

"I didn't? Hmm, well, those odd hills are some sort of Ancient burial mounds," I offered, trying not to blush thinking about what Lena and I had done after the Raiders fled.

Sectuib waved me back and zlinned Lena critically. He opened his eyes and shook his head, "Your field is growing at a faster than normal rate, but not at a Companion's level."

"Well, you seem well enough, Reez," Sectuib Ruit said with a grimace.

Sectuib's Companion stared at Lena in her borrowed Householding robe, then glanced at me in my just as borrowed clean white shirt.

"Pardon us a moment, Miz Lena," Sectuib said. Once the office door closed, he said, "Reez, do not for a moment entertain the idea you are somehow a channel. It doesn't take zlinning to see how you two feel about each other. Don't, for a second, forget a renSime can't offer transfer, and it's too dangerous to consider pairings like the House of Rior advocates,"

I nodded. "I understand that, Hajene."

Sectuib looked at his Companion, who frowned, "Ruit?"

"I just zlin something… odd about them."

I stared. "I, uh, really like her."

"That's not it, Reez," he replied, sounding exasperated.

His Companion said, "Sectuib?"

"Reez, you are not to attempt transfer with her, understood?"

"Of course, not." Yet, now that he mentioned it, my handling tentacles twitched.

"Reez, you have always been rather sensitive," he replied, pacing his desk. "I sent you to become a Gen hunter simply as a way to put that sensitivity to good use, rescuing Gens trying to flee across the Border, not to…"

I blinked.

Sectuib shrugged, "We've problems enough with the Raiders out there without spooking everyone in town with thoughts that there's a Wer-Gen, too."

His Companion cleared his throat.

"I know, Wynn," Sectuib muttered. "The best Companions are reputed to make the best Wer-Gens… and Lena might make a fine Companion one day. But get it out of your head, Reez. You are not, somehow, even half a channel, understood?" Sectuib glared at me.

I stared, thinking, *Half a channel?*

Sectuib Ruit suddenly turned, zlinning through Householding Muzu's too thin walls. "They've captured more Freeband Raiders and some of our Simes are wounded, too. Reez, keep Lena inside the Householding's walls."

"Yes, Sectuib," I replied as the Sectuib and his Companion hurriedly exited the office.

* * * *

Lena stared as the Simes and Gens of Muzu rushed down the corridors to help with the wounded. "Reez, what's happening?"

"The Raiders," was all I needed to answer.

Lena went pale.

"It'll be all right," I lied. "Come with me."

* * * *

"Reez?" said the greying Sime woman, answering the door.

"Hi, Aunt May, this is my friend, Lena," Reez said, smiling, gesturing me within as the Sime woman he called his aunt opened the door fully on an inner subterranean room of the Householding, which was made up of a long row of some of the oldest brick built buildings in

Colnzvil. There were no windows, but a number of landscape paintings of the Mizipi and one of the remains of the nearby Ancient ruins, particularly the two jutting horseshoe-like protruding curved metal forms the ruin was most known for. The apartment was three times as big as my home on the farm… I winced, knowing home wasn't the farm, anymore.

"It's lovely," I said, feeling like I was intruding.

May closed the door. "Reez, your room is as messy as you left it."

"Um, sorry, Aunt May," he replied, giving me a sidelong glance.

She didn't exactly zlin me, but she looked at me rather closely. "I'm the closest thing to a mother Reez has. I heard he brought you in. Actually, most of the Householding heard about your arrival. I arranged for that robe… and Reez's clean shirt."

"Thank you, Ma'am," I said.

"Oh, no thanks are necessary and call me Aunt May. You are our guest, at least until Reez hits Turnover, he's ahead of me, by-the-way. We've a cot you can have." Aunt May gave Reez a look. "Welcome to Householding Muzu and don't mind me saying, I'm happy to draw you a bath."

"I'd appreciate that," I replied, knowing I needed it badly.

"You'll use it next, Reez."

He nodded. "Yes, Aunt May."

* * * *

"We don't have much; you can sleep on the bed. We've a cot I can sleep on in the living room," I told Lena, opening the door to my room.

She looked inside. "Your aunt is right. What a mess."

"Oh." I hurried inside and began tossing everything I had elected not to take with me into my chest of drawers.

"That helps, but you do know it will all be wrinkled."

"Wrinkled?"

I grinned, "Yes, unlike that white shirt you're wearing."

He sat on the edge of the bed. "Uh, I'm not used to this."

"Used to what?"

"Having, uh, guests…" I said, feeling that twinge of recognition again whenever I met her gaze.

Aunt May did not bother to knock. "Uh, huh… Well, you two aren't exactly children. You are not living outdoors anymore. The bath will be ready soon. Here are clean towels. I'll get some sandwiches. Sectuib's passed word that the militia has captured more Freeband Raiders. We have more casualties on the way here. They've put the uninjured ones in the Pens for safekeeping. So, the channels are going to be working on healing all night. Miz Lena, the bathtub's ready down the hall on the left."

Only then realizing how rank I must smell, I said, "Thank you."

* * * *

I shook my head, "Aunt May…"

"Reez, you have always been an odd one. Sectuib's said you were just sensitive," she replied, "but somehow I think with Lena around, you're finding yourself at long last."

I shook my head. *Found myself?* I thought about that a moment. *Huh?*

"She's pretty," she said. "And won't be a child for very much longer."

"What?"

"Oh, perhaps, I'm a romantic… an old woman thinking you two look rather comfortable together. Well, never mind, clean up this room, then wash that stink off you."

I frowned, dreading having to follow both admonitions.

"One other thing, Reez. Keep her out of sight for now."

* * * *

A warm bath in a real tub, I thought, glancing over my shoulder and smiled. I felt… safe and at peace even knowing about all the Raiders outside of town. After rubbing off all the dirt and grime, I laid back in the tub, remembering dozing as I rode piggyback. I had fallen back into my old nightmare, but without the horror of seeing the teenager boy's form being loaded on a gurney and carted off the "plane."

I vividly remembered his eyes in the nightmare, his imploring desperate looking eyes, as he had fought to reach me too far back in the aisle. Passengers struck him as he lashed out… his Sime handling tentacles flailing.

He writhed, dying unable to reach me… as I felt slightly fevered, not knowing that selyn was now coursing through me.

I sighed, remembering more of the dream than I ever had before. No one could understand what had happened on the flying machine. My frightened mother hurried me through… the term-nal.

Images I didn't understand swirled: covered carts without horses on roads that reminded me of the Eyeway that we used to cart our produce to Colnzvil. A home that looked like nothing today. I remember stepping out of the horseless cart and hearing a harsh whining sound. A white vehicle with flashing lights pulled up next door. Medics ran from it to the front door of the neighboring house. My best friend's mother run out, screaming, "There's something wrong with my daughter!"

Momma tried to draw me away, but I wouldn't go. A few minutes later the medics brought out a gurney and they strained to hold my best friend down as she shouted, "Let me go!"

She turned her head and looked right through me, bolting past the medics who were knocked aside and she was leaping toward me, tentacles spraying fluid as they burst free. Her mother screaming in horror.

She was on me in an instant, handling tentacles lashing around my arms. I cried out as she grabbed me close and forced her lips on mine.

That's when I half woke; piggybacked against Reez's back, realizing dimly we had stopped. His whole body tensed. Blearily, I could feel how angry he was, half-glimpsed the Raiders over his shoulder, felt my anger echoing his. We've gone too far to fail now. How dare the Raiders block our way?

One of the Raiders met my gaze, brown eyes widened in recognition. My best friend's eyes filling with horror as I felt blackness well. Yet, instead of the cry I remember, she shouted, "The Wer-Gen!"

They fled and I… I had never felt so exhausted in my life, yet had never felt… so safe and… loved. I closed my eyes, and fell deeply asleep as Reez resumed his run.

There was a knock on the bathroom door. "You nearly drown in there?"

"Reez?" I whispered, my heart singing.

"Lena, you nearly done in the bath or not?"

I rose and grabbed my towel, feeling my cheeks warm, not certain why. "I'll be out in a minute."

CHAPTER 3 — GHOST OF SELYN'S PAST

"Reez, what am I supposed to do here in the Householding?" I asked sitting down with him in the living room. I was clean for the first time in a long time and realized he washed up rather nicely, too.

"Do? There's a great deal to do. You've a lot to learn, first of all."

"Learn? I'm farm raised. I can cook. Need me to milk a cow?"

I winced. "Well, this is a Householding, not exactly a farm. Muzu is known for the chemical concoctions we make."

"You make the fireworks?" she replied.

"Well, we have members who do. Those chemicals make lovely colored fires. We've been trying to get them to use them at the Territorial Capital. But they've been resistant to buying from a Householding."

"I saw them with Mama and Pappa at the town festival."

I smiled. "Hmm, can you read Simelan?"

"And Genlan, too."

"You read Genlan?"

"Mama's from out-Territory. She wanted to make sure I could live on either side of the Border." She switched to Genlan, "And I speak it, too. Although, she decried my writing in script."

"Excellent," I replied. "That's something the Householding can really use."

"You mean I could teach it?"

"Perhaps, some day. You've only recently Established and every Gen is, well, precious. We depend on each other here," I replied.

"I noticed."

I smiled.

"Thank you for saving me," she said.

"Uh, as I recall, you saved me. Really, Lena, I can't explain it. Somehow you have reached across time, out of my Need nightmare, and saved me."

She didn't laugh, just came over and hugged me, nodding in recognition, understanding completely.

* * * *

There was a knock on the door. Reez answered it. "Yes?"

"Sectuib wants you and… Miz Lena."

"Both of us?"

"All I know is we've an injured Raider, who's terrified of Wer-Gens…"

* * * *

The brown-haired raider was shackled. She cursed as we came into the shielded room.

Sectuib Ruit looked up, "She's little more than a child and won't allow us to help her."

"Pervert! I'll not let you turn me into a Gen!"

"I can't turn you into a Gen," Sectuib replied, exasperated.

"Leave me the shen alone!"

I met the young Raider's gaze.

She frowned, suddenly looking uncertain. I glanced at Reez, who muttered something under his breath, then said, "Sectuib, I recognize her."

Sectuib Ruit glared at him. "I thought you might. Now explain it to her, so I can deal with her injuries."

Reez sighed.

She bristled, "You're just going to make me die of Attrition!"

Sectuib shook his head, "The Council might sentence a hardened Raider, but you look too young to deserve such a fate."

"She can't break free, can she?" I asked, eying her shackles.

"No, and certainly not with that broken leg and her fractured ribs," Wynn said.

"What happened?" I asked.

"Her horse gave out and came down hard on that leg," Sectuib answered.

"Could you leave us alone with her for a few minutes?" I asked.

Wynn drew the insulating curtain closed as they left.

"So, you were at the Mounds," I said.

There was a terrified look in her eyes, "Leave me alone!"

"Reez, stand behind me," I said.

Frowning, he muttered, "Lena, you sure about this?"

I nodded.

He rolled up his sleeves.

"You saw something at the Mounds that spooked you and your friends," I said. "You zlinned someone atop the biggest Mound, didn't you?"

The girl stared at me. "What?"

"You saw something you couldn't explain... a young woman, half Gen with four arms." Coming up behind me, Reez slipped his arms under my armpits, peering over my shoulder and waved.

"Uh, hi," he said.

The Raider stared, zlinning, her eyes going wide. "It was you."

"Can't say we're sorry to have scared you off — since it saved our lives," Reez said, hugging me from behind.

The Raider covered her face with her hands and burst out laughing. "Oh, how could I of all people have been...?"

I frowned slightly as she laughed harder as the Sectuib and his Companion returned.

The girl wheezed, "Ow, it hurts to laugh... I'm such a fool. Fine, I won't fight your helping me... not after knowing what they pulled."

Frowning, Sectuib gestured and we left.

* * * *

I took Lena back to Aunt May's. Hours later, Sectuib sent for us again and told us to see if we could convince her to accept channel's transfer and get some answers, too. "I don't know why she thinks your fool stunt was so funny, but let's use it to our advantage. We need all the help we can get in order to deal with the Raiders. Understood?"

"Yes, Hajene," Lena replied.

"Yes, Sectuib," I said.

* * * *

The Raider was still shackled but visually better. "Come to keep me company?"

"Not exactly," I answered, glancing at Lena. "We've come to talk."

She laid back. "Talk? Why?"

Glancing at me, Lena admitted with a smile, "We wondered what you thought was so funny."

The Raider sighed.

"I'm Lena, and by your accent, you grew up in Gen Territory."

"For all the good it did me. Turning Sime wasn't exactly expected." There was a haunted look in her eyes I knew too well. She shook her head, "Name's Raish and I'm alive today because I hid like you did on that Mound. I played a ghost in the Ancient Ruins, barely managing to survive each month. Then the Freeband Raiders came…Look, I admit, being free of them is not something I regret. It was better being a ghost, which is why I can see the humor in your Wer-Gen act."

"Oh," I muttered as our gazes locked. She looked tantalizingly familiar… My eyes widened as did hers.

She swallowed, "Yes, that was me in the woods shouting: 'It's the Wer-Gen…'" She chuckled. "Somehow, I think we were fated to meet before I died… and why anyone bothered to fix me up, knowing I'm going to die in Attrition, anyway, is beyond me."

"You won't die, Raish," I said. "We've a channel who can offer you transfer."

"That's perv…" she shook her head. "It's no use. I've heard what the channels do. Never believed it, though. My family were proper Churchgoers. The idea of Simes not Killing? We knew it was a clever lie… but that doesn't matter now. My family and hometown's gone like the others."

"What are you talking about?" Lena rasped.

Raish shook her head, "Look, I had my own act. I learned to ghost in the Ancient Ruins. Carved out a nice trap for the unwary. Spooked Simes stalking fool Gen scavengers…"

I winced.

"It's not like I had a choice," Raish admitted.

"You have one now," I said. "You never have to Kill again."

Raish shook her head, chuckled in disbelief, looking at her healed leg, "What he did… it's as difficult to believe as the idea of not Killing someone like my sister, ever again."

Frowning, I said, "What's this about the Raiders coming to the Ancient Ruins?"

Raish sighed, "The Raiders had been wiping out towns across Gen Territory. They've herded a lot of Gens there and took over my haunting grounds... I figured if they had the Gens, it was time to join. I ended up with a place with their vanguard. We crossed the river and took out the Territorial fort, so the others could escape from the Gen Army after we had... disrupted the region first."

* * * *

"Reez, what do you think you're—" Wynn shouted as we ran toward them as they left one insulated room and were about to enter the next.

"Sectuib!" Reez shouted, as I ran to catch up.

Frowning, he paused, "What did you learn?"

"Her group was the lead element of a far larger group of Freebanders, who have forted up in the ruins across the Mizipi. They've taken a dozen towns near the Border and captured enough Gens to set up their own Pen."

"What?" he rasped.

"There are at least a thousand Raiders over there. Many are from the next Sime Territory. They hadn't received enough Gens and turned Raider, fighting their way across the entire territory. The Gen Territorial Army has them surrounded on all sides save the Mizipi."

Wynn paled, "Ruit..."

"I know. This is worse than we thought."

"Do they have food for the Gens?"

I glanced at Reez, who visibly trembled, "Raish said that, uh, the most hardened Raiders leading them said that wouldn't be a problem. They have plenty of water and, well, the Gens can either eat the rats in the ruins or the children they've taken hostage."

"Lorshes," Sectuib cursed.

* * * *

"You heard what Sectuib said. There's nothing we can do," Reez said as we sat in the apartment with Aunt May, who had brought soup from the main kitchens.

I shook my head. "If I'd made it across the Mizipi, I would have been Killed."

"Well," Aunt May said, "you, at least, managed to get that Raider girl to take transfer from the channels."

"She didn't exactly thank us for it," Reez replied.

"Well, you talk to her… explain about disjunction. There's still a chance for her and those young enough to…"

I was staring.

Reez sighed, "Lena, no one can disjunct after First Year. They can take some channels' transfers, but, well, they have to Kill to continue to survive."

"Many die trying to stop," Aunt May said.

"Oh…" I muttered, thinking of my parents, who I secretly hoped might come here for transfer. I would have given anything to see them again.

Reez met my gaze as I looked up. "Sectuib will think of something…"

Shaking my head, I muttered, "I hope so… Reez, I want to speak with Raish again. Perhaps, there's something she knows about the ruins which could help."

* * * *

"Lena, this is a real bad idea."

"What? After what Raish told us?" I asked as we knelt by the House-holding's outer wall. "The Raiders wiped out her hometown. She thinks her family's dead."

Reez stashed the coiled rope we had borrowed and the bags we had carefully packed from the Householding's stores. "Lena, be careful with those," he hissed.

"You just want to live forever…" she replied. "You know if we don't do this, those Raiders will swarm across the Mizipi and destroy this Householding, town, and entire community. I don't want my parents turning Raider after the Freebanders steal all the Gens in the area."

"Raish's a Raider. They'll say anything."

"You'd zlin if she was lying, wouldn't you? You think her tears over the fact she recognized some of the prisoners was an act?" I said, knowing how "perceptive" he was when zlinning.

"Uh, no, I don't think so," Reez answered.

"So, she really thinks you're cute?"

"Lena, stop it."

"Her thinking you're cute should help," I said as we headed toward the infirmary to gather the last thing we needed if we had any hope of success.

* * * *

Raish stared at the key in my hand and rasped, "Reez, you want me to what?"

"Guide us into the ruins so we can, well, rescue the Gens and children," I said.

"It'll never work," she said. "They'll zlin the militia, and us, for sure."

"It'll just be the three of us and, uh, well, Lena's rather good at praying. They won't zlin us crossing the Mizipi at night."

"Praying…" Raish muttered. Shaking her head, she said, "Fine, let's say we make it across. You want us to take on a thousand Raiders?"

"We just need to help the Gens escape and the Gen Army will do the rest," Lena replied.

"Just," Raish said, shaking her head. "Look, how can you even trust me around those Gens?"

"You know some of them," Lena said. "And there are all those children…"

"And you've just had transfer," I said. "You can handle this. Save their lives."

Raish did not look entirely convinced.

"It'll buy you a new life here in Sime Territory," I said, "Sectuib will see to that."

Raish frowned, looking into my eyes and sighed.

"You mentioned there are underground warrens that helped in your ghost act," Lena said.

"You think your Wer-Gen stunt with my ghost act is going to work?"

"It has a good chance of being the perfect distraction with the help of your ghost tricks," Lena replied.

"You are one crazy Gen."

"Raish, can we get the Gens out through some of those tunnels you told us about?" I asked.

Raish paled. "I shouldn't have told you that."

"All we need to do is get the Gens to safety and scare the Raiders out of the ruins," Lena said, smiling.

She is becoming a very convincing liar, I thought.

* * * *

Raish glanced at us as Lena sat mounted behind me as our two horses cantered through the countryside, wending our way through the least probable paths any Freeband Raiders might choose. The two of us zlinned for any danger as we rode to the one place the Freebanders were most unlikely to be… the Mounds.

Once there, Lena led us to all the thick branches she had gathered to build her raft. Reez was soon cutting our rope to lash the raft together. "It looks easier when you use that than try to make your own," she said.

Raish shook her head. "It's going to break apart in minutes."

I pulled a hatchet from my saddlebag, "No, it won't. I came prepared."

"We're just going to end up downstream," Raish replied.

"Not if we start far enough upstream," Lena answered, looking at me.

I nodded, "Raish, we'll need to make a litter to drag it along."

Raish gestured at the other bags we had brought. "Wonderful, I can't wait to see us carting those across the river."

"Oh, here are the oars," Lena said.

"She's funny calling those little paddles 'oars,'" Raish said. "Then again, anything for our Wer-Gen friend, here."

* * * *

I focused on my Starred Cross cupped in my hands as we crossed the Mizipi that night on the raft. Reez and Raish rowed, trying to be as quiet as possible. I prayed. I was not afraid. I knew the Gens and children in the ruins must be, though.

I was beyond fear and knew I likely could get myself Killed. But somehow with Reez at my side, I felt… fate was calling. I was a Gen in a world of Simes, and my dreams had long been of fear of their Need.

The world didn't have to be that way. Not if we could work together as the Householding showed was possible.

I could feel Raish's glance. My shoulders itched with it, knowing she thought she was crazy for joining us on this fool's errand.

She was atoning for I knew not what, though, perhaps, in my nightmares I did. At least, I hoped that was what she was thinking. Otherwise, she was going to Kill me the first chance she got.

When we reached the far bank, we hid the raft.

* * * *

"Reez," Raish whispered to me. I zlinned the direction she wanted us to go. We moved past the two curved broken spires jutting into the night sky and crept into the ruins beyond.

I put my hand on Lena's shoulder as she cupped her Starred Cross, focusing on it in such a way that I couldn't read her field. I gestured with a handling tentacle. Raish nodded, sensing the Raider sentry, half-dozing.

We edged past. Minutes later we heard the sounds of whips followed by screams and laughter. I glanced at Raish, who whispered, "This way."

* * * *

Reez touched my arm as we followed Raish between a series of heaped stones. "This leads into the first tunnel. We need to be quiet. Sound echoes."

I looked around, "Its pitch black in there."

Reez chuckled, "Not to us. Your field zlins bright enough for us to see by."

"Oh."

Raish muttered, "Loverboy, keep her close. You wouldn't want her tripping and breaking her fool neck..."

"Raish," he rasped.

She replied, "Ever wonder what it would be like with a Sime girl, like me?"

I cleared my throat, "Raish."

Reez muttered, "Raish."

"I can see you mooning over each other. It's unnatural. Then again, I'm helping you... Aw, come on," Raish said, "we've your Mound act to bring to a bigger audience."

* * * *

We came to a twisted metal door, Reez encouraged me to duck, helped me past. We went down tunnel after tunnel. The place was a warren.

Reez put my hands on the rung of a ladder. Someone slapped my... Raish chuckled.

Up I climbed and found myself at another level. Reez clasped my hand. "The floor's missing there."

Raish whispered, "Quiet. It's about to get rather loud. Follow me, and no talking."

There was a creaking noise. The sound of scraping metal and the faintest amount of light suddenly as a breeze began to flow past. Reez led me away to another ladder and up I went. I could suddenly see Raish as she opened a metal hatch.

Once under the stars, she closed the hatch and I could hear an eerie sound. Raish peered out between the twisted stone. "Well, some of them are noticing the moaning sound. Good."

"Raish?" Reez muttered.

"I'm doing my part. Can't wait to see you doing yours again," she replied, smiling at Reez.

I opened our saddlebags, "Oh, you're not done, Raish."

"What are you talking about?"

Reez sighed, "We've got to let those Gens know what to do."

"Why are you grinning at me like that, Lena?"

"We're partners, Raish. Ghost and Wer-Gen, aren't we?"

Shaking his head, Reez rolled up his sleeves.

Raish grimaced. "Oh, no, I won't."

"If Lena and I can do it," Reez replied, "you can do it... Now put on that iridescent paste on your jerkin."

I shook my head, "Also slaver it there and there."

"Like this," Reez said, applying it on their Sime companion's right arm.

"Wer-Gen," she muttered back, eying me in a way I liked not at all.

"Let's just hope this ghost thing works whether they are duo-conscious or not." I knew the Raiders below would zlin us soon as I glimpsed the faint outline of the top of the curved horseshoe-like shorn metal masses jutting from the ground at the edge of the Mizipi River. Desperately hoping this would work, I told myself, Householding Muzu needed to survive, even if the three of us didn't.

Reez looked at me with those eyes from my nightmare. His gaze resigned that we would be giving our lives saving those Gens and the Householding from the Raiders.

* * * *

Moments later Raish cursed. "I can't believe I'm doing this..." putting on her black robe.

Grinning, I said, "You know, you make a lovely ghost."

"Why, thanks, Reez," she replied. "Now, I get to sneak through the warrens and play good spirit to those Gens and the kids."

"There really is a tunnel entrance down there they can flee through?" Lena asked.

"Yes, one that isn't easy to find from down there."

"What do you suppose this place was used for?" I asked as she turned to leave.

"Idiot; isn't it obvious," Raish said, "this was an ancient Gen Auction fairground."

* * * *

Raish returned, seeming subdued.

"Is everything all right?" I asked.

"Raish?" Reez said.

She glared at us. "Those Gens are bigger fools than we are. I whispered from the tunnel entrance that I was with the Gen Army and this was the way out. The kids at first shied away, but one of them... a girl came closer. Good thing she couldn't get a good look at me in this robe. I convinced her it wasn't some trick. She told one of the adults. It seemed to take forever before the kids began slipping into the tunnel."

"So they…"

"The first should be reaching the end of the tunnel soon. I was just afraid that some of the adults were going to try to flee, which the Simes were more likely to zlin." There was a haunted look in her eyes.

"Raish, what's wrong?" I asked.

"That girl, Lena, she, uh, reminded me of my sister. The one I Killed in First Need."

Reez went over and hugged her. Shaking her head, Raish glanced down and said, chuckling, "Lena, I think he likes me more than you."

* * * *

Lena and I placed the jars with care, then set our robes aside. "They really work?" Raish asked, glancing at the jars I had half feared would break before we ever got here.

"Best chemical fireworks the Householding makes," I replied.

Raish said, "They better or this is going to be a very short act."

Peering over the lip of the ruined wall we now hid behind, I said, "That's quite a camp the Raiders have down there."

"Over a thousand Simes," Raish admitted, "and all those Gens penned behind that makeshift palisade, who could panic at any moment."

"Yeah, so let's get our act started, ladies," I said, taking my place behind Lena, putting my hands on her hips.

She glanced back, smiled, and whispered, "Hmm, I think you like me more than Raish."

Shaking my head, I prayed for the impossible.

Raish muttered, "Ready or not," and threw the first jar of chemicals.

* * * *

There was a blinding explosion and a burst of blue flame. Reez jumped us to the top of the flat outcropping structure that Raish thought our perfect stage.

Below the Raiders and Gens alike gaped.

"Come to me, Simes!" I shouted, my voice echoing across the valley. "I hunger!" I waved my iridescently glowing arms as Reez shook his own glowing arms and fists, mirroring my fury, while careful not to let his black robe slip free.

Raish cast another jar, which burst explosively in orange splattering flames.

I laughed maniacally, not feeling the cold breeze at all, as the eerie wind continued to howl through the ruin's broken structure, knowing we only had five more firework jars.

* * * *

Simes zlinned us as Raish cried, "Wer-Gen!" She then cast two more jars from hiding, which exploded. She made a blood-curdling scream, "NO! NO! WER-GEN!"

"COME TO ME, SIMES, I HUNGER!" Lena yelled.

Raish screamed again and squeezed herself between the twisted structure beneath us, radiating terror to all those below. She turned her arms, revealing they were glowing. "NO! WER-GEN, NO!"

The Raiders stared as they zlinned the Sime vanish, screaming.

Raish scraped skin, pulling herself back into hiding, then grabbed the next two jars and cast them against the far walls. They exploded spectacularly as she climbed up behind me. "Loverboy, nice knowing you," she whispered too loudly, as she climbed atop my shoulders and screamed, "I HUNGER!"

The Simes in the rear turned and ran. Those in the forefront gaped at our nageric glow and flow, uncertain of what they were zlinning. As Lena glanced up at Raish almost jealously, I grew furious at Raish's antics.

"MINE!" she cried, her field seeming to course with our anger, our railing against the death we knew our destiny.

They turned by the hundreds, screaming in fear. The Gens fled to the ruined stretch of wall serving as the back perimeter of their Pen. I could zlin them clearly vanishing down into the hidden tunnel entrance. I exulted as the Raiders failed to notice the mass escape, desperate to escape the valley, knowing that all Ancient ruins were haunted and perhaps had also gotten word of the Wer-Gen woken and risen from the Mound of Sime bones on the other side of the Mizipi.

I swallowed. "Um, it's working... I think we'd better get down."

"It is?" Lena muttered as Raish leaped down from my shoulders, vanishing from the view of those below. Soon the biggest and last jar went arching out toward the valley below. It shattered on the ground in a deafening explosion, brilliantly splattering fire upward in a mix of colors and smoke. The Simes pushed each other out as they clambered over the far wall in their mad flight.

Soon we began hearing gunfire ring out. "Well, the Gen Army is going to have their hands full," I said.

Raish grinned as I jumped back down with Lena, who turned and hugged me, "Reez, it worked!"

"Hey, stop that, loverboy!" Raish rasped.

I turned to her, grabbed her hand, and pulled her close, drawing her into our hug.

"This isn't what I had in mind," she said as Lena chuckled.

I bent my head and kissed Raish, who I realized was crying. "What?" I murmured.

"I'll never Kill again," she swore. "I'm never going to be a ghost again in a place like this."

Lena smiled, "Good, then we better get out of here. We need to get back across the river before someone finds our raft."

"You most definitely are a Wer-Gen," Raish muttered. "A bossy one."

"Me? Bossy?"

"Yeah, all I ask is that you don't come up with any more crazy ideas like this."

"Um," I muttered, meeting Lena's gaze, as she shook her head, smiling, though her nager belied that. "Let's just get back to the raft before... the Raiders decide to do the same."

Raish asked, "Lena, how about I give you a piggyback ride this time?"

"I can walk just fine from here," she replied.

"We'll get to the river so much faster and it'll spook any Simes but good."

"Uh, ladies," I said, feeling distinctly uncomfortable for some reason.

They glared at me, then at each other.

I swallowed hard, urging them back the way we'd come, realizing it had been much easier running on selyn alone. But somehow, I knew my life, and the nightmare that haunted me, was never going to be the same again.

"Blood Taint" first appeared in *A Companion in Zeor* #16 (2001-2002):

http://www.simegen.com/sgfandom/rimonslibrary/cz/cz16/blood_taint.html

BLOOD TAINT

KATHERINE X. RYLIEN

Garrett Brunson sat on his narrow bed staring out the window, though there was not much to see. Just a stretch of pale dusty grass and the corner of one of the other buildings. At least there were no bars on the windows, like there had been at the last place. Nothing to prevent him from walking away. But of course, he had nowhere to go.

He heard his roommate turn a page of the textbook he'd been reading for the past hour. Without looking up, Garrett knew that Jamal's attention was no longer on the book. "Garrett, unless my sense of time has suddenly become defective, it is five minutes past the hour and you are late for your appointment."

"I told you already, I'm not going."

Amusement rippled through Jamal's nager. Several days short of turnover, his field dominated the room, though Garrett would have been stronger if both were at the same point in their cycles. "Here now, it's your transfer appointment. You can't just skip it. Do you think you'll get a better assignment that way? Won't work. The Tecton has its charms, but flexibility is not among them. Better run along now, and perhaps they'll overlook your tardiness."

Garrett didn't answer. He wished Jamal would mind his own business. His roommate was six months younger than Garrett, but had changed over earlier, and was near the end of his First Year as a Sime. Here in Sime territory, they were regarded as coming from similar backgrounds—both were from out-Territory, both had Killed in First Need and then successfully disjuncted, and both were channels. But from Garrett's point of view, the other boy came from a different world. Jamal was the son of a wealthy banking family, while Garrett's parents were farmers, struggling year to year with the possibility of starvation.

When they were alone in their room, they tended to lapse into English, and Jamal's upper-class manner of speaking was particularly noticeable then. Usually it didn't bother Garrett, but today, he found everything about Jamal irritating. Jamal had done very well here at the Institute of Alternative Arts, where channels who were considered unfit for actual channeling work were sent for training, and would probably graduate soon. Whereas Garrett, who had arrived a little less than three months ago, was in trouble.

Through the unshielded door, Garrett could zlin a powerful and familiar Sime nager, which flared in a preemptory demand for admittance. Jamal replied by projecting an invitation, followed by an unconvincing effort to seem absorbed in his studies. Garrett's supervising channel, Martya Dunne, opened the door and stood there radiating disapproval. "You are expected to remember your appointments, Garrett. You have inconvenienced me, and also Sosu Thorne, who, as you may recall, was scheduled to give you transfer."

From Jamal, a momentary outburst of jealousy and indignation quickly stifled with a wary glance at Hajene Dunne. Garrett hadn't told Jamal that he had been assigned to a Gen Donor this month. Jamal felt it was beneath his dignity to accept transfer from other channels. He treated all Gens with a solemn courtesy that he did not always extend to other Simes, but toward the technical-class Donors, his attitude came close to reverence. Garrett respected the professional Donors, but also thought that they had to be at least a little crazy. If he'd been lucky enough to be Gen, the last thing he would have been interested in doing was letting some Sime put its tentacles on him. Particularly one that had already Killed somebody.

Garrett didn't answer out loud. He projected Need at Hajene Dunne, not caring that Jamal would find this behavior amusing. Surely she would like to give him transfer herself, instead. She knew what he Needed, and she was one of the ones who could make it work.

"Garrett, come with me, please."

He followed her through the halls to her office. Branden Thorne was nowhere in evidence. Martya Dunne closed the door of the heavily insulated room, leaving them in a bubble of privacy. She took one chair, and Garrett flopped into the other one. "Garrett, I know you don't want this assignment, but simply failing to show up is not the answer. You had a miserable time of it last month, and we have to do better for you. But we have to reduce your dependence on the therapeutic technique. Every other month is simply not an acceptable prescription. You've been doing very well in your classwork, especially considering the problems with your last transfer. But no matter how well you do with your studies, you cannot be certified as a med-tech unless we can get your DJS symptoms under better control."

Disjunction Syndrome. It was a phrase Garrett had heard many times before, and it filled him with despair, because he didn't think it was likely to improve. "Maybe I should just switch to the other classes."

"You've already put three months into the medical program. Now you want to just give up and try the industrial curriculum instead? I want to encourage you to stick with it. Your counselor at the disjunction clinic recommended you for the medical track, and I concur with his assessment. You can make better use of your natural abilities in that field, and you would be offering a valuable service by reducing the burden on working channels, freeing them for other responsibilities. While it's true that a channel's sensitivity can be very valuable for a variety of industrial applications, those classes are offered primarily for those who are not capable of functioning in the medical work."

Garrett did not think it was any disgrace to be enrolled in the industrial classes. Some of the students there hadn't even Killed anybody. He sometimes peered through the door of the industrial labs, and it looked interesting. He knew the students were an odd mixture of the more unstable disjuncts, and a number of nonjunct students at the Institute, who were there because various physical infirmities prevented them from being trained as working channels, or as medical technicians for that matter. Many of them came from inbred channeling families that could trace their ancestors back to well before Unity, and they had a reputation for dying suddenly for no apparent reason.

"If I switch to those classes, can I get the other kind of transfer?" The kind I need, damn you.

"Your course of study is partly your own decision, though I will not approve a change based on an impulsive decision, particularly in your current condition. Your transfer assignment is another matter. You have no say over that, but must accept the Controller's decision. All of us are in the same position, as far as that is concerned. And there are good reasons for that. Now, I have told Sosu Thorne to meet us one hour from your original appointment. Should I dismiss you now, with the understanding that you will, of course, show up this time? Or would it be better for you to wait in one of the secure areas? We have already extended your cycle in the hope of alleviating some of your problems. Another hour will not put you into hard Need, but it will be the closest you have come to that since disjuncting. Give me your self-evaluation, please." She sat back and looked at him, waiting to judge him by his answer.

Distantly, Garrett could feel a storm of emotion trying to build up inside him. If not for the seawall of Need he might have been in danger of bursting into tears of frustration. "This is not a good idea. Why can't you give me transfer?"

"We discussed this before. I understand you're afraid you will hurt him. Your concern for his safely is commendable, but misplaced. Listen to me, Garrett. You will never be put in the position of being assigned to any Gen that you could possibly injure in transfer. Never. Sosu Thorne is highly trained and experienced at this type of work, and has capacity and draw speed tolerance beyond anything you will ever require. He has no fear of you whatsoever. And that confidence is not misplaced. And I will be right there in the room with you."

"But what if…" How could she possibly move fast enough to stop him if he acted without forethought, without conscious intent? "I mean, look, what if someone grabbed him hard enough to break the skin on his arms? Under augmentation, you could drive your fingers right to the bone. That would hurt really bad. Do you really think he'd be able to remember his training if something like that happened?"

Hajene Dunne went very still. "Is that what you think you might like to do?"

Her inflection and nager were neutral, opaque, and Garrett had a sense that he was a few ill-chosen words away from getting himself locked up in some secure facility for the rest of his life.

"No! No, I…" Surely she could zlin that he was telling the truth, and that thought caused his panic to recede a little. But what if she could read something in his soul that he had hidden even from himself?

Perhaps he deserved to be locked up. Perhaps it was the only way to keep him from hurting anyone else.

"What you just described; is that what you are planning to do?"

"No. It was just… you said I could never hurt him. I just don't think that's true."

She twined her fingers and tentacles in an intricate pattern. "In answer to your question, my best guess as to what might happen in a case like that, is that the Gen would let loose a nageric shock that would Kill any Sime in close proximity—certainly, anyone who had made lateral contact. Trained Gens such as Sosu Thorne do have certain defenses. It's not a question I ever want to learn the answer to, really. Since I'm sure you don't, either, we will drop the matter. Now, what are we to do with you until your transfer appointment? Give me your self-evaluation, and I will tell you whether or not I concur."

The storm burst through the seawall, not tears but dry rage. "You can go to hell! You can take your Gen with you!" He took a deep breath, trying to calm himself, and settled back into the chair from which he had half-risen. "I told you last week, I am not doing this. I won't feel any different about it in an hour. I guess you can probably make me do it.

That's what you'll have to do, because that way, whatever happens will be your fault."

She took one of his arms and briefly touched one of his partially extended laterals with her own. "I would estimate two to three hours before you are truly in hard Need. Perhaps you don't remember what that's like. You say you will feel no differently about this in one hour; what about in another six?"

She looked at him, and he thought that she expected him to break then, to panic and beg her to reconsider. He made no reply. She was projecting the certainty that in another six hours he would do whatever she wanted; anything at all. And he was not at all sure that she was wrong.

"No comment?"

Garrett shook his head, not trusting himself to speak.

"All right. Let me get something for you to occupy your mind, and I shall inform your instructors that you will have to miss your classes for the rest of the evening." She grabbed a half dozen books from her shelves, so rapidly that the selection seemed random, though he doubted that it was. She thrust these into his arms, then led him once more through the halls. As they walked they passed a variety of people. Unlike the disjunction clinic, there were a fair number of general donors wandering the halls, unescorted by renSime guards. Garrett and his fellow students were supposed to be no threat, now that they had disjuncted. No threat, most of the time, and for when it was judged otherwise...

Past the infirmary, there were a row of isolation rooms. Garrett had never seen the inside of one, but was familiar with them by reputation. This was where you got locked up if they decided you couldn't be trusted. Hajene Dunne unlocked one of them, and Garrett went obediently inside. It was smaller than the room he shared with Jamal, and the only furniture was a padded bench that was bolted to the floor.

She stood in the doorway looking at him, her nager revealing little of what she might be thinking. "Six hours should not be outside your capabilities, as long as you don't augment too much. Simes do have a tendency to do that if they allow themselves to panic. We don't intend to let you die of Attrition, Garrett, even if you handle this very badly. I will alert the staff on this end of the building, and they will help me keep an eye on you. If you feel you can't handle it, push the distress signal beside the door and I will come and evaluate your situation. Sosu Thorne will remain your transfer assignment, regardless. In six hours, in twelve... this time tomorrow, if you feel you can hold out that long. You seem to feel transfer is an optional activity for Simes. You will learn otherwise before you leave this room." She gave him one last, considering look, and closed the door.

He heard the key turn in the lock.

He flipped through the book on top of the stack, a text on Gen anatomy. It was interesting, but what was the point? He would not be able to meet the standards for the medical certification anyway. Particularly not to practice on Gens. She'd made it clear in their last meeting that his control would have to improve a great deal for that, and that she would require some improvement before he could even be certified to work with other Simes.

Pointless or not, he became absorbed in the book. Precisely one hour had passed when he sensed Hajene Dunne standing outside the door. Had she decided to let him out early? He doubted it. He waited until he was sure she was not going to unlock the door, and sensed that she was about to walk away. Then he projected a cheerful defiance at her. She could read through his showfield, of course, but in his mind the gesture still counted for something. And in truth, he did not really feel that bad.

Garrett set the book down. It was beginning to make him edgy, looking at all these pictures of Gens. He didn't want to think about that. The next book was a general text on Sime physiology, but he didn't feel like reading about that either. The third one was a study of the physical manifestations of Disjunction Syndrome. Drawn by the same grisly fascination that might have caused him to nudge a dead animal with his foot, he opened that one and began glancing at the illustrations, not uncovering any new information on a topic with which he was already intimately familiar.

Artist's renderings, which he had previously encountered, attempted to depict the subtle changes in nerve bundles that were thickened irrevocably by Killing. In truth, these changes could only be detected by a sensitive channel who knew what to look for.

It was these nerves that the therapeutic transfer was designed to stimulate. Informally, the technique was sometimes called a simulated Kill. This book, like others he had seen on the subject, took care to point out that it was actually nothing of the kind. Because anything that resembled an actual Kill too closely could weaken or destroy the disjunction conditioning. And the channels performing the treatment only had a theoretical knowledge of the Kill, even if they had wanted to recreate the experience in its totality. The technique had been developed with the goal of simulating the effect of Gen pain and fear on those nerves, without recreating those sensations too closely. It was an experience with a strange feel to it, an artificial taste that was as different from the real thing as the way Garrett's memory of the taste of meat differed from the bean-curd steaks that the cafeteria tried to foist off on out-Territory kids who missed foods that they would no longer be capable of digesting properly anyway.

This artificial feel of the therapeutic transfer mingled oddly with the undercurrent of Gen contentment that the channels could not help projecting, because it was so deeply associated with their own experience of transfer. A strange combination, and yet it worked. Garrett had never had any problem accepting these transfers. They were wonderful. But it was the policy to use such techniques as infrequently as possible, because it was feared that using them too frequently would cause excessive dependence on them, and might weaken their effectiveness as well.

Statistics were not ordinarily a source of fascination for Garrett, but he became absorbed in table after table of information about the effectiveness of this treatment on both channels and renSimes. Two to four times a year was typical for those Simes who required the technique, which not all disjuncts did. This was new information, and dismayed Garrett. That was not nearly often enough.

The students had another name for the technique: the blood taint. When he'd first heard the term, Garret had found it curiously apt, even though no blood was spilled when a Gen was Killed for selyn. Still, it fit.

Absorbed in the book, he barely noticed when Hajene Dunne came to stand once more on the other side of the door, marking the end of his second hour of confinement. But once she had left his concentration faltered. He resented both her assumption that he would find this subject of interest, and the fact that she had proved correct.

He didn't feel like reading. He felt like pacing. Instead, he closed his eyes and practiced one of the relaxation drills he had learned at the clinic. When he felt able, he began trying to review some of his classwork. Why hadn't she taken the time to let him get his own textbooks? The pace at the Institute was merciless, and he could not afford to fall behind.

What little concentration he could summon was shattered when she appeared once again, marking the halfway point. He was annoyed, and strove to ignore her. Maybe when she came back in another three hours with the Gen in tow, he would tell her he still wasn't interested. That might wipe some of the smugness from her nager.

He picked up the Disjunction Syndrome book again, not bothering to open it, just bouncing it in his hand. When he realized what he was doing he made himself stop and set it down. Severe and atypical DJS, that had been one of the phrases he'd seen in his file, which he'd sneaked a look at one time when Hajene Dunne had turned her head to speak to someone at the door, the day she'd started all this by assigning him the Gen. Let her blame the Controller if she liked, Garrett was her patient and he knew she had a great deal of say in the matter.

She'd told him that he would not only have to reduce his dependency on these treatments, but also show more control when they were administered. Because once the channel giving him transfer began to stimulate those nerves, he attacked in something not far short of Killmode. What did they expect? But apparently other channels who received this treatment responded differently. The attack reflex was not triggered until after commitment to transfer, so at least it did not cause him to be viewed as a threat to public safety. At least, not until he had started talking about ways to provoke a panic reflex in a trained Donor through the use of physical trauma. He'd felt sure that when he said that, she would at least stop this transfer, whatever the other consequences.

Severe and atypical. Nobody's fault but his own, because he'd had plenty of warning. He'd known for months that he was going to change-over, or would have known if he'd allowed himself to.

But he'd shut out the premonitions of his impending changeover, fought them with all he'd been taught, through prayer and hard work and more prayer. For surely thoughts as disturbing as the ones that haunted his dreams were the whisperings of a demon. That was what he had been taught; that such awful ideas came from outside his own mind, and that sufficient faith would purify him of them.

He had never been told that some Simes knew they would change-over... or what such knowledge meant. The Church of Man Descended had a great deal to say about Simes, much of it tinged with more pity than condemnation. They paid scant attention, however, to the distinction between channels and renSimes. Thinking back, he could recall only one passage, committed to memory like so much of the church's teachings:

"A Sime is a Sime. The distinction between so-called channel and any other Sime is nothing but Tecton propaganda. They would have us believe these 'channels' are Simes that do not Kill, and can prevent other Simes from Killing. But it is obvious to any but the Deceived that all Simes Kill, for that is their nature."

In a way, he had proved the church right, at least in his case. He was a channel, and yet he had Killed—matricide, which the Church held to be one of the worst crimes anyone could commit.

He had refused to admit what was happening to him until the first, faint striations appeared on his arms. It looked as though he'd scratched at them with his fingernails, but he knew he had not. By then he had been weak and feverish, finding it difficult to think, but he knew what had to be done.

He pulled the small metal token from beneath his pillow, the one his oldest brother had shown him on his eleventh birthday, a little over two years earlier. Much like a coin in appearance, these tokens were distributed by the Tecton. The familiar and reviled Tecton Seal was on one side; engraved on the other was the phone number of the nearest Sime Center. This token, along with a battered pamphlet that some of the children had kept hidden in a dead tree until it was ruined by the moisture there, was all the changeover training Garrett had ever received. Even that much was strictly forbidden by the Church. Children who turned Sime were to be humanely destroyed, not given the chance to earn a more final damnation by Killing and then going on to create others of their own kind.

He held the token in one sweaty hand and realized he did not have the strength to make it into the next room and use the telephone there. He was not even sure he could remember how to operate it. The high fever was making simple things seem complex. So he called to his mother. She often worked with her husband and sons in the fields during the early part of the day, before going back to the house to begin preparing supper. But on that day, Garrett had been too ill to work, so she had stayed home with him. It was understood that she would do whatever needed to be done for him.

When she came into the room, he took his arms from beneath the covers and showed her, pressing the coin into her hand and asking her to call the number engraved on it. He heard her walk into the front room. That was where the telephone was… and also the short-barreled shotgun she was expected to use on him now. He turned his back to the door, hiding his arms once more beneath the blankets. If she came back with the gun, he did not intend to make her look him in the face when she did it. A great sense of peace came over him then, because it was out of his hands. An interminable moment later, he heard her dialing, then speaking softly. He began to cry. Then he heard her come back and slide shut the heavy bolt on the outside of his bedroom.

"They said they can be here within a couple hours," she told him through the thick wooden door. "They said you should be all right until then. God help us, Garrett." As far as he could recall, those were the last words she had ever spoken to him, or to anyone. His memories of what had happened next were distorted by fever and by new perceptions he hardly knew how to interpret.

The bolt on the door was sturdy enough, as was the door itself. It was the frame which had given way. Later, he saw the door lying intact and useless on the hall floor, hinges twisted and still fastened to part of the splintered frame. The dish that had been in his mother's hands when he'd caught her had not fared as well, but lay shattered near her feet. She had begun preparing the evening meal, and a neat row of vegetables lay on the counter next to the metal token Garrett had given her. The expression on her face was unbearable.

He went into the front room where a shawl her own mother had knitted lay over the back of the sofa, concealing a rip that had been imperfectly mended. Behind the couch, of course, was the gun. It had been kept there ever since Garrett, the youngest child, had been old enough to understand that it was not a toy.

He could not understand why she had not kept it near her, brought it into the kitchen so that she would have a chance. Surely she had not given such absolute credence to what some faceless stranger had told her over the telephone. That would not be like her. He stood looking at the gun for several minutes, thinking that it might be simplest if he were to use it, now, on himself.

Instead, he took the shawl into the living room and covered her body. Then he sat down to wait, taking a place on the floor beside her. Had it been two hours? He didn't think so. Not unless that strange, surrealistic sequence of events had taken much longer than it had seemed. He didn't think so. It had all gone so much faster than it was supposed to. Not that it mattered, now.

If the Tecton came to get him before his father and brothers returned, let them do what they liked with him. And if they did not—well, he had little doubt as to how his father would see fit to handle a situation like this. Garrett could only hope that he would have the courage to stand his ground and take what was coming to him, as if it were nothing more than a switching. He thought briefly of running away; he knew the woods well enough to avoid capture for quite awhile. But to what end? If he stayed free long enough, he would only end up Killing again.

So he sat there until a sharp rap came at the front door, and then he went to answer it. Pulling open the door, he saw two men. The one in front held a clipboard, and was just in the process of lowering it, as if he'd used one corner of it to knock. "You're too late," Garrett told them, but before he could even complete his sentence he felt a sharp stab of dismay. It took him a moment to realize that it was not his own emotion, but came from the smaller of the two men, who stood behind and slightly to one side of the one with the clipboard. He didn't fully understand the reasons behind this reaction until much later. Out-Territory response teams hated scenes like this, of course, arriving as quickly as they could only to find a dead Gen and a junct Sime and little they could do to remedy the situation. But it was worse when the Sime was a channel; one of their own. Channels had a significantly lower chance of successful disjunction, in comparison with renSimes. And even for those who made it, the damage was greater. Disjunct renSimes could usually do just about anything they'd be able to do if they were nonjunct. Whereas, a channel with the same history was forever barred by Tecton policy from doing most of the things nature had designed channels to do.

Garrett knew what Jamal thought of this policy, because he'd been subjected to an embittered tirade on his roommate's last turnover day. Jamal thought there was nothing wrong with him that could not be cured by the Gen-transfer privileges enjoyed by working channels who would not be expected to take transfer from another channel except under unusual circumstances.

As far as Garrett knew, Jamal might well be right in his insistence that there was no good reason he should not be licensed as a working channel, as would have been permitted routinely in the days before Unity. But in his own case, Garrett did not need some phrase like severe and atypical symptoms to tell him there was still something inside him that could do harm, if it were allowed to get free. Call it DJS, or call it a demon. A demon that had been bound with chains and confined in some deep cavern, but could never be slain, like some immortal monster out of a dark fairy tale. He agreed with the Tecton's position that an innocent, nonjunct renSime ought not to be exposed to such a thing in transfer, and did not see why they would want to run the risk of letting him touch one of their Gens.

It wasn't as if they didn't know what he required. Hajene Dunne knew. Not anything a Gen could give him, not without paying the ultimate price and completing Garrett's damnation in the process.

Severe and atypical. Garrett wasn't surprised that his symptoms were considered unusual, after comparing his changeover experience with the other disjunct channels at the Academy. He had told them things that he did not think he could ever tell his Supervising Channel, or any other nonjunct Sime.

His memories of Killing were clearer than he would have wished, and Hajene Dunne encouraged him to explore these memories and analyze them—even though she must have known he was not sharing all of his conclusions on the topic with her. If his disjunction was sound, she assured him, thinking about it would not reawaken anything more than a ghost of the desire to Kill. Hanging unspoken between them was the other half of that thought; that if he turned out to be one of the unfortunate few who were technically disjunct but too unstable to be permitted to walk free among vulnerable Gens, it was better to find that out early, while he was still in a supervised environment where his condition could be detected before it got out of control. Despite the looser security at the Academy, Garrett knew they were there for more than just vocational training.

Four hours had passed, and if he hadn't been so acutely aware of the time already, he'd have been reminded by Hajene Dunne's silent and momentary presence on the other side of the door. All the mercy she could show him, he decided, but still worth a great deal. It was a promise, an assurance that she had not forgotten about him. That she would not leave him to die here. He no longer entertained any thought of telling her to go away. As his father would have said, all the fight had been beat out of him, though nobody had raised a hand to him. All they'd done, in effect, was to send him to bed without his supper. It was more than enough.

Comparing his experiences to those of the other disjunct channels, Garrett had begun to realize how unusual his own changeover—and subsequent Kill—had been. Atypical, to use the phrase from his records. No wonder his symptoms were, because...

None of the others he'd talked to about it had found their Kills truly satisfying. Some had gone on to Kill more than once, and for those who had not, either great self-restraint or else lack or opportunity had played some role. Garrett had come out of the berserker mode in a state of shock, filled with guilt and despair—but he'd felt no urge to go looking for another Gen.

He'd learned part of the reason during his studies in the disjunction ward, in the process of learning basic facts that any in-Territory child knew long before the age where changeover became a danger. His mother must have been an unusually high-field Gen, the kind that would have been encouraged to train as a professional Donor if she had been born in Sime Territory. The very fact that she had been able to bring him to term, and survive giving birth to him, attested to that. But he didn't think that was the whole explanation.

Because she hadn't died right away. It was not only the most satisfying Kill that he'd heard any of the others describe, it had been the most prolonged experience. He believed now that she had tried to cooperate—had tried, without really even understanding what the word meant, to give him transfer. But of course she hadn't really overcome her fear, just pushed it aside. He had been able to taste it, telling him there was something more, and he had gone after it. It was a moment of greed he had been paying for ever since, and would continue to pay for until the day of his own death.

He wasn't quite sure what he had done that caused her nerve to break. But as good as it had been up until that point, it became immeasurably better. By far, the most intense pleasure he had ever known, before or since.

"Nothing so evil should feel like that," he whispered aloud in the isolation room. He hadn't meant to speak out loud, and was embarrassed.

It would not surprise him to learn that the room was wired for sound, and the little he'd said was enough for them to figure out what he'd been thinking about. He was surprised to find his lips dry and cracked, though his mouth was watering to the point where he had to keep swallowing. His arms were seeping ronaplin, and there was nothing he could do about that besides wipe them occasionally on the tail of his shirt. He wasn't as embarrassed about that as he was about the verbal slip. No one was likely to see him in this condition but other Simes—and Sosu Thorne, who was presumably used to this kind of thing.

As he approached his sixth hour of confinement, his resolve began to falter. He'd been so confident that, knowing when this torture was going to end, he could endure it. But it was too much. He tried to keep still on the padded bench, knowing it was foolish to waste selyn by pacing, but the urge to move around was strong. A couple of times he found himself on his feet and moving without having made any conscious decision to get up. Once on his feet, it was almost impossible to keep from augmenting. He made himself sit down, although the bench was starting to seem to him like some kind of trap, a grave above the ground that would spell his death if he remained there.

The fifth time he sensed Hajene Dunne outside the door it no longer seemed like a reassurance. Nothing but mockery, and it was only her superior nageric strength that kept him from zlinning the pleasure she was doubtlessly taking from his suffering. He projected his rage and his hatred at her, hoping to hurt her at least a little. She left after a pause of exactly the same duration as the other times, and he began to shake.

It had been stupid to make such a futile attack on her. What if she decided to extend his punishment? What if she came back at the end of the next hour and just zlinned him through the door again, instead of letting him out? He wouldn't be able to stand that. He wasn't sure he could even hold out until then. But he would not press the signal. He would sit here until he lost control altogether, and began battering at the door in a mindless attempt to get out. Unlike the door to his childhood bedroom, this one had been knowledgeably designed to withstand a Sime operating under high augmentation. He probably could not break through. But he had no doubt that he would reach the point where he would not know any better than to try, burning up the last reserves of his strength.

Far more efficient, and sensible, to exert a small pressure on the metal plate marked emergency signal with his hand. But he would not. For one thing, he was fairly certain that she would just examine him and conclude that he was not as bad off as he thought he was.

He lay down on the bench. Again the image of a coffin came to his mind, accompanied by a feeling of claustrophobia. He imagined, instead, that it was one of the narrow cots in the bedroom he'd shared with his two brothers. He remembered lying there during the winter nights that had started so early in the day, and when they had all gone to bed early not from fatigue but for lack of anything better to do—and to conserve energy. There was never quite enough food in the wintertime, not if they wanted to be sure and keep an adequate reserve against the possibility of a late spring. Often, he had lain there in the darkness, drowsing but unable to sleep, and thought about summer.

Summer was always better. There was no shortage of food then, and also no shortage of things to do, hard work that taxed his young muscles and left him exhausted from trying to keep up with his father and brothers. But even in summer, there had been times of leisure. After church he and his brothers had been free to spend the rest of the day as they pleased, for work was forbidden on that day. And it was the pond that he recalled the most clearly. Muddy and bug-infested, the cool water had been such a welcome balm on the hottest days. The time he and his brothers had spent there had a timeless quality, and it was the pond that had comforted him during those long winters. The same image came to him now, and it was as if he were there once again, beneath the shade of the willow tree, splashing in the shallow water.

That last hour passed as if in a dream. He felt feverish, as he had in changeover, but the water from the pond cooled him. He could feel it, smell it, and taste the hot sun on his skin. The isolation room became a thing of shadows, rising in his consciousness like the memory of a bad dream that he recalled only vaguely. The pond was far more real, and through his closed eyes he could see it, could perceive it with all five of the senses he'd possessed as a child. Only his newest sense told him he was still locked up in this other place, so very far from home.

When he sensed Hajene Dunne outside the door once again, he was almost reluctant to leave the safety of these memories behind. But she had the Gen with her, and was in the process of unlocking the door, so he sat up and wiped the excess ronaplin off his forearms, then tucked his shirt back in. It was the closest he could come to making himself look presentable.

Hajene Dunne came in first. She'd done something to make her nager dull and uninteresting. Branden Thorne followed, a blazing beacon of life and promise. It was something like a reenactment of his disjunction trial, only they had changed all the rules on him. He clung to the edge of the bench to keep himself from rushing at the Gen. For one thing, Hajene Dunne was standing in his way. He didn't think he would be able to get past her unless she let him. And he could tell from the vibrations in her field that she was speaking, but could not tell what she was saying. Doubtlessly there were more formalities to be gone through before he could have what he Needed. With an effort, he pulled himself duoconscious.

"...up until now, but—ah, there he is. Hello, Garrett. How are you feeling?"

Surely she could zlin for herself how he felt—at the very edge of death. He did not doubt that the Gen could see that as well, with his eyes, and perhaps sense with that shadowy awareness of nager that he'd read the higher-order Gens often developed. He thought of making some breezy remark to the effect that he felt fine, but they'd both know he was lying, and he was terrified that she might leave again if he did. So he said nothing.

"Garrett? Talk to me, are you ready for your transfer appointment now?"

"Don't be absurd, Martya, obviously he is." Slowly, the Gen moved closer and laid a cool hand on Garrett's arm, soothing the agonizing fire that ran the length of his lateral tentacles. Handling tentacles whipped around the Gen's hand of their own accord, and Garrett was trembling with the effort it cost him not to reach out with the other hand as well. Instead, he continued to cling to the side of the bench. Abruptly, his mind flashed back to the pond, and it seemed that the water was over his head and he was choking on it, and one of his brothers reached out with a dead branch for him to hold onto, and used it to pull him from the water. A very early memory, if it was real at all, because the deepest part of the pond barely came up to the level of a man's waist.

"Careful, Branden, he's not entirely with us yet. He may attack. Be ready."

He had the feeling she was speaking more for his benefit than for the Gen's, and again he had the impulse to say something, but could not. It was all he could do not to attack, and he wondered if Hajene Dunne was at all impressed by the self-control that allowed him to hold short of actually doing so. More likely, she thought it was pathetic the way he was sitting there shaking, barely able to keep from springing at his assigned Donor like a berserker. He could read nothing in her field. It was almost impossible to tear his attention away from the Gen anyway.

He still held one of the Gen's hands trapped against his arm, where one pair of laterals were in blissful but frustratingly incomplete contact. Thorne ran the other hand gently down Garrett's forearm, bringing his intil down to a reasonable level and making it possible for him to remain duoconscious without a constant struggle. He projected gratitude, then remembered that the Gen could not read the nageric thank you in his field. But maybe he could pick up a little of it, or read the emotion in Garrett's face.

Thorne sat beside him on the bench, and Garrett realized that he would not be expected to move into one of the transfer suites. Relief made his muscles turn weak as he zlinned that the Gen was as committed to this transfer as he was. He managed to relax his grip on the Gen's hand so that a more suitable transfer position could be established.

"Good, now give me your other hand." Garrett did, more than willingly. The Gen knew what he was doing, and was in firm control of the situation. This was not his mother; nobody was going to get hurt. The Gen's lips touched his, completing the circuit.

The first, life-giving flow of selyn was better than any clean transfer Garrett had ever gotten from a channel. He drew greedily, the last vestiges of his self-control slipping away in the pure pleasure of the onslaught. But with this loss of control came terror, and he drew back, desperate to escape. The Gen tried to hold him, but Garrett came back to duoconsciousness curled into a fetal ball, face averted from his Donor but with his arms still trapped in a full transfer grip. He felt Hajene Dunne touch the base of his skull with one lateral, then she withdrew.

"Try again, Branden."

It ended in much the same way. Just like all the times a channel had tried to give him a normal transfer, when what he Needed was the other kind.

Branden Thorne was radiating frustration—and physical pain. He had a headache to match the one Garrett could feel pounding at his own temples. Just as Garrett had always feared would happen if he tried to take transfer from a Gen. He'd hurt the Donor. Thorne was so focused on Garrett that he didn't even seem to be aware of his own discomfort, but it magnified Garrett's own pain. And it horrified him when he realized the significance of what he was zlinning. If he did succeed in taking transfer from Thorne now, when he was in pain—and if he enjoyed it…

"These don't feel like spontaneous aborts, Martya. I'd almost swear he was doing it on purpose. Garrett, did you go through all the trouble of disjuncting just to die of Attrition?"

Garrett tried to pull away from the Gen's grasp, and finding it too much trouble, just buried his face in the crook of his elbow. He could feel Thorne trying to stimulate his intil. "Come on, Garrett, you've got to stop fighting me."

"No, let him go. It won't work. Let me get you both some fosebine."

Thorne didn't argue, but released Garrett's arms and began to stroke his back as Hajene Dunne went to a locked supply cabinet built into one wall. It helped, and Garrett wished there were something he could do in return to ease the Gen's discomfort. "I'm sorry; I didn't mean to hurt you."

"Here, drink this."

As Garrett swallowed the foul-tasting mixture, he was aware of Hajene Dunne taking the Gen into position for a lateral contact probe.

He felt a faint sense of outrage, because on one level he still thought of Thorne as his. But the feeling was blunted by pain. Garrett set down the empty glass and massaged his temples. Need still chewed at his nerves, Need unaccompanied by any trace of intil. He wished he were dead.

"You'll be all right, Branden. Get some dinner, and then come to my office in a couple of hours. I'll take another look, and give you a little therapy for any remaining discomfort... and in the meantime, I'll talk to Dhar about getting you another assignment. If we can't find one without messing up the schedule too badly, I'll have to take your field down, as well."

Once the Gen had left, she turned to Garrett, and her field was no longer dull or unappealing. He knew from the faint air of resignation in her nager that she was going to give him what he had wanted all along. The feel of the other Sime's laterals twined with his spelled safety, because he did not believe that any buried part of him wanted to hurt her. He thought it likely that he could do so, if he tried, but he would gain no satisfaction from it. She would drop the Gen showfield in a hurry, and quite possibly hurt him back. Knowing this, he had no fear that the demon would break free of its place of confinement and strike out. He gave himself fully to the transfer, control slipping from him once again, but this time there was no panic.

Relief and satiation singing through his nerves, he dropped his head to rest on his channel's shoulder, maintaining all four lateral contacts because it felt so good. He breathed in deeply. Even without reference to his other senses, he could have told from the faint smell of her skin that she was Sime, and female.

He could feel her gently trying to disengage her laterals.

"Garrett. Let go of me, now." He did, and she took his shoulders and held him at arm's length, "Look at you. After two aborts, no power in this world could get me as post as you are right now. The resilience of youth."

Abruptly, his mood plummeted. "I'm sorry. I tried, I really did."

"You did very well."

Why would she say such a thing? Two goals had been set for him; to reduce his dependence on these therapeutic transfers, and to maintain control. He'd accomplished neither of these. His inability to accept the

Gen had left her with no choice but to provide him with the blood taint, despite all her efforts to substitute something more wholesome. And once she'd offered it to him, he had retained no control whatsoever.

"You understand why you aborted, don't you? You were still afraid that you would hurt him. That speaks well of you, that you would be concerned for a Gen's well-being on such a deep level, even in hard Need. It proves to me that the assessment was correct, when you were recommended for the medical program. Because for you to do that kind of work, we have to be very sure you have a significant degree of ability to resist the temptation to attack a defenseless Gen, even under circumstances that test your control."

"I would die first." Garrett muttered, as much to himself as to his supervising channel.

She gave a barely perceptible nod, as if to signify that she understood completely. But she didn't. How could she? She was nonjunct. Oh, he'd heard the argument that it was not that much different for Simes who had never Killed—that they had to face the same instincts that existed in him. But it wasn't the same. It couldn't be.

"At any rate, you withstood the delay as well as I had hoped you would. Very encouraging. What if I suggested pushing it a little further next time, not as a punishment, but as part of your training? Do you think you could do that?"

"I don't know. I kept thinking I would never make it… I don't know if I could have gone on much longer. I'm not even sure I could do that again. What would you have done, if I had pushed the signal?"

"Come in and evaluated you. There is a point beyond which it is nothing but torture to demand self-control, when it is impossible. That point varies widely, and depends as much on mental attitude as remaining selyn supply. At a regular channeling school, you know, students are routinely pushed well into clinical Attrition as a testing procedure. to their breaking point. We rarely go that far with disjuncts, because we have found that the procedure can shatter their self-confidence. But there is perhaps no group more diverse than this handful of disjunct channels here at this school. I have had a few students here who benefited greatly from pushing it to that point." She looked at him appraisingly.

His mouth was dry. Attrition. The word itself had the power to terrify him. Not because it meant death, but because of the loss of control that would inevitably come first.

"Well, we can discuss all of this later, after I have a chance to discuss your case with the Controller. There is no reason you ever have to suffer hard Need again if you don't want to—it's largely up to you. But you are far from the first of our students to elect transfer delay as a method of honing the will." She spoke without irony, as if he had filled out some form requesting such a course of training. Perhaps, from her point of view, what he had done was not much different than that.

"For now, go clean up and you can meet Sosu Thorne and myself in my office a couple of hours from now. I will show you how to look for, and treat, any residual damage from those aborts. Don't worry, he's in no danger—if he required serious intervention, I would not have let him leave this room, nor would I be making this into a training exercise. Between the fosebine and the little bit of therapy I gave him already there might not be much left to treat. But follow-up care is always a good idea for any kind of transfer trauma, and a little hands-on experience will be good for you. And I'd like to take another look at you as well."

Garrett had mixed feelings. He didn't really want to have to face the Gen again, but was glad of the chance to make up for what he had done. Not that his feelings mattered much in any event. She had not phrased it as a suggestion. "Yes, Hajene."

After he'd showered, changed and endured a certain amount of disbelieving raillery from Jamal about the lengthy transfer delay, he realized he was famished. He headed for the cafeteria, where he decided to sample several dishes he had not tried before, mostly from the black serving bowls that warned they were for Simes only.

The cafeteria never closed, but it was between regular mealtimes, and the dining area was almost deserted. At one of the few occupied tables, he saw Branden Thorne, who was eating alone. Before he could decide whether to retreat back into the serving area, the Gen saw him and beckoned to him, and at that point there was no polite way to refuse.

"Come on over and sit down. Are you really going to eat all that? I have got to see this with my own eyes."

"Is your head feeling any better?" As he took his seat, Garrett forced himself duoconscious so that he could zlin the answer for himself, and so that he would know if the Gen was being candid with him.

"It's fine, really. I'm sorry things didn't work out better. It's not your fault. Martya told me that you weren't too wild about the assignment to begin with. Sometimes I think they should give a little more weight to individual preference when they make these decisions."

Still duoconscious, Garrett could not help knowing that the Donor felt as though he had failed. His head wasn't giving him much pain, but his pride was bruised, something neither fosebine nor channel's functionals could treat.

"It's not you." Garrett lowered his voice, glad there was nobody at any of the surrounding tables. "If I were going to get transfer from any Gen, I can't think of one I'd rather have than you. But… look, it just reminds me too much of, of my changeover. The Gen I attacked—and Killed—you were projecting some of the same feelings as she did." He could hardly believe he was discussing a thing like this with a Gen. But it was suddenly important to him that Thorne understand that the problem with their transfer had been Garrett, and not himself.

But Thorne was radiating indignation, as if Garrett had accused him of some ghastly faux pas. "I find that difficult to—look, I enjoy transfer. I find it hard to believe that your—the Gen that you attacked in changeover felt anything like that."

"My mother," Garrett acknowledged. "You read that in my file, I guess. Yes. She did, at first."

Thorne paused for a long moment before saying anything more. Garrett, lost in his own thoughts, did not bother to stay duoconscious to read the Gen's reaction.

"Have you told Martya that part of it?"

"No."

"Maybe you should."

"Maybe." He reached out and touched Thorne's hand with the tip of one handling tentacle. Thorne seemed to find this completely unremarkable, and just went on eating with his other hand. He was probably used to Simes wanting to touch him.

Garrett resumed picking out choice bits of fruit from his own plate with a two-tined fork, leaving the tentacle in place. There was something inherently comforting about all that selyn.

He didn't know if he would be assigned a Gen Donor again in an effort to control his problems; he wasn't even sure if he wanted that, and didn't plan to worry a great deal about that question, because he knew that his wishes meant nothing one way or the other as far as that was concerned. But if they did give him that kind of assignment again, he did not plan to make such a big deal about it. Because his worst fear, that he would lose control and try to hurt his Donor, had not come true. Not even after the six-hour delay. The experience had given him that much, at least.

The demon still lived somewhere deep inside him, he did not doubt that, dreaming its dreams of pain and fear and death, somewhere beneath the waterline of conscious thought. But its chains were not so easy to break as he had imagined.

The realization came over him that this was the first time since his changeover that he had touched a Gen without feeling uncomfortable about it. Not that he'd had many occasions to touch one at all, but in some of his classes, doing examinations and practice functionals on Gens as well as Simes was part of the lab work, and he had never cared for that. Now, he felt as though he would be able to face doing that, under any reasonable circumstances. Unreasonable conditions, such as a Gen that was terrified or in severe physical pain—well, his instructors had already made it clear that he would never be required to face anything like that. And he believed it. The Tecton could be harsh, but he thought they could be trusted to keep their promises.

He drifted back into duoconsciousness, still basking in the radiance of Thorne's nager. He was reminded again of the farm, where there had been a hill, a gentle slope of cultivated land behind the barn. The land his family farmed was mostly flat, but from that one spot with its slight elevation, it had seemed like he could see for miles. Pausing there and looking out over the fields, he'd sometimes felt a great sense of peace and freedom. Sitting in the Institute's lunch room with his tentacle still resting on the back of Branden Thorne's hand, he felt the same way.

With the demon drugged into sleep for awhile by the medicine Hajene Dunne had so reluctantly prescribed, he savored this fragile contentment. Just short of his fourteenth birthday in natal years, eight months past changeover, Garrett was old enough to know such feelings were always temporary. All the more reason to appreciate it, and enjoy it for as long as it lasted.

R.K. Hageman had several earlier stories appear in *A Companion in Zeor*, many years ago, under another name. This is a new story crafted for this anthology.

MORE THAN MEETS THE EYE

R. K. HAGEMAN

The afternoon wore on as Jefri and Denrau ambrov Kelin rode side–by-side along the road that led home from Arensti. They had just reached a village that appeared to be entirely deserted or abandoned.

Denrau was old enough to remember when Enorel was a lively little community. What had happened to them all? Had they simply given up on getting government-supplied Gens and gone renegade? Or had the villagers dispersed to larger, better-supplied towns? There was no way to know, now. Dust and dry leaves blew in little gusts down the main street.

Jefri, his coal-black hair falling in his eyes, reined in his horse and looked intently around him. "Listen! Someone's here," he exclaimed. "A child, I think. I can't detect any selyn field, but I can hear a voice." He turned to his Companion. "Can you hear it?"

Denrau closed his grey eyes and listened. "Yes, I think so…that way?" The older Gen motioned toward the south; in the direction he thought he heard a human voice.

The young Sime nodded in agreement. "Yes— I think so, too…" They searched the area, looking up and down empty dirt streets and peering into windows looking for the child whose voice they had heard over the wind.

At last, Jefri caught sight of movement in a yard behind one house. He easily scaled the fence, and slipped around the corner of the building to see what he could, and stopped short, appalled.

Sitting in the dirt playing with tufts of grass and humming to herself was a little girl. Not all that little, Jefri realized; she might have been nine or ten years old, in fact, judging from her physical size. But she acted like a child much younger, maybe three or four. In a few moments, the back door of the house opened, and the First Companion emerged from inside. "They're gone, Sectuib," he said, tightly controlling his voice, but his rich field flared with anger and outrage. "The house is empty. They went off, wherever they went, and left her here to starve. A little child!" Dismayed, he ran a hand through his thick brown hair.

"We don't know that this is her house," Jefri mused. "She may have been lost and let herself in here. There's water in the trough there. She might have come in the yard to get some…" His voice trailed off. Startled at the sound of the men's voices, the girl sitting on the ground suddenly covered her ears and wailed piteously, rocking back and forth. That's not normal for a child that age…that's why they abandoned her, he realized. Something's wrong with her.

There was no point in searching the tiny hamlet. There were no adults remaining here. We—Kelin—are the only chance she has. "You know, we don't know that they went off and left her. She might be a runaway. No telling how long she's been here, or where she came from," Jefri mused. "She's not starved, after all—she must have been eating something." What that might have been didn't bear thinking about. He hoped she'd just been scrounging food from houses.

She had stopped wailing, but was still not looking at them, rocking back and forth where she sat. We can't just leave her here; we have to take her along with us. Denrau went calmly up to her where she was and knelt down facing her, at her eye level. "Hello," he said softly. "We're here to help you. This place isn't safe for you now, so we'll take you with us. Come along now," he said. "My name is Denrau ambrov Kelin, and this is Jefri Farris ambrov Kelin."

She didn't meet his eyes, or give much of a sign that she'd heard him at all, but her head moved slightly in what might have been a nod. The experienced Companion helped her to her feet and lifted her up in his arms, as she was small for her age.

The next thing he knew, she was fighting him with all her strength— hitting, kicking and clawing like a wildcat. "Hey!" He let go of her, and she landed on her feet, still striking at him with her fists.

Like a flash, Jefri stepped in, seizing her arms with hands and tentacles. "No!" he said firmly in a tone that expected to be obeyed. He addressed her in Simelan, in words of one syllable, turning her face towards his so she could not avoid his eyes. "You may not hit him. Hit me if you like—though I'd rather you didn't—but you will not hurt him… ever." He indicated Denrau with a tentacle. "Understand?"

She did not speak, but nodded slowly. "Good," said the young channel and let go his tight grip on her. "Are you all right, Denrau?"

"More or less," his Companion replied ruefully. "She didn't actually bite me, though she tried to." There were bloody scratches on his right cheek from the girl's nails, and a fresh bruise was swelling rapidly above his left eye. "Now what do we do, Jefri? Any bright ideas? We can't tie her up and throw her behind our saddles, but we can't just leave her here, either." He dabbed at his face with a handkerchief.

"I'm thinking." Jefri eyed the young girl, whose tawny tangled hair partially hid her greenish-hazel eyes. He noticed her necklace, a silver pendant hanging from a battered leather cord. Carefully, he reached to look at the pendant, making no sudden moves. There was writing engraved on the oval medallion: Ten-lee, he sounded out. "Tenlee," he said slowly to the girl. "It's a pretty name. Is that your name? Tenlee?" She nodded, and then looked away from his face, avoiding eye contact with him. "She seems less afraid of me than of you," he added. "I guess that makes sense. She's probably never seen an adult Gen in her life, except…"

"…except in a Pen tunic and a neck chain," Denrau finished, stowing his handkerchief in his back pocket. "I didn't even think of that. I went to pick her up because most people in-Territory don't regard Gens as dangerous."

It hadn't occurred to the Sime either, that she would have been terrified of his affable and good-natured Companion. "Let's hope she's not afraid of horses." Jefri got to his feet and took Tenlee's hand to lead her with him. "Come on, Tenlee. We're taking you home. It's a nice place. Plenty of food, nice sheep to play with, and acres of pretty orange flowers," he said, describing the fields of deep orange-red cosmos that made Kelin's signature dye color.

She followed him warily. It took nearly half an hour before Jefri could get her to stand next to the horse and touch his burnished-gold fur shading to black on his legs. But no matter what he tried, there was no getting her onto the buckskin gelding's back.

"Wait, Jefri, I have an idea," Denrau said suddenly and rummaged in his saddlebags. "All kids like sugar candy, right?"

"Barring my mother, yes," Jefri agreed.

Denrau took out a paper packet of the hard-sugar lollies that he used while traveling for sweetening his tea, and offered it to Tenlee. Her face lit up and she reached for the proffered treat, but he didn't give it to her. He reached up and took Jefri's horse's lead rope and put it in her hand. She dropped the rope, not liking the rough feel of it, but he picked it up and put it back in her hand. The message was clear: keep hold of the rope and you can have the candy.

It worked. She eyed him warily, and took hold of the rope. "Good girl, Tenlee," the First Companion said with a smile, and gave her the watermelon lollipop. Communication had occurred.

"Sectuib, we are every parent's worst nightmare," Denrau observed ironically as they headed off down the road with Tenlee walking alongside Jefri's horse. "Doesn't any good mother teach her children not to go anywhere with strange men who offer you candy?"

"Well, if that's the only way to get her to come with us, it can't be helped." They both knew the alternative was to bring her by force, which neither of them really wanted to do. Abandoning her was not even a remote possibility, no matter how much of a problem she was.

"You do realize, at this pace, we won't be home for ten days, if that?"

"Oh, I have no intention of continuing at this pace," Jefri explained. "When her feet are tired enough, she will have enough reason to get onto the horse."

By mid-afternoon, Jefri's prediction had proved true. After an hour or more of walking, the girl clearly showed signs of being tired and foot-sore, and Jefri wordlessly offered her a hand up. Apparently she had decided to trust him, for she allowed him to hoist her up into the saddle in front of him.

They rode on silently until they came to the next town. "I should get more provisions," said Jefri thoughtfully. "What we have isn't enough for three people for a week." They rode along the main street, ignoring the stares of the locals, until they saw a building whose sign read "General Store."

His Companion nodded, considering. "Nuts, dried fruit, some more bread…while you're in there, you might see if they have any ribbon. A piece of soft leather might be good too, a foot or so long and half that wide."

Jefri nodded, heading into the store.

Tenlee gazed around her with a look of astonishment. Denrau dismounted from his grey mare and tied both horses with enough freedom to move their heads, and offered them both some water, keeping a wary eye out for any trouble.

He'd been here years before: the same street, the same store, on the same horse. However, he'd worn a blue cloak in those days, not a cinnamon-brown one. Now First Companion in Kelin, he shook his head at the memory. He still missed Klyd; he probably always would. But there was no way back to his old life, nor would he take it now even if there was. He was no longer the same man, nor was Klyd Farris. Valleroy saw to that, he reflected with a touch of sadness.

A tug on his sleeve brought Denrau back to the present. Tenlee was still seated on Jefri's horse, but she had reached over to touch him; that was a step in the right direction, he thought. She tugged his sleeve again, and pointed to his saddlebag. Denrau smiled back at her. "Clever girl," he said. *She knows Jefri isn't the one who packs sugar for his tea.* "You've been a very good girl, riding on the horse all this way with Sectuib." He opened the saddlebag and fished in it for the packet of sweets, and gave her a yellow one. "When he comes back, we will ride a little farther and then we'll stop and make camp. If you help, you can have another piece of candy then. All right?" He watched her eyes to see if she understood what he said. She looked from him to the door and back again, nodding slowly. She pulled the paper off the yellow sucker and put it in her mouth. I wonder—when was the last time anyone gave her sweets? Someone must have loved her once, surely. Unless she could speak to them, there was so much about her life that they would never know.

The door of the store opened, and Jefri came out with a number of parcels. "Sorry I took so long," he said. "I got food and the things you wanted, but I also got some things for Tenlee. She needs clothes that aren't worn to rags."

"Can she dress herself?"

"Guess we'll find out in the morning."

As they rode on, at an easy trot, twilight was falling and the bright planet Venus shone like a precious gem in the southeastern sky. After about eight miles, the road they were on passed through a grove of trees. "This looks like a good spot," Jefri said, as they moved away from the road. He lifted Tenlee down from the horse, and then dismounted. "I'll manage the tent, you do the fire. I'll go and get water."

"Yes, all right. And Tenlee?"

"Maybe she can help me with the tent when I get back."

When Jefri was getting water for tea and soup, he heard a rhythmic *crack... crack... crack* sound from the direction of their campsite. That's odd. When he arrived back there, he saw what was making the sound. The little girl, Tenlee, was sitting by herself a few feet away, rocking herself back and forth and pounding one stone on another, to no apparent purpose. *Crack... crack... crack...*

The channel watched her for a minute or two, still steadily banging the two rocks together in a rhythm that never varied. "Fascinating," he observed.

Denrau looked up from busying himself with the fire. "Can you find something else for her to do? Please?"

The Sime smiled. "I'll see if I can get her to help me with the tent." Jefri motioned her to come with him. She put down the rock, got up, and followed him.

He unrolled a coil of rope from behind his saddle along with a large canvas tarpaulin. Stretching the rope firmly between two trees, he flung the canvas over the rope, and staked down its edges to make a tunnel-shaped tent. He showed Tenlee how to crawl into the tent. She shrank away from the darkness inside it, though. "Does that look scary?" he asked. "What if we have a light in there?" He got out a candle and the camp lantern from Denrau's baggage, and lit the candle inside the glass chimney. When he placed the lantern on the ground, it cast a golden light that illuminated everything. The girl looked curious, but she still refused to come inside the tent.

The sounds of a crackling fire told Jefri that dinner would be on soon. In another ten days, he would have no appetite, but right now something to eat would be welcome.

Supper that night was freshly made nut bread from the shop, along with a roasted squash and onion soup. Tenlee ate the bread and some of the dried fruit, but she refused the soup, making a face. After they'd eaten, it was still early evening.

"How about 'Three Times Three'?" asked Jefri. "Our match isn't ended yet."

"True," said Denrau. Three Times Three was a simple game, but it served to pass the time. He pulled a small leather pouch out of his pocket and spilled out the three dice. The game combined luck and strategy, and it was usually played for money, but they used a number of small stones in place of coins. "Perhaps Tenlee might want to play, too, sometime," the Gen said thoughtfully.

Jefri looked surprised. "You think she can?"

"She's a bright kid." They divided the gaming stones between the two men, and rolled one die to see who would go first. The first play went to Denrau. He rolled 2, 2, and 5, and grimaced. He kept the five, and rerolled the other two dice. They came up 4 – 2. He held back the 4, and rerolled the last die hoping for something higher than 2. His turn ended with a total of 12. "Not too bad," he said. He put six stones into the center, his bet.

Tenlee looked at the three dice, and held up both hands with all fingers, and then two more fingers. "Exactly," said Jefri. "He got twelve. Now let's see what I get." He put in six stones as well, and rolled the three dice in his turn. The dice came up 6, 5, and 1. "Ha! I got 12 on one roll...I can't lose." He kept back the two high dice, and rolled the one. It came up a three. Before he could say anything, Tenlee clapped her hands with glee and pushed all the stones to Jefri's side. "That's right; I won that one, but the game's not over yet." He pushed all the stones back into the center. She still wasn't looking either of them in the eye, but she was certainly interacting with them.

While they had been setting up camp, she had wandered about, picking up pretty stones, a pine cone, and a few flowers. She had all of those in a little pile near her, like a private cache of beautiful things. Now, she peered closer at Denrau, without actually meeting his gaze. She looked at the angry red scratches on his cheek and the bump she had raised on his forehead, and slowly touched her own face in the same places. She looked away, seeming to be sad.

"Huh," murmured Jefri. "Does she realize she did that to you?"

Apparently she did. She searched through her little treasure trove, and chose a stone that sparkled with flecks of mica. Still looking down, she offered it, on her palm, to the grey-eyed Gen.

"Naztehr, I think that's an apology."

"I think you're right." Denrau took the pretty stone from her hand and gravely put it in his own pocket. "Thank you, Tenlee. But it's all right. I'm not angry. You were scared, and you didn't know what else to do." He offered her two fingers. "Friends?"

She reached out and touched her fingertips to his for just a moment, and withdrew her hand. "Well, that's progress," Jefri said.

"Jefri," Denrau said, "what did you do with the rest of the supplies? The things you picked up at the general store?"

"Here." He passed the paper bag to his Companion. "You didn't say what you wanted with them."

"Well, I had an idea." Denrau reached into the bag and pulled out the piece of soft leather. With his pocket knife he cut a wide strip from the leather piece. Then, he cut the leather lengthwise so that it hung in three strips and deftly braided the three strips together into a firm braid about the length of his forearm.

"What's that for?" What it looked like was a quirt for a horse.

"A toy." He put it down on the ground in front of Tenlee, without looking at her.

Jefri eyed the Gen skeptically. "Don't little girls like dolls? Or fuzzy toy kittens?"

"I'd almost forgotten about this, to my shame," the First Companion explained, "but years ago, there was a boy in Zeor who was a lot like her. He didn't speak, either, but he was very clever...let me see, his name was...Ayden. Anyway, he would get attached to one plaything, or one object, and carry it with him everywhere. If Ayden liked something, he would do the same thing over and over and over. Anyway, one time, Klyd's father gave Ayden a ring puzzle that the blacksmith had made. None of the other kids in that age group could figure out how to work it. Ayden did it in three minutes flat."

"That's something."

"Yes. And it became his favorite thing. He carried it around with him, and he would work it and unwork it and work it again, and again, and again, for hours on end. It made him happy." He shrugged. "So I wanted to see if Tenlee would like playing with cords or leather or something soft like that."

"Good call," said Jefri with a smile. "Look at her."

Tenlee was completely absorbed in the leather braid, turning it over and over in her hands, slowly undoing the braiding to see how it was done. Then, the strips hanging free, she wove them again until the whole strip was braided once more. She made a small sound of glee, and looked up at the two men, her thin face illuminated with the first smile they had seen from her.

Jefri and Denrau kept playing their dice game. Gradually they had inched farther and farther inside the tent, and little by little, Tenlee had moved with them until she also was inside the makeshift canvas shelter. *She's decided that being in here with us is better than being outside alone in the dark,* Jefri thought. Before bed, they made one last pan of tea over the embers of the fire, and shared the steaming trin among the three of them. Denrau took out two more candy lollies, stirred his cup with one to sweeten it, and gave Tenlee the other one.

She considered for a while whether to eat the candy or put it in her tea as Denrau did. Finally, she put it in her pocket. Before long she curled up like a small kitten in the blanket they gave her, and was fast asleep.

"So whatever happened to that boy, Ayden?" asked Jefri quietly.

"He Established," said Denrau, "and to my recall was a good donor. He worked in the kitchens as a prep cook. His job was chopping vegetables."

Jefri's eyes widened with surprise. "With a knife?"

"Yes. I watched him dicing yams once. He cut every slice the same thickness, and then cut each slice into strips, and then crosswise into tiny perfect cubes. The cooks said Ayden chopped better than the machine did, and better than most of the other kitchen workers. If you were looking for models of excellence, Ayden ambrov Zeor was a shining example." His tone was pensive. "That's what Grandfather said at his funeral."

"What you're saying is that we shouldn't rule out any possibilities for her."

"Exactly. I suspect there is a great deal more to her than meets the eye."

The next morning brought a new problem—what to do about Tenlee's hair. "I suppose we could just let it be," Jefri mused. "Let the women in the House take care of it when we get home."

"Hmmm. What worries me," his Companion said, measuring out the grain for the morning's porridge, "is that if her hair is neat, and relatively clean, it won't attract attention as we go through towns. But if her hair is a rat's nest like it is now, people will wonder why we're not looking after her properly, or worse, whose child we've abducted. They won't wait around for us to explain that she was like that when we found her."

The Sectuib made a face. "You're probably right. So, are you going to do it or am I?"

Denrau shrugged. "She trusts you more, I think."

"Any suggestions?"

The middle-aged Gen shook his head. "None, I'm afraid. Just guesses. You could try brushing yours first to show her it doesn't hurt and then brush hers. That's why I wanted those ribbons." Thanks to Jefri's work during the night, he looked much better this morning than he had the night before; the scratches had closed and the discolored patch above his eye was much diminished.

"Resorting to bribery, are we?" The channel smiled.

"That's all I can think of. It seems to work."

Not sure how she'd react, Jefri gently patted Tenlee on the shoulder to wake her up. Her eyes opened, and a look of fear crossed her expression for a few moments until she remembered where she was. Then she sniffed the air and smiled. Breakfast was cooking and she was hungry.

"Before we eat," the Sime went on, "we get ready for the day." Here goes nothing... "First, we wash up." He washed his own face by dipping a cloth in the bowl of warm water that he had heated on the fire, and calmly handed her another cloth and indicated that she should do the same.

She took the cloth from his hand and slowly copied his action of rubbing it on her face. Unexpectedly, she smiled. "That feels good, doesn't it?" he said, and took it from her when she stopped. "All nice and clean." So far, so good...now for the hard part. "Now we have to brush our hair," he went on. "If we don't we might scare him," he gestured to Denrau outside the tent, "and he might run away." He heard a deep chuckle from the First Companion, tending the fire. Jefri pantomimed himself as a wild-eyed monster. Tenlee giggled. He had deliberately left his own curly Farris-black hair unkempt and unruly, so he took a brush from his bag and stroked it once through his hair, and handed her the brush. "Your turn, Tenlee. Now you do it." She did the same, flinching as the bristles pulled at the tangles in her hair. She handed it back; then he brushed his own hair two strokes, and handed the brush to her again.

After several minutes of swapping the brush back and forth, her tawny brown hair was still not perfectly untangled, but it was better than the disheveled mess it had been. It was longer than Jefri had expected, hanging below her shoulders. "Very good," he praised her. "Young girls like you get to wear pretty ribbons in their hair. Which one do you want?" He held out the three colored pieces of ribbon he had gotten the day before; green, pink, and purple.

When they came out of the tent, Denrau was surprised and pleased. Jefri was accompanied by a young girl with a clean face and a purple ribbon tied neatly in her wavy golden-brown hair. "My word," he exclaimed, astonished. "Well done. And I didn't hear any, er…protests."

Jefri explained the turn-taking idea he'd had. "I thought that would work better than trying to comb it for her by force. I was just happy she let me put the ribbon in," he added.

"Anyway, breakfast is ready when you are." By the fire sat a pot of cooked porridge and another pot of stewed apples with raisins. Three mugs of steaming trin tea stood ready as well. Denrau unfolded his legs from his seated position and went to get Tenlee. Carefully, he touched her arm, trying not to startle her. Then he went back to the campfire and she followed him. The three of them ate, and Jefri began to relax. *She's not throwing fits, she's willing to ride on my horse—perhaps we'll only be a day late getting home.*

But as soon as the men started striking down the tent, Tenlee shrieked aloud and grabbed onto the rope so Jefri couldn't untie it from the tree. She wrapped both arms around the tree and wailed in anguish. "Oh, shen," the Sime muttered, exasperated. "Now what?"

Denrau turned around from packing. "What's the matter? Oh…" He breathed deeply as he used his nageric field to calm his channel, wishing it worked on kids as well as Simes. The little girl sank to the ground rocking herself sobbing, and still holding on to the tree. "I'm guessing she thought we were staying here. She didn't know we were leaving this place."

"What?!" Jefri exclaimed, incredulous. "But this isn't home! It's just a campsite! You don't stay in the place you're camping…everyone knows that."

The Gen shrugged. "Who can tell what Tenlee knows, or doesn't know?" He stacked the cooking gear back together, one pot inside the other. "Anyway, you pack, and I'll see what I can do. You're angry, and that will scare her." The Gen walked slowly over to the tree where Tenlee still clung, whimpering. "Hey, Tenlee. We're almost ready to leave. We're on our way home." *Something to remember—she hates surprises,* he thought. "Here, I'll draw you a picture."

Denrau smoothed a flat space on the ground with his palm, and used a slender stick to make an X in the dirt in front of them. "Here we are, right here." He drew stick figures of two horses and three people—two big and one small. "That's Jefri and me, and that's you, with the long hair. See?" She reached with her finger and added the triangle shape of the tent. "Yes; and our tent. Very good. But this place," he pointed to the ground where they were sitting, "is not home." Then he walked several yards away, and drew a circular shape of interwoven arcs on the ground. "Here is our home, this is Householding Kelin. We're going there." How could he get her to understand how long it would take?

Then he had an idea. One fourth of the distance there, he drew a tent shape, and another at half the distance, and another at three-fourths. With his hands, he mimed sunrise and sunset four times. "Three tents from now, then home." She had stopped crying and was looking at the line he made to represent their path. He walked his fingers along the path. "We ride and ride today. Tonight, we camp again." He mimed putting up the tent with the shape of his hands.

It worked. Tenlee nodded, and wiped her wet face with her hands until Denrau gave her his handkerchief. "See? We're all ready to leave now."

Jefri stood there, astounded as his Companion rejoined him with Tenlee calmly beside him.

The young Sime was at a loss for words. "How did you do that?"

"I finally understood what she was trying to tell us. Jefri, look at it from her point of view—she has no idea where we are or where we're going. This spot is familiar to her now, so leaving it terrified her." Her tantrum forgotten, the nine-year-old was stroking the long silky black mane of Jefri's gelding. "So, we have to think ahead and not surprise her. We know now surprising her is a very bad idea." He gestured toward the scratches on his face. "But I think she understands. I told her that when the sun stops, we stop. The sun comes back and we go."

"You should be a teacher," muttered the channel as they saddled up.

"I was, in Zeor," Denrau explained. "One of my various jobs—besides chasing Klyd across the landscape—was teaching basic Simelan to other Gens. So I got good at explaining things in very simple ways."

To the men's surprise, Tenlee chose that morning to ride with Denrau instead of Jefri. By mid-afternoon, she had turned around to face him instead of facing forward, and had gone to sleep in the saddle, with her head resting on his chest and his rust-colored cloak wrapped around her.

"Paxton is about 4 miles," said Jefri. "Should we go through, and take our chances, or pass around it?"

"Normally, I'd say go through," Denrau replied. "But in this situation I'm inclined to think that 'the longest way round is the shortest way home.' The fewer people we have to deal with, the fewer explanations we have to make."

A mile or so farther along, the road divided in a fork. Jefri led the way as they took the fork that led around the nearby town instead of into the town itself. They rode on, aiming not to attract undue attention. However, they could not completely avoid all human habitation even if they avoided going through towns. A couple of miles beyond Paxton, they passed by a homestead where several Simes were working in a large garden, hoeing out weeds and watering the vegetable crops.

They intended to pass on by, but a group of Sime men—some mounted, some on foot—approached the Householders and blocked their way. "Hold it right there, perverts. What's your business?" demanded the oldest one in the group, who appeared to be in a position of authority. "And what are you and your pet Gen doing with that child?"

Jefri put his hand on Denrau's arm in an age-old gesture of Sime ownership. *Mine.* At the same time, he used his field to mask from them any pain his Companion felt. "We are from Householding Kelin. I am Jefri, Sectuib in Kelin. This Gen is my Companion. We are returning from exhibiting at a trade show." He paused, allowing them to zlin him without objection. "She was abandoned and we rescued her."

"What do you mean, 'abandoned'?"

"What I said. There is a town back that way, a day's ride or so, and not a living soul was there except for this little girl. We wouldn't leave her there to starve, so we are bringing her home with us."

Denrau said nothing, except to gently wake Tenlee who rode nestled against him in his cloak.

Another man, armed with the usual stock whip, advanced on the Householders. "It's unnatural, what you people do there, and you're going to use this innocent young 'un for your own filthy purposes. She should stay with her own kind. You shouldn't have taken her."

"If there had been a family to look after her, we would not have. It was a matter of saving her life."

The men had been joined by others, women as well as men, so that the two men from Kelin were now surrounded by a small crowd of people. "What do you mean, 'look after her'?" growled one old woman. "She's no toddler."

"Frankly, she might as well be," explained Jefri bluntly. "She's a nice enough child, but her mind is impaired in some way." *I hope Tenlee doesn't understand what I'm saying...* "True, she can feed herself and she knows not to soil herself. But she can't speak, and she fears almost everything." He shrugged. "That's just plain speaking. In our Householding, she will be well cared for, no matter whether she becomes a Sime or a Gen in due course. But it is almost certain she will never be a functioning adult in any sense."

"Then what is it to you?" demanded another. "Why does your kind care about some idiot child? She's a waste of supplies, probably why they left her."

The two Householders exchanged glances. What Jefri was about to say was probably going to get them in trouble, but it couldn't be helped. "Because we believe that all human lives are valuable and precious," he answered. "Simes, Gens, children, all. And she's certainly not an idiot, at any rate."

"Seems like a nice little girl," said a woman in a faded blue dress with an apron. She was not yet middle-aged, but no longer young. "We would take her, wouldn't we, Nalon?"

"Might be," her husband said slowly, stepping out of the crowd and approaching Denrau's horse. He reached as if to lift Tenlee down from the horse, but Denrau shook his head and backed his dappled grey mare a little.

"I wouldn't do that if I were you," said Jefri. "Not until she knows you a little more. She attacked him yesterday when he tried to pick her up. As I said, she's easily frightened."

He considered. Maybe this would be all right; one of these families would probably be very much like Tenlee's own family had been. He heard someone in the group mutter, "She did that?"

Nalon turned to his wife and they spoke briefly in murmurs before he addressed Jefri again. "You—all of you—why don't you come with us and stay for a meal? Civilized folks don't handle family matters in the middle of the road." He made a welcoming gesture that included both the Householders and Tenlee as well. She started to cry, a soft whining sound.

"Sh-sh-sh-sh," Denrau said, comfortingly, as he lifted her down into Jefri's arms. "It's all right, little one. No one's going to hurt you. Are you sure about this, Sectuib?" he asked Jefri softly as he dismounted and they walked behind the farmer and his wife.

"Maybe it would be the best, a life that's more familiar to her..." the young channel said, uneasily.

"Can you imagine what it will be like when she changes over? If she changes over? She won't understand what's happening, and she'll be terrified. We know how to handle her now, but do they? I doubt it very much." His grey eyes were clouded with concern.

"I know, Naztehr, I know." Jefri was downcast—he knew his Companion was right, but he wasn't sure how to keep these people from insisting on adopting the orphan girl, without just taking her by force and making a run for it. That would be impossible; they were vastly outnumbered. He sighed. Diplomacy and negotiation were his older cousin's forté, not his. "They'll just have to learn."

When they reached the farmhouse, roughly half a mile's walk, Nalon opened the gate and let them all in. The footpath led to the front door, and another path led around to the back of the house. "We don't mean to be impolite," he said, "but we'd appreciate it if…that one…" he flicked a tentacle in the Companion's direction, "doesn't come in the house. There's a nice bit of shade around back, and the pump has plenty of good sweet water. Drena—my wife, here—will show you where. You can water the horses, too."

"Nalon, it's a warm day, it's going to be stifling inside. Why don't we all take our lunch out back?" Drena offered.

"I suppose that would be all right, but what about…" The Sime man looked uneasy. He couldn't bring himself to call Denrau 'him,' but he didn't want to insult Jefri by calling his Companion 'it.'

"Don't worry," said Jefri. "We understand these things." Still holding Tenlee by the hand, he followed Drena, walking around the farmhouse to the back. These people might not be wealthy, exactly, but maybe they could take care of the lost child after all. Would she stay there, though? Jefri had a sudden vision of Tenlee wandering off.

The man, who had introduced himself as Nalon Sewell, showed Jefri and Tenlee to a picnic table under some trees and pointed in the direction of the pump. "Water's over there," he said, and went inside with his wife, leaving the three travelers alone in the farmyard.

"What do you think, Jefri?" asked Denrau, perching unperturbed on a nearby hay bale. Nalon's gesture had made it clear he wasn't welcome to sit at the table. "Should we leave her with these people? I don't want to."

"Nor do I. But I've been thinking. We've all been talking as though Tenlee has no say in the matter. I think she should. Let her decide."

"Is she able to make that decision?"

"Guess we'll find out."

Presently, a Sime girl emerged from the farmhouse, bearing a tray with six glasses on it, as well as a pitcher of water with mint leaves in it. She set the tray down on the picnic table along with the pitcher. "Hello, Tuib," she addressed Jefri. "I'm Jana. Mother said you're passing through and you found a lost little girl on the way."

"Yes, we found her yesterday afternoon." Tenlee had looked up for a moment when the older girl came out of the door, but paid her no further attention; she was completely involved in braiding and unbraiding her leather toy.

"Where are you from?" Jana sat down at the table with Jefri and Tenlee, not disturbed by the little girl's ignoring her altogether.

"We come from a Householding called Kelin. It's about three days' ride from here, to the northwest. At a walk, that is."

"I think I've seen it," said Nalon as he and his wife, Drena, came out of the house to join them. Drena carried a large bowl of some sort of fruit salad. "Isn't that the place with the big field of them orange flowers? What are those for, anyway?"

"This," said Jefri, fingering his rust-colored cloak. "We have other dye plants for other colors, but our own House color comes from those orange cosmos. Different techniques determine whether the final color is yellow, orange, tan, brown, brick red, or this."

"What do you folks do, anyway? Besides…er…"

Besides being perverts? Jefri thought to himself. "We're an artisan textile firm, basically. We don't make large scale or industrial work, but small-scale limited productions. We're known for handmade lace, among other things. For wool, we also raise sheep and 'pacas, and the sheepdogs which help us tend them."

"My goodness. I had no idea…" Drena served out portions of the salad, composed of chopped apples, celery, carrots, walnuts and raisins with a tangy-sweet dressing to bind it.

Tenlee was still involved with her leather toy, and seemed to be oblivious to the plate set in front of her. "Isn't she hungry?" asked Jana.

"She might not eat in front of so many people," Jefri said. "It took us a while yesterday to get her to eat with us." He took a bite of the salad. "This is delicious. Thank you!" He watched Tenlee out of the corner of his eye. "Don't watch her so closely," he said to the others. "It upsets her."

Jana, who must have been about fifteen years old, suddenly got up and filled one of the empty glasses with mint water and carried it to Denrau on the hay bale, who smiled by way of thanks. Her father glared at her disapprovingly. "Daughter…" he said in a warning tone.

"They're guests, Daddy, even this Gen," she answered back, meeting his eyes with a hint of teenage rebellion. "Aren't they? You always say to treat guests better than anyone in the house."

"That's enough backtalk from you, girl," he growled. He stopped when he realized Tenlee was shrinking away from him. "What's the matter with her, anyway?"

Jefri's reply was frank. "We don't know. One thing for sure—she can't read fields, but she picks up emotions very well, almost as if she could. And angry voices make her anxious. It's all right, Tenlee," he said. "It's not about you. Go on and eat."

"Tenlee," said Drena aloud. "It's a pretty name; did you name her that?" To Jana, she said, "The casserole should be done now. Go on in the house and get it."

"No, her name's on her necklace," explained Kelin's Sectuib. "I'm assuming her family did that because she can't speak to introduce herself."

Jana got up and went into the farmhouse. Denrau met Jefri's eyes and twitched an eyebrow. Normally there were nageric ways to get a channel's attention, but he wasn't about to do any of those things in a junct Sime's house. Jefri got up and walked over to his Companion. Denrau mutely held his glass up for Jefri to see. Floating on top of the water and mint leaves was a tiny bit of paper, which said in pencil, 'Take me with you.' "Oh, no! Get rid of that, quick." he murmured.

The First Companion nodded, took a drink of the cool mint water, and swallowed it, paper and all. After a slight cough, he asked softly, "What do we do about it?"

Jefri whispered, "I have no idea." Jana came back out again carrying a rectangular baking dish. The casserole consisted of rice combined with two kinds of squash, along with mushrooms, spinach, peas and pine nuts. It smelled delicious, and all the adults served themselves a helping.

Nalon fixed Jefri with a firm gaze. "So is she feeble-minded, or not?"

"No," Kelin's Sectuib replied firmly. "I don't think so, not in the least. She's done some things that show she is very clever, but on the other hand some of her behavior is very strange unless you understand why she is doing it. It's true, though, that Tenlee may need to be looked after all her life." He took a deep breath, knowing that he was about to be skating on very thin ice. "If I may ask a question of you…"

"Ask it."

Jefri met the older Sime's gaze. "Why do you want to take her in yourselves? If you were expecting that she will be able to help you with the farm work, for example, you should be aware that she may not have the ability to do that." He added, "Dealing with her takes a great deal of patience."

Nalon nodded. "I see that. Our children are nearly grown, except for our youngest, and we are not yet old. We could give her a home—a simple one, true—but a home for all that."

The young Sectuib decided to be more direct. "And what will you do if she turns out to be a Gen a few years from now? Turn her out? Take her to the border? Leave her at a Pen?" The farmer did not answer. "With us, in Kelin, no matter what happens when she comes of age, she will have a home and be cared for as long as she lives, Sime or Gen. Can you say the same?"

"My wife and I have discussed it. If the girl here is willing to stay, we are willing to have her. If she turns Gen, we'll have to cross that bridge when we get there. No point worrying about what hasn't happened yet."

Time to ask her what she wants. Jefri tapped Tenlee on the wrist. "Tenlee, do you like this place? Do you want to stay here?" As usual, she looked in his direction without actually looking at his face or in his eyes. "This family wants you to live with them, Tenlee." He used a tentacle to indicate Nalon, and said, "Father," and motioned to Drena, who had come to sit down next to Tenlee, and said "Mother."

I don't like this at all, thought Denrau, carefully keeping his field neutral. *Even with all the trouble she's been, I like her. I like her toughness, how she figures out the world in her own way. I want to see her grow up, even though she's not my child. But there's no good way to say that to these people.*

The family's youngest daughter, Rael, had come outside to see the 'lost little girl.' Rael had given Tenlee her doll to play with, and Tenlee let Rael handle her braided leather strips.

"Probably you should leave now," said Drena softly, "while she's not watching you."

Jefri didn't agree. "No. We'll tell her goodbye, briefly. She hates surprises."

"What do you mean?"

"She gets very agitated about things that she doesn't expect to happen." To Tenlee he said, "Tenlee, this family would like you to stay with them. Denrau and I are going away now." He gestured to his Companion and himself, and their horses, and made the typical Sime gesture for 'goodbye' with his tentacles. Tenlee nodded as though she understood, the ends of her purple ribbon brushing her shoulders along with her gold-brown hair.

The two Householders rose from the table, and thanked Nalon and Drena for their kindness and hospitality. With heavy hearts, Jefri and Denrau walked to the tree where the horses were tied. Jana called out, "Wait a moment, let me bring you some water for the road." As they were leading their horses, the burnished gold and the grey, toward the farm gate, Jana caught up to them, bringing them the water. "You saw my note? Can't I go with you?"

"Not now, not yet," said Jefri softly. "Your parents would feel we had violated their hospitality, with good reason. You heard me describe where Kelin is. If you wish, you may come." Aloud, he called out, "Farewell, and thank you!" as he swung himself into his saddle, handing Jana the package with the clothes they had gotten for Tenlee the day before.

Denrau opened the gate for Jefri, then closed it and mounted his horse as they moved off down the road. "Did we do the right thing?" Sadness now colored his showfield.

"I don't know, Naztehr. I hope so. But surrounded by a crowd of juncts, accusing us of kidnapping her against her will, I'm not sure what else we could have done. I didn't want to make a decision that would make the locals even more hostile to us than they already are." The channel sighed. *Strange,* he thought. *We only had Tenlee with us for a day or so, but she had already become a part of us, so that we miss her when she's gone.*

"We must go back and check on her soon." Denrau's tone was firm. "She could be unhappy there. Or they might be unkind to her."

"Yes." There was nothing further to say about it, and both men fell silent as they headed for their next spot to camp.

A chilly wind was picking up by the time twilight fell. Despite Kelin's good showing at Arensti, neither of the Householders could shake off the melancholy that settled over them like a heavy cloak. The weather seemed to match their mood as well.

When sunrise came, it was shrouded in grey cloud, so it lent little warmth to the morning. Jefri went to get water from the nearby creek, while Denrau coped with the fire. "Be on guard," the channel said. "I can zlin people on the road, though none of them seem to be threatening. I'll be right back." With a shiver, the middle-aged Gen fastened his lined wool jacket and knelt to his task. For breakfast and tea, they needed only a small fire, not an all-evening fire. Soon, he was using his breath to encourage the tiny flame to grow and catch among the twigs and sticks.

A sound caused him to drop his striker into the leaf litter on the ground. There were hoofbeats coming up the road from some distance, and the rider was coming fast. *Now what?* The Companion came to his feet in a few seconds, prepared for trouble. "Hurry up, Jefri!" he called out.

However, his heart leaped for joy when he heard Jefri's answering shout. "It's Drena Sewell coming! She has Tenlee!" The channel dashed into the clearing a moment later.

Denrau's face lit up, and his fields glowed like a prairie sunrise. "What? I can't believe it! But…what could have happened?"

"We'll find out soon enough." Jefri set down the water container and went out to the road where Drena and Tenlee could see him. The reason for Drena's arrival could not have been more apparent. Her young passenger flung herself off the saddle and ran to the rust-cloaked Sime standing in the roadway, throwing her arms around him.

"Good morning, Mrs. Sewell," said Jefri formally, greeting her as she dismounted. "This is quite a surprise."

"For you and me both, Sectuib Farris."

Tenlee looked around, clearly wondering where Denrau was. She started to wail, but Jefri stopped her. "Don't worry, he's right over there." To Drena Sewell, he said, "Yesterday, you kindly welcomed us into your home. Please, allow me to invite you into our home... well, home away from home."

As they came through the copse of trees and approached the campsite, Tenlee pulled away from Jefri and ran into the First Companion's arms, sobbing. These were no cries of anxiety, fear, or frustration; she was weeping real tears into the fabric of his jacket.

"There, there, it's all right. That's my brave girl," Denrau said, patting her back. He had discovered she liked that.

Drena's field registered shock as she heard Denrau's voice—a real Gen speaking Simelan. "You—you can talk..."

"Of course I can," he replied calmly with an engaging smile. "In some circumstances, like yesterday, it's safer for everyone if I don't. But this is my home."

Nonplussed, she looked around what was obviously just a campsite.

"A Companion's home," he explained, with a twinkle in his calm grey eyes, "is wherever his channel is. Even if that's a leaky tent in the woods."

Jefri pulled out a camp chair and unfolded it for her. "Please, have a seat." He turned to Denrau. "Is she all right, Naztehr?"

"Seems to be. Looks like she felt the same way we did, Jefri." He dislodged Tenlee from clinging to his chest, and took her over to where the water was. Together they carried the pan to the crackling fire. Now that the fire was going, he placed an iron grate on top. "Put the pan there." She did. "Let's play a game, Tenlee," he said. "Can you find my tea box? It's this color," he told her, pointing to the blue shirt she was wearing today. "Go find it..."

She dived into the tent and started rummaging, while Denrau began preparing their breakfast. Jefri turned back to Drena Sewell. "Tea will be ready soon. So ... what happened?"

"Well, it's like this." She smiled at him, ruefully. "Turns out, Nalon didn't really believe you about her. He thought you were exaggerating about how... damaged she is," the Sime woman explained. "He said you were saying those things about her being not right in the head as an excuse to keep her and take her off to...that place of yours."

"Then what?" He noticed the little girl emerging triumphantly from the tent, with Denrau's battered old Zeor-blue tea caddy, and smiled.

"Funny, she didn't act any different when you left, until a while later, after supper or so. Guess she just figured we were babysitting her and you'd come back from someplace. Then she realized you were gone, I guess. She threw a panic fit, and was trying to climb over the gate and come after you." She shook her head. "And you were right about her being strange. Rael, our little one, was trying to play with her, and she just kept fooling with that leather thing. Later, Rael was playing some little tune on this musical toy she has, and Tenlee covered her ears and screamed, and ran outside. Later, she grabbed the toy away from Rael and broke it. On purpose."

"I think there are some sounds she can't stand," Denrau said. "I was whistling yesterday when saddling the horses, and she did the same thing—screamed and held her ears."

The Sime woman didn't reply; just sipped at her tea. Clearly she wasn't coping too well with being conversationally addressed by a Gen.

"You said she was clever, and she is that," she went on, talking to Jefri. "This morning we woke up and we couldn't find her. Not anywhere in the house. Then Jana saw that this little squirt had managed to get out of her window. She ain't afraid of heights, I'll tell you that. We searched the place till Nalon saw the stable door was open. That little wretch was in there, might and main, trying to put a saddle up on Brownie here! She couldn't do it, she's too small. But, how does she know how to saddle a horse?"

"Watching us, I suppose."

"By then it was almost sunup, and Nalon told me, 'well, this won't do, with her trying to run away twice and she hasn't even been here a whole day. You can't help me run the farm if you've always got to be watching her every minute. She'll drive us all mad.' Anyway, Jana managed to get her hair brushed out, but we couldn't give her a bath without a fight. It was like trying to wash a barn cat! So Nalon finally told me, 'take her quick and catch up to that Tuib Farris. He can have the girl and welcome.'"

"Did you have any trouble then?"

"Not a bit. You see, she kept trying to draw this thing on the ground or in the dust," said Drena, pointing to the Kelin emblem on the back of his cloak. "We didn't know what she was doing until Jana realized it was your House symbol she saw on your cloak. So I pointed to that one she drew, and pointed down the road, and said, "We're going to find your friends, that a way. And she lifted her arms up to be put on the horse, pretty as you please. So here we are."

Jefri shook his head, with a sigh. "That's quite a story."

"What will happen to her, now? What will you do with her?"

"Whatever makes her happy. If that means she spends all day roaming in the cosmos fields, or brushing the sheepdogs, so be it. She will be safe, and well looked after, and happy." He paused, and added, "Drena, thank you and your family for trying. We know she once had a family, and I thought maybe she could have a family again."

"To be frank, Sectuib, she already has one. With you." She gulped, and took a deep breath before continuing. "And you," she added, addressing Denrau directly for the first time. "And your people."

EPILOGUE

Sectuib Kelin, to Sectuib Zeor, greetings—

Dear Klyd—

The most astonishing thing has been happening here. You remember that three years ago, I and Denrau came upon the abandoned little girl, Tenlee, and we took her into Kelin. You were very helpful in finding some Ancients' writing about her condition, describing such children as 'locked inside themselves.'

Jefri smiled as he paused to dip his pen in the bottle of rust-colored ink. How could he possibly describe this?

He continued to write. "Since that time, she has settled in here remarkably well under the circumstances. She took to spinning, both with spindles and a wheel, as though she were born to the task. Not only is she extraordinarily skilled at spinning, she clearly derives great pleasure in it. Denrau's theory is that it is the repetitive nature of treadling the wheel or turning the spindle that appeals to her so much—it's the same motion, over and over. Watching her twirling a cotton spindle in its wooden bowl, seemingly conjuring thread out of the air between her hands, is incredible. She's a good knitter as well. However, she cannot weave on the loom; something about it is abhorrent to her, and the constant noise of all the looms in the weaving room will drive her out of there in seconds. Her other great talent is with the animals. She loves to help care for the sheepdogs, and she also is very good with the rabbits and sheep. Sadly, we had resigned ourselves to accepting that she never would be able to speak more than a few words and names.

However, since her changeover two months ago, Tenlee is not the same girl! Changes have happened that we would have never even hoped for. Her anxious behavior of rocking herself or repeatedly pounding on things has nearly ceased, and she looks at people's faces now, where she never would before. The accelerated development of First Year seems to be making dramatic improvements for her. She is even talking a little! As far as we can tell, because she isn't able to explain, it seems that her physical senses are distorted somehow—for example, she cannot bear many ordinary sounds that are barely noticeable to others. But as a Sime, hyperconsciousness gives her a new set of senses that are reliable to her and that her brain is able to process. Her whole demeanor is different now. It is, frankly, a miracle, and something wonderful to see. It will be exciting to discover what else her First Year will bring.

A strange thought comes to me. Being a Sime has not 'cured' Tenlee exactly, but her improvement is so significant, that it makes me wonder. It is said that the mutation into Sime and Gen was caused by experiments that went awry in the Ancient days. Do you suppose that some of those experiments could have been an attempt to improve life for such children as Tenlee, by giving them hyperconsciousness and so bypassing their sensory system which had malfunctioned? Of course, we will never know, but it's an intriguing idea.

Hoping all is well with you and with Zeor.

Jefri Farris, Sectuib ambrov Kelin.

THE BOX

LAURIE POLLACK

The yellow ribbons for her hair
She preferred to dress in overalls like a boy
She loved it when he taught her how to hunt.
He said she was a good shot just like him.
But still she loved to braid these ribbons in her hair.

Her green and purple dress, so long outgrown.
He bought it for her birthday when she was ten
Though times were hard. She used to love
to wear the dress to church.
I put the ribbons and the dress inside the box.

Her rag doll, Molly, sitting on the shelf
I sewed it when she was five, and it's been years
Since she's played with it.
When she sang to the doll he used to laugh.
The doll, and also her prayer book go into the box.

"Donate them to the church!" he said last night,
And handed me the box. His eyes and voice were dry.
"The drought is hard, and others are in need."
"We have no children. Others can use these clothes and toys."
He held the rifle in his other hand.

And then we knelt and prayed.

And now I look into the box,

And think about the man I used to love.

Mary Lou Mendum has contributed this new story in her Eskalie and Talin series, which is available for free reading on simegen.com. "The Problem of the Pilfered Pen" is one in this series. It may also be seen here:

http://simegen.com/sgfandom/rimonslibrary/PILFERED.html

PRELUDE AND FUGUE IN FOUR CHOICES

FROM THE ILL-TEMPERED CAVALIER

MARY LOU MENDUM

PRELUDE

Eskalie Morlin hadn't intended to see her father at all that fall afternoon, much less to have him meddle so spectacularly with her life.

She had been whistling as she guided her little black mare down the main road out of Sommerin, heading for Tormin, and home. As far as she was concerned, life didn't get any better than this. The sky was blue, the air was crisp, the trees were brilliant with fall colors, and the empty road stretched before them. The message she had been hired to deliver in Sommerin had been eagerly awaited by its intended recipient, and the reply she carried was not likely to be of interest to anybody else. Thus, there was no reason to anticipate that any third party would interfere with its rapid delivery and the bonus that would likely accrue on that happy occasion.

It was a far cry from her first few months as the junior member of Kirlin Security and Investigations, when she and the senior partners, Amsil and Sesfin Kirlin, had struggled each month to pay their Pen taxes. Several highly profitable cases had increased both the firm's reputation for quick, confidential and honest service and its bank balance.

At the top of the next rise, she paused to inspect the road before her. The last, least outpost of Sommerin was just ahead: an old barn that had been converted into a disreputable shiltpron parlor by a trio of ex-thieves, now mercifully closed for business in the early morning. Its day-laborer clients were hard at work in the fields surrounding the town, harvesting grain to feed the Gens and horses through the coming winter. Behind her was the haze of smoke and reflected selyn that drifted over every human settlement.

A long arrowhead of geese flew south overhead, honking loudly, so high she couldn't zlin them. She remembered her father telling her that the Ancients built machines that could fly as high as a goose. Small child that she had been, she'd wanted to believe him and had spent many hours imagining what it would be like to soar through the clouds in pursuit of the formations.

Now, as an adult, she shook her head at such childish fancies. Why would even the Ancients build a machine to chase after geese in the sky, when it was so much easier to wait for the blasted creatures to land in the nearest marsh, if one happened to have a use for a large, noisy, ill-tempered bird in the first place?

Star's ears pricked forward and she danced, impatient at her rider's woolgathering. With a chuckle, Eskalie let the mare move into an easy canter.

Preoccupied with the riddle of the Ancients, she almost missed the approach of a more recent progenitor. In her defense, she had not actually zlinned her father more than two or three times. She had left home almost directly after her changeover, fleeing a boring, conventional existence as a junior banker under her parents' exacting tutelage. All things considered, and despite the occasional hazards implicit in the profession, the life of a private detective, security guard, and courier suited her much better. Her father might think it was a grand adventure to zlin the Territory's biggest notables cringing before him in his office, begging for loans, but Eskalie had experienced the real thing. She knew her father's life for the dull, humdrum existence that it was.

Eskalie's mental image of her father, then, was that of a child: she remembered him as a tower of strength, sometimes stern and sometimes forgiving, but usually willing to lend a tentacle to her childish enterprises when asked. Her childhood memories did not contain any nageric component, and the few times they had met since her precipitous departure from her childhood home had been insufficient to replace the childish shadow-father with a more realistic, nager-based, adult impression.

When she zlinned the frail old man riding slowly past the barn-turned-shiltpron parlor toward the outskirts of Sommerin, his well-bred horse wandering a bit from side to side as if lacking in direction from its rider, her first thought was simply to offer assistance. She pulled Star to a halt and asked, "Are you in health, Tu...." He looked up, and while his face might be thinner and his hair greyer than it had been in her child-hood, it was still undeniably that of her, "Father!"

In her defense, her father had aged dramatically in the two months since she had last zlinned him. Then, he had been a formidable man, not young but still strong and hearty. Now, what had been a small flutter in his nager had become an unhealthy quaver that made him zlin weak and old.

Rossil Morlin zlinned her stiffly, his nager no longer flexible enough to blend smoothly with hers. "Eskalie! What are you doing here?"

"Courier run," she answered succinctly. "High profit, low risk."

"Good for you."

He did not, Eskalie noticed, fill the conversational void as good manners required, by volunteering the reason for his own presence in Sommerin.

"Your mother is well," he said instead, "though she worries about you."

Eskalie nodded. "Tell her I'm doing fine."

Another awkward pause stretched until she could no longer bear to leave the question unasked. Instead, she blurted it out like an awkward, unmannered child. "Father, you don't zlin at all well. Have you seen a physician lately?"

Displeasure at her rudeness made her father frown. There was also a hint of…guilt?…in his nager that she couldn't figure out. It was almost as if he'd been caught getting falling-down drunk in a fancy Kill parlor, not riding down the public eyeway in pursuit of his perfectly respectable, boring business interests

"I'm old, girl," he snapped at her, in lieu of answering her question. "Almost eighteen years past changeover, when most Simes are lucky to live ten. There's no cure for that."

"But surely, something can be done?"

"I've just been having some rough turnovers," he said. As if in dem-onstration, the fluttering in his nager grew suddenly worse, wasting selyn in bright sparks. He doubled over the pommel of his saddle with a hiss of pain.

"Father!" Alarmed, Eskalie jumped off Star and ran to him, helping him slide off his horse before he fell. She walked him toward the closest refuge, which happened to be a splinter-filled plank resting on two bat-tered crates under the big oak tree that grew beside the barn. He stumbled on a clod of dried grass—at least, she hoped it was dried grass; the other possibilities were much less wholesome—and she blinked sudden tears from her eyes.

Fathers weren't supposed to be old and frail. They were supposed to be immortal and indestructible. Surely this was just some passing illness, easily cured by any competent physician?

She settled her father on the plank and ran for the barn. It might be closed for business, and she could zlin no Sime nagers through the thick boards, but she could see smoke coming out the hole in the "kitchen" roof and hear the sound of dueling flute and shiltpron. That suggested the presence of at least three people to her detective's mind, two more than was necessary to fetch a physician.

She tried the door, discovered that it was barred from inside, and gave it a few sharp kicks. "Hallo, there!" she yelled. "Open up!"

The music stopped. A moment later she heard a voice grumbling, "Can't you see we're closed?" and a thud as the heavy bar dropped. The door opened a crack and the careworn face of Zilmor, the shiltpron player, peered through. "What's the shedoni-doomed emergen... Eskalie? What are you doing here?"

"My father is very ill," the detective explained, pointing behind her and letting the condition of his nager speak for itself. "You must fetch him a physician, and quickly."

"I'll be right back," the ex-thief said, ducking back inside.

Eskalie returned to her father, whose field was still fluctuating, sending a plume of wasted selyn into the ambient. At that rate, he'd waste two weeks of selyn in a day or so. She tried to mesh her nager with his, in hopes of dragging it into something approaching a normal rhythm, but she couldn't get a proper hold on it. Instead of calming the vibrations, her own field was being overwhelmed, making her too dizzy to zlin straight.

"Not like that," a calm, familiar male voice said behind her. A nageric fog swept through her field, steadying the chaotic ambient. At the same time, cool Gen hands grasped her shoulders, moving her firmly aside.

Eskalie turned, unsure whether to cheer or to flee: her usual reaction when encountering Tallin, the Giant Killer Gen. While it did explain the flute music she heard, this particular Gen had no business visiting a disreputable shiltpron parlor after hours. Yet there it was, standing beside her and looking down at her ailing father with every appearance of concern.

"You'll only make things worse if you let your field be unbalanced like that," the Gen lectured her, as if it had the right. "You've got to provide a steady field no matter how his fluctuates, like this."

Before Eskalie could intervene, it reached for her father's hands. Its fingers slid up to close lightly on his wrists, perilously close to the openings to the sheaths that protected his vulnerable laterals. The slender tentacles emerged under the coaxing, licking blindly at Tallin's arms.

"Don't fight me," the Gen warned the ailing Sime. At the same time, the fog evaporated, exposing the blazing furnace of selyn production that Tallin usually kept hidden. It swept through her father's weakened, chaotic field, imposing order with the same ruthless efficiency with which the Morlin family butler directed the staff in cleaning up after a large party.

When it was done, Rossil Morlin sat for a moment, adjusting to having his selyn system so unceremoniously rearranged. Then he opened eyes that had regained their customary sharpness and inspected the Gen closely. It looked calmly back at him, the furnace of its inner nager once more shielded by a haze of fog.

"I see you were not completely forthcoming on the provenance of your 'pet Gen' last summer, daughter of mine," the elder Morlin said dryly.

It was only then that Eskalie looked at the Gen with her eyes. Tallin was wearing the turquoise and grey livery of Householding Dar, not the nondescript costume the creature and worn when her father had last seen it. At the time, she had been so desperate to make her Pen fees that she'd taken a job for the perverts at Dar, only to discover that the deal included having Tallin join her investigation, posing as her pet Gen. When she had encountered her parents, she'd been equally desperate to prevent them from learning of her circumstances. She still wasn't sure why the Gen had gone along with the charade as far as it had, but any hope of maintaining the illusion of prosperity was now gone.

"No, Father, I wasn't forthcoming," she admitted. "It was a matter of client confidentiality." The Morlin bank had a Territory-wide reputation for discretion. Eskalie fervently hoped her father would accept her reluctance to explain before she was forced to admit that the Gen, itself, had hired her over the objections of all concerned, including Eskalie herself.

Rossil Morlin, however, kept his attention on Tallin. A close inspection by the banker had been known to make seasoned politicians and business leaders blanch in terror. It had no impact whatsoever on Tallin's composure.

"Tallin ambrov Dar," Eskalie's father ventured, and the Gen nodded politely. "It never occurred to me that you might still be alive, after so many years. Last summer, I thought that my daughter had managed to get her tentacles on a son of yours."

Eskalie looked accusingly from Gen to parent and back again. "You two know each other?"

Tallin graciously deferred to Rossil, who looked at his daughter and sighed, too tired to deny the obvious. "When I was in First Year and your Uncle Rabin was still a child," he began, "your grandparents left me in charge of him while they made a trading run to Gulf Territory. Being young and eager to sample all life had to offer, I went haring off to visit friends who lived outside of Sommerin, dragging my little brother along. Rabin promptly contracted a particularly bad case of whooping cough. Sommerin was much smaller, back then, and there wasn't a physician worthy of the name in the whole town. So, I took your uncle to House-holding Dar, and we ended up staying there for almost a month before his cough finally eased."

Eskalie's eyes widened at this admission. "You? Stayed at..." She looked at Tallin for confirmation, hoping that her father's wits had suddenly started to wander, but the Gen nodded.

Such things happened, of course. But mostly among the desperate poor, who couldn't afford a real physician and had no social standing to lose by associating with perverts. For Rossil Morlin, the son of prominent traders, founder of the most influential bank in Nivet Territory, to admit doing so was a scandal of monstrous proportions.

Another thought occurred to her. "If Uncle Rabin was still a child, that must have been almost twenty years ago."

"Seventeen, actually," Tallin agreed. "My wife, Nilba, had been Sectuib for five years with me as her First Companion, and our son, Califf, was four."

"But that's impossible!" Eskalie objected, calculating the numbers. "Califf zlins my age, and if you had a four-year-old son, seventeen years ago, then you must have Established at least..."

"Twenty-three years ago," the Gen agreed.

Tallin's nager showed no hint of any intent to deceive, not that it couldn't zlin as sincere as it cared to. However, her father's story corroborated at least part of that outrageous claim. She inspected the Gen more closely. It had some streaks of grey in its hair, but far less than her father, whose hair had turned mostly white in the past year. Its face had lines, but not the wrinkles her mother was beginning to show. It zlinned, looked, and moved like a person about ten years past changeover, or Establishment, rather. She'd assumed it was a little older only because it had an adult son. Who, himself, was quite a bit older than he appeared, it seemed.

"Do the Householdings have some mysterious, secret Elixir of Life that they've somehow neglected to share with the rest of us?" she asked Tallin.

"We've been trying to share it with the rest of you for hundreds of years," the Gen said, with a weariness that had nothing to do with either age or physical exhaustion. "It's the Kill, Eskalie. The shock of it wears out a Sime's body so that you die of old age long before you should.

Householding Simes who have never Killed can live thirty or forty years past changeover before they start suffering from the complications of old age."

Eskalie knew that the Householders were very different from normal Simes, but she'd never thought they were hiding something that momentous. Although now that she thought about it, it explained a lot about how the perverts managed to prosper despite widespread revulsion at their lifestyle. If they could realistically expect to live three or four times the normal lifespan, they could afford long-range planning in a way that only the most prosperous, multi-generational families could approach. Only more so, because the people who did the original planning could expect to live to see its results, and even try again if the first attempt was unsuccessful.

Tallin had turned its attention back to Eskalie's father. "I've stabilized you for now, Rossil, but the underlying problem remains," it said, using the lecturing tone of a physician advising a patient. "I'd estimate that you have two, perhaps three more Kills before you can no longer recover from the shock."

It was unreal, Eskalie thought, to hear a Gen issuing a Sime's death warrant so calmly.

Rossil did not zlin surprised. "I thought it was something like that," he admitted. "Gretta wanted to be sure that it wasn't a treatable illness, though, so I promised her I'd get an expert opinion."

Eskalie knew very well that there were no less than three learned physicians living within ten miles of the Morlin mansion. Her detective's instincts came to an absurd conclusion. "You were going to ask the channels at Dar for help?" she blurted.

Her father turned his head to look at her. "Yes, of course, Eskalie. When you want an expert opinion, you seek out the best expert available. Whatever their... personal proclivities." He looked back at Tallin. "Although it appears that my journey was unnecessary, after all, because there's nothing to be done."

"Not nothing, exactly," the Killer Gen corrected him. "You could gain a year or more by alternating your Kills with a month or two of channel's transfer. It wouldn't be quite as satisfying, but it would let those injured nerves heal a little before the next onslaught. Talk to Sectuib Califf if you'd like to pursue that option."

Eskalie fully expected her respectable father to turn on the Gen and discipline it for making such a suggestion. She was preparing herself to intervene before one or both of them were injured, but to her surprise, Rossil Morlin just shook his head.

"I've had a good, long life," he said, becoming once more the father Eskalie remembered, strong enough to face anything without flinching. "I'm not so afraid of dying that I have to set aside every principle I've lived by. Give your boy my greetings."

"I will," the Killer Gen agreed. For a wonder, it seemed willing to accept his decision, although its regret was plain to zlin. Eskalie wondered how her father managed that trick. Tallin tended to brush aside her own attempts to refuse its "help" like so many cobwebs.

"There's something else you can do for me, too," Rossil Morlin continued. His nager and expression reflected a new tension, as if what he intended to ask was very important to him, but he was unsure how his request would be regarded by the Gen.

"What might that be?" Tallin asked.

Her father nodded toward Eskalie. "Promise me, by your oath to Dar, that you'll look after my little girl when I'm gone. She's young yet, and following a dangerous profession. The young often get into situations we canny old foxes would avoid."

"Father!" Eskalie objected, but it was too late.

"I promise," the Killer Gen agreed, "unto Dar."

Rossil Morlin leaned back against the trunk of the oak tree, still more tired than a Sime ought to be, but strangely content. He even smiled at Eskalie's indignation.

"Catch my horse for me, Eskie," he ordered. "I've got to get home to your mother. There are arrangements to be made."

Her mind full of protests and objections that neither her father, the Killer Gen, nor the universe at large cared to hear, Eskalie obeyed.

FUGUE, IN FOUR CHOICES

SIX WEEKS LATER.

Eskalie looked over her shoulder as the first flurry of snowflakes swirled past her, carried on an icy blast of wind. The mass of black clouds that she had been racing all afternoon had finally caught up, and seemed intent on avenging the insult of her attempts to elude them.

"We made it over the top of the pass," she told the shivering black mare beneath her. "But there's no way we're making another twenty miles to Quidden's Roost today. Or tomorrow, from the look of things."

Star whuffled in agreement, placing her hooves carefully on the rough, steep trail. It would be slippery as well as rocky before much longer, and the flying snow wasn't going to improve the mare's vision.

"We'll have to find a place to wait out the storm," she decided. "Maybe that shepherd's shelter a half mile ahead; it should be empty this time of year. Mon Ergest will just have to resign himself to the delay."

Her reputation as a fast, honest, and discreet courier had continued to spread. It was now a more reliable source of employment than the detective and security work that had been the main support of Kirlin Investigations, previously. People tended to want those services in the summer, when travel was easy and trade was active. In late fall, however, taking to the open road was less appealing and there was more call for messengers, as long as they were trustworthy.

It had been a gamble, accepting the run to Quidden's Roost so late in the year. She had driven a hard bargain with the irascible old jeweler: enough to pay a month's rent on her firm's new, larger offices, which actually had a separate room in which Eskalie and her partners Amsil and Sesfin could sleep and store their personal belongings.

When she set out, it had been cold but the skies had been clear. She'd taken the shortcut through the pass because it was early for one of the area's notorious blizzards.

"That's the thing about weather," she complained, wiping snow out of her eyes. "It keeps changing and it's no good at reading the calendar."

The delay in delivering Ergest's message didn't concern her unduly. No one would blame her for sitting out a storm like this. No, she and Star would rest in the warmth of the shelter and move on in the morning, when the storm had passed. They would reach Quidden's Roost in another day, she would deliver her message, and then hurry home the next day if the weather zlinned reasonable. If it did not, she had enough money with her to pay the surcharge the Quidden's Roost Pen would charge her for claiming her Gen at a Pen at which she was not registered.

First, however, she had to reach shelter. The snow was now hock-deep, and Star waded through it with her tail tucked underneath her and her ears back. She stumbled, unable to see the ground, and Eskalie dismounted to lead her. As a Sime, she could zlin the path under the whirling white carpet and guide both of them around the worst of the loose rocks. It was hard work, though, with her field dimming down toward Need and no other travelers on the road.

The desolation fit her mood. Soon after changeover, she had realized that the father of her childhood, the infinitely strong and wise protector, was a fallible human being. When she had truly accepted that he was mortally ill and would soon be leaving her to make her own way without his support and guidance, it had shaken her world. Despite her yearning for the adventurous, independent life she had built, she had raged against the unfairness of it all: that her father would soon be gone and she would lack his advice and protection.

An hour later, the light was starting to go, but the trail had finally leveled off. The footing improved, too, as they left the pass and entered a mountain meadow. It almost made up for the increased exposure to the howling wind as the rock walls receded, leaving a wilderness of lifeless, frozen snow. Giddy with relief, she turned down the side trail that led to the shepherd's shelter. It was a sturdy building, she remembered from a visit the previous spring, built out of the stone that was so plentiful in the area, with a thick door made of untrimmed logs. Definitely an improvement over stumbling through the storm on increasingly numb feet.

The first hint Eskalie had that she was not the only traveler seeking shelter from the storm came when a swirling backdraft carried a faint hint of smoke to her nostrils. She would have thought she was imagining it, but the mare also lifted her head, nostrils flaring, and stepped a little faster. The second hint came when she rounded the last curve and a momentary lull in the curtain of flying snow let her make out two wagons drawn up close to the door.

She pulled the mare to a halt and zlinned, but the stone walls kept their secrets. "Star, my girl," she observed, "we have a dilemma. Those might be perfectly innocent fellow-travelers, caught by this early storm just like we were. On the other hand, this is a lonesome spot and not all fellow-travelers are innocent."

There could be no turning back. Neither she nor the mare could make it to Quidden's Roost in this weather, nor was there any other reasonable shelter within reach. However, she had not gone through changeover yesterday, despite her youthful appearance, and there was no reason to be stupidly trusting. She took Ergest's letter out of her courier's pouch and hid it under the scraps of used paper in her tinder kit. Few bandits were literate, so they might not recognize its value during a casual search of her belongings. The coins in her purse were more problematic. After a moment's consideration, she hid the three most valuable in the lining behind the tools in her repair kit, then placed it among the spare buckles and straps, extra stirrup, hoof pick, brushes, and other clutter in the bottom of her saddle bag. A quick zlin confirmed that they were not immediately obvious.

The rest of her money she left in her belt pouch. If the people in the shelter were thieves, better they had something easy to steal. With luck, that would content them and they wouldn't look further.

"Now we'll see if they're willing to share shelter," she told Star. She tucked her cape around her closely, took the mare's reins, and resumed their slow plod toward the log door.

When she was about five hundred feet away, the door opened and a wheelbarrow of stable sweepings emerged, pushed by a heavily bundled Sime wrapped in a grey cloak. After so long alone, the impact of his nager burned across her laterals, a brilliant spark of life among the deadly cold.

It was obvious that the man had not expected a fellow traveler any more than Eskalie had. He shouted back through the door and several of his comrades appeared to gawk at her, also wrapped in grey cloaks. None of them zlinned threatening, so she continued toward them, keeping her own desperation out of her nager as much as she could.

"Hallo, the shelter! I'm Eskalie Morlin, out of Tormin. Is there room for a half-frozen courier by your fire?"

"Could be," the first man admitted. He zlinned her thoroughly, in a fashion that might be taken as rude in a town, but which was only common caution under the circumstances. She must have passed his test, because he introduced himself as, "Akib."

With a sigh of relief, Eskalie volunteered her own name again and settled into the necessary task of negotiating the terms of her stay. Five minutes later, she was admitted to the barn portion of the shelter. In the spring, the big, dirt-floored room would be used as a lambing pen, or perhaps for shearing. Now, it was crammed with a dozen horses, dozing on a picket line. Some of them woke enough to greet the newcomers, but Star was too tired to nicker in return.

Eskalie was sympathetic. Now that she was no longer being battered by the wind, she was starting to feel her own exhaustion. It was that, perhaps, that kept her from being as observant as usual. Then again, the grey cloaks the strangers were wearing were of good quality, but not otherwise particularly unusual.

The horses were also of good quality. One particularly fine chestnut at the far end of the picket line, next to a door that must lead to the living quarters, caught her eye. The animal looked almost familiar, as did the grey beside it. Eskalie was trying to cudgel her half-frozen, Need-impacted brain into remembering where she'd seen such horses before when the door to the living quarters opened. Two figures in turquoise-and-grey livery stepped through. The first zlinned like an odd almost-Sime, and the other was an all-to-familiar Gen whose nager zlinned like the sun shining through fog. The ambient nager in the barn skewed, then settled into a bright glow as the newcomers approached.

"No," Eskalie protested under her breath to the Fates who insisted on making her life difficult for reasons known only to themselves. "You couldn't have managed a nice group of ruthless bandits instead? Or perhaps some Freeband Raiders?"

As was their usual custom, the Fates did not deign to answer her. No doubt they were much too busy snickering at the predicament they'd landed her in.

Sighing, Eskalie turned to greet Sectuib Califf, the Pervert-in-Chief of Householding Dar, and his father, Tallin, the Killer Gen.

"You're not frostbitten," Califf told her a little later, as she repossessed her still-numb feet and extended her toes toward the welcoming warmth of the stove. "It was a near thing, though. Another half hour out in that storm and you'd have had significant damage."

Eskalie endured the pervert's fussing and pointedly ignored the concerned look that Tallin was throwing in her direction over his Sectuib's shoulder, in favor of basking in the life-giving heat. The inner room of the shelter was about half the size of the outer pen, with a floor of rough-split logs worn smooth by years of dirt and wear. The primitive nature of the décor didn't stop it from feeling like a paradise in comparison to the inhospitable frozen wasteland outside.

At the moment, it was crowded with a half-dozen men and women dressed in Householding Dar's turquoise-and-grey livery. Two travel lanterns provided a bright light to supplement the stove and the nagers of the five Gens the perverts had brought along created a cheerful, reassuring glow in the ambient nager. Under its impact, her Need had receded to a mere nuisance and her stomach had settled enough to allow her to sip the mug of hot tea she cradled in her chilled hands.

"Whatever possessed you to travel these mountains so late in the year, Eskalie?" Tallin scolded, as if it had a perfect right to do so.

She had long since given up any hope that the Killer Gen would learn proper manners. How could it, when its owner treated it like a parent? So she shrugged and answered, "I was offered a substantial bonus if I could get a message to Quidden's Roost and a reply back within a week. The chances of a major storm this early were small, as you know."

"The risk…"

"Was much less than risk you lot were taking," she pointed out. "One person on a good horse travels much faster than a pair of wagons over these roads."

This silenced both the Gen and its parent. The border with Gen Territory was not far off: in fact, on which side of that border the pass Eskalie had crossed belonged had been a matter of dispute over the decades. While the paths on the current Sime side were primitive, there were some reasonably decent, wagon-friendly roads on the Gen side, for those who didn't worry overmuch about the constant Gen patrols. Eskalie had learned over the past year that the Householders traveled freely on the

Gen roads with the help of their highly trained Gens, who could pass close inspection by marauding Gen patrols.

Such border-hopping was, of course, quite illegal: an executable offense on both sides of the border. After due consideration of the ammunition she could bring to a discussion of travel routes, Tallin decided to abandon that topic in favor of another that was also favored by Eskalie's partners, Amsil and Sesfin.

"You're too close to Need to be traveling, especially so late in the year."

An hour ago, zlinning the storm eating away at her waning reserves of selyn, Eskalie would have agreed with it, albeit privately. Now, however, warm and surrounded by lush Gen nagers, much of the urgency of Need had disappeared.

"I'm fine," she assured the Gen, extending her handling tentacles to wrap around her tea mug to demonstrate their steadiness. "The storm will blow over by tomorrow morning. I'll have plenty of time to visit the Pen in Quidden's Roost while my client's employee composes her reply."

"If the storm doesn't blow itself out quickly enough, you don't have to face Attrition," Califf offered quietly. His nager shifted to zlin more imitation-Gen than imitation-Sime, making his meaning clear.

Eskalie recoiled, her laterals retracting painfully against her Need-swollen ronaplin glands. "I'm no pervert!" she spat at him.

The Pervert-in-Chief looked at her calmly, undeterred by her reaction. "No, you aren't a Householder," he agreed, "and you're too old to become one. Leaving the Kill behind entirely is only possible during a Sime's First Year. However, older Simes can skip Killing occasionally without ill effect. There are several isolated communities close to Householdings that rely on channels every winter to stretch out their Kill cycles when Pen deliveries are delayed."

"I come from a respectable family…" she began, only to stop at the amusement reflecting back at her from both Califf and his Gen. In light of what she had recently learned about her own father's prolonged stay at Householding Dar in his youth, it was probably justified. "Well, we're respectable now," she corrected herself. "So you can just forget about your perverted 'offer.' I'm not going to come begging to you for a fake Kill."

Once again, her anger and revulsion seemed to roll right off that infuriating calm. The Pervert-in-Chief merely nodded. "I won't force you unless you become an immediate danger to the other people here," he promised. "And by that, I mean our Gens as well as our Simes."

Eskalie wondered if one became inured to being insulted, with sufficient practice. "I'm no thief, to steal a Gen that belongs to someone else."

"See that you don't," Califf said, in stern warning. "The law might be willing to make allowances for someone with your family connections, under the circumstances, but I and my people are not. Every Sime and Gen here is quite capable of defending against such an attack."

"Your meaning is quite clear," she told him stiffly. It was, too. If she tried to steal a Kill, they would murder her.

"Good, then we understand one another." His nager softened. "And if you decide that you'd rather not face the twenty miles to Quidden's Roost in Need, after all, then I am at your service. You have only to ask."

They left her then, to think over what Califf had said. When she got up to check that Star was comfortable, nobody followed her into the improvised stable.

Esklie slept well that night, undisturbed by her usual Need nightmares because of the steady beat of selyn production surrounding her. She woke warm, refreshed, and confident in her ability to take on the challenge of continuing her journey.

It gave her a hint of why the Simes who joined Householdings were willing to associate with their deadly Gens. It would be pleasant to have Need reduced to a minor inconvenience. The freedom to think about something not directly associated with obtaining one's monthly Kill was worth a great deal. The price that the Householdings demanded for such comfort was, of course, out of the question. Still, there was nothing preventing her from enjoying a free sample.

She helped herself to tea—as long as she was free from Need-induced nausea, it was healthier to drink as much as she could—and started folding her bedroll, quietly so as not to startle the sleeping Gens into waking.

It wasn't long before there were others stirring, moving about the small chores of organizing the space, packing odd bits of clothing and equipment, and preparing a meal for the Gens.

A cold draft wafted through the shelter as Akib came in from the stable. He saw the bustle and shook his head. "You might as well enjoy a lazy morning, all of you," he announced. "The wind's howling as bad as ever and the snow is knee-deep and still coming down. Nobody's going anywhere today, is my guess."

To the Householders, it meant an extra day or two in the safety of the shelter, facing nothing worse than a little boredom: a minor disappointment, but not a disaster. Eskalie didn't share their equanimity. She had twenty miles of frozen snow to cover and was running out of time in which to do it. As the others discussed the merits of a storytelling contest, she noticed Califf zlinning her, no doubt wondering if she was going to beg him to share his talent for perversion. With a shudder, she moved to the corner of the room farthest from the fire, away from the others, and settled down to consider her options.

It was too much to hope for that her obvious wish for privacy would be respected. Tallin's Gen bulk settled beside her, mostly obscuring the nagers of the others.

"You do have a second option, if you won't take channel's transfer," the creature said, its quiet voice and steady, sun-through-fog nager calming her in spite of herself. "I told you once before that I would give you selyn if you wanted it."

"You not only have a death wish, you think I share it," she said, with the dry sarcasm that was all the humor she could muster in Need. "Or did you miss what your…son…threatened to do to me if I Killed one of his Gens?"

"I'm not offering to let you Kill me," Tallin answered. "I'm a Companion. I can serve a channel's Need and not be harmed by it. Your draw is slow and shallow in comparison."

It was surreal, hearing a Gen discuss being attacked by different Simes as if they were different blends of tea. She came from a world in which Sime attacks on Gens came in only one flavor: instantly fatal to the Gen.

"Mind you, Califf could probably give you more satisfaction," the Gen continued, blithely ignoring her inability to believe the entire conversation. "He can simulate Killbliss quite well, I understand, while that's a trick I've never had occasion to learn. Still, if you can't accept Califf, I'm willing to give it a try. At worst, you'd be less satisfied than you might wish. Either way, though, you'd be able to travel to Quidden's Roost without worrying that any small delay could be fatal." Tallin's voice was calmly unconcerned about the prospect of being attacked. Its nager showed concern, but only for Eskalie.

That seductive combination was a practiced act that the creature used to lure Simes into its power. Once under its control, she would be at its mercy. Sometimes, it used that power to the benefit of the Sime it controlled. She knew from personal experience that its attention could ease turnover and the related discomforts women often suffered. For that matter, her father might not have survived without its intervention.

However, she also knew from personal experience that the Gen had little compunction about using its training to manipulate the Simes around it, controlling their actions by controlling their moods…and that it did not always use its talents for the benefit of its victims. She had zlinned Tallin lure Yosum Forst into attacking it, at which point the Killer

Gen had crushed the hapless Genfarmer's laterals with somewhat fewer misgivings than a cat would display when dispatching a fat and tasty rodent. Her own laterals retreated far up their sheaths at the memory.

When she didn't respond to its offer, the Gen shook its head in what was almost a paternal gesture of fond exasperation. "Think on it," it advised her, "but don't wait too long to make your choice." Its nager disengaged from hers as it stood, in a strange way that her Needing body didn't interpret as a potential Kill escaping.

Smart body, to recognize that this Gen was more likely to be Killer than Killed.

She huddled in the corner, setting herself to endure until the storm was over.

When the woman assigned to night watch on the horses came back into the shelter on the morning of the third day, she reported directly to Califf. Eskalie's hopes that one of Dar's horses had suffered an injury were dashed as the Pervert-in-Chief's attention flashed immediately to her. The meaning was clear: the storm hadn't lifted, and so there would be no break for Quiddon's Roost, not even on foot.

As that unwelcome news sank in, Eskalie bolted for the stable. The heavy, insulating door closed behind her, cutting the ambient nager of the perverts and their deadly Gens. Without the comforting presence of that selyn, unattainable as it was, Eskalie realized, with dawning alarm, that she was out of time. Even if the storm were to end this morning, she could not wade through twenty miles of frozen snow to the Pen in Quiddon's Roost before she died of Attrition. She had exactly four options, and if she didn't choose between them, and quickly, her body would choose for her as she fell into the insanity of near-Attrition.

If she did nothing, and just stayed where she was, she would attack the first Gen—or Sime —who came through the door to check the horses. Ordinarily, that would leave her with a criminal record and the lifelong shame of being a Sime-killer or a Gen-stealer. However, given the enthusiasm with which the fellow occupants of the shelter practiced their deadly arts, it was more likely that her intended victim or the other Householders would slaughter her in retribution before she could stand trial. They might, or might not, go on to destroy her reputation as well.

She had some sense of decency left, she discovered, even this close to Attrition. "Whatever else I am, I'm not a thief," she told Star, walking over to put her arms around the mare for what comfort that might bring. Star turned her head to look at Eskalie and cocked one ear to indicate her agreement: option one was not acceptable.

No, if Eskalie had to die, she should do it with honor and walk out the far door into the storm, covering as much distance as she could before her body gave out. The cold would take her quickly, although not quickly enough to spare her from the horror of Attrition entirely. "The Householders would take care of you, Star, and let Kirlin Security know what happened to me," she explained.

Reassured that her life would go on, even if Eskalie's did not, Star went back to munching her hay. That was less consolation than it ought to have been. Eskalie discovered that she didn't want to die, even with honor. Not of Attrition, surrounded by the cold and blowing snow, and not a hint of life as far as she could zlin. No, option two was not much better than option one, in the end.

To live, however, she had to have selyn. There were two sources within her reach that might not be immediately fatal to her. Tallin, the Killer Gen had offered to let her take selyn. The Gen might have been trained to survive having one of Dar's channels draw from it at Need-slaking speed, but Eskalie had seen Califf working with his Gens. The channel always approached them slowly and gently, with care taken not to startle or frighten them. Knowing that they were not being attacked, the Gens felt no impulse to defend themselves.

Eskalie was long past the point at which she could be polite. She would attack Tallin like a berserker, given half a chance. Would the Gen's training in serving channels hold through a violent assault? If it didn't, would the Killer Gen revert to the other training Dar had given it? Would its cool Gen fingers clamp down on her arms, crushing her laterals as they lay helplessly exposed, shenning her out of her Kill, to die in convulsions? She had seen Tallin do that to Yosum Forst, zlinned Yosum's pain, horror, and disbelief as his prey turned on him and became the predator.

"Yosum was an arrogant fool and a thieving traitor, but no Sime deserves to die like that," she told Star, as the mare whuffled against her shoulder in search of a treat.

Eskalie certainly didn't want to risk such a death. She wanted to live, and the Need gnawing at her didn't care about laws, or dignity, or consequences. Which left her fourth option: accepting Sectuib Califf's offer of a fake, imitation-Gen Kill. It was the ultimate perversion: taking her Kill from another Sime who wouldn't even have the decency to die afterward.

She wouldn't die, either. No, she'd have plenty of life in which to remember how all her vaunted principles had meant nothing when it came to the test, and she'd gone groveling to a pervert for a fake Kill the first time she couldn't get to a Pen. She doubted that Califf would spread the story around—that was the sort of thing that might provoke the townsfolk of Sommerin to finally toss the whole nest of perverts out—but he might use the information to force her cooperation on some other issue. Even if he didn't, she would know. And if she couldn't look at herself in the cracked bit of mirror Amsil kept next to the washbasin, what was the point of living?

"There isn't one," she said, and Star's tail swished in agreement. She muttered a curse and started pacing back and forth along the picket line, running through her options again and again. They remained the same. A cold and lonely descent into Attrition, wandering in the storm. Execution for attempted Gen-stealing or Sime-killing at the hands of her fellow travelers. Califf's tentacles entwining with hers, his false Gen projection offering degradation and the death of honor. Tallin spooking as she attacked him, his hands clamping down on her laterals. Death by storm, by shame, by smashed laterals or outraged fellow travelers. Her Need-starved body could zlin no hint of life in her future, no hope of survival among her options.

She couldn't force herself to choose as Need clamped down harder, death gnawing at her. As her body tried to consume the last bits of selyn in her reserves, she discovered that she was not, after all, able to face death before dishonor. At least, not death by Attrition. Dishonor, after all, could sometimes be lived down, given enough time. Her father had managed it, after all.

She was turning toward the door back to the inner shelter, ready to beg Sectuib Califf for an imitation Sime-Kill, when it opened. Warmth and light hit her, a furnace promising life, and her body attacked reflexively. In a burst of augmentation that drained her meager reserves ever further, she grabbed the source and snatched the life into herself with no thought beyond filling the empty void inside of her.

Some part of her, the thinking part that had been debating choices, finally noticed that the rest of her was attacking the selyn source that had entered the stable, and vaguely registered its concern for future consideration. Shortly thereafter, as the incoming selyn reached her brain, she experienced a nagging feeling that something was missing. The pain of Need was fading, but there was no matching pain echoed in the selyn that flowed so easily up her laterals. That was fundamentally wrong, and she teetered on the edge of rejecting the selyn entirely, despite the life it offered.

Her handling tentacles clamped down harder, seeking that elusive satisfaction, and the pain that evoked combined with the lingering pain of near-Attrition. It wasn't what she really wanted, but it was enough.

She opened her eyes as her awareness of the selyn fields around her faded away. In the light of the lantern, she could see that the arms she clutched with such bruising force were, at least, not Sime ones. That was the only normal thing about the situation. Instead of a limp corpse dangling from her hands, Tallin was very much alive, grinning down at her in insufferable self-satisfaction.

She dropped the Gen's arms quickly, before it changed its mind and decided to murder her after all. "What the shen did you do that for?" she demanded. "For that matter, what the shen did you do to me, anyway?"

Tallin shrugged, with no sign of apology. "You couldn't accept channel's transfer, or you'd have come to Califf yesterday. He could have forced you, as close to Attrition as you were, but you'd have had a hard time living with yourself afterward. You didn't have any moral objection to taking selyn from me, though. The only thing preventing you from accepting my offer was that you were afraid of me. I just had to wait until you were close enough to Attrition that you couldn't chicken out and shen yourself. It worked, didn't it?"

Eskalie supposed that, technically, she had violated the law by attempting to Kill a Gen who belonged to another. On the other tentacle, the Gen was alive and well, and had deliberately precipitated the whole affair. Given the way Califf deferred to his parent, Eskalie could reasonably hope that he wouldn't bring charges. Brimming with the selyn she had stripped from Tallin, she could now afford to wait until the storm cleared completely before making the run to Quiddon's Roost in relative safety.

The realization that she was going to live, after all, finally penetrated her confusion. Relief made her throat choke closed, her eyes watered, and she began to cry. Like most Simes of her family's class, Eskalie was accustomed to waiting out the usual post-Kill burst of emotional instability before leaving the privacy of the Killroom. This time, however, she was not alone. Gen arms gathered her close and held her as she bawled into Tallin's bulky chest.

When her sobs eased, the Killer Gen let her go. "You're fine," it said, with the complacent attitude of an expert contemplating its handiwork. "You should come into the shelter now, though. Califf will want to check you over."

Eskalie bristled at the arrogant creature's high-handed assumption that it could issue orders to her. "Who appointed you to run my affairs?" she demanded.

"Your father." The Gen grinned at Eskalie's indignant glare, and reminded her piously, "As you'll recall, I promised him I'd look after you."

Tallin's expression left no doubt of its intent to step into her father's role, poking its overlarge bulk into her affairs. If the Gen was correct about its potential lifespan, it could easily outlive her. The prospect of having a near-immortal Giant Killer Gen as a self-appointed protector was comforting, in a twisted sort of way. What person in a dangerous profession wouldn't want such a dangerous weapon by her side, ready to inflict mayhem on anyone who threatened her? For that matter, what Sime wouldn't want to spend time close to a Gen with such a spectacular nager, whatever its ownership and degree of Killability?

"Once Califf has finished with you, we'll get you a bowl of soup to drink," Tallin continued, providing a clear demonstration of the drawbacks of such an arrangement.

She couldn't fool herself into believing that the Gen was dangerous only to those who threatened her. The mayhem the creature inflicted on Simes, wherever it went, could just as easily be turned in her direction. Since its owner, Califf, had no will to discipline it, the best survival strategy for handling a Killer Gen like Tallin was to follow its wishes in the small things, in hopes that she could escape from its sphere of influence before a larger issue came along.

After all, losing the support of one's parents was a normal and necessary, if unhappy, part of growing up. How else could the younger generation grow and thrive, except by taking the places emptied by those who had died before them? Someone would eventually take her own place. If she was very lucky, she would have the chance to pick and mold that person into a worthy successor. Would that successor also have the Giant Killer Gen concerning itself with her affairs?

"Come, Eskalie," the Gen repeated, herding her toward the inner door.

The detective preceded her self-appointed father substitute into the shelter, already planning how best to make her break for independence.

SHADOWS

ZOE FARRIS

WC 6703

"I will tell you a story of our people."

The old woman sat by the fire, naked and unashamed. The flames cast flickering light on her dark skin, dancing patterns in red, purple, green, and blue. Her teeth were startling white and her hair was wild, like a nest of red belly black snakes.

"It's a good story told to me by my mother's mother, and told to her by her mother's mother. Now I tell to you, although I not your mother's mother." She laughed and her white teeth flashed.

"This is a story of one from the Separated. In the world of the Separated, Sime and Gen could not live together without death. The Gens—they did not live with Simes and when a kid went through the Becoming they either Killed or were hunted and put down. The old woman shrugged. The Simes of the Separated hunted the Gens for the Kill so they could live. From far away across the big water, a Healer—Tumoo—came to us from the Separated. But the way she came, that's what makes this a good story…"

* * * *

The People had waited for the Separated to learn in their own time. The spirits had told them that it was only a matter of time before the Separated accepted that the two types of people, Sime and Gen, must live as one.

But now the time had come for the People to help. All the signs pointed to it. The rains came early and there was food in plenty and no one went hungry. The clouds told stories during the day, and at night the stars continued them, dancing across the sky in new patterns.

On a night of a half moon, beneath the Life Tree, the elders talked. The next day two men, a Healer and a Life Giver, and two women, a Healer and a Life Giver, went walkabout. They knew where they were going. The scrubs and the rocks told them. When they were uncertain, a wallaby showed them a way. A nest of ants, taller than the tallest of men, pointed the direction and the birds called to them when they were near. The Healers zlinned the truth in the pattern.

Maki, the male Healer pointed, "Zlin there." He told the woman, pointing in the direction of the rising sun.

"I zlinned already," Anka, the female Healer, told him "So many attacking one and she is badly hurt."

"The Separated cannot be blamed," Illa, Anka's daughter and a Life Giver, said, "they are children."

"Even children should be punished." Anka clenched her fists in anger.

Maki had already walked away. He stopped and took a long length of cord with a slim piece of wood tied to it from his belt. He started whirling it in rapidly increasing circles above his head. The others went silent as the bullroarer increased speed. The rhythmic sound pulsed out, travelling further than any Sime could zlin, its voice loud in the still, dusty, ancient land.

They watched as the attacking Simes raced to their horses and sped away, leaving behind one lone, bleeding body in the dirt.

The female Life Giver, not much more than a young girl, looked at the fleeing figures. "They run from Shadows fast enough!"

Maki stopped the bullroarer and put it back in his belt. "We must hurry now, you follow as fast as you can," he instructed the two Gens.

Maki and Anka covered the ground quickly, augmenting as only a Sime Healer could, until they neared the energy field that lay, oozing selyn, on the red dust.

"She is powerful" Anka said in awe.

"She is hurt," Maki said shortly, and knelt beside the small form.

Where the small body was not covered in blood, it was covered in bruises and whip marks. Maki could zlin the broken ribs and the damage to several organs.

Anka started to croon, as a mother to her child, manipulating their fields together as Maki started to heal the worst of the girl's wounds.

It wasn't long before their Life Givers joined them, fitting themselves into the moving selyn fields of the two Healers with the knowledge only the special Life Givers had.

* * * *

A groan came from the small body, and her tentacles writhed, seeking to know what was happening before her lesser senses, her ears and her eyes, gained enough strength to start working. What she zlinned comforted her. Channels, Companions, friends. Her eyes opened and widened in confusion.

Four dark figures surrounded her. They wore little more than a piece of cloth as a covering that was tied to their waist by string. All were barefoot.

"Who are you?" she said, croaking the words out of a throat that was bruised and dry.

"Be still," the Woman said, "You are hurt, Maki heals."

"Who are you?" The girl repeated. She looked past the woman to the two Gens who stood watching from behind the two Simes. "Where am I?"

"I am Anka, of the Munara People but your people call us Shadows." The woman's smile was reflected in her nager. "What is you name?"

"My name is Tamro."

Hearing the strange girl's name sent a ripple through the ambient as the two Healers and two Life Givers responded with a mixture of surprise and pleasure.

"What's wrong? What did I say?"

The woman looked to Maki and they both smiled. "Tumoo is our word for Healer. Your name, Tamro, in our words mean One Who Heals."

"Nothing is wrong child."

"I am not a child; I am nearly two years past changeover." The frown on the woman's face told the girl that her words were not understood, "Since I became Sime." Tamro added, her tentacles moving slightly.

"You are not of the People; you do not have the understanding, and in that you are still a child. Now be still and let us work." Anka fell silent and added her nager to Maki's. Their Life Givers adjusted their fields smoothly so that Tamro felt no discomfort.

At an unseen and unzlinned signal the two Healers strengthened their fields around Tamro. Maki raised a hand and crossed the middle fingers as two of his handling tentacles touched the tips of the crossed fingers. Tamro did not know the meaning of this but zlinned in the Gens a sense of satisfaction.

"You're a channel? I didn't know there were channels here." Tamro asked when silence became too loud for her mind.

"Shanal?" Maki shrugged. He took her hands into his own and closed his eyes, "I am Healer, like you. Don't know shanel word." He settled himself in the red dirt and started to chant, running his hands gently over her as he zlinned for other damage inside her body.

"Yes, Healer, that's what a channel is. What do you call your Companions?" She gestured toward the two Gens with a tentacle.

"Life Givers." Maki said. His voice and nager radiated reverence as he spoke the words.

As unfamiliar as these people were, Tamro, the healer from the Separated could zlin they were helping her. The nagers of Healers and Life Givers were unmistakable. She could not remember what had happened to her, but the pain throughout her body told her to stay still and let them work.

"And my people, my friends, where are they?"

"Later" the woman said, "You rest and heal."

"No, I must find them. I have to have my Companion—my—Life Giver." Tamro fought the rising panic that was clear to see and zlin.

"We will take care of your Need when it comes. You let the healing work." Anka began crooning softly, easing the girl's mind, "Maki, make her sleep."

Maki locked his field with the girl's, overriding those of Anka's and the two Gens, and put the young Sime into a deep sleep. "We can move her now."

"Her people, there are more of them?" Orad, the male Life Giver said.

"I zlin none" Maki said as he picked up the young Healer, the white skin of the girl contrasting against his own black skin. "She needs water."

Together the small band set off towards their camp, but not directly. There was a water hole not far, and the girl was not the only one to require water.

The sun had hardly moved in the sky before they reached the water hole, but the smell of blood told them this was no longer a good place. Maki stayed, holding the girl while Orad went ahead.

"It is her people," Orad told them when he returned.

"There is no life," Maki said.

"This is wrong," Anka said. Her voice held a sob.

Illa comforted her mother with hands and nager, her field blanketing the older woman in a soft comforting fog.

They left the dead behind, explaining to the spirits that the water there was no longer good. Silently the women used stones to make marks on trees. The knowledge of this would be spread.

* * * *

Tamro awoke in an ambient of calm. There was a soft crooning voice close by, which stopped even as she became conscious of it.

"You are awake, this is good." Illa said softly. "Drink."

A vessel was held to her mouth, and thankfully she drank the cool water, realizing even as she did that her pain was much lessened.

"Thank you." Tamro looked around and added, "Where am I? How did I get here?"

The Gen looked at her quizzically. "You don't know? You can't tell where you are?"

The question was an honest one. As a Sime, Tamro should be able to tell. Since she had Become Sime, her sense of where she was in the universe had been unmistakable. She closed her eyes and felt for it. "I know I am here, but I do not know where here is. I know where home is, but I don't know how it would be possible to get there from here."

Tamro grasped the Gen's hand. She did not feel sick; this was not the psycho-spatial disorientation she had learned about. Realization came to her in a moment of shock. "I can't remember!" Her horror reflected in her nager for any Sime to zlin.

"Can't remember? What is it you can't remember?" Anka asked as she and Maki approached.

"I can't remember what happened to me. How did I get hurt? Where are my friends, my family?" Tamro closed her eyes. She felt a deep guilt, but did not know why.

Immediately the ambient was filled with uneasiness.

"They are gone." The Healer said.

"Where?" Tamro choked back tears. They wouldn't leave me alone in a strange land, would they?

"They are with the spirits"

Tamro looked at him in horror. "Do you mean that they are dead?"

The Healer nodded. "Dead, yes. Gone to the spirits."

"Liam, Aharo…"

Illa quickly put a hand over the girl's mouth.

"You must not call them here. You will see them again, very soon, but they must not be called here." Anka said firmly.

Tamro looked at her and fear well up, "see them again—very soon" was that a threat of death? But there was no threat in the woman's kind nager.

"What do you mean?"

"You will understand." Anka run a tentacle gently down the girl's cheek and smiled. "You rest while Maki works."

Tamro lay in silence while Maki focused his field, zlinning for any remaining damage. The male Gen, Maki's Life Giver, sat cross-legged beside the Sime.

Illa gave Tamro's hand a gentle squeeze and smiled as she stood, leaving Tamro in the care of the men. Tamro watched as mother and daughter walked towards another group of women.

Clouds drifted overhead. The wind danced through the sharp grass. Insects sang their songs. A large bird, black with yellow feathers under wings and tail, landed in the branch of the shade tree and screeched down at the People. In the distance other birds answered. Soon the small tree was full of the black birds.

"It is time," Maki said, and his nageric hold on Tamro eased.

"Time for what?" Tamro felt some of the pain return but now it was easy to bear and she sat up slowly.

Anka and Illa returned carrying a woven bag.

"Illa will say with you," Maki said. Maki, Anka, and Orad walked toward a group of waiting Simes.

"Where are they going?" Tamro asked the Gen in concern, zlinning something at the edge of the ambient.

"They go to take care of your friends." Illa spoke softly, almost in a whisper, "They will return tomorrow."

Tamro jumped to her feet and paused, feeling nauseous. She wiped the sweat from her face and took a tentative step forward. "Wait!"

"No, Tumoo, you cannot go. You must stay here." Illa said. "They will come back."

Tamro felt herself held by the Gen's field and for a moment she stood swaying. She tried to follow the others but was pulled back by that strong steady field. Her thoughts were of her own people, and her Need for her own Companion, her own Life Giver, was stronger than the hold the Gen had over her. She forced herself to go hypoconscious—the state of using only the five senses that Simes shared with Gens—until she could no longer zlin the Gen by her side.

"You must not follow," Illa said.

"You stay here if you want to, but if they are going to my people I am going with them." Tamro walked away from the Gen with tears in her eyes and determination in her heart. Her body ached from her healing injuries and approaching Need but she buried the thought of it and kept moving.

They can't all be dead. Maybe some escaped, she thought. She approached the group, which had stopped. "I am coming with you. Someone might still be alive."

"You cannot. The spirits will be restless if they feel their friend close to their bodies so long after death and they may be vengeful." Maki pointed back to the tree, "You must wait."

The group turned away from the distressed channel.

"I am not staying here. They are my friends, my family. If there is any chance…"

"You cannot come!" Maki's voice was loud and firm; the birds waiting in the trees rustled their feathers as the air rippled. "You do not understand these ways. You must stay." The command was backed by a nager as un-swaying as rock.

Think! Tamro knew both Healers and Life Givers could overpower her by nageric manipulation alone, but she was not sure if they would physically restrain her if she continued to follow them. *I have to make them agree to take me.*

Something the young Gen had said earlier came back to Tamro, "If I cannot go to them, I will call them to me!"

Tamro took a deep breath and opened her mouth, "Ahar…"

"STOP!" Maki's voice scared the birds from the tree and his nager rang with anger.

He looked at the young girl in front of him, her cheeks stained with tears, and the rock of his nager melted with compassion, "Maybe I am wrong. Your ways are not our ways. You are strong enough. You are a Healer. You can come."

They walked silently as the day turned to night.

The half-moon's weak light was enough for all to see. Tamro wished they could go faster, but they could only go as fast as the slowest Gen in the group.

When the moon was directly overhead Maki stopped, "We will rest here."

Tamro realised that Illa was automatically taking on the role of her Companion; positioning herself where she could best offer the Healer support and the young Sime let herself hope.

Maki and Anka exchanged knowing glances and Anka nodded at Maki's wordless question.

"Yes, she will be the one."

* * * *

The group headed off again before first light. No one spoke. Overhead several of the large black birds flew past and into the distance. Ahead a line of trees outlined the path of a river. As they drew closer the small noises of waking birds grew louder and the dry desert air seemed to relax with a sigh of moisture.

At the edge of the tree line they stopped.

Maki stood with eyes closed, muttering softly to himself. The others waited for his signal.

Tamro was torn. She wanted to rush ahead and find out the truth but was afraid of what that truth might be.

A blanket of calm settled over Tamro as the two Gens moved to stand either side of her. She felt the Companions' nagers connect with her field and form a bubble of protection around her.

"It is safe for us to go now." Maki said, "The spirits will not know you are here." Maki moved off and the rest followed.

The group rounded a clump of bushes and Tamro froze at the sight before her. A wagon, their wagon, was lying on its side, its contents spread out on the grass, wheels shattered and useless. Her knees gave way and she fell to the ground, her fingers and tentacles clutching the earth as her eyes beheld the trail of carnage. A body, beaten and disfigured, lay across the roots of a tree, "Wi..?" She began, but a shift in the blanketing nager reminded her not to call them and she closed her mouth over the name.

Tamro looked past the body of the channel and saw other bodies scattered throughout the area. She zlinned, but there was not a trace of selyn anywhere. The Gens appeared to have died in the Kill. Her Sectuib's Companion was dead a few feet from him, his neck broken. All those who had come to this land to start a new life were dead. All except her.

Illa, crying silent tears helped the Healer back to her feet.

Tamro walked amongst them, their spirits unaware of her presence, and searched for the one she called Companion.

"I can't see my Companion. He must be still alive." She said with hope.

No one spoke as she searched. The Gens kept close to Tamro and the Healers walked behind them.

She went from one body to another, memories returning with each battered face and broken body, but there was no sign of Aharon, her Life Giver. Despite the brutality all around her, Tamro felt hope.

Tamro found a body that she did not recognize, a stranger, their clothing odd and different to the Householders. Their tentacles grasped the muscular arm of a male Gen. Tamro turned away, unable to look further.

"You were right." She sobbed, "They are all here; they are all dead. My people are gone." She fell to her knees again, her hands and tentacles covering her face, "What's to become of me?"

Illa put their arms around the distraught Sime."

Anka spoke softly, her nager adding to the soothing affect from Illa, "What is the custom of your people?"

"I have to bury them." Tamro looked around the debris strewn area, "I can't leave them like this."

The other two Simes looked at each and Anka nodded, "They are her people, we will do this their way."

"We will bury them and sing their spirits home." Maki's voice shook as he spoke the final words.

They buried Tamro's people together, but dug a separate grave for the raider. When they were finished, Maki placed a large stone on the mound.

Tamro stood at the grave for a long time, crying.

With a gentle touch of her nager, Illa led Tamro away from the place of sorrow.

Tamro laid her hand flat against the dirt and said, "I will find out what happened here."

By the time she stood and turned to leave the others had began to walk out of the line of trees, back toward the desert. As Tamro and Illa walked away together, those that had come to help sang the spirits to rest. Illa added her soft sweet voice to the chant and Tamro felt comforted.

The group walked the red dirt for half a day, following the sun across the sky until it gave way to the moonlit darkness. Illa stayed near Tamro, her field a soothing balm on the channel's grief.

"Thank you." Tamro spoke the words of gratitude with sadness in her voice and field.

"Who could have done that to them?" Tamro wondered aloud.

"Illa gently took the channel's hand, "You didn't see what you looked like when we found you. Without Maki and Anka you would have died."

Tamro put her hand to a spot on her head that was still sore and said, "Maybe that's why I don't remember."

"You will remember if the spirits need you to remember." Illa replied.

The air warmed quickly as the first hint of sunrise lightened the sky. Tamro looked around as the landscape opened up in the morning glow. Flat. That was how she saw the land. Flat. That is how she felt. She did not see the small hills or the gullies that hid water, the bushes and scattered trees that gave home to many animals. All she saw was flat red dirt.

Tamro zlinned ahead. She zlinned the fields of more people than she remembered.

"We are home," Illa said, her nager a swirl of joy and excitement.

Tamro was too close to Need to feel the joy or excitement that the Gen felt. She could not even deeply feel the grief that she should be feeling from the loss of her people, or the fear that came with the uncertainty of her future.

Tamro felt the Gen's instant nageric response as her field dropped into a quiet steady stream of calm and support. The excitement was gone but the joy remained, unobtrusive but there.

As they arrived at the camp they were greeted with smiles and laughter. In the distance behind the approaching people, Tamro saw smoke rising into the air and the aroma of cooking drifted to her nostrils, but she was too far into Need to anticipate the feast that was obviously being prepared.

Maki turned and spoke to Tamro, "Go with Illa and rest, and soon she will share her life."

Illa's face lit up. "Am I the one?"

Maki just smiled and walk away.

Tamro zlinned pleasure in the Gen and felt a great burden lifted from her shoulders. She had suspected—no, hoped—that Illa would give her transfer and now it seemed official. She followed the Gen through a group of people and observed that while many of them were as dark as Illa and her mother, some of them had skin that was even lighter than her own.

"These are your people?"

"Not all. There are people from many groups. They have come for the Corroboree."

"What is a Corroboree?" Tamro asked.

"It is a gathering of all the People. We share stories and songs and celebrate the Joining." Illa looked at the channel and smiled, "And they have come to see you, too."

Me? I'm not important, Tamro thought as she looked across the camp.

"We'll rest here," Illa said, crawling into a lean-to made of bark. On the ground lay several grey and red-brown animal skins.

The shade from the tree and the breeze sweeping over them was a relief from the heat and sun. Tamro sat cross-legged and watched as people prepared for the celebrations. Illa was lying beside her, instantly asleep, exhausted from the long walk.

Tamro steeled herself for the Gen's nager to let go its support, to feel her Need to its full extent, but even in sleep this Gen's field remained linked to her. *She is a strong and caring Gen. I didn't know Gens of such strength would be found here.* Tamro thought.

She held the girl's hand and wrapped a handling tentacle around her fingers. The touch gave her a strange sense of comfort in this overwhelming place.

As Tamro sat beside the sleeping Gen she wondered how much more powerful Illa would be with proper Householding training.

An eerie quiet settled over the campsite as voices dimmed to a soft murmur. Tamro sat and watched.

Men, both Sime and Gen, stood at the far edge of the clearing. They began to clap decorated sticks together, chanting softly. The group began to dance, isolated jerky movements that matched the stick clapping. Three young men moved to the front.

From the other side, women, both Sime and Gen moved into the clearing. They danced forward, taking one scraping footstep after another as they clapped the same beat as the sticks. Three younger women led them. The women sang a song that weaved with the men's chant.

A third group sat midway. Tamro zlinned that those seated were both Sime and Gen as well.

These were the Healers and Life Givers from the different groups. Sitting with them were the Elders.

Those not involved in the dance stood around the circle and watched. Some children mimicked the dancing.

The ambient grew stronger with anticipation.

"Illa, wake up," Tamro said.

The young Gen stretched, sat up, and rubbed her eyes.

"What's happening?" Tamro asked, gesturing at the clearing with two tentacles.

"It is the Joining." Illa shimmied a little closer to her charge and leaned against her, shoulder to shoulder, "We will have our Joining soon."

"Joining?" Tamro felt the a thrill go through the Gen's nager and she zlinned Illa's willingness to give her selyn grow. "You mean Transfer? They are going to have Transfer—there—in front of everyone?"

"Not all." Illa said. "Those in front..." She pointed to the three of each group who lead the dance, "The spirits have said they can be joined. The Gens will be Life Givers to the Simes."

"But, they're not channels—Healers," Tamro leaned forward, raising herself up, "it's not safe."

The Gen laughed; a gentle laugh that carried on her field, "They are matched. The Healers would not allow the Joining if they did not match."

Tamro watched as the groups met in the centre of the clearing. The six that were meant for the Joining left the dancers and went and stood before the Healers.

Maki raised a hand and with word and a nageric flourish signaled. All movement stopped. The music sticks ceased and the song faded.

Maki spoke the words of the People, and then spoke words that Tamro would understand. After a brief glance toward Tamro he looked back at the six, "You have been tested. The Elders have spoken to the spirits. Share and receive life as the ancestors tell us."

The six left the clearing in pairs. Tamro realised that they were going to have transfer in private.

One of the other Healers stood forward and raised her hands, her tentacles spread to her fingertips, "These Joinings also join our families. We will be strong because of this. We will share lands and food. We will welcome each other into our camps. We will provide life to our new brothers and sisters when they Need."

Another Healer spoke, "The ancestors told us of one who would come. One who has the knowledge of the Separated ways, but is not truly Separated. One who will help us to teach the Separated the ways of the Joined." The Healer paused as people muttered amongst themselves. When they did not cease he called them to quiet, with voice and nager, "Maki—our brother—our cousin—Tumoo to the Munara People, has found the one."

Tamro flushed and looked around as every head turned to her. She felt Illa's protective nager tighten around her. *What do they expect me to do?*

"Tamro!" Maki called.

Tamro rose uncertainly, encouraged by Illa's hand and nager to move forward. People around the clearing broke into a murmur at the sound of her name, so close to their own word for Healer.

Maki began singing, Orad joined him, adding his light tones to Maki's deep voice. Anka gathered two bunches of leaves and handed one to Maki. The ends were smoldering from sitting in the fire.

Tamro and Illa stopped in front of Maki and flinched as he waved the smoldering leaves around the two girls. Maki stood back, Anka took his place, and passed smoldering leaves in front of Tamro and Illa

Illa used her hands to capture the smoke and wash her face and body as if she were washing in the river. Tamro copied the Gen's motions, unsure of their significance.

All the other Healers moved forward, their combined energy fields closing to form a bubble of calm around Tamro and Illa. The People fell silent again.

Illa faced Tamro and held out her arms and smiled, "Take from me and be strong again."

Carried on the soft words came the solid and profound offering of a Companion. Tamro could no longer resist, her Need too deep, her life ebbing away. All thoughts faded. The only thing now was Illa, and the Gen's Need to give.

Tamro's tentacles latched onto the Gen's arms, holding them too tight, half afraid that the offer of life was going to be withdrawn at the last moment.

But she need not have feared, Illa was the one who leant forward to make fifth contact.

In that instant of physical contact, the two, Sime and Gen were bound together. Illa was bound by the Sime's tentacles; Tamro was bound by the Gen's nager.

In that time—in that split second before fifth contact was made—before their lips were joined—the air stilled—time slowed, and the world shifted.

* * * *

A bright yellow sun shone against the pitch black sky above the red earth. Tamro stood stunned as stars appeared and pulsed slowly, growing larger and becoming solid forms as they touched the ground in front of them.

The pleasure in the Gen's nager ran through their still connected systems and calmed her, easing her apprehension.

Two thin black figures, backlit by the yellow sun, stepped forward. They seemed out of focus, as if they were very close and very far away at the same time.

One raised a tentacled hand toward Illa. The other stood silently. Behind them was an uncountable number of grey shadows. Illa stepped forward.

The shadow Sime touched her shoulder, "It is good you came to visit the Old Ones."

Although Tamro did not know the language the spirit spoke she had no trouble understanding it.

"It is good to see you, grandfather." Illa turned to Tamro and smiled, "I bring Tumoo from far away."

The figure stepped closer and held his hands out to Tamro, "You are with us, as we knew you would be," he said. "We must give you the memories."

His thin bony fingers and thread-like tentacles stretched out touching Tamro, lightly on the temples.

A sealed section of her mind opened and she saw—no—felt the presence of her friends, she could not see them, but she knew they were there, somewhere behind this figure in front of her.

Memories came to her.

She had been beaten and left in the desert to die. She remembered the people of the town torturing her.

Liam's death entered her mind—a knife in the back.

Another memory, a Companion—her Companion—standing with his back to a tree. Simes circled him waiting to attack. Too many Simes. Violence followed, until he had no more selyn to give, and death came.

A shimmer—and Tamro remembered being a Sime of the Separated ready to Kill, bearing down on a terrified Gen.

Tamro remembered being an old man, crouched beside a fire, chanting his dead wife to the spirits while tears ran down his face.

She remembered being a woman huddled under a lean-to struggling to give birth.

She remembered being a child writhing in agony, arms cut from elbow to wrist, knowing that she was dying in changeover, and knowing it was the Separated who had mutilated her.

She remembered being a boy, only three months past changeover, running before riders as they hunted him down.

And she remembered when she was a young girl, out alone in the desert, feeling the first signs of Becoming; of changing over and knowing she must call for a Life Giver.

The memories crowded in on each other—a young boy of thirteen, his tentacles on the verge of breaking out—a Gen approaching a new Sime—a young girl playing—a father teaching his child to hunt—a woman making food for her family.

And she remembered—a time where there were no Simes, no Gens, a time before, a dark time of confusion.

"No further." said the old man, now so sharply in focus that he seemed more solid and real then anything Tamro could remember. "It is time. When you receive Illa's selyn you will be of the People."

Tamro felt the ground beneath her feet as the images and memories settled into her mind. Illa's cool Gen hands were still on her arms and she felt the soft lips on hers. She was still in Need. As soon as their lips touched and selyn flowed, Tamro realised that it had all happened in less than a single heartbeat. Tamro felt the selyn being poured into her starving system, not waiting for her to take it.

Her mind protested the Gen controlling. A Gen should not control transfer, the thought warned, that is how you became junct, joined to the Kill. Tamro tried to listen to her mind's warning, but she could not hear through her body's Need for selyn.

The Gen's life-force filled Tamro like the dry billabong after the rain. It washed the darkness before it, forcing open barriers that had never before allowed selyn to pass. The Gen's nager, as hot as the red land, surrounded and embraced Tamro. Flecks of red, orange and green danced through the ambient, highlighted by specks of silver. The wind swirled their joined fields into dancing spirals that reached out and picked up the joyous ambient of the People.

For the first time she felt alive, truly alive. She felt the touch of energy on her skin, her hair and even in the breath she took. No transfer had felt like this.

Tamro looked up into Illa's bright eyes. She felt hours had passed but it had only taken a moment. The yellow sun had gone and taken the spirits with it, and it was night again—true night. She gazed down at their joined hands, light and dark, her handling tentacles still holding them together. She had to make a concerted effort to release the Gen—her Companion—her Life Giver.

All those people. All those memories. Tamro tried to hold onto those memories, but they were rapidly fading as a dream fades upon waking.

Maki lifted his arms and spoke, "You are of the Joined. The Ancestors have brought you to us."

Toora stepped forward and placed a small stone in Tamro's palm, clasping her hand around hers, "This is the mark of Healer."

The stone felt warm in her hand and she could feel the lines melt into her skin. Tamro looked at the intricately carved stone. Five lines splayed out from one end like rays of the sun, the centre line longer than the others.

"This is the mark of Life Giver." Toora said as she placed a stone, carved with a spiral design, on her daughter's palm. The Healer's pride glowed in her nager.

Behind them the People danced and chanted. The young laughed and stamped in the dirt while others took up the music sticks.

She had the knowledge of what it was like to be Gen and be Killed, and what it was like to be Sime and Kill. She had the memories of her friends and she had the memories of the People. And she remembered what she had done, and what it had meant.

That memory hit her like a solid wall.

"It's all my fault. My friends died because I disobeyed my Sectuib," Tamro gasped between sobs, "I know why there are no channels among the Separated, they murder them before they can learn their own potential. They destroy the only hope for their future survival because they are afraid."

Tamro cried into the young Gen's chest, "Because channels Need more selyn, they would Need more Kills, so they hunt their channels down like animals. They hunted us. They Killed and murdered my people because we were different, and it's my fault that they knew we were different. If I had done what Lia…Sectuib had told me. If I hadn't tried to rescue that boy…"

Illa wrapped her arms around the crying Sime.

"We will speak to the Spirits," Maki said. "We will find out what purpose they have for you."

Tamro stood up shakily, "No. Now I know what to do," she said.

* * * *

The moon was low in the sky and the horizon was starting to get light. Most of the people, and all of the children, had left to find a place to sleep. Maki, Anka and the Elders sat with Tamro and Illa around the remains of the fire.

The glow from the fire lit Tamro's face, matching her strong nager with it's red-gold glow.

"I was a child, now I am an adult" Tamro said. "Your spirits taught me many things, but I am not of the People." She smiled at Maki. "You knew that, didn't you? But even if I am not of the People, I am part of the People. Alone I can do nothing, but with you I can start."

"Start what?" Anka asked.

Tamro looked sad for a moment. "It is my fault my people died. We came to this country hoping that it would be a place for us to find a home. But it is too different for our type of life. The Separated have no Channels, no Healers. They are junct—joined to the Kill—and they can see no other way of life. They destroy their only chance at life every time they murder a new channel, not realizing what it is they do. Because of my mistake, my disobedience, they saw that we were different, like the ones that they murdered in changeover—in the Becoming. Your spirits showed me that there must be a balance, and because of this it up to me to teach them. But I can't do it without you, the People who are wise."

"I can help find others like us," she said. "I can find them, help them learn who and what they are, teach them to be what they should be, the way to survive, for all of us, Simes and Gens."

"Together we can teach the Separated to live as one people."

* * * *

"What happened then?" asked a small voice.

"All stories have a beginning and an end. That is the end of the story of how Tamro came to us. How Tamro became the first Sectuib in this land, and helped the Joined and the Separated to become one people is another story, for another time."

The fire had all but died. The air became chill and a sudden wind whipped red dust into a tall Willy-willy before it danced off into the distance. When the dust had settled the old woman was gone.

VINCENT OF THE GATE

R. K. HAGEMAN

It was as hot as a firing-kiln inside the office, but at least it gave a respite from the glaring Southwestern sun. I approached the grey-haired Gen official seated at the desk. He had a silver star pinned on his blue chambray shirt, and the turquoise ring on his right middle finger was the same color as his eyes. There was a silver medal with some intricate design on a leather thong around his neck.

He looked up and smiled at me, first giving a long look at my retainers. "What can I do for you, Hajene?"

"It's like this. The statistics — the census figures — for this area are, well, unusual, and I've been sent to investigate," I explained, showing my credentials. I wasn't going to come right out and say they'd been murdering their changeover cases, but it sure looked that way to the Nivet Census Bureau.

"Well, you've come to the right place. I'm the sheriff. My name's Robert Bigelow. Unusual, in what way?"

I accepted the chair and the cup of coffee he offered me. I hate coffee, but I'd learned to drink it for diplomatic purposes just like this one. "The statistics for this area, roughly a fifty mile radius, are unbelievable on the face of it. They show that there have been very few changeover cases sent from here to any Sime Center, and no deaths from attacks in First Need. That's impossible."

"I see. It may be improbable, I'll grant you, but it's not impossible. It happens to be more-or-less true."

"More or less?"

"I said it was true, ma'am, I didn't say it was simple. That's pretty much the way things are, all right, but the story's long and complicated."

At least he acknowledged that there was a story. "Fine. Let's hear it."

"I'm just trying to decide whether I'm the one who should be telling you, and whether it is any of your business. After all, young lady, this is not your Territory."

I sighed. His entire field rang with obstinate resistance. "No. But by law, any Sime is a citizen of my Territory, and if something's happening to them, that is my business, Sheriff."

He nodded, acquiescing. "True." He fingered the medal around his neck, and sat there for several minutes, thinking. "However, you will have to wait until this evening. I'm on duty, and there are certain calls that I have to make."

I didn't like this; it was getting fishier by the minute, and his field had gone stony and unreadable. He was hiding something, but I was on his turf; and diplomatic immunity or no, there wasn't a lot I could do. "When and where shall I meet you?"

"Here. At six o'clock?"

"Very well."

"Good." He rose to see me out.

Once outside, I stood there for a few minutes, thinking what to do next. I wanted to follow him if I could; it sounded as though he intended to check the "official story" with someone else before telling it to me. On the other hand, I wanted to do some quiet asking around town.

Stymied for the moment, I decided to get myself something to drink, if nothing else to get the taste of coffee out of my mouth. How Gens could drink the stuff, and enjoy the experience, was beyond me. A building down the street seemed like some kind of public-house, so I went down to see about it. It turned out to be a shabby little café, but it would probably serve the purpose. Outside on the steps, some little girls were playing a game with a small ball and some pebbles. The point of the game seemed to be picking up a certain number of the stones while tossing the ball into the air, and then catching the ball again in the same hand.

I watched them for a few minutes. They seemed happy enough, playing in the sun, with the peaceful innocence of children who have nothing to fear. This far out in the boondocks, distant from a Sime Center, that was a very rare quality in any child, much less three of them. Before long, one of the girls won the game, and looked up at me with an expression of triumph. The sun blazed in reflection from a medallion around her neck; it was the same as the one the sheriff had. "That's a pretty necklace," I said, and waited to see what would happen.

"Oh, this is San Vicente," said one of the others. "We all have one, see?"

"Why is that?"

"He protects us…San Vicente means 'Saint Vincent'," the third one, apparently the oldest, explained as she gave me hers to look at. I turned the medal in my hands, studying the design. It showed a boy squeezing himself through the bars of a wrought-iron gate. Around the edge of the oval, read the caption, San Vicente de la Puerta… I was able to recognize the language as Spanish, but I couldn't read it.

I knew what a "saint" was: some kind of holy man in one of the Ancients' major religions. *Oh, no…Don't tell me this is all mixed up with out-Territory religion!* All I knew about most of the Gens' religion was that it was bad news. Generally, it involved them believing in a God who spoke to them and told them to do things: usually kind and loving things like murdering children in changeover, along with harassing the kid's parents for whatever "sins" had caused their child to "turn Sime" at puberty. The Church of the Purity was the obvious example, but it was far from being the only one. I played dumb and kept asking questions. "What does he protect you from?"

"From changeover," said the same girl, implying that I was more than a little bit dense.

I still didn't know what was going on around here, but the more I heard, the less I liked it. "How does he do that?"

"He helps the brothers to pray for us, and he helps us to be brave like him and not afraid."

This was getting more confusing by the minute. "The brothers? Who are they?"

"They belong to God. They live by themselves in the desert, and they pray many times every day. If you're very, very good, they choose you to come and help them pray and protect us. And no one ever gets Killed here, or turns Sime. Not ever."

Well, at least someone around here was explaining the statistics, even if it was a little kid. "Brothers are boys. What about girls like you?"

"It's the same…there are sisters, too. The brothers make wine, and honey, and medicines. The sisters make yarn and rugs and soap, and different kinds of food. Then they sell it. But their real job is to pray for all of us, and to choose the ones who will join them."

I was becoming more interested in this "brothers" and "sisters" thing. Maybe it made sense to these kids, but it sure didn't to me. And I figured if I stuck with it long enough, I'd hear something about "demons" or "monsters" eventually; that's what out-Territory religious types usually called Simes, in my experience. "How do they choose? What if you don't want to go?"

"But everyone wants to go! It's a great honor, to be chosen as one of them, you see."

"Do they choose grownups, or just kids, or what? Can anybody be one of them?"

To my surprise, two of them dissolved into blushes and giggles. The oldest one blushed a little, too, but answered. "They choose kids because…well, they want them before they're old enough to be married or have sex or anything. To be one of them, you have to be pure, so your body can belong to God." Pre-puberty, I thought: in other words, pre-changeover. She eyed me with curiosity. "Where are you from?"

"A long way north, and a long way east from here. But I work in Capital now. You know where that is? The big city, near the mountains."

"Aren't there brothers and sisters there?"

"Not like that. Just the regular kind— our parents' other kids."

"Then who protects you?"

"From changeover? Nothing. In Sime Territory, it's OK to be a Sime, just like me." I let them see my retainers. "My little brother is one, too, but my older brother's not. He's a Gen. Where I come from, it doesn't matter. All of us are valuable just the way we are." There, give them a little taste of life in a non-prejudiced society. "Do you know anyone who was chosen?"

"Sure," said the youngest girl, the one who had spoken first. "My cousin, Angela, is with the sisters now. They say she's the fastest weaver of them all."

"I bet you miss her, don't you?" Maybe the chosen ones were simply taken away and put to death or something, and this 'brothers and sisters' thing was just what they told the locals.

She looked at me, uncomprehending. "No. Why? I saw her last market day."

Well, now I was at a loss. If the chosen young people had vanished in the night, never to be heard from again, I would have had the missing piece of the puzzle. I had another piece, all right, but it didn't fit any of the gaps. "That's nice," I said to cover my confusion. "I'd better be going, though, I've got work to do. Thanks, girls." I needed time to sort out all this strange stuff. The more I found out, the less sense it all made. Children usually were good sources of information because they don't know what not to tell, so they tell everything. On the other hand, they were easier to deceive. It was entirely possible that the adults in this community knew exactly what was going on, and all this religion business was what they told the kids until they were old enough to get the real story. Whatever. I wasn't going to find out about the missing Simes from this region by standing here in the dust.

The little one, Angela's cousin, stopped me as I turned to go inside, tugging my skirt. "What kind of work?"

The oldest one frowned. "Hush, Lucia. Don't be nosy."

"It's OK," I said. "I'm traveling through areas far from big cities to find out where we should build a Sime Center. Then we can take care of all the Simes who change over, and no one will get hurt."

"But we don't need one of those. There aren't any Simes here."

"I know. But you're lucky; not every town has the brothers and sisters to protect them," I said, going along with their make-believe game. I smiled at them and went into the little café. The air was thick with the aroma of good food. I was still pre-turnover, so it was making me hungry.

"Good afternoon." I said to the woman behind the counter.

"Afternoon." Her field was suspicious and not a little annoyed. "What were you talking about with the kids out there?"

"Oh, just chatting. I noticed how happy they were. Usually in rural areas, kids that age start having a lot of anxiety, either about getting attacked by a berserker or becoming one, themselves."

"Those kids out there ain't never seen a berserker. There ain't none around here."

"So they were telling me. Any idea why?"

"Nope. Don't care, either, so long as they don't bother us. Guess there was one a few years back, though…but it wasn't one from around here. On its second or third Kill, the sheriff said." She looked me up and down, noticing my retainers. "You're one of them channels, aren't you? What you doing in town, anyway?"

"Looking for areas where we should build a Sime Center. I'm with the Census Office, so we check population data and things like that. We want to put one where it will be the most convenient and serve the most people." OK, that was only partly true, but a Gen wouldn't have any way of knowing that.

"Well, this ain't the place. I dunno, maybe it's true what the padre says; the abbey protects us from them. Whatever it is, it works. I moved here twenty years ago, and I've never seen any Simes but just that one that I mentioned. It's a real nice peaceful little place."

"I'm sorry, I don't speak Spanish. What's a padre? And an abi?"

"Padre means 'father.' You know; a priest. And abbey isn't Spanish—it's spelled a-b-b-e-y. It's the religious house out there in the desert about ten miles, with a big wall around it. They been there hundreds of years. It's a double one, which is kinda rare, they say. Half of it for the monks, half for the nuns, and a wall down the middle so they never get together for any hanky-panky." She chuckled. "Anyway, the priest rides into town every Sunday to have church; there's a young priest here in town, but he's kind of an apprentice, I guess. I don't go, but most of the town does. And every market day, some of the monks and nuns come and sell stuff they make. All the cups and dishes in here are from the abbey. Better than the ones you buy in the general store, and cheaper. And why not support them? They're good folks." At some point, she'd stopped being suspicious of me, and got talkative. Probably they don't have new people to talk to very often. "Anyway, what can I get for you? You didn't come in here just to talk, did you?"

"I want something to drink, but not coffee. And I'm hungry, but I can't have anything with meat or animal fat. Can you help me?"

"If you can have beer, I got some of that. And there's lemonade, too. The water around here's pretty good; that's why the place is called Agua Dulce…you know, 'sweet water.' As for something to eat, let's see. I got tortillas that the nuns make, and those have oil, not grease. They say they keep better that way. There's soup, with tomatoes, beans, corn and hot peppers. No grease in that, either. And there's honey. There's always honey. The monks keep bees, you see."

So I had some of the soup, which was amazingly good, with one tortilla and honey, and lemonade. She watched me, and shook her head. "You sure don't eat much. That ain't enough to satisfy little Lucia out there."

"It's fine for me, thanks. I'd better be getting back to work, though. Thanks for lunch and the conversation."

"Don't mention it. Have a nice trip back."

"Oh, yes, one thing I was wondering about. A friend of mine makes a habit of studying different religious beliefs, and I wanted to tell him about this San Vicente that the girls were talking about. Who's he?" One thing I like about out-Territory Gens; they can't tell whether you're lying or not.

"Well, I don't suppose he's a real saint, like the Saint Benedict that the abbey says they follow. I guess he's just a local saint around here. But lots of people in these parts have a Vincent medal. There's a guy named Bernardo Aragón a couple streets over who makes santos — religious figures and carvings. He does some silversmithing, too. Jewelry and stuff. But every year in October, the 21st is Vincent's day, and the only work Señor Aragón does that day is striking Vincent medals. He strikes other medals, too, of other saints, but that day is just for Vincent. They have a special service in the church."

"So, what about him? What did he do?"

"I'm not real sure. Like I said, I'm not a religious person. But I think the story is that he turned Sime and ran away, miles and miles out in the desert, so he wouldn't Kill anybody. That must have been some kind of miracle, if it was true, for a berserk kid to run away from folks instead of toward them. Anyway, the kids believe that if they pray to him, he'll keep them from turning Sime, or else if they do, they'll be brave like him and not Kill anyone. There's a shrine to him out at the abbey, I guess."

"That would make sense. Thanks again." I paid her for the food along with a suitable tip, and went back outside. The two younger girls were still playing on the steps, but they were playing with little cloth dolls now, and the oldest girl was nowhere in sight.

This situation was beginning to remind me of watching my sister knit. She'd be pulling away at the skein of yarn, and it would be nice and straight, then all at once she'd pull it and it would come out in a big messy tangle. Every time I thought I had this thing figured out, it got so tangled I couldn't see where the thread went. Determined not to let it get past me, I headed over to the shop of Bernardo Aragón. Turned out, he didn't speak English, and I didn't speak Spanish. And he certainly didn't know Simelan; no one did, out in the sticks like this. That's why the Bureau sent me, as my English is pretty good.

As I left his place, I realized I'd slipped up. I couldn't zlin the sheriff's nager anywhere. I had meant to follow him, to find out who he was going to talk to before talking to me, but my attention had been focused on the woman running the café, and he'd left without my noticing him. A lot of the buildings were made out of adobe or stone, which shielded fields pretty well, and that made it even harder to keep track of people. And retainers left any channel half-blind in the first place.

I went back to the café, got some more lemonade, and then went to find a shady spot to drink it in, and think. I tried to remember what we'd studied in sociology class about Ancients' religions. If I remembered right, the one that had saints and crosses for important symbols was all about a man who was supposed to be the son of their God (that sounded impossible on the face of it), who had been publicly executed for being a political nuisance. Then he'd come back to life or something, and if people believed in him, their souls would live forever. And saints were supposed to be people who had been executed for following him, or had done miracles, or been especially good at following him, or some crazy thing like that. I could kind of see how a kid in changeover who had chosen Attrition in the desert, rather than Killing someone, might qualify for sainthood to people who believed in this system. But what that had to do with the weird census statistics, or the firm opinion of the locals that nobody here ever changed over, I couldn't figure. It was beginning to look as if I was going to have to settle for the "official story," whatever that would be; I sure wasn't getting anywhere by asking questions. And the idea that this abbey place was "protecting" the area from Simes was just silly. Something else was going on. But I hadn't found anyone so far who zlinned as if they were lying or hiding something. Just the sheriff. That gave me an idea, though. I went back out on the main street, and walked down to the end of town where the church was. You couldn't miss it, as it had a big cross on the roof, and I knew that in Gen towns, the burial ground was always near the church if there was one. I wandered around and looked at the stones, which usually had their own tales to tell.

I couldn't believe it. Not one of the epitaphs indicated that the deceased was a berserker victim. Usually in out-Territory graveyards, a lot of markers said "Killed by demons" or something similar. And once in a while graves of teenage kids with no cause of death given, or else something vague like 'fever,' meant that they had actually died in changeover, but someone was looking the other way and burying them in hallowed ground anyway, Sime or no Sime. Neither of those patterns were visible here. And Agua Dulce was obviously a very old town; some of the grave markers actually looked old enough to be pre-Chaos. I sat down on a bench, feeling like tearing out my hair. Everywhere I turned, I ran into a stone wall. There had to be an answer somewhere, but what was it?

A solid and sweet Gen nager surrounded me, and I looked up. A man stood there, in a long black gown with a white collar. He wore a black leather belt, a wooden cross around his neck, and battered leather sandals. "Can I help you, Hajene?" Aha! He knew a channel when he saw one.

"I wish you could. I must have the answer to one question. What is happening to the kids in changeover?" Suddenly, there were tears running down my face. "I have to find them and take care of them…where are they? Are they here?" I waved my hand at the graves around us.

He said nothing for a long time. "I am Father André, and I am telling you the truth. They are not buried here. Our Lord looks after them, and us." He made a gesture of touching his forehead, his chest, and each shoulder — whatever that meant — and then sat down in the grass facing me. "Be comforted, my child, they are safe. They have come to no harm, and they harm none."

Right, I thought bitterly. A sneaky way of telling me that they're dead. "At least you admit that they exist." I searched for a handkerchief. "But your God is no comfort to me. There are Gen towns where children in changeover are beaten to death, and all in the sweet name of the same God you're talking about."

"No." His field backed up the firmness of his statement. Just being around him was making me wish he were on the Tecton rotation rolls; he would make the kind of Donor that First Order channels would fight over. There was something about his nager that was more beautiful than any transfer I'd ever imagined. He glowed like a warm fire on a cold night. But I was a Third; the only way I'd get a Donor like him would be in my dreams. "That does not happen here. Our God hates murder and violence. And those who commit violence, even in His name, do not know Him, nor He, them."

"I wouldn't know anything about that. But it doesn't matter what crazy fairy tales these people have been taught to believe — it's a statistical fact that thirty-three percent of the children of two Gen parents are Simes. Where do they go when they change over? They don't come across the border in-Territory from this region, and the Sime Center in Tuson doesn't report them, either. And I can't get a straight answer from anyone."

Apparently, I wasn't going to get one from him, either. The young brown-haired priest shook his head. "God loves them, and cares for them, and they are no concern of yours."

"They are my people."

"They are our children. And we do not harm them in any way." He wasn't lying — but what was he doing? "May I pray for you, Hajene?"

"I don't believe in your God."

"I know that, and so does He. Will you allow it?" I shrugged. Then he went into a state that made his nager glow like a clear summer sunrise. He held his hands above my head, without touching me, and spoke softly to himself for a few minutes. "You may stay here as long as you like, out here or in the church. It's cooler inside, and quiet."

"No, but thank you. I have an appointment." It was almost six, the time I had arranged to meet with the sheriff.

When I went back to Sheriff Bigelow's office, he was waiting outside, with his horse and mine saddled and ready to go. "Good, you're early," he said. "Did you have a pleasant afternoon?"

I ground my teeth. Small towns had lively gossip networks, just like Sime Centers did; he probably knew exactly what kind of afternoon I'd had. "It was…interesting."

"Did you find out anything?"

"Nothing that made sense. No one will tell me what I have to know."

"That's because most of them don't know any more than what they told you."

"Father André knows." I was sure of that.

"That's right. Did he tell you?"

"No. Are you going to?"

"No." He slung a canteen of water over his horse's saddle horn. "I'm going to show you. Coming, Hajene?"

Great. This is just like those Gen murder-mysteries where the villain tricks you into following him somewhere, and then shoots you and hides the body. However, I was on to his game, and if it happened to get me any closer to solving this impossible problem, then I had no choice but to play along and keep my wits about me.

We rode for an hour and a half in all but silence, punctuated only by his occasionally pointing out local landmarks and beauty spots. His laconic travelogue was mostly lost on me, however. I prefer cities to arid, rocky wastelands. I noticed that as we rode, we descended gradually between hills until we were riding along in a shallow canyon. After some distance, we forded the stream and began to ascend the other side on a narrow trail that looked barely wide enough to ride on. To my astonishment, I could see the tracks of wheeled carts or wagons in the dirt of the path, and silently acknowledged the skill of anyone deft enough or crazy enough, to drive a wagon on this trail. I followed the sheriff single-file and let my mind wander, tired and confused by everything that had happened this day. Would I ever find out what was going on?

Therefore, I was unprepared for what came next. We rounded a curve in the trail, and found ourselves suddenly looking down into a valley whose chief feature was a large walled fortress with a tower. The trail dipped down at that point, and descended into the valley by a series of switchbacks and curves.

We approached the main gate, and I had a sudden moment of feeling that I'd somehow seen this spot before, but that was impossible. We were expected, for there was a white-haired man in a black robe waiting inside the gate for us. He opened the gate, and with a shock, I perceived what I had been unable to zlin from a distance — this old man was one of the most powerful channels I'd ever seen. "What? What is this?" I blurted.

"Robert tells me you have asked where all the Simes are," the white-haired Sime replied. "I am Abbot Gregory of this house, and I will give you your answer. They are here." He gestured around him to the busy groups of monks doing various tasks and errands. Black-robed like he was, they would look alike to Gens, but not to any Sime; there were both Simes and Gens here working together — renSimes and channels and Donors, unrestricted, without retainers, and free.

I could barely speak, I was so shocked. "What is this place?"

The old man gazed at me with an air of dignified authority, mingled with compassion. "Come inside. We will talk there." Silently, he turned and walked toward the doors.

The sheriff and I followed him, as one of the monks closed the gate behind us. I turned to glance back, and got another shock: this was the gate depicted on the Vincent medals. It was obviously the same gate, and seen from this angle — not from the outside but the inside. That didn't make any sense, but then, nothing had made any sense about this whole business.

Once we went through the heavy ancient doors, it felt good to be inside. It was wonderfully cool, compared to the broiling heat of outdoors.

How they could stand to wear those heavy robes, I had no idea. We walked through the stone hallways, decorated with ornate religious art that I didn't understand. We came around a corner, and were face to face with a niche containing a life-size statue carved out of wood. It was a nearly naked young man, with iron spikes driven into a heavy beam through his wrists, right where a Sime's selyn-transport nerves would be... I recoiled so fast that I backed into the sheriff, wanting to vomit just from thinking about it. "Who's that? What a horrible thing to have a statue of!" Even though the man — whoever he was — must have been a Gen, or an Ancient, it was still revolting to contemplate.

The Abbot murmured softly, "That is our Lord, and yes, it is horrible. That is how he died, and we must never forget." He held one tentacle to his lips. "Please keep silence in the hallways. We will talk in my study."

I had been so unsettled by the sight of that grisly statue that I didn't pay attention to much else that I saw in the halls. Presently we came to a door, which the Abbot opened to reveal a good-sized but sparsely furnished room, with many books, several chairs, and a desk that would have brought a fortune from any antiques dealer. He closed the door. "Now, we may speak freely. Within the abbey and the grounds, we keep a rule of silence. Robert has told me about your reasons for coming. We could think of no other way to solve this problem, except to show you."

I had one question. "Why is this place such a secret? If you've really solved the problem, why not make it known?" As soon as I'd blurted it out, I realized why not.

"Think. What would most of Gen society do if it found out that we were 'harboring dangerous Killer Simes' here? These buildings were designed not to be burned, but someone would find a way to burn them... and us."

"When did this all begin? How?"

Abbot Gregory nodded. "That is what I intend to tell you. You must realize that you are getting a privilege; there are very few outside these walls who know what goes on here. Sheriff Bigelow is one — he found out about us when we brought his daughter here, and we were unable to help her. She died in changeover. Father André is another; he was an orphan who was left at the gate, and he grew up here. He lives in the town, so in case of an emergency changeover, he can serve any Need." He reached over and pulled a cord which rang a small bell outside the door. When a boy appeared at the door, he said, "Bring us tea, please, Pablo."

When the tea, fragrant with mint, arrived, he poured some for me and the sheriff. He leaned back in his chair and began to speak. "The story I will tell you is an oral tradition, from centuries ago. It was long, long ago, in the first years of the Chaos. . ."

* * * *

Vicente Ruiz looked back over his shoulder at the two black-robed figures leading the donkey — Brother Antonio and Brother Diego. Antonio told good stories, his white hair ruffled by the dry wind as he used his strong brown hands for illustration. And Diego always looked as if he were the happiest man in the wide world. He was always kind, even though he didn't talk much; all the same, there seemed to be a light that glowed within him, behind his eyes, somehow.

"Vicente!" His father's voice suddenly got his attention. "What are you doing? You've spilled out half the water!" Then he followed his son's gaze to the two monks walking down the road into the distance. "Vicente, mi hijo, what have I told you? You don't want to go with them — they have nothing there for little boys like you. They do nothing there but sing and pray, and work very hard, all day long."

"Why, Papá?"

"Because that's what it is to be a monk. You promise to give up everything you have and live inside the walls all your life. That's not all — they go to the church seven times every day. You don't even want to get up for Mass once a week on Sundays! Forget about them, Vicente. They live a different life, in a different world."

He couldn't understand this. Was his father saying bad things about such good people as Antonio and Diego? "But they're so good to me, Papá."

"Oh, yes, they are, that's true. They are very good and holy men. But you will have a better life than that, hijo. You will come into the business with me and your uncle Gilberto, and you will find a pretty muchacha, no? You're old enough to start thinking of that, now."

"Yes, Papá." He knew that tone; better to let it drop for now. He finished filling up his jugs with water, and they turned and walked out of the village square toward home. Even with all the terrible things that were happening nowadays, Diego looked peaceful. Vicente wanted to know why.

Late that night, Vicente was awakened by pounding on the door. Sitting up, he could hear dogs baying and men's voices. Then his father's voice said, " Sí, sí, I'm coming." The door closed then, and the howls and voices faded away into the night. He tried to go back to sleep but could not. Finally, he crept down the steep stairs. "Mamá? ¿Qué pasa?"

"Ah, Vicente. Did that frighten you? It's all right, we're safe here. They are looking for Rosalba Chavez." Señora Ruiz's eyes were red from weeping. "She Killed her sister and ran away before anyone could stop her. And she loved Lorena so…how could this happen? Madre de Diós…"

Fear clutched at his vitals. "Could she hurt Papá?"

"Probably not. When these poor children go mad this way, they usually only Kill one person, and even then it is a brother, a sister, a cousin, a friend...not the adults. But now, she has become something terrible in her madness — she can see in the dark, so it will be hard for them to catch her. Come here, and we will pray together that Papá and the other men will find her soon and come back safely." She beckoned Vicente to her side, and they knelt together before the little retablo in the corner. When they finished, she sat back on her heels for a moment before getting up. "There, now we shall not worry anymore," she said firmly. "We have put everything into the hands of the good God, who watches us all."

When he got up the next morning, he heard clearly his father's deep voice, and he ran downstairs. His parents and Uncle Gilberto were there around the kitchen table, along with several other men of the village. The smell of fresh warm tortillas filled the air. All the men had tired eyes; clearly they'd been out all night. "¡Papá!" cried Vicente, and flung himself into his father's arms. "I was so afraid..."

"Ah, Vicente, you're a good boy. I am well, we are all well, and poor Rosalba...she will harm no one else." He continued with what he'd been saying. "We must have some kind of system, so this doesn't happen again. If another one of the young ones becomes loco, we need to be able to warn the village sooner. What shall we do?"

"We could send someone to the church, to ring the bell, perhaps," said Señor Moreno, thoughtfully. "But if the mad one were out already, that person would be in terrible danger."

"Perhaps not," replied Uncle Gilberto. "So far, the crazy ones have only attacked other young people. They ignore us adults, and an old man who can still run swiftly would probably be safe. But, when it happens, it happens so suddenly. How can we tell everyone whose house it is, whose child it is?"

"We could give each house a special code, for when we ring the bell," said Vicente.

"That's very clever, hijo." Vicente's father smiled wearily. "It might work. Let me go and talk to the sexton about it. He might know a way to make it easy."

Before long, the town of Agua Dulce had developed a system just like Vicente had suggested. Each house had its own signal. A few months after Rosalba Chavez had gone mad and Killed her sister Lorena, the system was put to the test. Hoofbeats were heard galloping down the street, and soon thereafter the church bell rang out — four rings, followed by three rings. It was the Aragón house, and men turned out into the village square to deal with the problem. However, for once, the precautions were unnecessary. Pedro Aragón had been in the process of going berserk, and then had gone into convulsions and died. The priest, old Father Eduardo, bent and examined young Pedro.

"Pobrecito," he said, his voice filled with compassion. "He did not ask for this. In the morning, bring him, and we will prepare him for his burial."

"In consecrated ground, Father? Surely not, for he is one of los hijos diabólicos, the devil children," said Rosita, the Aragóns' neighbor.

"Now, Señora Rosita, shame on you. You know that there is only one devil, and he is Satan himself, not poor Pedro Aragón, who did not wish harm to anyone. He has harmed no one, nor committed any mortal sin that I can see, and so he may be buried as a good Christian youth who has received his First Communion, which he did only last spring. He has become ill, and died, and that is all." The priest's tone was firm, forestalling any argument.

The old woman would not be put off so easily. "But, Father Eduardo, do you know of any illness that causes that?" She indicated young Pedro's arms with the long blistered areas on them.

"No, I do not. Yet he has recently confessed and been absolved, and he has committed no sin."

Over the next several months, three more young people suffered from the strange feverish madness. Once, when he saw Father Eduardo in the street, Vicente had the courage to approach the tall priest and ask a question. "May I ask something, Father?"

"Certainly, Vicente." Eduardo knelt down so that he could be at eye level with the boy.

"Do…uh, do the ones who go mad know that it's going to happen? Or are they surprised, too, like us?"

"No one knows, Vicente. No one has ever been able to speak to them; when they go mad, they seem to become both blind and deaf. Why do you ask, my child?"

"I don't know. But I have been wondering about it. What does it feel like, to them, I mean?"

The old priest shrugged, palms upward. "No one knows. But I believe it must be very frightening for them, as for us. I don't think that they understand what is happening to them."

"I wish that we could do something to stop it all."

"Ask God, Vicente, ask God. He is the only one who can help us now." What he knew, but did not tell the boy, was that the problem wasn't only here in Agua Dulce and the surrounding areas. The news was spreading that the same terrible thing was overtaking young people in town after town, in the cities and on the farms.

"Yes, Father. I will." That night, as Vicente knelt beside his bed and went through the prayers with his wooden beads in his fingers, he added an extra thought — an intention in the direction of nuestra Señora, la Virgen de Guadalupe. She, blessed Mother, would not want to see such a dreadful thing happen to her own Son, so she could understand the grief and suffering of these mothers who were losing their own children, either as the loco ones or their victims. Perhaps she could stop this terrible thing, so no more young people would be lost this way.

* * * *

One autumn night, the howling of a coyote awakened Vicente. He opened his eyes in a cold sweat; had he awakened from a nightmare? No. He moved his head, and realized all at once that he was going to be sick. That's what the nightjar was for, among other things, and he grabbed it just in time. His neck ached, and he felt strange all over. He huddled under the rough woolen blanket on his wooden bed and half-dozed, feeling altogether miserable.

Sometime later, he didn't know how long, he woke abruptly and flung off the blanket. It was making his arms sore just to touch it. Then he knew. "Madre de Diós, it's happening to me," he said aloud, his heart racing with fright. He had seen José Salazar, and he'd heard about Rosalba Chavez and Pedro Aragón — he knew what was going to happen now. It was inevitable. And now he thought he understood why…there seemed to be a brilliant glow coming from upstairs, from Lupe's bedroom down through the ceiling. *It's so beautiful, I want it, I Need it… is that why they Kill them? Because they are beautiful beyond reason?*

He stopped himself, suddenly. "No. No one is going to shoot me like Rosalba or José. And I will not Kill Lupe. She's getting married in the fall, and Papá must have a grandson from them, as there are no sons but only me, and I'm dying…" What should he do? What could he do? Then he realized, all in a flash — Brother Antonio knew everything. He would know what to do, and he could explain it to Vicente, just like he always did. Father Eduardo was kind, but white-haired Brother Antonio, old as the trees, was wise. Vicente grabbed up his rosary, tucked it into his pocket, and slipped silently out of the window.

As he crept down the street, barefooted and soundless, he found that not only Lupe's room glowed with that delicious sparkling light; other houses had glowing people in them, too. He passed the house of his grandparents: no glowing there, nor at the schoolmaster's house — of course not! There were no young people there. So that's it, Vicente thought, glad of the knowledge, but wishing he'd found another way to learn it. Other children turn into starlight, and the crazy ones Kill them for it. And grownups don't do either; they only mourn us all. 'Holy Mary, Mother of God, pray for us sinners, now and in the hour of our death,' young Vicente repeated silently as he moved past house after house, fighting off the sudden attacks of cramps that knotted his insides. I want that light, I Need that light... no. Go to Brother Antonio. He will help me, I know he will.

He was nearly out of the town, when a dog barked and someone looked outside. He tried to duck behind a wagon, but it was too late. Having no choice, he began to run. That was a bad idea — it gave him away at once. Lights came on, bright to others' eyes, but pale flickers compared to the ever-more-brilliant glow coming from some of the houses where Vicente's friends and cousins and playmates lay asleep. "Stop him! Stop him! It's the Ruiz boy, gone mad!"

"No! No!" he shouted, "I won't hurt anyone!" But he gave that up. He could either run, or yell, but not both at once. So he ran, knowing that he was running into the deepest darkness in the world, away from the beautiful light that his sleeping, innocent sister gave off, and little brown-haired Alana with the laughing eyes — he knew which house was hers — and Roberto, and Manolito...no. If he kept thinking about them, he would turn back and his promise to God and the Blessed Virgin would be all undone. He ran on, on, into the darkness, turning his back on the light. Ahead of him, nothing glowed except for the remnant of a child's trust that Brother Antonio's wisdom would save him. *I will not Kill anyone.*

He could hear them coming now, dogs baying on his trail, and voices shouting. "Holy Mary, Mother of God," Vicente began again, this time aloud; no reason to keep quiet now. What strength kept him running, he did not know. Behind him, far back, one of his pursuers had that same glorious light — he could turn back, hide, spring upon him like a puma, and have the light all to himself. "Jesus Christ, son of God, have mercy on me, a sinner; help me, I'm losing. I can't run away from that any longer, I've got to have it...is that a sin?" Cramps assaulted him, and he fell down, retching. He had to get up, had to keep running. If he lay there, the dogs would reach him. On foot, he could outrun them all. He could outrun the world.

His feet pounded the dirt road as he flew. With a burst of energy, a new idea came to his mind. Even if Brother Antonio couldn't help him, the monastery was a safe haven. If someone claimed sanctuary there, then no one could come in and take him away, not for any reason. He knew, instinctively, that such a sanctuary would be his death. *But I want to be like Pedro Aragón who didn't Kill anybody. I will not Kill my friend, not even to save my own life.* "Dear God, help me..." Still running, he began to recite the rosary prayers, wondering if he could actually say fifty Aves before he reached the gates. The road wound around the hill now, where the footing was the most treacherous. However, it would start downward soon, into the valley where the abbey nestled in the sandstone hills like a piece of turquoise cupped in an old woman's brown and leathery palm. Once the road headed downward, he would be in greater danger as the dogs and men would be gaining on him, and he would soon be within rifle range.

At the abbey gate, the doorkeeper heard the commotion from the hills. He rang a bell that hung by his side, and squinted with his age-dimmed eyes into the night, trying to figure out what was going on. In a moment, another monk, young James, appeared out of the gloom with a torch. "What's happening, Brother?"

"Don't you hear it? Dogs baying, men shouting?"

James listened. "Ah, yes. I hear it now. I suppose the villagers are after some sort of criminal; perhaps he stole a sheep."

"No, Brother James, I think that the one they're chasing is coming here. Go and waken the Abbot. He should know what is happening."

By the time that Abbot Tomás arrived, it was obvious that the object of the villagers' pursuit was headed for the abbey gates. They could hear his voice, ragged and hoarse, whimpering "Jesus Christ, Son of God, have mercy on me, a sinner…" even as he fell down in the path fifty yards away. With the dogs practically at his heels, he lurched to his feet and with a superhuman effort flung his slim body at the bars of the abbey gate and squeezed through them. "Brother Antonio, Brother Antonio," he murmured. "Help me, please…"

Antonio made his way to the youth who was collapsed in a shudder-ing heap on the ground, dirty, and with bleeding hands and feet. "Here I am — why, it's young Vicente!" he exclaimed in shock. "What are you doing here, child?"

"I told you, did I not? I would come here, someday, and stay as long as I lived?" He showed them his arms, the telltale striations showing in the lamplight. "Father Abbot, there is no one here that I can harm. I ask sanctuary."

* * * *

"What happened?" It took me several moments to come back to the here-and-now; the old man's story was so vivid that I was reliving my own changeover at the same time as I was hearing about Vicente's.

The Abbot sighed heavily. "He was granted sanctuary, and locked himself into a cell, to wait for the end. Antonio and Diego kept vigil with him, outside the door of the cell. They prayed the rosary with him, and gave him last rites, and sang to him until he died."

I shuddered. These people, supposedly so kind, had let him die of Attrition under their very noses. "They could have at least done something to make it easier for the poor kid."

Gregory replied. "There was little they could do for him, all the monks being adults, and not Gens. We believe that it is wrong to take the life of any living human being, even when there are some who would call it mercy. You must admit that taking his life cannot be a murder without the walls and a mercy within them," he chided gently. "You can't have it both ways. In any case, he received another benefit that he asked, as well. Abbot Tomás granted his desire to take the vows of a postulant of our order. Normally, we would not accept the vows of a dying man, but Vicente confessed that he had wished to join us for some time although he had deferred to his father's wishes. He was buried here within the abbey walls, and was at once hailed as a hero for sacrificing his own life to protect the lives of others. Over the centuries, Vicente has become revered as a local saint, of which you are, no doubt, aware."

"Then what happened?"

"The villagers were, of course, grieved and saddened. Some time went by before any more changeovers occurred; Agua Dulce has always been a small town and it didn't happen as often as it might have in more populous areas. It was nearly a year before the next changeover happened; the boy, Manuel, chose Vicente's way and ran here. But, though no one knew it, the situation had changed. One of the novices, a youth named Joseph, had been left with the abbey some years before as an orphan, and he had recently begun his novitiate."

"Let me guess," I said. "He'd Established."

"Indeed. Manuel was unaware of Joseph's existence until he had already taken refuge behind the walls and gate. Then, with no warning, he attacked Joseph, who had little idea of what was happening; he'd grown up inside the abbey since infancy, had little experience with the outside world, and had never seen a Sime Kill. His chief concern was to help Manuel, and both of them survived. Manuel Salazar was the first Sime brother of this order. He was definitely not the last."

I thought back to what I had heard during the day. "So when you go to the kids' houses, and ask them to come, it's because they're in Stage One of changeover."

Abbot Gregory nodded. "Yes. Or, because they've begun producing selyn in extraordinary quantity, and are required here to help take care of the Simes. Our prior, Father Paul, walks through the village every day, blessing all that he meets. The eager children run to be blessed by him, believing that it will keep them safe from changeover. It does not keep them from changeover — but it does, indeed, keep them safe. Father Paul is what you call a channel, as am I…the sleeves of a monk's habit can conceal many things, especially tentacles. As he signs the cross on each child's forehead, he zlins them for incipient changeover."

I tried to absorb this, feeling as though I'd wandered onto another planet when I wasn't looking. "But, how…how do you handle…do you serve everyone, or what?"

"We handle each one as he Needs. Some have partners; others, who have found no partner or are unstable for some reason, are looked after by me or by Father Paul. Look here," he said, opening the large book on its stand beside the desk, near the end. He used a tentacle to indicate the words: *And my God will meet all your needs according to his glorious riches in Christ Jesus.* "We believe that when God promised to meet all our needs, he meant exactly that: all. He is infinite, omniscient, and omnipotent, and there is no condition or circumstance for which the Almighty has not made provision in His grace. He takes into account every situation produced by the actions of His creatures. The Sime mutation was a surprise to mankind, but God supplied a way to cope with it. Knowing this, we pray for each new Sime that he — or she, among our sisters — shall be provided for in the way which is best for that person. And I will have you to know, that in the centuries that we have done this, there have been no Kills within these walls. Not one."

"That's impossible."

"In your world, yes. Here, no. With God, nothing is impossible." Gregory met my eyes resolutely. "I ask you, what are you going to do with what you now know?"

I shook my head, confused. "I don't know. I had imagined all kinds of terrible things going on here, but this is incredible — if I hadn't seen it with my own eyes, I wouldn't believe it. Are you the only ones?"

"Who knows? We have no communication with any other religious houses, and the world lost touch with Rome over a thousand years ago. I would hope that others have found the same path, or a similar one; I can think of no other way to reconcile what we believe with the situation in which the world now lives."

"One thing. I know what you have told me in this office, but I have to observe for myself. I must monitor someone's transfer." That was the only way I knew of to make sure they weren't going to be branded as Distect — it didn't matter whether they'd ever heard of the Distect or not.

Gregory frowned, and his disquiet rippled the ambient. "This is a solely male community. To have a woman present…you realize we regard the transfer as a sacrament, a holy rite, even though it was not instituted by Our Lord. I can take you, or Robert can, to the convent, and you may observe one of the sisters' transfers. But not ours."

He had a point, though out-Territory attitudes toward sex always mystified in-Territorials. It was perfectly necessary for psychological and physical health, and doubly so for channels. Their celibacy was dooming them all to a lifespan more like Gens' than like any Tecton Simes, but after all this time of living that way, this austere old Sime was not about to take advice from me on it. "I have another question, if I may…though it isn't really on this issue."

"Ask, and I will answer if I can."

"What is that horrible statue all about? The male Gen with spikes through his…" I couldn't even say it without feeling sick.

"Ah. He is no Gen; he is an Ancient, the most Ancient of all. In his physical body, he was God become human, to share in our humanity."

"Why would he…" I started to ask, and then decided that I didn't really want to know. I didn't have time to get tangled up in Gen religions or Ancient ones, either, and that answer sounded like it would take a week, or maybe a lifetime, for me to understand. I still didn't know why the poor man had been executed in such a vicious way, but I wasn't going to ask: that answer probably wouldn't make sense, either. "Never mind."

"In that case, I have a question for you. With one word in the wrong ears, you can destroy everything we have here, everything God has done for these people; everything that young Vicente died for. Is that what you intend to do?"

He was right; that was the question, no doubt about it. What in the flaming shen was I going to report? I couldn't lie, obviously. And I couldn't stonewall; I had to report something. I said as much to Abbot Gregory.

He waved a tentacle in a cautionary gesture. "I remind you, madam, we are outside the borders of Nivet Territory, and Tecton law does not apply here."

"That's not the point. The government of your own territory is a signatory to the treaty that states any Sime out-Territory without retainers may be shot on sight, as presenting a public menace."

"Do I look — or zlin — like a public menace?"

No, he didn't. But that didn't help.

* * * *

The next day, having done what I came for, I left. I still didn't know what I was going to put in my report when I got back to Capital, but at least I had the next few days to try to figure it out, or find a loophole, or something. I told the Abbot, and the Mother Superior, that I'd do my best not to let them get wiped out by the retainer laws, but I couldn't promise anything. The sun was shining brightly, as I rode north to the nearest train station, but I didn't notice. I was too busy thinking.

Those people had been doing their thing, religious fanatics or not, for a long, long time. That monastery was far older than Zeor; they'd done no harm, and a lot of good, for the last several centuries. What I had zlinned was a lot of healthy, peaceful, happy people. Whose business was it to tell them they had to disband? I had gone down there, expecting to unearth a lot of murders; and there hadn't been a single one. Every single Sime for miles around had been taken in, and provided with selyn for a lifetime. How could I destroy any community with a success rate like that? On the other hand, the retainer laws were specific in the extreme. All it would take would be for one of those monastics to lose his or her partner, or be unable to reach a priest, and attack one of the townspeople in desperation…no matter how careful they were accidents do happen.

While waiting for the next train eastbound for Capital, I saw *The Tecton Star* on the newsstand, with a sensational headline: "Zeor Sectuib Accepted By Out-T Med School." I bought a copy and stood reading it; I kept reading even after I'd boarded the train. Apparently Digen Farris's dorm room would be officially considered Sime Territory, so he wouldn't be in violation of the retainer laws.

That just might work! What would it take to declare Agua Dulce part of this Territory?

* * * *

Philippians 4:19
Paraphrased from C.S. Lewis,
Letters to Malcolm: Chiefly on Prayer.

Author's note: I owe a considerable debt to Dame Edith Pargeter, OBE. All these characters are fictitious and of my own creation, but if not for her series of twenty novels, *The Chronicles of Brother Cadfael*, (written under the pen name Ellis Peters) it would never have occurred to me to hide Simes in a cloistered monastery, or that Benedictine robes can conceal quite a number of things, including tentacles. The actual monastery which inspired my fictional one is the Monastery of Christ in the Desert, Abiquiu, NM (www.christdesert.org). A newspaper feature in the *Rocky Mountain News* about their community gave me the idea for Vincent's story.

DESTINY

N. EILEEN O'NEILL

Every morning, Pramod went to the old slave that sat in a corner all day, and most of the night, spinning thread and wearing a filthy shift of no particular color or shape. But always, the slave just looked at him with filmy eyes and shook its head to indicate that it was still unable to tell Pramod his destiny.

Would he be a slave, or a master like his parents? It was a question every child asked with increasing frequency as childhood neared its end.

He yearned for the day he would be accepted into the ranks of the masters, and could begin to learn the ways of magic. A child could command a slave to obey, and the slave usually would, out of fear of the child's parents. But when a master fully versed in the ways of magic gave the order, the slave could no more disobey than it could walk on water. If it showed defiance it would be struck down by a force that could not be seen by the eye but could give slaves pain or even death—the force of magic.

But on that morning, Pramod did not need to go to the old slave. When he woke, his fingers found the aching welts that ran from his elbow to his wrist, six on each arm. His question was finally answered, though not happily. He would be a slave.

Soon he would have great strength and would need little sleep or food. He would be able to see in the dark and perceive invisible forces. But these things were of little comfort, because they were all given to him so that he might better serve his masters. He would even receive extra limbs, to help him perform the toil that would be his lot until he died. He allowed a tear to run down his cheek, knowing that soon, even his emotions would not be his own to command. It was said that slaves felt only what their magic-wielding masters desired them to feel.

Would he be permitted to see his father one final time? Pramod was not sure whether or not he hoped this would be so, but he knew that his wishes were of no significance. He rose and looked around, bidding a silent farewell to his beloved home immaculately maintained by slaves who always managed to leave the room before they were seen. From this day, he would no longer live as a son in the house of his parents. They would mourn him as dead, and he would be sold far away, so that his mother would not have to see the slave with her child's face and be reminded.

Pramod knew that he must go to the overseer now, and follow whatever orders he was given. He took nothing with him, as slaves owned no possessions. He would receive nothing for his labors but coarse unadorned clothing, a few scraps of food—and life itself.

For on the night of each full moon, every slave was embraced by a master, whose magical touch bestowed the gift of continued life. And any slave who was denied admittance to this ceremony was soon observed to go mad, and then to die a lingering and agonizing death.

But there would be no life for Pramod, not even as a slave. When the time came, he was taken to a room where a master waited to give life to the new slave for the first time. As that moment neared, however, the overseer could sense that this was one of the dangerous ones. The ones possessed, not just by one demon hungry for life, but by two. If any but the strongest master tried to give life to a slave with two demons, that master could die. And the wrath of the other masters would be great and would fall upon all the slaves.

And so, though its heart was made heavy by the knowledge of what it must do, the overseer motioned for the master to step away. The master, who had once had a son named Pramod, left the room as the overseer pulled the knife from its belt.

THREE MILESTONES IN THE FOUNDING OF CORDONA TERRITORY

MARY LOU MENDUM

Introduction: In my novel-length S~G fan fiction *A Test Of Courage*, (http://simegen.com/sgfandom/rimonslibrary/cz/cz18/courage01.html) I introduced the warlike South American Sime Territory of Cordona. At the time of the story, 125 years after Unity, the Simes of Cordona live and think much like the juncts of the early Sime Territories of the northern continent, before the Pen system was formalized. They form bands of Simes that survive by raiding the surrounding Gen Territories, Amazon and Zillia, for selyn and supplies. The only functional difference between Cordonans and Freeband Raiders is that the Cordonans are technically non-junct: they use channels to avoid Killing. However, since their rocky mountain home can't support agriculture, Cordonan bands must capture, strip, and release new Gen victims each month. The only Gens who live with the bands are the Companions, who are viewed as the band's most prized possessions rather than as members, and what few children are born are fostered out among the Gen villages on which they prey.

In a twist of irony, Cordona was founded by Householders just before Unity. How and why Householders would adopt a raiding lifestyle makes an interesting story.

NEW ORTLAND, NORWEST TERRITORY, SIX MONTHS BEFORE UNITY

Siskyu ambrov Shaeldor hissed as her swollen arms started itching again. The temptation to scratch was almost irresistible, but she knew she must not, or she would injure the developing tentacles underneath. The itch did provide some distraction from the yawning emptiness that was growing inside her, however. She knew it was "just" Need, but changeover training was no preparation for the reality.

Cool Gen hands reached to rest on the itching skin, soothing both discomforts. "You're doing fine," Riftan encouraged her. He was portly despite being only ten years older than Siskyu, and the hair on the top of his head was starting to thin. Siskyu felt lucky to have him, even so.

Riftan had actually come to New Ortland only the week before, as the spare Companion to a channel who was on her way to set up a trading post further north. With Siskyu's premonitions of changeover growing ever more acute, and no sign of the Companion who was supposed to have come to take care of her, Grandfather had persuaded Riftan to stay and serve her First Transfer instead.

Beyond the Gen's comforting bulk, Siskyu could feel encouragement echoing back to her from her grandfather, and from the other Simes and Gens who were gathered in the common room of Shaeldor's New Ortland compound to witness her elevation to adulthood. Most of them were Householders, Shaeldor sailors who had chosen to spend some time away from the ocean, but who couldn't bear to leave it behind entirely. Some were retired, some were raising families, and a few were recovering from injuries, for the sea could be harsh and unforgiving and those who trusted to her mercy were sometimes betrayed.

Not all the observers were Householders, however. There were no native Householdings in Norwest Territory and only a few dozen adults in Shaeldor's trading outpost, so of necessity they had a great deal more interaction with the local juncts than normal. Some had even become friends of sorts.

Captain Givryn of the *Skyver's Hope* had a place of honor, his first mate Ewart grinning behind him. They didn't appear too upset at the thought of witnessing "perversion." Come of think of it, they'd probably cadge many a free drink by telling the lurid story of how Riftan didn't die like a proper Gen.

Siskyu didn't mind. Captain Givryn had always had a kind word or a trinket for her, since the day three years ago that he had seen her arrive in New Ortland, a quiet child still stunned from the loss of her parents to plague. If she could repay his kindness with free drinks, it was fine with her.

"It won't be much longer now, Siskyu," her grandfather assured her, zlinning her deeply. "Remember, you mustn't rush breakout. Wait until I tell you to start trying."

Siskyu nodded. She knew the drill as well as any well-trained child. Before she could answer, however, a commotion outside caught her grandfather's attention, followed by the clang of the gate bell. Entrusting her to Riftan's care, he went off to greet the new arrivals.

Through a window, Siskyu caught a glimpse of a dozen lathered horses being led into the courtyard and a flash of grey and turquoise livery. The new arrivals were not ambrov Shaeldor, then. The horses were fast, well-trained animals, and tired and road-stained as the visitors were, there was a well-practiced air of menace about them. Even without the turquoise and grey livery, Siskyu would have known them for Dar guards.

There was no reason why Householders visiting New Ortland shouldn't stay at the Shaeldor-run safe house, of course. That was its purpose: to provide a sanctuary in a town that lacked a resident House-holding. New Ortland was the busiest port in Norwest Territory and despite the drought of the past few years, there were enough people passing through that Grandfather Elman never complained of entran.

Which begged the question of what such an expensive, elite military force was doing so far from their home in Nivet Territory. There seemed to be an ominous darkness hovering around them, which fascinated Siskyu until Riftan placed himself firmly between them, and the darkness disappeared.

"I'm zlinning," she realized, and felt the Companion's indulgent amusement.

She could feel the breakout contractions gathering in increasingly strong waves that rippled down her arms. The sense of urgency was reinforced by the anticipation of the guests, as they rearranged themselves for the best view. Wistra hurried in from the kitchen, where she had been preparing a feast for the guests, drying her hands on her apron. She exchanged a quick word with Paigan, who ran the chandlery down the street, then reflexively checked to make sure that her twins, Broza and Almid, were not getting into mischief. Even Captain Givryn paused in the story he was recounting to watch.

Soon, Siskyu was holding tight to Riftan's arms with bruising strength, straining to extend her new tentacles. She chuckled in triumph for a breathless moment as they finally burst free, then the yawning emptiness of First Need reached to claim her. Driven by instinct, she attacked Riftan, no longer really aware of him as a separate being. He was life, and she reached to take him in.

When she opened her eyes, Riftan's face swam before them, a soft, tender smile curving his lips as he looked at her. He would continue on his journey as soon as her own Companion arrived. Even if they never met again, however, she knew that his nager would always define the essence of Gen to her, just as she would become part of the way he defined Simeness.

Then her grandfather was there, a proud grin almost splitting his weathered face in two. There were new faces scattered among the guests, too: the newly arrived Dar were mingling with the other guests. She let go of Riftan and grinned back at her grandfather, then sobered as he pulled a ring from his pocket.

In a clear voice, she offered to her grandfather and to the assembled Householders her provisional pledge to Shaeldor. Her final commitment to House and Sectuib would have to wait until she could travel back to Shaeldor for training, but she didn't think even that would mean more to her than seeing the pride on her grandfather's face, and better yet, feeling it through her new senses.

Later, she was to remember that timeless interval as the last truly happy, innocent moment of her childhood.

As her grandfather placed the ring on her finger, a tsunami of pain and terror engulfed her, part of her but somehow separate. Then the pain abruptly disappeared, leaving a hole in the universe where it had been that was somehow even worse. Someone was screaming, and she couldn't tell if it was her or someone else.

Then she was herself again, restricted to the five senses she had known since birth. The information they were giving her, however, was no less horrifying. Captain Givryn was lying in a boneless heap on the floor, his limbs splaying at odd angles and a pool of blood collecting underneath him. Across his body was Ewart's, face down. Or rather, it should have been face down, but wasn't: His neck had been twisted until his sightless eyes stared up at Siskyu accusingly.

Their murderer stood over them with every appearance of calm, despite the fresh blood that stained her train-worn Dar livery. Her dispassionate gaze swept the room, meeting the eyes of the assembled guests. Her weather-beaten features looked incapable of smiling, and the implacable glint in her eyes made Siskyu want to run and hide.

The young channel looked around for an escape route, and discovered that Captain Givryn's death had been no accident. Every non-Householder who had come to celebrate her changeover was dead, from Captain Givryn and his mate to Paigan the chandlerer and Borvan the longshoreman.

Siskyu was still trying to comprehend the situation when the Dar woman spoke, in a harsh voice that combined grief and iron-clad determination.

"Your pardon, Naztehrai, for this grievous breech of Shaeldor's hospitality. We bring urgent news that cannot be allowed to reach junct ears."

Siskyu's grandfather was staring around at the carnage in shock. "You couldn't have waited until our guests left?" he asked plaintively. "You had to murder them instead?"

"We could not, and we did," the Dar said firmly. She paused, as if to determine whether anyone else was bold enough to challenge her, but with dead bodies and Dar fighters scattered about the hall, no one was moved to complain.

"Naztehrai, I am Vrappa ambrov Dar," she said, when it was clear no one else would object. "My team and I were hired to guard Gens being shipped to New Ortland from the main Genfarm at Yarrow. We find ourselves unexpectedly at liberty, however, because there are no adult Gens left to ship."

A babble of voices broke out, and Vrappa impatiently signaled for silence. "I tell you, we managed a thorough inspection. The big Genfarm at Yarrow can't have more than a half dozen adult Gens in stock, and what staff remain are fighting to claim them. The last of the breeders were shipped off over the past few weeks."

"Surely you are mistaken, Naztehr Vrappa," her grandfather protested. "The farms at Bink's Point and Gorget will make up the shortfall."

"How?" the harsh voice demanded bluntly. "They couldn't support the whole of Norwest even if they were at full capacity. And…well, tell him, Asaka."

"Vrappa is correct, Hajene Elman," a male voice said apologetically from across the room. His respectful tone contrasted oddly with the limp body of Renna the laundress that lay crumpled at his feet. He was as formidable as his leader, with almost as much bulk on him as a Gen would have, and all of it muscle. "I managed to get a look at the records. Last week, a dozen Gens were shipped to Gorget. Not to the farm, as new breeding stock, but to the Pen."

"To the Pen?" her grandfather asked. "But that means…"

"That the entire Pen system of Norwest Territory has collapsed." Vrappa's harsh voice was grim. "Half of the staff at Yarrow have already run for Nivet, and the rest will be doing so as soon as they Kill the last few Gens."

"It's Zelerod's Doom," Siskyu said in a small voice, breaking the ominous silence. She had learned about the famous junct mathematician in her history classes back at Shaeldor, before her younger brother and her parents had died and Sectuib had sent her to stay with grandfather in New Ortland. Back then, she had viewed Zelerod's predictions as a justification for the Householdings, something that might persuade the juncts to see reason and forsake the Kill while there was still time. She had never let herself dwell on the consequences if they did not.

"You're right, youngster," Asaka said grimly. "It is Zelerod's Doom. Not the localized disasters that happen from time to time when winter storms block the roads and delay Gen shipments, but the real thing."

"There are no storms blocking the roads, this time," Vrappa's harsh voice continued. "In a week or so, when the government has quietly disappeared and people learn that no more Gens are coming, they will go hunting for Kills. All of them. The Gen Army is good, but they're trained and equipped to stop small bands of Raiders. They won't last long against an entire Territory of desperate juncts and when their first desperate Need is quenched, the raiders will look for a secure base."

"Nivet," Riftan named the obvious choice, and Siskyu felt a shiver go down her spine. Nivet was Shaeldor and home, the home she hadn't seen in far too long. "We must go home and warn them," he continued, echoing Siskyu's thoughts.

"It's too late for that," Asaka said, with a forcefulness unusual in a renSime contradicting a Companion. "The drought has been worse further south, and Nivet's Pens are strained to the limit and beyond. There isn't enough selyn to drive off a whole Territory's worth of berserkers. Nivet's Pens will collapse before the end of summer, and its junct Simes will scour the continent until it becomes one vast wasteland."

"Shaeldor and every other Householding on the continent are doomed," Vrappa stated coldly. "They will be destroyed before winter can close the roads. Our Naztehrai will give a good account of themselves, I'm sure, but even Dar can't fight off a whole continent's worth of juncts."

"So it's all been for nothing," Grandfather said heavily, burying his face in his hands and tentacles. "Five hundred years of hope, pain and sacrifice, building towards a future that isn't fated to be."

"Not as we imagined it, certainly," Vrappa said, with a kind of brutal compassion. "But perhaps we can still salvage something from the ruins. How many of your Naztehrai here are sailors?"

Elman blinked at the apparent change of subject. "Perhaps a dozen have worked ships on voyages, although most have retired to the shore. Ship handling is a job for the young. We elders take care of business."

"Is that enough, with the assistance of the rest of us, to sail a ship south?"

"It might be," Elman said, shaking his head, "but Shaeldor has no ships due into New Ortland for the next ten days."

"We can't wait that long," Asaka said. "The news that the Pens are empty will circulate within a day or two. At that point, the only available Gens will be here."

None of the ambrov Shaeldor had thought that their personal end would come quite so soon. Siskyu could feel them absorbing the knowledge, the Simes instinctively moving closer to the Gens, even though they knew full well that no protection they could offer was adequate.

"We'll have to use the shipping that's available," Asaka said grimly. "What about that two-master I saw in the harbor?"

"The *Skyver's Hope?*" Her grandfather shook his head, his eyes resting on the limp carrion at Vrappa's feet. "The ship could make the trip, but…"

"I don't think her crew will be very happy about letting you have her," Siskyu interrupted, unable to contain her bitterness at having her future snatched away just as it was beginning, "seeing as how you've just murdered her captain and first mate. Captain Givryn was a decent, hardworking man, and one of Shaeldor's closest friends in the city."

Vrappa turned to skewer Siskyu with a look that sent her shrinking back to press against Riftan's bulk.

"I hadn't planned to ask permission." The quiet words exploded in the packed room like Gen gunpowder, all the more so because their speaker was quite confident that she could execute them.

"But that's piracy!" Riftan burst out, his outrage echoed by every sailor in the room. No one who made a living from the sea was ever completely safe from piracy and all viewed it as a crime morally beneath even the worst of lorshes.

"Yes, it is," the Dar leader agreed. "It is also necessary. We couldn't allow the ship's rightful crew to come along, anyway. We can't take more Simes than we have Gens to support, and we must give priority to Householders."

"You would turn criminal, for a few weeks more of life, at best?" Siskyu had never seen her grandfather so disappointed. "I would have thought your oath meant more than that. It is far better to die with honor intact."

"Our oath to Dar is just as sacred as yours to Shaeldor," Vrappa insisted. "We would gladly die before dishonoring it, if we didn't have an even greater responsibility to humanity itself."

"If you are right, there will soon be no humanity toward whom one might feel responsible," Riftan pointed out.

"It is summer, and the drought has been widespread," Asaka countered. "The deserts to the south will stop land-based raiders. A good ship, however, might sail beyond the reach of Zelerod's Doom."

"The pirated *Skyver's Hope*," Grandfather said flatly.

"Yes. With it would sail the knowledge of how to live without Killing. And of what happens when you don't."

"We'll rest a few hours,." Vrappa said calmly. "That's enough time to then take the *Skyver's Hope* gather what supplies are available for the voyage. Isn't the next tide supposed to be an hour before dawn?"

"…yes," Grandfather agreed, his shoulders slumped in defeat.

In the mad scramble that followed, someone took the time to collect the bodies scattered about the hall and arrange them in a neat row, with curtains for shrouds. It was likely that no one would bother to bury them in the brief days before New Ortland became a wasteland, but it was a gesture toward civilized behavior, nonetheless.

A few hours later, the bodies of the night watch on *Skyver's Hope* were unceremoniously dumped in the harbor.

ANCIENT RUINS BETWEEN AMZON AND ZILLIA TERRITORIES, 4 MONTHS BEFORE UNITY

"Get up, girl," a harsh voice grated in Siskyu's ears, and a boot prodded at her back. She whimpered, wrapping her arms around her body, and assessed her condition. The beach was no longer spinning and jumping around with disorientation and her abused stomach seemed inclined to stay put for now. Beyond that, there was no particular reason she could zlin to open her eyes.

"Go away," she told the voice. "I want Grandfather."

"He's dead," came the response. "He drowned when the ship hit that rock and broke up."

"Drowned?"

Siskyu sat up too quickly and moaned as the world started spinning again. It lasted long enough for her to conclude that bad as having Vrappa scowling down at her might be, having three of her was much worse.

* * * *

Three hours later, the survivors of the wrecked *Skyver's Hope* gathered around a small fire in a partially sheltered nook among the Ancient ruins that dotted the landscape. There were only a dozen of the refugees left alive. Riftan huddled next to the fire, staring woodenly into the flames, his nager dull and unresponsive with shock. Three of the Shaeldor sailors had survived, as had Wistra, the Gen woman who had managed the kitchens at the New Ortland compound two months and a lifetime ago. All of the children had drowned. Vrappa and five of her

Dar guards had also managed to survive the waves, although her second in command, Asaka, was injured and would soon need an early transfer.

That was likely to be difficult. Besides Riftan, there were only two other Gens in the group and eight renSimes.

"We'll have to head for the nearest Sime Territory," Vrappa decided. "Zelerod's Doom shouldn't have reached this far. There is plenty of metal in these ruins. We can mine enough to buy Pen Gens to make up our numbers and land on which to found a new House."

The six renSimes spent the next two days salvaging what supplies they could from the wreckage that washed onto the beach and mining some of the best of the chunks of metal hidden under the riot of jungle growth that covered the ruins. The Gens sorted through the salvage, except for Riftan. The Companion had taken the news that every person or thing he'd ever known was dead or destroyed even harder than the rest of them. He couldn't seem to muster any interest in the mechanics of survival. Instead, he spent hours gazing into the fire, his nager collapsed into a fog of despair.

On the third day, Asaka and two of the other Dar guards captured a junker, a huge Gen with shaggy hair and trail-worn clothes who had been careless enough to wander into the ruins alone in search of easy wealth. Like most Householders, Vrappa spoke some of the Gen language, although the local dialect was very different from that spoken by the doomed Gens of New Washington Territory. She questioned the man for three hours, persisting in spite of her victim's fear and confusion. At the end, though, she could only shake her head in disappointment.

"He doesn't know of any Sime Territory nearby that might have Pens," she reported to the others in more civilized Simelan. "All the Simes he's heard about seem to be the sort of lone juncts or small bands of raiders that any Gen Territory produces." She turned back to the prisoner and told him, "One more thing we want, then you free."

"What is that?" the junker quavered. His nager showed considerable skepticism, and a faint but growing hope.

"Your selyn," she said, reaching out to grab the Gen by the back of his collar as he tried to bolt for freedom. "Come, Siskyu, we've spent long enough here," she added briskly in Simelan.

"But I can't!" Siskyu protested in the same language, as she tried to put Riftan's detached but strong nager between herself and the panic-stricken Gen. "He's no donor. Taking first donations from Wild Gens is a Sectuib's job."

"You're the closest thing we have to a Sectuib," Vrappa pointed out, forcing the Gen a step closer to her. "Perhaps the closest thing left alive in the whole world."

The magnitude of her ignorance seemed suddenly overwhelming. "I don't know how," she admitted. "My control isn't good enough to risk it. I might hurt him!"

"Asaka can't wait while you practice your control," the Dar leader said implacably, dragging the Gen another step closer to Siskyu. "He must have selyn soon. If you won't take this Gen's field down, Asaka will Kill him."

The blunt announcement caught Siskyu by surprise. "But he's a Householder, sworn to die rather than Kill!"

"Dar is dead," Asaka said. The effort it required him to speak coherently so close to hard Need was clear to zlin. "You are the only working channel left. We are too few to protect you as it is. If I must, I will live as a junct until you are safe. And then I will die."

Siskyu looked at the renSime in horror, then squared her shoulders. "All right," she agreed. "I'll try it."

"Riftan, help her!" Vrappa ordered. The Companion continued to sit, staring blankly, until one of the sailors shook his shoulder. He looked up, then got to his feet. His attention, such as it was, focused on Siskyu, cutting the Wild Gen's nager considerably.

Siskyu looked up at the much bigger Gen struggling in Vrappa's hold and tried out her primitive English. "Be calm. Not hurt you."

She tried to explain what she intended, but her English wasn't up to the task. The Gen didn't believe her, and although Riftan's nager shielded her from the worst of it, his reaction was raising Asaka's intil dangerously.

Finally, Vrappa's patience gave out. "Stop stalling and do it," she demanded. With her handling tentacles, she tore the junker's sleeves off, and shoved him forward into Siskyu's arms.

Siskyu caught him, Sime instinct and her truncated training combining to get her a proper grip. The Gen screamed as she made lateral contact and she had to augment to restrain him. "Be calm," she pleaded once more, and completed the contact.

It was much harder to maintain her concentration with the Gen's field flaring panic under her tentacles. She'd never had to immobilize a struggling Gen before, either. Fortunately, Sime instinct intervened in time to protect her laterals, although the Gen would have some nasty bruises to show for it when she was done.

She couldn't glean as much selyn through the junker's resistance as an experienced donor would yield, but she persisted. When she finally retracted her laterals and released him, it was with a certain sense of satisfaction that she turned to Asaka and held out her hands in the traditional channel's offer of transfer.

Afterward, Vrappa's mood was much improved, with the most immediate crisis overcome. Although she insisted on relieving the junker of some of his supplies, she offered payment of a sort.

"Metal there," she told him, pointing to an overgrown mound. "So deep…" she indicated the distance. "No other Sime here. Safe working. Much money."

The junker stared after them as they left, but when Siskyu looked back from the next ridge, he was already tearing into the mound.

CORDONA, 23 YEARS AFTER UNITY

"You came."

Siskyu shifted under the pile of blankets that shielded her from the chill of the spring morning. It never got truly warm in the caves, but this spring the cold and rain seemed particularly endless.

"Yes, I came."

Riftan's cool Gen hand reached out to take hers, falling into the Companion's habits that had been drilled into him so long ago. "You're much too thin," he complained, with the querulous tone Companions had used for generations, back before the world changed. "You haven't been eating properly."

Filmor, her second in command, took offense at this insolence in a mere Gen, but Siskyu waved him back when he would have punished it. Truth to tell, she found this reminder of what had been more comforting than offensive. "It's hard enough to get food up here for our Gens to eat, in winter," she reminded the Companion.

It had been one of the reasons why he and Wistra had left the band to settle in Gen Territory, ten years before. Another had been her development of the technique that allowed junct Simes to survive several years without Killing, by deliberately exposing them to Gen fear and pain. Life with a modern channel was much easier for a Companion who did not expect to be regarded as an equal by the Simes around him.

"Even Simes have to eat."

By failing to accept Siskyu's dismissal of the subject, Riftan again demonstrated his inability to adapt to modern life. Siskyu had to wave her followers back from the Gen once more.

"Riftan, food isn't going to cure what's wrong with me. "

She took what strength she could from the Gen's unguarded sympathy and pulled herself to a sitting position, braced against the cave wall. "Leave, all of you, "she ordered. "I want to speak with the Gen alone."

There was a certain amount of grumbling, but in the end even Filmor was persuaded to go. When there was no one to overhear, Siskyu indulged herself and zlinned Riftan deeply. Even after more than a decade of not working, his nager was distinctively Shaeldor: a taste of her lost childhood.

"Do you ever wonder what your life would have been like, if Zelerod's Doom hadn't come?" she asked wistfully.

The Gen's sorrow matched her own. "There are mornings when I'm convinced that it was all a dream; then I wake up."

Siskyu knew that she would never have a better chance. For that matter, the chronic grinding pain in her gut was a constant reminder that she would have no chances at all, soon.

"We are the last two people alive who even know what Shaeldor was and what it tried to accomplish," she started tentatively.

"Shaeldor is dead," Riftan said, his voice harsh. "Its Sectuib and all the membership who stayed true to it died twenty-three years ago. We poor tattered remnants who survived betrayed it."

"Not quite," Siskyu corrected him. "The House lives as long as its last pledged member survives to keep its ideals alive."

"It might as well be dead, then," Riftan said. "I'm a simple Gen farmer, now. My children think that I'm making up stories when I tell them about what was. In another generation, Shaeldor won't be anything more than a myth. As it should be. A House that consists of one lone Companion, who can't stay true to his pledge, is nothing."

"You kept your pledge to me, until my actions made you withdraw it. You even kept your ring. I can zlin it hanging from that thong around your neck."

The Gen pulled the thong out from under the collar of his shirt, revealing a battered but still identifiable Shaeldor crest ring. "Somehow, I can't bear to just sell it," he said softly. "Even though I certainly could have used the money."

"You're ambrov Shaeldor," Siskyu said again. "And while you live, Shaeldor isn't—quite—dead." She shifted once more, but there was no position where the gnawing pain in her belly didn't grab her. "I don't have the right to demand anything of you," she began tentatively. "I don't know if I'm worthy enough even for a ghost House. But I would like to give Shaeldor more than a provisional oath before I die."

Whatever Riftan had thought she would demand of him, it wasn't this. "You have led a band of bandits and highway robbers," he objected weakly. "You deliberately beat and terrorize innocent Gens for the enjoyment of junct Simes."

"I stood between renSimes and the Kill, in the only way this new world of ours allows," Siskyu corrected softly. "That hasn't stopped me from remembering that there was once a better way. I couldn't live my life by Shaeldor's principles because the future of humanity demanded that the knowledge of channeling be preserved, at all costs. My death, though, is my own."

She extended her handling tentacles to wrap around Riftan's wrists. "I would like to die as Siskyu ambrov Shaeldor, not Siskyu the bandit. As the last Companion and the last living member of Shaeldor, will you accept my oath?" She looked up at the startled Companion, putting all the pleading she could into her eyes. For a long moment, his determination wavered.

Then he removed the thong from around his neck, and placed the ring in Siskyu's withered fingers. "Pledge, then, if you will. I suppose you've been as true to your provisional oath as I was to my full one, at that."

Siskyu could feel her cracked lips curving in a smile, then she grasped the ring as firmly as she could. Her voice was surprisingly strong as she began, "Unto the House of Shaeldor, I pledge my life, my property, and my future. And Unto Riftan, First Companion in Shaeldor, I pledge my loyalty, wherever the winds may blow me, until the sands of time come to claim me…"

Afterward, Siskyu asked him, "Was I right, to preserve the techniques of channeling when circumstances force channels to be bandits? It didn't matter so much, back when I thought it would be temporary, but there can never be a proper Householding, here."

"No, there can't," Riftan agreed. "I hoped for a long time that something had survived in Nivet, but there's been no word from the north in all these years."

They talked for a while longer, taking comfort in shared memories that seemed more and more like a dream. Then Siskyu drifted off to sleep, clutching Riftan's hand.

When Riftan left the cave an hour later, Siskyu's emaciated husk was already starting to cool.

A SHORT LIFE

ELIZA AMBROV HALWYN

I know there is no use running, but still, I run. I'm running for my life.

My breathing is laboured, my lungs and my legs ache. I push on, stumbling over the rough ground.

With no warning I am suddenly stopped in my tracks by a grip like steel. I fall, inertia dragging the predator down on me. Sheer terror kicks in and I scream and struggle wildly, all reason gone. I am flipped around as if I am nothing more than a doll.

For the first time I see my attacker. Small, thin, little more than a child. Its eyes are glazed as if it is blind, but its aim is unerring as it grabs my forearms.

Strong tentacles wrap around my arms and I scream again as I feel muscle and blood vessels break below the skin.

My scream is cut off as my mouth is covered by her mouth. I find myself paralyzed, unable to move my head away. Her breath stinks. My fear is overwhelmed by such exquisite pain that I think I am going to, hope to, beg to pass out. I am on fire, burning from the inside out.

It seems impossible for the pain to get worse, but, unbelievably it does. There is nothing but the pain.

I know this won't last much longer, there is no way I can survive this torment, but it seems unending.

Blackness starts to descend. As it engulfs me I wonder if this Sime will remember me.

Regretfully, I know she won't.

Controller's Dilemma originally appeared in *Ambrov Zeor* #16, (1988) and can be found in Rimon's Library:

http://simegen.com/sgfandom/householding/chanel/cd.html

on the domain. There are several stories online that feature Frevven, and others that feature the characters of Householding Chanel.

CONTROLLER'S DILEMMA

MARJORIE ROBBINS AND K. L. SCHAEFER

"House of Zeor offers respect to House of Chanel, Sectuib Aran."

"Chanel returns Zeor's respect and welcomes you to Cedarcity." Aran smiled warmly as he extended his hands to the Gen. "I didn't expect to see you this soon, Chaynek. Our transfer is still two weeks away." As the Donor touched his fingers and tentacles, Aran zlinned a slight uneasiness, quickly squelched, in his nager. "Something wrong?"

"No, no," replied Chaynek lightly as he glanced around the small overcrowded room. "Surely a Controller rates a bigger office?"

Aran chuckled. "Chaynek, Chaynek, will you never change? I like my office as it is."

It truly was a small room, boasting only one window which was dressed with blue gingham curtains, lopsidedly tied back to reveal the midsized farm town of Cedarcity, the largest town in the Iway District, Upper Midwest Territory. The walls were covered with needlepoint pictures, mostly farm scenes, giving the room a warm, homey air. A massive wooden bookcase graced one wall.

"Now, answer my question," the channel insisted gently.

Chaynek grinned. "You might tell me what you're doing out here on the edge of nowhere first, Sectuib — er — Controller."

Aran nodded understandingly. "It does take some getting used to. Controller isn't a job I would have volunteered for." His dark blue eyes grew even darker, as he ran a restless hand through his reddish-brown hair. "But when Chanel donated the hospital complex to the Tecton, District Controller Sunlan asked me to stay here and take over as Controller for the Cedarcity area." He shrugged. "It more or less made official the work Chanel's been doing in this area for years."

"But why here? There's nothing but cows, corn and a lot of wide open spaces. Besides, it's hot," complained the Gen as he wiped his sweaty brow.

Aran grinned. "A grateful patient donated the land. As to the weather, don't fuss. It could be worse."

"There's nothing worse than this heat."

"You'd better hope it stays warm. A sudden cool spell could mean trouble. This is thunderstorm and tornado country."

Chaynek groaned. "Then why in shen didn't you pick a civilized spot for your Center?"

Aran chuckled. "I can see I'm going to have to work on your attitude, my friend. Country life is kind of nice once you get used to it. Now," his voice deliberately grew stern, "tell me why you're here this early. Is Muryin up to something?"

Chaynek's eyes widened in simulated innocence. "Why, Sectuib Aran, are you accusing Zeor of chicanery?"

"Zeor, no. You and the Sectuib, possibly. What nasty do you have for me this time?"

Chaynek sighed. "Truly, if I didn't know better, I'd swear you were reading my mind. I'm a few days early because Muryin wanted me to bring Frevven Alymeer to you." Pulling a sheaf of papers from his jacket pocket, he tossed it across the desk. "I left him in your reception area. He's a disjunct channel who's insisting on being trained."

Aran's brows went up. "But the Tecton doesn't go for that much anymore. After all, it's been almost twelve years since Unity. We're just not that desperate for channels. Hasn't anyone explained it to him?"

"Of course we have. But he won't listen to anyone, not even Muryin. He's obsessed with the idea of being a working channel."

"Um." Aran was lost in reading the report from Zeor. "Raised out-Territory. Killed his sister in changeover. Managed to reach a Center and then Killed an inexperienced Third Order Donor who tried to help him." Aran raised a skeptical brow. "Sent to Zeor for disjunction and just barely succeeded, after initially displaying a hostile and uncooperative attitude." Aran shook his head, raising puzzled eyes to the Gen.

"Surely he must realize how impossible this is. With this record the Tecton will never train him. They make fewer and fewer exceptions every year, and then only for disjuncts with a good record and a much better attitude." He tapped the report with one tentacle. "But not for someone like this."

Settling back in his seat, he met Chaynek's eyes. "Why did you bring him here? There are orientation centers closer to Zeor."

"Yeah," grunted the Gen, "but Sectuib Farris feels it's going to take a lot of counseling to convince him to give up his obsessive ideas. She wanted you to work with him."

Aran shook his head. "I'm not the only psychologist in the Tecton."

"Perhaps not, but Chanel's specialty is psychology, and you are Sectuib in Chanel."

The Sime rose, chuckling, as he carelessly tossed the papers into his immediate problem basket, which was already full to overflowing. "That sounds like a Zeor con job, and I'm just egotistical enough to accept the challenge. All right, I'll do what I can. But Muryin owes me one. Come on. I'm anxious to meet this 'problem' of yours." He paused a moment, then smiled warmly as Kareen ambrov Chanel, First Companion in Chanel and specialist in Adolescent Psychology, entered the room. She was a short stocky woman, with close-cropped black hair, speckled with the grey of middle-age. Founder and one time leader of Chanel as Sosectu, she was now content to serve her House and the Tecton as Companion and psychologist.

"Hi, Mother," Aran said softly.

"Aran, I just met the most interesting young man. Frevven Alymeer is — Oh, hi, Chaynek. Welcome to Cedarcity."

"Thank you, Kareen. It's good to see you again." Chaynek half rose as Kareen perched on the arm of her son's overstuffed office chair. "We were just discussing Frevven."

Kareen's eyes darkened as she regarded the Companion from Zeor. "I'm sure. He had a few things to say about you, too. Aran, you're going to get permission to train him, aren't you?"

Aran shook his head. "I can't, Mother. The Tecton has pretty strict rules on that."

"Policies, not rules," Kareen snapped. She gave her son a stern look. "Aran, you know what Chanel's policy is towards people who are being treated unfairly."

"To redress the wrong, if we can. But nobody is wronging Frevven."

"Ha! Denying him the chance to train as a channel? Denying him the opportunity to be what he is?"

The Sectuib took a deep breath, trying to still his slowly rising temper. As the Tecton rules gradually grew stricter, this type of argument with House members was becoming all too common. "I honor my pledge to Chanel to the best of my ability."

"If you did, you would try to get permission to train Frevven," urged Kareen.

"Mother, it isn't quite that simple, and you know it."

"You've already made up your mind and you haven't even met the young man." Taking a deep breath, Kareen added softly, "Look, Aran, I know as well as you do why the Tecton has that stupid policy."

"It's not a stupid policy, Mother." Aran gave her a stern look. "As a general rule, training disjuncts is a very dangerous practice."

"So suppose Frevven is the exception to the rule? Do you want to ruin his whole life out of blind loyalty to the Tecton?"

Chaynek had kept silent throughout the discussion, but his nager reflected his increasing impatience. "Have you considered that training Frevven might also ruin his whole life?" he finally asked. "Zeor has done a lot of studies on disjunct channels. They can't handle the pressure, Kareen. And that's not all. Even when they serve transfer, they—"

"Oh, shen, Chaynek, not long ago a large number of the Tecton's channels were disjunct," Kareen interrupted, throwing the other Gen an annoyed glance.

"Exactly, but Zeor has always felt—"

"All right, all right, enough you two. The ambient is giving me a headache," Aran said, hoping to put a stop to the argument. "Mother, I know all about your famous intuition—"

"Then why not listen to me?" Kareen's eyes flashed.

"Because Frevven's record doesn't inspire me with confidence." He raised a silencing tentacle as she started to protest. "There is no point in discussing this further. We're not considering Frevven for training and that is that. But I'm not ignoring my pledge to Chanel. Our virtue is service. We're going to serve Frevven by teaching him how to make a new life for himself."

"Right," said Chaynek. "Truly, Kareen, training Frevven would not be in his best interests."

She shrugged her shoulders in defeat. "I still think you're both wrong."

Aran rose, gently dislodging his mother from her perch. "I haven't even met the young man. Let's go see him." He grinned at her. "Maybe the record is wrong or misleading. Perhaps I'll change my mind."

Chaynek shook his head. "No, it isn't. But zlin for yourself."

Threading the maze of channels' offices known as the Executive Suite, they proceeded towards the small lounge at the end of the corridor. The Executive Suite, changeover evaluation and juvenile psych wards comprised the second floor of the converted hotel that served as both Sime Center and hospital.

Almost immediately Aran sensed something wrong. He went duo-conscious to zlin. Gen terror and a Sime in Killmode assaulted the channel's senses.

Aran ran off down the corridor under augmentation, bursting into the lounge in time to see two young Simes struggling. One was in Killmode, obviously straining to reach the terrified Gen woman cowering in the corner. That must be Frevven, judging by how easily he was provoked into attacking. Before Aran could intervene, Frevven shoved the other youngster violently against the wall and sprang at the Gen.

So much for Mom's intuition that this disjunct might be different, Aran thought bitterly, as he swiftly intercepted and served transfer.

As the transfer ended, Jorn Frigg, a channel who worked on the changeover ward, entered the room on the run. "Controller, what—why did you serve Trazee?"

Confused, Aran glanced from Jorn to the young man before him and back again. "What are you talking about? This is—"

"I'm Trazee Seward," the youngster said proudly. "I'm a channel now." And in a fairly typical post changeover reaction, he sat down to play with his tentacles.

Oh, shen! thought Aran. *Now we have a real mess.* Aloud he said, "Then where is Frevven Alymeer?"

"Over here, Aran." Chaynek had just arrived and was kneeling by the other Sime, while Kareen had gone to comfort the frightened Gen woman.

Aran immediately joined Chaynek and was surprised to notice that the youngster was wearing a pair of wire-framed glasses, now slightly askew. He gently pushed them back into place before making lateral contact. A moment later he raised his head to look at Chaynek, who had enveloped him in a supportive field.

"He has a concussion," said Aran softly as he projected Genness to arouse the youngster. "And some swelling of the brain, but he should…" He paused to study his patient.

Frevven moaned as he opened greenish-gold eyes to focus weakly on the channel's face. He raised one hand and re-adjusted his glasses on his nose with a tentacle, then squinted at Aran. "Who — who are you?"

Aran smiled reassuringly. "Hajene Aran, Sectuib in Chanel and local Controller. Lie still a moment. You've suffered a concussion."

"Yes, Sectuib Aran," whispered the youngster.

"You're going to be just fine, though you will require some further treatment. You may have some pain and dizziness for a few days, but we can control that with medication."

Frevven nodded, apparently not much interested in his condition. "The Gen, is she all right?" he asked.

Aran nodded, "Yes, she was just frightened. You lie still for a few minutes. Chaynek, watch him."

Rising, Aran crossed the room to where Trazee was sitting on the floor complacently studying his tentacles.

Kneeling beside him, Aran said, "I'm Hajene Aran, Controller here. Congratulations on becoming a channel."

The youngster grinned. "Do I get to start my training now?"

Aran shook his head. "Not for a while. Taking transfer from me instead of a Donor could cause you problems."

Trazee pouted. "But I want..."

Aran held up a hand. "This isn't an issue for argument, Trazee. I'm sorry for what happened, but it can't be helped now. You'll undergo evaluation and if everything checks out okay, then I'll admit you to the First Year channel's school. How did this happen anyway?" He glanced over at Jorn.

The other channel squirmed uneasily. "I'm sorry, Hajene. We were admitting Trazee when he just ran. He was fixed on his mother, but I thought he..."

Rising, Aran said sternly, "So you let her stay here?"

"I told her to go downstairs."

"Please don't be mad," interjected the Gen woman softly. "I disobeyed him. I wanted to be near Trazee."

"I understand, Mrs. Seward," Aran said. He fixed Jorn with a stern look, biting back the rebuke that was on the tip of his tongue. "Hajene Frigg, I want to see you in my office in fifteen minutes. You've got some explaining to do."

"Yes, Hajene," replied the other channel. "Shall I take Trazee to his room first?"

Aran shook his head. "No, leave him here. I'm moving him to the evaluation ward."

"Yes, Hajene." Jorn left the room, taking Mrs. Seward with him.

Aran knelt by Frevven's side. "How are you feeling now, young man?"

"Much better, Hajene. I mean, Controller." Frevven wriggled restlessly. "Can I get up now? Chaynek keeps stopping me." He glared resentfully at the Gen, who had a restraining hand on his shoulder.

Aran frowned in puzzlement as he zlinned Frevven's definite hostility towards Chaynek. "He's just doing his job. But, yes, I think you're recovered enough to get up. And please, call me Hajene or Aran. I'm not too fond of Controller."

"Yes, Hajene." Pushing away Aran's helping hands, Frevven stood up.

"Now," Aran said softly, "tell me what you thought you were doing. Intercepting any Sime in Killmode can be dangerous."

Frevven sighed, absently smoothing back his somewhat unruly light brown hair. "I'm sorry, Hajene. I just grabbed Trazee and tried to hold him until help arrived, but I couldn't keep him away from the Gen."

"I wouldn't have—! I mean, I couldn't help—" Trazee's voice trailed off. He glared at the other boy, fierce anger and shame burning in his nager.

Frevven flinched. "Hajene, I just wanted to defend the Gen. That's what a channel's supposed to do, isn't it?"

Aran bit his lip as he studied the two youngsters a moment, searching for just the right words. Finally, he said softly, "Frevven, that was a brave thing you just did. But if Trazee had turned on you and attacked, you could have gotten Killed."

Frevven shrugged, "I'm not sure that matters."

Aran frowned. "Would you care to explain that remark?"

Frevven shook his head. "That would be pointless, Hajene. Someone like you wouldn't understand."

Defiant words, but Aran read a desperate plea for understanding in the younger channel's nager, a plea that Frevven was trying unsuccessfully to hide.

Suddenly doubting everything in Frevven's record, Aran found himself momentarily looking at the world through Frevven's eyes. "I might surprise you. But this isn't the time or place to discuss it." He gestured towards his mother. "Sosu Kareen will take you to your room in the Orientation Center, and I'll be by after I finish rounds. Then we'll talk."

"I don't want orientation," muttered Frevven rebelliously. "I want training."

Aran sighed. "Nevertheless, you will go with her, and do as she says. We'll talk later."

Frevven's nager flared brief defiance, but then he lowered his eyes. "Yes, Hajene," he replied stiffly.

"Come, boys." Kareen herded the youngsters from the room while Aran sank wearily into a seat.

Chaynek sat down beside him, focusing a relaxing field.

Aran smiled, "I hope you're ready for some serious work."

"Of course. That's what the Tecton pays me for."

"Good. We have rounds to make. But first I have a question for you."

"What?" asked the Gen, warily.

"Why does Frevven have so much hostility towards you? I've never known you to be a bad guy."

"You're not a rebellious youngster, either." Chaynek's characteristic smile faded and Aran caught a quick flicker of what might have been unease in the Gen's nager. "Let's just say that his disjunction was a bit of a struggle. I had to teach him a few lessons the hard way. Sure, he resents me, but he'll get over it."

Aran was silent for a moment. "He may very well resent me, too, by the time this is over. Changing his mind isn't going to be easy."

"Truly, Aran, if anyone can do it, it's you." Chaynek's nager was filled with encouragement.

"I hope you're right. Well, let's get started. I still have to see Jorn, then rounds could very well take all afternoon."

Chaynek frowned. "That bad?"

Aran regarded him somberly. "It gets worse every year. Sometimes I wonder if the Tecton knows where it's going. Or what it's doing." And with that cryptic remark, Aran led the way from the room before the Gen could reply.

* * * *

It was late in the day by the time rounds were completed. Sending Chaynek off to unpack, Aran went across the street to the large red brick building on the campus of the Center's First Year School that served the entire Iway District as Orientation and Counseling Center for new Simes from out-Territory.

He paused to exchange a few words with the renSimes on duty at the main desk in the spacious lobby before proceeding to the third floor. When he got to Frevven's room, he found the young channel sitting by the window, a very melancholy expression on his face.

"Hi, Frevven. May I come in?"

The youngster regarded him with a decided lack of enthusiasm. "If you wish, Hajene."

"How are you feeling?" Aran asked carefully as he sat down on the bed.

"Just fine," Frevven said sarcastically, staring at the floor. "How should I feel? I'm a channel, but I can't get the training I require."

"I meant physically." Aran extended his laterals to zlin. "You did get hurt this afternoon."

"It was worth it," Frevven muttered. "I prevented a Kill. If I get the chance, I'll do it again."

"You were lucky that time, my friend," Aran said grimly. "Now, please come on over here and lie down. You may think that you're feeling fine, but you do require more therapy."

Silently, Frevven obeyed him, holding out his arms for Aran to make lateral contact.

Aran zlinned him carefully, finding that while there was still some trauma, the damage from the blow to the head was reversing itself nicely. He also noted that it was Frevven's turnover day, the midpoint in his Need cycle. Releasing the youngster, Aran began projecting as a Gen, to encourage Frevven's healing processes.

Immediately, Frevven frowned. "How do you do that?" he demanded, and began fumblingly to copy Aran's shift.

"You've read some manuals, I guess?"

"I found them lying around," Frevven answered, but his defenses were melting under Aran's field therapy, and his eyes drooped shut.

"Hardly, but we'll overlook that for the moment. Now stop trying to copy me. You're upsetting the field balances."

Frevven opened his eyes, grinning sheepishly. "Sorry, Hajene. I was just curious."

More than curious! "I'll make you a deal. Relax so I can finish this job and I'll explain the theory later."

For a moment Aran thought Frevven was going to refuse, then the boy sighed. "All right. But you promise you'll explain it later?"

"You have my word."

Closing his eyes, Frevven yielded.

There was silence for a few minutes, then, retracting his tentacles, Aran smiled. "Take it easy for a few days and there'll be no permanent damage."

Frevven sat up. "Then can we talk about the possibility of training me?" he asked hopefully.

Aran sighed. "How many times do we have to say no before you hear us, Frevven? What you want is impossible."

Stubbornly Frevven shook his head. "It's not impossible. I'm a channel. I should be trained to function as one."

Folding his hands in his lap, Aran stared thoughtfully at the young man. "I can understand and sympathize with your desire to serve as a channel. It's a beautiful thing. But I don't think you've considered carefully. You just can't do it."

Frevven's eyes grew hard. "I know what you're going to say, Controller. I've heard it before."

"Oh? What's that?"

"You're going to remind me that I'm disjunct. That disjuncts can't be anti-Kill conditioned." Frevven met Aran's eyes, challenge bright in his eager. "You think I'd Kill somebody, someday."

"Well, statistics show—"

"Shen the statistics! I'm never going to Kill again. I'll die first."

"I'm sure you believe that." Aran decided to take another tack. "Look, you're six months into First Year."

"So what? Where in the manual does it say that a channel can't learn after First Year?" The youngster fidgeted. He pushed his glasses more tightly against the bridge of his nose with the tip of a dorsal tentacle.

Aran shook his head. "You're not thinking clearly. Six months is not enough time for the training, nor the learning. Your secondary system will lose its flexibility."

"I can do it." Frevven was doggedly determined. "If I work real hard, I know I can do it. Maybe I won't be the best channel in the world. Maybe I'll never be more than Third Order. But I know I can do it, regardless of what Sectuib Farris says."

For the first time Aran zlinned a flicker of uncertainty in Frevven's field. "And what did she have to say?"

"Well—" Frevven looked away. "She says disjunct channels shouldn't serve nonjunct renSimes. Disjuncts do something not quite right when they serve transfer and that's not good for the nonjuncts."

Aran almost laughed. "Zeor's been saying that for years, but they haven't been able to prove it convincingly."

"You don't believe it?"

"Well, I wouldn't go that far. She could be right. But I don't think it matters at this point in history. Someday, maybe when there are no disjuncts or semi-juncts and the world is more civilized than it is now, it might be worth worrying about. But not now."

The relief suffusing Frevven's nager was almost palpable. "Hajene Aran, I know I could be a good channel. I could learn to do it right." He looked at Aran hopefully.

Maybe he could, thought the older channel. *Maybe Frevven was the exception to the rule. Maybe it was wrong not to train him.*

Aran cut off that train of thought abruptly. The Tecton didn't run on 'maybes.' "Frevven, I'm sorry but what you want is impossible."

The young Sime turned away, leaving the bed to go stand by the window, his nager tightly closed against the Controller.

Aran rose. Going around the foot of the bed, he put his hand gently on Frevven's shoulder, attempting to link nagerically with the other channel.

Frevven stiffened. "You're not going to change my mind, Hajene. I'm going to train as a channel. I have to."

"Why? Why is it so important to you?" Aran let understanding and compassion flavor his field.

"You wouldn't understand." Frevven pulled away, his nager radiating total rejection of the support Aran was offering. "I see no point in discussing it. All I want you to do is get me into a training program."

"Believe me, I wish I could. But it's not allowed."

Frevven made no reply, but his nager flared a poignant despair that Aran found hard to ignore.

Taking a deep breath, Aran said firmly, "Look, what you want and even what I want has little or no meaning to the Tecton. What I can offer you is a chance to make a new life for yourself."

"Doing what?"

"Whatever you want and are suited for. We have some excellent job training and placement programs. We'll test you to see what you're capable of, then—"

"I'm capable of being a channel."

Aran shook his head, "Give up on that idea. It's just not an option."

"I don't want job counseling," Frevven snapped. "I want to be a working channel."

"Very well. Obviously you're in no mood to listen to reason." Aran's field slowly returned to neutrality. "We'll discuss this again another time." Receiving no reply from the youngster, he left the room, pausing at the front desk to write some medical orders for Frevven's care.

Aran then went to the library and picked up a book on the history of Zeor which he had been trying to read for several months. Settling himself on the window seat of the big bay window overlooking the Center's lavish gardens, Aran wearily leaned his head against the window frame and closed his eyes. The book lay unopened on his lap. Unbidden, his thoughts returned to the unhappy young channel in the Orientation Center.

How am I going to reach that kid? Shen, but he's stubborn. Aran shook his head. "Frevven, Frevven," he murmured aloud. "It's madness to consider training you as a channel, but how do I get you to see that, and make you understand what a mistake it would be?" With a deep sigh, Aran opened the book and tried unsuccessfully to lose himself in the history of Householding Zeor.

* * * *

During the next week Aran worked hard to change Frevven's mind. He gave him books to read on the history of the Tecton, arranged for him to talk to instructors from the First Year School who had had first-hand experiences working with disjuncts, and spent many hours himself counseling him, but to no avail.

The kid was proving to be very uncooperative. And while he did grudgingly submit to the standard vocational and psychological tests, he refused to participate in any group activities or listen to any counseling from the Orientation Center staff.

One night Aran was again in the library, still trying to read his history of Zeor. Sensing the approach of a familiar field, he put down the book and smiled as the library door opened. "Mother, what are you doing up this late?"

Kareen smiled wanly, as she quickly crossed the room to settle down on the floor at her son's feet. "I could ask you the same question."

"I'm never in bed this early."

"Especially a week from transfer," murmured Kareen, focusing her field warmly. "Are you all right? Where's Chaynek?"

"I'm fine and I sent him to bed. I don't require constant attendance." He frowned at her serene knowing smile. "You're awfully smug for a Gen. Have you completed your evaluation of Trazee yet?"

"Of course," she replied loftily. "Trazee checks out just fine, Sectuib. No psychological problems that I can detect. Except—"

"A rather arrogant attitude?" guessed the Sime.

Kareen frowned. "Most unbecoming for a channel. And it could get him in a lot of trouble."

"Do you recommend we admit him to the First Year School?"

"Yes," Kareen replied hesitantly, her brow furrowed in thought. "Except for his attitude, there's no reason to deny him the training. I've put a recommendation in his chart that he be given psychological counseling while in training." She looked up and met his eyes. "But his attitude is causing problems. Especially with Frevven Alymeer."

Aran sighed. "Frevven has enough problems. What's Trazee been doing?"

"He taunts Frevven about being disjunct and thus, no good."

"That statement isn't even true. Can't you separate them?"

Kareen sighed. "I've tried. But Trazee has made a lot of friends at the Orientation Center, so I have no reason to keep him away. And Frevven makes things difficult. He refuses to attend his counseling sessions. He mopes around the Center, or wanders the campus of the First Year School watching the students. Some of the instructors have complained."

"How's he taking Trazee's harassment?"

"He's pretending it doesn't affect him, but I can tell he's deeply hurt."

"And refusing your help," finished Aran softly. "Want me to talk to him?"

Kareen shook her head. "No, right now it won't do much good. The only thing Frevven wants to hear you won't tell him."

"I can't tell him," amended Aran.

"You could if you wanted to."

"Don't you think I want to?" Aran said softly. "It would not be wise. And you know it."

Kareen was silent a moment. "What about your oath to Chanel? You're not serving Frevven by being stubborn like this."

"And you're not being logical. If Frevven were trained, there's an excellent chance he'd lose control and Kill somebody again."

Kareen frowned. "Are you sure that's your real reason for being so stubborn? Not just that District Controller Sunlan is a stickler for the rules and would most likely lower the boom on you?"

"Both reasons are valid, Mom. As Controller, I can do a lot of good for a lot of people."

"True. But in the long run, which is more important? Your position as Controller, or your oath to Chanel?"

Aran was silent a moment. Technically, his mother was correct. Chanel always put the rights of individuals above all other considerations. But in this case — "My oath, of course. I'm just not convinced that letting Frevven train as a channel is in his best interests. As I said, I don't think he can handle it."

"Well, I think he can." Kareen's nager was doing a slow burn. "At least consider it. Controller Sunlan will be here in a couple of weeks for his annual inspection tour. You could ask for a hearing on Frevven's case."

Aran was silent a moment. He knew there was only one way to get Kareen to drop the matter. "Very well, Mother. I'll write to him in the morning and ask for permission to convene a board. We'll let the other controllers rule on this. But don't expect Sunlan to agree. You know how he feels about the rules."

"Then you'll find another way. We will train Frevven," she replied confidently.

* * * *

The next morning, Aran sent for Trazee.

Breezing into the Controller's office, Trazee took a seat without waiting for permission. "What do you want, Aran?"

"You will address me as Hajene," Aran said sharply.

"Aw, Hajene, don't be so fussy. It's a beautiful day, and all's right with the world." He stretched luxuriously.

"I didn't send for you to get a weather report." Aran carefully kept his tone neutral. "When you are with me, or any other channel for that matter, you will behave appropriately. Do I make myself clear?"

"Yes, Hajene," Trazee muttered unwillingly.

"Good. Now, I sent for you to tell you that I've decided to admit you to the First Year School. However, I want to warn you that your training will not be easy. You're going to work as you've never worked before."

Trazee shrugged. "It'll be no problem for me. I know I can do it."

Aran took a deep breath, trying not to react to the youth's smug arrogance. "Trazee, in these few minutes you've given every indication that you may not make it through at all."

Aran zlinned a sudden surge of uncertain fear and almost subliminal agreement with his assessment. Immediately, the youth suppressed this, putting on his façade of boastful self-assurance.

He doesn't believe in himself. It's nothing but a show. Aran quickly made a note on Trazee's chart.

"That's an unfair statement, Hajene." Trazee met Aran's eyes defiantly. "I'll be a very good channel. Now, take Frevven, for instance. Someone like that will never make a decent channel."

"We're talking about you, not Frevven." Aran paused a moment. "I might point out that the only difference between you and Frevven is opportunity and circumstance. Had your mother not brought you here, you most likely would have Killed. Frevven had no such good fortune. As far as that goes, you were lucky he was here. Frevven kept you from Killing."

"Oh, sure. I wouldn't have Killed my own mother. You're making a big deal out of nothing."

Three weeks, four at most, and he'll have learned just how big a deal it really was. Aran made another note on the boy's chart and handed over his enrollment papers. "Pack your things and get over to the school. It's right across the street. Dean Johnstone is waiting for you."

"Yes, Hajene." Trazee's eyes flashed rebelliously, but he grudgingly obeyed Aran.

It was with a sense of relief that Aran turned to the mountain of paperwork before him. Somehow, today it didn't seem such an onerous chore.

* * * *

A week later, it was time for Frevven's transfer. Aran met him in the transfer room reserved for their use.

He found the younger channel sitting on the transfer couch staring at the floor, his nager filled with deep depression. Frevven didn't look up as Aran entered the room.

"What's wrong?" Taking a seat beside the younger channel, Aran attempted to put a friendly arm around him, but Frevven pulled away.

"You know the answer to that, Hajene."

"I suppose I do." Aran considered for a moment. In the mood Frevven was in, any attempt at transfer was probably doomed to failure. Then he hit upon an idea that might raise the youngster's intil. "Tell you what. It's about time I kept the promise I made to you the day you arrived. Would you like me to demonstrate the functional mode?"

Frevven's eyes widened as he looked at Aran for the first time. "You remembered!"

"I may be slow at times, but yes, I remembered. Should have gotten to it sooner, actually. Do you still want the demonstration?"

Frevven nodded eagerly. "Yes, Hajene."

"All right." Rising, Aran pulled down a wall chart. "This is a diagram of a channel's systems, primary in red, and secondary in blue." He smiled to himself as Frevven rose and came to stand beside him.

"This is the vriamic node, right?" The youngster pointed to a purple spot in the center of the chest that seemed to overlay both systems.

"Right. It connects the primary and secondary systems, and controls selyn flow."

Frevven's eyes were bright with excited interest. "How do you control it?"

"It's partly by reflex, and partly under the control of the conscious mind. I'll demonstrate in a minute. Now, you'll notice that though both systems circulate throughout the body, they are separate and distinct."

Frevven nodded. "But I've read that you can move selyn from one to the other. How?"

Aran suppressed a chuckle. The youngster wanted more than just a simple demonstration. "By what's called an internal shunt. Through the vriamic node. But that's a subject for another lesson." He pulled down a second chart. "But before we proceed I want you to take a look at this. It's a diagram of a junct's system."

Frevven frowned. "It's got more pathways."

"Right. And with more places for the selyn to go, it moves faster during transfer. Most Kills are made on speed alone."

"Yeah. Sectuib Farris told me." He looked away from the chart, uneasily adjusting his glasses on his nose. "My junct pathways were sealed during disjunction."

"Right. Any questions?"

Frevven had several that Aran answered indulgently. Finally he said, "You're probably the most inquisitive youngster I've ever taught. But I truly don't have a lot of time. Go and sit down and I'll show you how to do a functional."

"Yes, Hajene." Obediently, Frevven sat beside Aran on the transfer couch and watched the older channel.

"All right. Zlin me." Aran extended his laterals as he slid into functional mode. "Secondary system active, projecting as a Gen—" He grinned as the other channel attempted to mimic him. "Frevven, you can't—"

Without warning, Frevven sprang at him, laterals outstretched and reaching eagerly for his own. Reacting smoothly to the unexpected attack, Aran let the younger channel find his transfer grip, prepared to serve his Need.

Frevven drew savagely. Caught off balance, Aran juggled the fields, taking firm control of the flow, but by that time, Frevven had caught the feel of vriamic control by going with Aran.

By the time Aran realized what Frevven was up to, selyn was flowing through the youth's vriamic node from his primary to his secondary system. In his state of Need, he shouldn't have been able to do that — but he was doing it.

Knowing an abort could be dangerous, even fatal, for the other channel, Aran let Frevven draw for a few moments before he attempted to end the transfer.

But Frevven resisted, desperately trying to prolong it. Then suddenly he lost vriamic control and selyn pulsed chaotically between his primary and secondary systems. Surprised at the unexpected pain, Frevven aborted and went into convulsions.

Overriding his own reaction to the abort, Aran linked with Frevven nagerically. At last he captured Frevven's wildly flailing arms and reestablished lateral contact, fighting the systemic chaos. A few minutes later and Frevven was still, staring up at Aran, eyes wide with fright, but nager defiant.

"You'll be all right now," Aran said reassuringly. Taking a blanket from the storage compartment at the end of the couch, he covered the youngster, then went to a cabinet in the corner and poured a hefty dose of fosebine. Sitting down by Frevven, he said, "Here, drink this. It'll make you feel better."

As Frevven reluctantly complied, Aran zlinned unobtrusively. The youngster would require a proper transfer in a couple of days, but wasn't in hard Need. Aran decided to wait, give the youngster's system a chance to stabilize.

"Don't you realize you could have gotten hurt?"

"I — I just had to. It seemed the only way." Frevven turned his head.

Suddenly Aran understood. "You think this'll force me into training you, don't you?"

Frevven just nodded.

"Well, it isn't true."

"But—" Frevven's face went even paler than it was. "But I figured you'd have to train me."

"Why?"

"Well, there's entran and all sorts of other nasty things that happen to a channel who doesn't use his secondary system, once he's begun."

"Very true. But the Tecton is under no obligation to protect you from the consequences of an ill-advised action."

Frevven's eyes went wide. "But — but I could die."

"Um-hum." Actually, Aran was fairly sure that he could get Frevven back into secondary dormancy, though it would be difficult for both him and the other channel. But he wanted to gauge Frevven's response to having possibly risked his life. *Did it really mean that much to him?*

"Well, maybe I don't care," the youngster retorted. "Maybe Trazee's right and I'm nothing but a worthless disjunct."

"Leave Trazee out of this," snapped Aran with more vehemence than he intended. "Half the time that young man doesn't know what he's talking about. Being a disjunct doesn't make you worthless."

Frevven plucked at the hem of the blanket with two tentacles. Then he pushed his eyeglasses up against the bridge of his nose and glanced up at the older channel. "It's keeping me from being a working channel. That's pretty worthless."

"Tell me something. What's so important about working as a channel that you should be willing to risk your life to do it?"

Frevven hesitated, staring at the Controller suspiciously. "Does it matter?"

"It obviously does to you. Explain it to me. I really want to know."

"I want to do something important with my life. If I can stop other Simes from Killing, stand between them and the Kill—" Frevven met Aran's eyes. "It's what I was born to do."

Aran shook his head. "That's not all of it, is it?"

The youngster turned away.

Overwhelmed with compassion, Aran began to gently rub Frevven's back and shoulders. "Talk to me, Frevven. Maybe I can help."

The youngster shook his head. "Nothing you can say will change things, Hajene. There's only one way…"

Aran waited. In a few minutes Frevven whispered, "I've Killed two people; my sister, and a Companion who only wanted to help. I'm a murderer. Don't you understand?"

Aran bit his lip. Never having Killed anyone himself, he had never fully understood the depths of despair and anguish suffered by those Simes who had Killed, though he had dealt with many of them over the years. He knew that the only salvageable ones were the ones who suffered that remorse most deeply. Apparently he'd misjudged Frevven's intensity of suffering.

He hesitated a moment, not wanting to express this to Frevven. "Is that why you're so determined to be a working channel?"

"It's the only way I can atone—" Turning to face the older Sime, Frevven raised anguished eyes to Aran's. "If you're never going to let me be what I am, I may as well have died in disjunction. What do you think kept me going all that time, Hajene? The chance to be a waiter in a shiltpron parlor?"

"I understand." Aran's nager filled unbidden with aching sympathy. "You feel there is nothing else in life for you. Shen." He fell silent as he attempted to regain control of his feelings. Upcoming transfer or no, Frevven's plight was causing him deep pain.

Frevven was watching him closely. "Please, Hajene, find a way to let me train."

Aran reluctantly shook his head. "Frevven, that's not an option for either one of us. There are a lot of things I can do to help you. Counseling, job placement and so on. All the resources of this Center are available to you. But until you decide you're ready to start making a new life for yourself…"

"You're not listening, Controller! I said I don't want to live unless I can be a working channel." Frevven turned away, ignoring the understanding and compassion in Aran's field.

"Very well. If that's the way you want it," Aran said regretfully. He rose to his feet. "I've got to go, but I'll send Kareen to sit with you for a while."

Going to the door, he signaled the attendant and told him what he wanted. He was about to leave the room when Frevven turned to face him, a desperate plea in his nager if not his face.

"Hajene Aran, what's going to happen to me now?"

"I don't know, Frevven. But I do know that you didn't improve your chances by what you did today. The Tecton doesn't like people who break the rules."

Sitting back down, he put his hand on the youngster's shoulder. "Please believe me when I say I wish I could give you what you want."

"Then why don't you?" asked Frevven defiantly.

"Because the Tecton won't allow it. Besides, it wouldn't be in your best interests. You've got to accept that what you want just isn't possible."

Frevven turned away.

"All right, we'll drop it for now. I've got to go for my transfer." Aran rose as his mother entered the room. "Kareen will sit with you. And we can talk more later if you wish."

Receiving no answer, he gave Kareen brief instructions, then left, heading for the room just down the hall where Chaynek was waiting.

"Aran, what's wrong?" Immediately Chaynek enveloped the channel in a comforting field as he led him to the transfer couch.

"I'm beginning to think that I should train him no matter what," Aran muttered softly as he allowed himself to be settled, his Donor by his side.

"What in shen are you talking about?"

"I'm talking about Frevven." Succinctly the channel explained what had just happened. "Damnit, Chaynek, the kid is willing to die for what he wants."

"That doesn't mean that training him is in his best interests." Chaynek's nager became guarded.

"Who are you to say?" the channel challenged.

"Sectuib Aran, please. You're overdue for your transfer. Let me—" Chaynek reached for Aran's hands, but the channel pulled away.

"Don't patronize me. You weren't there. You don't know how much he's hurting."

When the Gen didn't answer, Aran began to zlin. "All right, something's on your mind. What?"

"I'm worried about Frevven, just as you are. But this isn't the time to discuss it. Let me serve you first." Again reaching for Aran's arms, Chaynek gently massaged the lateral sheaths, encouraging the tentacles to emerge.

"Very well then, get on with it. But afterwards you're talking." Knowing that Chaynek could be very determined in the pursuit of his duty, Aran surrendered, letting his tentacles lightly caress the Gen's wrists.

A faint smile crossed Chaynek's lips. "Truly, Aran, you're so tense you wouldn't get any real satisfaction from our transfer. Let me work a little. Just a little."

Suddenly extending his handling tentacles, Aran immobilized the Gen's fingers. "I said don't be patronizing. It's your evasiveness that's making me tense. What are you hiding anyway? Don't you agree with me?"

Chaynek relaxed completely, though the channel could see he was making a tremendous effort, giving Aran an amused smile. "I said I'd explain after our transfer. This isn't the best time to argue. Now, are you going to be stubborn and deny me a perfect Chanel transfer?"

Aran was silent a moment, exploring the emotion in the Gen's nager, reading only friendship and an intense desire to serve. Whatever Chaynek was hiding, he was doing a very good job of it. Releasing the Gen, Aran made a conscious effort to relax. "Better than at Zeor?" He attempted a teasing tone.

"Well, different anyway. Chanel has a certain style, a flair. I can't explain what it is, but it's there."

"Um." Aran closed his eyes as the Gen went to work, giving himself up to the comfort of Chaynek's ministrations.

After a few minutes Aran said softly, "Now, Chaynek. This is as relaxed as I'm going to get."

Obediently Chaynek held out his arms for Aran to find his transfer grip. The channel knew his Donor wasn't completely satisfied with his condition, but he didn't care. The Chanel transfer would have to wait until their next encounter. He was too concerned about Frevven to worry much about the quality of his own transfer.

As Chaynek made lip contact, Aran began his draw, swift, controlled, totally Tecton in nature. The transfer left him full of selyn, satisfied, and yet not satisfied.

Chaynek frowned as the channel retracted his tentacles. "Was that necessary, Sectuib Aran?"

Aran shrugged, "If you're going to play games—" His eyes widened as the Gen dropped the tight control he'd been maintaining on his nager. Chaynek was as worried and concerned as he was.

"I guess I owe you an apology," the channel said softly.

"No, I was holding out on you. I didn't want to spoil your transfer completely." Chaynek took a deep breath. "We received a letter from Controller Sunlan this morning."

"He turned down my request for a hearing, didn't he?" As the Gen nodded, Aran slammed his fist against the side of the couch. "Shidoni! What do I do now? Chaynek, not training Frevven is pure shen. Do you know why he wants to be a channel so badly?"

"I have a pretty good idea. So does Muryin. But you can't do it."

"Oh, Chaynek, don't tell me what to do." Against his will, Aran began to cry, for Frevven, and for his own helplessness to do anything to ease the younger channel's pain.

"I'm sorry," replied the Gen softly as he handed Aran a clean hand-kerchief. "I wasn't trying to give you advice. But Aran, you are reacting emotionally now. Not a good way to make such an important decision."

"And you're being logical, I suppose?" Aran blew his nose.

Chaynek squirmed. "I admit I'm having trouble."

"You really care for Frevven, don't you?"

The Gen nodded. "Yes, I do. That's what makes it so hard. I'd like to agree with you. But the studies Zeor has done—" He forced a grin. "That argument isn't going to impress you, is it?"

The channel ignored the question. "He should be trained." Aran's voice held a conviction that made the Gen tense.

"No, he shouldn't. He—" Chaynek stared at the channel a minute. "You're not seriously considering —"

"Why not?" snapped Aran. "Maybe Kareen's right. Maybe not train-ing him is unnecessarily cruel."

"Sectuib Aran, I hate to argue with you when you're post..." He hesitated a moment as the channel laughed mirthlessly.

"Post, shen. That's the worst transfer we've ever had."

"Nevertheless, you won't be doing Frevven any favors if you train him."

Rising, Aran stared at the Gen a moment. "That's a matter of opinion. If I thought he could handle the pressure I'd honor my oath to Chanel, train him, and to hell with the Tecton. But— oh, never mind. I'm not thinking clearly. You're probably right. Frevven couldn't handle it." He left the room before Chaynek could reply and returned to his office.

Taking his seat behind his desk, Aran glumly contemplated the stack of case files before him, all requiring a Controller's decision.

Oh, Frevven, I wish I could give you what you want. I hope you never know how much it hurts, to deny you what should be yours by right. Aloud he said, "But I have no choice. The Tecton stands against the Kill. I can't do anything to jeopardize that." He sighed deeply as he chose a file from the big pile. "If only I could be as sure as you are that you'll never Kill again."

Shaking his head, he attempted, not entirely successfully, to banish Frevven from his thoughts in order to better concentrate on his many other problems.

* * * *

The next few days passed uncomfortably for everyone. Though Frevven stabilized physically, he was very miserable and still refused to cooperate with Aran or the Orientation Center staff. Aran himself began to slide into depression in response to Frevven's misery. Being naturally empathic, he found himself more and more involved emotionally with the young channel in his care, and more and more inclined to do what his heart dictated. But that would not be a wise move and he knew it. So he hung on grimly, continuing to try to change Frevven's mind, though he knew that, too, was likely to be a losing battle.

One day he was outside the Center's garden area when the wind began to pick up. *Uh-oh! Feels like a tornado coming.*

Running back to the center under augmentation, Aran shouted crisp orders to the gardeners to get inside. As he did so, the sky turned a very violent shade of sickly green. Turbulent clouds scooted overhead, twisting and turning in savage fury. In the distance he could see several funnel clouds, grey twisted tentacles of destruction reaching down from the sky to devastate the ground below.

He was met in the hall by his secretary. "Hajene, the emergency bell's ringing! Funnel clouds have been sighted!"

"I know. I saw them. Is everyone safely inside?"

Before she could reply, there was a tremendous crash. The old building began to vibrate alarmingly, as the glass broke in several windows, sending shards in every direction.

"Get down!" yelled Aran, taking a dive for the floor himself.

The roaring and shaking seemed to go on forever, then suddenly everything was quiet.

Aran rose and zlinned the people in the area. Miraculously, there were no injuries. "All right, everybody. Let's get to work."

Aran issued orders for his channels to make a quick check on all the patients and visitors currently in the Center, then assemble in the reception area with emergency gear.

Running across the street with his channels, Aran paused a moment to assess the situation.

Though he had seen the aftermath of tornadoes before, he was shocked at the extent of the destruction. Every building on the First Year School Campus had suffered some damage, with some completely blown away. Only the Orientation Center and the Sime Center had survived unscathed. Debris was everywhere. The street was torn up in places, as if an avenging angel had passed by, destroying everything in its wake. The pain and fear in the ambient was overwhelming.

For the next several hours Aran was busy directing rescue operations and healing the injured. Fortunately, there were only a few deaths.

As things were winding down, Chaynek reported that Frevven wasn't in his room.

"Then where in shen is he?" snapped a suddenly worried channel.

"Probably he's out helping the rescue teams, but I'm not sure where."

Aran considered a moment. "He shouldn't be exposed to all this, in his condition. But I doubt if he'd come back for anyone else. I'll look for him myself."

But it was longer than he expected before Aran could turn control of the rescue effort over to another channel and search for Frevven.

After questioning several people, he discovered that Frevven had last been seen heading off in the direction of faculty row at the far end of the campus.

Going in that direction himself, Aran zlinned something abnormal. Breaking into an augmented run, he rounded a corner.

Almost a block away, an injured Gen woman lay half covered with the remains of a collapsed porch, projecting pain from a shattered leg mixed with stark terror. A channel — no, two channels — stood facing each other, both in Killmode and fixed on the Gen. With a sinking heart, Aran recognized them as Frevven and Trazee.

Letting his showfield rise to pure Genness, Aran ran still faster, hoping against hope he could entice them away from their intended victim. But he was too far away to have much effect.

Even if he could reach them in time, if he intercepted one of the youngsters, the other would go for the woman before he could stop him. The only hope was that Trazee would pull out of it and somehow manage to stop Frevven. After all, Trazee had started his training, and though Aran knew he hadn't had his anti-Kill conditioning yet, he should have some self-control. Frevven certainly couldn't be expected to do it.

Time seemed to stand still for Aran as he zlinned the delicate balance of terror between the two boys and the Gen. He wouldn't get there in time. One of them would attack the woman any second now.

Come on, Trazee! You can do it!

Then Frevven moved towards the Gen, tentacles reaching for her arms. Aran groaned. A little longer and he could have been there—

Dancing lightly on his feet, Trazee cut Frevven off, moving between him and the Gen.

Frevven feinted to the left, trying to get past Trazee, but Trazee moved to block him. The two young channels squared off again.

Suddenly, Frevven's field went quickly, even violently, from Sime Killmode to the Gen simulation and enticement of a working channel.

Aran's breath caught in his throat. What he was seeing was impossible, and yet—

Trazee hesitated. He had a clear shot at the injured Gen, but he turned towards Frevven, wavering between two potential victims.

But Frevven hadn't enough selyn in his secondary system to serve another channel. Surely he must realize that. Trazee would Kill him.

If Frevven knew that, it didn't seem to make much difference. He stood his ground, still projecting Gen. And the simulated Gen terror in Frevven's field was enough to overwhelm the flesh and blood Gen woman's nager entirely. Trazee leaped on Frevven, his face set in an expression of feral greed.

Aran was almost upon them now, but Frevven didn't seem to be aware of his presence. He was set to try to serve Trazee and never mind that he'd die trying.

Aran pulled the two channels apart, shoving Frevven roughly backwards and taking Trazee in transfer position. He poured selyn into the boy before he'd even begun to react to being shenned out of the transfer with Frevven.

"Hajene, wha-what happened?" Trazee came out of transfer confused at finding himself in the Controller's arms.

Releasing him, Aran said softly, "Frevven kept you from Killing again, then I shenned you out of a transfer with him to serve you myself."

Trazee groaned as he put a hand to his head. "No wonder I feel terrible."

"You'll live," replied Aran wryly. "Now go get some help. We require another channel and a stretcher. Fast!"

"Yes, Hajene."

As Trazee ran away, Aran went to the injured woman, who was now unconscious. He examined her, then carefully freed her from the wreckage.

Then he returned to sit by Frevven, who was sprawled semi-conscious on the ground. Gingerly he made nageric contact as he worked to assist Frevven in recovery.

Now that the immediate crisis was over, it hit him just what an incredible thing Frevven had done. With no training or conditioning, he had acted in a manner worthy of Aran's finest channels. *I have to train him now, or I'm not worthy of the title of Sectuib in Chanel.*

Gently, he helped Frevven to sit up.

"Trazee. Did he—?" Frevven adjusted his glasses as he met Aran's eyes. "The Gen—?"

Aran smiled reassuringly. "The Gen's fine, and so is Trazee. I got here in time to shen him out of his attack on you and serve him transfer. Do you realize you could have gotten Killed?"

"I really didn't care. I just couldn't let him Kill that Gen. He didn't want to Hajene, not really." Frevven wearily rested his aching head on Aran's shoulder. "I suppose I'm in trouble again?"

"No. I would be a fool to chastise you for what you just did. But I have decided—"

"What?" Frevven interrupted warily, raising his head to stare at the older channel.

Aran took a deep breath. "If you still want to be a working channel, I'm going to do what I can to bring that about. Bear in mind that I can't promise you I'll succeed. The Tecton could overrule me. But I'm prepared to offer you a choice. Either I can serve you here and now, and you can forget about training, or I can arrange a qualifying transfer with Kareen. That could be dangerous if I'm later overruled. It's your decision."

Frevven was stunned. "Why, Aran, why? You've been telling me it's impossible."

"I would have done this all along, Frevven, if I had thought you could handle it. Now I'm sure."

"But won't you get into trouble?"

"Don't worry about me. Do you want to take the risks?"

"But the Tecton—"

"I am ambrov Chanel. Tecton rules and regulations just don't mean as much to me as doing what I know in my heart is right."

Frevven absorbed the significance of that quiet statement. "I'll do it, no matter what," he replied.

Aran nodded. He had expected no other answer. "Help is coming," he said softly. "Let's go back to the Center and arrange that transfer."

It wasn't quite that simple. A million and one details clamored for Aran's attention when he and Frevven finally made it back to the Center. But he refused to get involved, insisting that his senior channels continue to direct the rescue operations while he accompanied Frevven to the transfer room and sent for Kareen.

Ignoring his mother's smug "told you so" look as she quietly entered the room, Aran took a seat by Frevven's side and reached for his hands. "Since this is going to be your qualifying transfer, I'm going to take readings before and after to determine your rating."

Frevven nodded and silently extended his laterals. Aran made lip contact then released him.

Relinquishing his position to Kareen, Aran retreated to a corner of the room and watched as Kareen took Frevven in transfer position.

"Now, Frevven," she said with a smile. "I want you to know that I'm a First Order Donor. Nothing you can do will hurt me."

"I know," whispered the boy just before he made lip contact.

The transfer went surprisingly well, though at first Aran thought Frevven's tight control would prevent him from getting much pleasure from it. Then, half way through, Aran zlinned Frevven's delighted response to the extra dimension of concerned, loving, personal compassion Kareen was feeding him along with the selyn; the extra dimension of a Chanel transfer. The young channel relaxed and, while he didn't relinquish complete control, he moved with his Donor into the spiraling peaks of shared pleasure that culminated the transfer.

Aran chuckled as he moved in to sit by Frevven. "That wasn't what I ordered, Mother."

"I know," replied the Gen complacently. "But I may never get another chance." She smiled at Frevven who was staring at her in wonder. "How are you feeling now?"

"That was — is it always like that?"

Ruffling his hair in a motherly gesture, Kareen said regretfully, "I'm afraid not, honey. What we shared was unique. Call it a Chanel specialty."

Aran held out his hands. "You're a working channel now, Frevven. See if you can link fields with me." As the younger channel put his hands in Aran's, their fields merged in the unparalleled timeless communion of working channels.

Frevven's eyes widened. "Hajene," he whispered in sheer delight.

"I know. Welcome to the club." Aran, pleased to be the first to welcome Frevven to the fraternity of channels, made brief lip contact then smiled warmly at the younger channel, now his colleague.

"Congratulations. You're now officially a Third Order channel. Roughly mid-range. You might even be able to make Second Order someday."

Tears filled Frevven's eyes. "Thank you, Aran. I — I —"

Blinking back his own tears of happiness, Aran took Frevven in his arms, enveloping him in a field of friendly compassion. "Don't thank me. You did this yourself." He held the boy a few minutes longer, then said softly, "I have to go back to work now. But Kareen will stay with you as long as you want her. Come to my office later and we'll see about getting your training started."

"Yes, Hajene," Frevven whispered as Aran relinquished him to the waiting Gen. Reluctantly, Aran returned to dealing with the effects of the tornado.

* * * *

The next day Aran personally enrolled Frevven in the First Year School. Though most of the buildings were damaged in some way, the instructors found new locations and resumed classes immediately, though not without some grumbling about having to work around reconstruction projects.

A few days later Controller Sunlan arrived for a routine inspection, and put an end to Aran's good mood. For a while the District Controller was kept busy with the aftermath of the disaster, but Aran knew the calm couldn't last forever. Late the next afternoon, Sunlan burst into Aran's office, Frevven's file in his hand.

He threw it violently onto Aran's desk. "What's the meaning of this?"

Aran smiled placatingly. "We're training a new channel. What's wrong with that?"

"A disjunct channel. You know that's against the rules."

Aran shook his head. "No, Controller. Against policy, perhaps, but not against the rules."

Sunlan's lips tightened. "It's against the rules to train a disjunct channel without the District Controller's permission. You don't have mine." He took the chair by Aran's desk. "I want you to stop his training immediately and put him back into secondary dormancy."

"Why?" asked Aran. "Why should it matter to you? I mean, so we train one more disjunct channel. Is that such a catastrophe?"

Sunlan sighed. "I know you don't care much for politics, but you might at least pay attention to current events. I'm up for re-election in a few months. If the newspapers find out we're training a disjunct, in defiance of policy, they'll have a field day. It could cost me the election. So he's not going to be trained."

"Yes, he is," replied Aran firmly. "I'm not going to sacrifice his future for your career."

"Then it'll be your career for his future. I'll relieve you of duty here and now, and re-assign you somewhere out-Territory. Then I'll take care of Alymeer myself."

"Oh, no, you won't," replied Aran calmly. "I can't let that happen. Perhaps we should discuss this with the Territory Controller. If I were to ask him to convene the board you refused permission for—" He let his voice trail off meaningfully.

"You wouldn't dare!"

"Zlin me and tell me I wouldn't." Aran put as much firmness into his nager as he could.

Sunlan was silent for a long moment. Finally, he spoke. "All right, all right. Publicity is the last thing I want right now. I'll sign the necessary permission, on two conditions. One, you voluntarily resign your position as Controller and accept a disciplinary assignment out-Territory. And, secondly, you send Alymeer to Desmaines for his training, out of my district."

It was Aran's turn to hesitate. As Cedarcity Controller, he was in a position to help a lot of people. Was it really such a good idea to throw all that away for one person, no matter how deserving that person?

A line from an ancient book of wisdom, now part of Chanel's Book of Philosophy came into his mind. *The needs of the many must never be*

*allowed to outweigh the needs of the few or the one, else we lose our
basic humanity.*

Resolutely, he met Sunlan's eyes. "You have a deal, Controller. My resignation will be on your desk in the morning."

Sunlan rose, smugly satisfied. "You're a fool, Sectuib Chanel. A real fool." He left the office without another word.

Aran rested his head on folded arms and gave in to the tears. Leaving Cedarcity would be one of the hardest things he'd ever had to do.

He raised his head as he zlinned a familiar nager. Chaynek was quietly entering the room.

"Aran, I just saw Sunlan in the hall. He was looking awfully pleased with himself and rather snottily suggested you might require the services of a Donor."

"Well, I could use a friend," Aran said softly as he wiped the tears from his eyes. Waving the Gen to a seat, he summarized his conversation with the District Controller.

"You knew this might happen. Is it worth it?"

"Yes. If Frevven succeeds as a channel, it'll be worth it. Even if he doesn't — I did honor my oath to Chanel. Tell me something, Chaynek. Does your oath to Zeor ever get in the way of your pledge to the Tecton?"

"Not so far. But then a Donor doesn't have to make the decisions a channel does. That might be a question for Muryin."

"Um. I just might take it up with her someday. In the meantime, I have an idea."

"What?" asked the Gen, warily.

"Do you think you can wangle an assignment at the Desmaines training facility? I know they're looking for First Order Donors for their faculty. You can tip the scales in Frevven's favor. It's going to be very hard for him to succeed." He paused a moment. "Sunlan's seen to it that I can't help him anymore," he finished bitterly.

"Truly, Aran, Frevven isn't going to like this," Chaynek replied. "He'd be quite content never to see me again."

"Yes, I know. But with you pushing him to accomplish all he can—"

Chaynek shook his head ruefully. "I've got to keep playing the bad guy, don't I? The stern taskmaker that he can't stand. I don't dare tell him how much I—"

Aran nodded as Chaynek's voice trailed off, acutely aware of the pain in the Gen's nager. "He'll have a better chance if he's challenged to prove himself. I've seen it work before. He'll succeed, my friend; if for no other reason than to prove you wrong."

Chaynek forced a smile. "I'll speak to Muryin. I'm sure she'll agree and arrange my assignment."

Aran nodded, satisfied. He'd done the best he could. Now it was up to Frevven.

The next day Frevven came to Aran's office to say goodbye before boarding the stage for Desmaines.

The youngster's nager was filled with guilty regret. "I never meant for it to turn out this way," he said softly. "Costing you your post and all. It's not worth it, just for me."

Deeply moved, Aran went around his desk to take Frevven's hands and merge fields one last time. "Don't ever say that, Frevven. I'm Sectuib in Chanel. My House is dedicated to helping the one, for only in this way can the many be strong. I did what I had to do."

"I understand, Sectuib Aran," Frevven replied, subdued. "But it still seems unfair."

Aran forced a grin. "Don't worry about me. I'll manage. And one way or another I'll get my Center back. You'd better go now. The stage is waiting."

"I suppose." Reluctantly, Frevven headed for the door. Then he turned back and ran over to Aran. Throwing his arms around the other channel, he declared fervently, "I'll make you proud of me someday, Aran. I swear it."

Aran hugged him tightly. "I know you will, Frevven. I know you will."

Andrea Alton has written for *A Companion in Zeor* in the past, and we are delighted to have her participation in the Anthology after many years' absence.

The characters in her many stories, which include "Belling The Cat," "Icy Nager," "Partners," and "Dunbren,"— all of which can be found through the *A Companion in Zeor* website, have Sime~Gen abilities and methods of transfer that differ from those explored in the published novels (canon) and in much of the rest of our fan fiction.

This is attributed to a different culture and training methods for the Simes and Gens in Andrea's writings.

Her work is entertaining, and these differences should not detract from your enjoyment of *The Gift of Alauno Light*.

THE GIFT OF ALAUNO LIGHT

ANDREA ALTON

Boy opened his eyes to the absolute darkness around him, returning from wherever his mind had gone wandering. He heard himself muttering the phrases his mother taught him when he was scarcely more than a baby. Genish words. The sound gave him a moment of stomach clenching fear. He'd received the worst beatings from his father those times when, as a young child, he'd used a word that was not Simelan.

His father's beatings had been meant to make him forget those Genish phrases. It had not worked. Those words were the only anchors he had to memories of being cuddled while a soft gentle voice spoke above him. His only surety that once he'd been loved. He did not know what those words meant. As a child he clung to those sounds with the tenacity of a shipwrecked sailor clutching a mast. He told them over to himself every night when he knew his father slept, whispering nearly soundlessly with his head under the covers.

For a moment he was lost in a confusion of past and present, then sorted the pain into the pain in his broken leg where an ancient wooden support pinned him to the uneven cold rock; followed by thirst, and then, far from the least of it, the rising urgency of Need skittering down his nerves like white hot ants.

He'd done everything he could to free himself. His efforts hadn't served. He was going into Need. All that was left was the waiting…

And the Remembering.

* * * *

From his work as a Junker he'd picked up quite a bit of the Gen language, both written and spoken, but for all the time he'd spent in Gen territory, he had heard only a few of those precious words spoken by a Gen. Nevertheless her words were Genish. Their meaning was Genish. He knew this, because her words weren't Simelan. Therefore, she would have been Gen, and, therefore, kept in a Pen with no escape. She would be long dead by now, he thought suddenly. All he had of her was her voice and her words which would die with him. Her gift unused. Her words unspoken. Her life erased along with his.

Staring into the dark, he wondered why those words had been so important to her that she made sure he would remember them. Suddenly his tentacles spasmed. Selyn rose in lazy spirals from the tips of his tentacles, little wispy ghosts only apparent because he lay in absolute darkness. It put him in mind of butterflies and moths taking wing.

Words also, could take wing. Could fly elsewhere. Could be heard and understood, and perhaps added to other words, and produce offspring. His mother's words could take flight. All he had to do was set them free.

His father would so hate that.

With a blurry sense of great and grand freedom he shouted his few Genish phrases until the tunnel rang with them. Stopping to take a breath he could hear a distant ominous cracking and then, closer, the quiet slither and slide of rock and dust falling from gently creaking tunnel supports. He laid back, mouth bone dry, shaky from Need and pain, and decided he'd probably freed a flock of Gen words, several times over.

Was he hallucinating? The mine tunnel seemed to be glowing with a haze of light. The effect of his mother's words? Or...

He leaned back with a sigh. Nothing magical here. There was merely a very high field Gen loose in the mine. He could hear the faint sound of footsteps coming toward him from the entrance. Oh, joy. Now stretching before him like a macabre banquet was the choice between dying of thirst, loss of selyn, crushed under a half mile of rock, being shot, stabbed, or beaten to death. On the tail of that thought, the wavering flame of a torch blinded him.

A deep voice called out in the Gen language, "Hallo....? Do you need help?"

Help? Feeling himself on the raw edge of hysteria, he muttered, "Come closer, my Precious," repeating something his friend O-onry, had, for some reason, always thought amusing. "I'm caught under a support beam," he called back in the same language. It was so dark in here, a Gen wouldn't see his tentacles even if he waved them in front of his nose. "Thank you, Ma," he breathed into the darkness, feeling the ronaplin wetting his arms, preparing him for a Kill.

The light moved closer, carried by a tall, stocky, wide shouldered shape wearing a heavy jacket. A broad brimmed hat obscured most of his face except for a square chin, dark and bristly with several days' growth of whiskers. Calmly the Gen walked toward him, his nager steady. On his hip, under the jacket, an occasional glint of metal told of either a knife or a handgun. The Gen stopped near the end of the beam, just out of reach, and with the torch held high, stood contemplating the situation before swinging a canteen off his shoulder and dropping it within Boy's reach. From the way it sloshed as he unscrewed the lid, he knew it was full. Boy drank about half of it before putting the screw top back on.

"How bad are you hurt?" the Gen asked.

* * * *

That close, the Gen's high field, strong and steady, bumped against his field, like a dog nudging for attention. Selyn flowed lightly as golden perfume over Boy's tattered nerves. He'd never felt anything like it and wanted it more than he'd ever wanted anything in his life.

The Gen spoke sharply, asking a question he'd apparently already asked at least once. "The leg...how bad?"

"Broken."

"Well, let's see what we can do about this..." Carefully sticking the torch into a hole in the wall, the Gen wrapped his arms around the beam and strained upward. The wood shifted an inch off Boy's leg. "Stick a rock under the post," the Gen ordered, in a strained voice. "To take the weight."

Boy scrabbled in the debris near him, found one that felt right, thick, but flat. He leaned forward, the movement escalating the pain as it pulled the leg. He tried to push the rock under the wood, but it needed more room. "Higher?" he suggested, gasping.

With a groan, the Gen straightened his legs, the wood came up a bit and Boy, with a sense of deep relief, pushed the rock under, felt the wood come down and *Oh, Glorious*, the wracking, throbbing pain was dulled. He fell back, panting.

Coming closer, the Gen crouched down...but still just out of Boy's reach. "One end of the beam is wedged up against the wall. We'll try again, in a bit." Giving a nod, in Boy's direction, added, "I'm Gordy Merryweather of Wide Plains Sept. Who are you?"

Boy offered up the Gen word he'd long since chosen for situations like this. "Banjo."

The Gen sucked a tooth, looking thoughtful. "Banjo what?"

The Gen was demanding a last name. Gens so seldom did this. His mind went blank. He grabbed the first Gen word that came to him. "Music."

"Banjo... Music." Gordy repeated, in an introspective tone, followed by another tooth sucking pause. Suddenly the Gen stood, making Boy flinch. He took down his torch and holding the light where it could fall on Boy's face, looked down at him, his expression intent, his nager sharpening. The Gen's attention spurred Need unbearably. The Gen did something, and the scream of Need subsided. Replacing the torch, apparently satisfied about something, the Gen squatted beside Boy.

Boy forced himself to stillness, heart thudded with growing anxiety. He suspected what little hold he'd had over the situation had just evaporated. He didn't know how or why, only that the Gen knew, and was thinking of doing...something.

Ignoring him, the Gen, studied the new fallen rocks in the tunnel and around where Boy lay. "You from the Quachita Mountains?" He sounded as if he were just making small talk, but his nager had shifted once again. Changed in a way Boy had never felt before.

To answer could be to set off a trap, but so would not answering. Truthfully he replied, "No."

"I only ask because you have the look of the Quachita Cherokee. It's the cheekbones." Pause. "Their territory is about five hundred miles from here." Another pause. "There's no clan there with a last name of 'Music.'"

"What are you accusing me of?"

"Not being named Banjo Music for one thing."

His heart thudded painfully. Carefully, keeping his voice level Boy asked, "What would be the second thing?"

"Trying to pass yourself off as Gen," was the placid reply.

Boy's heart thudded so hard it hurt. "What..."

The Gen held up a restraining hand. "Don't try to deny it. The closer I get to you, the faster your tentacles slide in and out. You're going into Attrition. Before we get you out of here, we'll have to do something about that."

Boy was shocked numb, and currently, somewhere on the other side of fear. He watched as the big Gen slipped off his coat, rolling up his shirt sleeves in a businesslike manner. "What are you going to do to me?" He congratulated himself on sounding so calm.

"I'm going to give you a transfer."

"Huh...!" He was so surprised he felt gut punched. "You'll die," Boy said flatly.

"Had years of bad transfers, have you?"

"If by bad, you mean they died. Then, yes."

"I'm a Merryweather. We don't die easy."

"What you are is three wheels short of a wagon."

"We'll find out, won't we?" Unperturbed, the Gen held out his arms.

Unable to stop himself Boy grabbed his wrists. Tentacles flashed out of hiding, wrapping fiercely around the Gen's well-muscled forearms. When nothing happened Boy snarled. "You going to let me draw or just talk me to death?"

The other shrugged. "This has to be done slowly. You've never had a Merryweather Gen before."

Made desperate by fear, Boy hardly heard the Gen's warning. His body grabbed at the selyn with greedy insistence.

And still nothing happened.

No. Not nothing. A tiny trickle of selyn seeped gently into his ravaged nerves. His attention focused on that golden thread, and everything else faded to smoke.

The Gen's approval manifested in an increased flow of selyn. Boy wanted that approval.

Every Kill Boy had ever taken had thudded into his body. It felt as if he was being hit with a wall of mud slamming flint shards into his nerves. This was so different, his whole attention focused on the golden movement — and he felt the tendrils of surprise and maybe a bit of sorrow etch into the flow.

This was the best selyn he'd ever gotten and at every moment he expected the slashing pain that had never failed to accompany a Kill. Yet, the soothing, sating, beauty went on and on. Boy could never exactly say how long it lasted when there was a loud CRACK and a shower of dirt. The Gen jumped slightly. The transfer ended then...but not abruptly. Smoothly, gently.

"So now we're done here...."

"And you're going to finish by slitting my throat..." Boy snarled, angry because now he knew what he'd been missing all his life and was deeply resentful at its loss, as well as frightened.

"Now that would just be a waste of my energy," Gordy said, already moving a larger rock to the beam. He shoved the rock under the wood with one hand and heaved. "Get your leg out!"

"Hey! A few minutes ago you were scarcely able to shift the beam with both arms!"

"I lied." There was long roar of a distant collapse in the depths of the mine. "Move! Move!" Gordy urged.

Boy scooted free, seeing but not feeling the leg scrape against the splintered beam. Rolling onto his stomach pulling himself over the debris to the rough wall, and with selyn coursing through him lifted himself onto a rock in the light from the torch. There he sat, zlinning through the thickening dust, feeling the sharp throb of agony in his leg and wondering how he was going to get to the entrance.

A strong hand was extended. He took it, and was pulled up to be half carried down the tunnel where dust hazed the distant sunlit entrance. Around them the cracking, rumbling sounds got stronger. "Seems the mine is going," Gordy said matter-of-factly, just as he stumbled, tripping over a pile of rocks Boy could clearly zlin.

The Gen was blind in the dark. Gens didn't zlin. Ahead, the way out was a tangle of fallen supports. Behind them dust rolled up from the depths. But, just a few steps ahead there was a side tunnel he'd made note of on his way in. The Gen couldn't see it. "Listen you," he snarled. "Go ahead two steps, turn to your right."

The Gen moved, following instructions.

"Keep going, it has a clean floor. It's narrow," he shouted above the increasing noise level, putting out a hand to keep them from running into a wall. "It starts to rise about six steps ahead…"

Supporting Boy with one arm around him Gordy followed the directions Boy shouted. The ground shook, the tunnel roared and around them dust and pebbles fell like rain. Up they went, with the ceiling ever lower. Gordy kept hitting his head until Boy feared the Gen would knock himself out. Boy yelled at him when to duck. As they struggled upward, the Gen's breathing was coming rough and labored. They spilled out of the dust laden darkness, into the air, collapsing onto a rock shelf covered thinly with grass. Dust and rock shards slid off them as Gordy regained his feet, pulling Boy up with him, and limped up a path that went off at an angle into the forest. Finally the Gen stopped beside a group of trees, letting Boy lean against a trunk, while he bent over, hands on his knees, breathing hard, and spitting dirt. They took stock of each other in the sunlight.

"Yep, Boy, you've got the Cherokee nose, as well as the cheekbones."

"You look like a hairy red bear," snarled Boy in return. In the sun, Gordy had a thick head of curly red hair, and several days' growth of an equally red beard. For a moment Boy, who had never seen a redhead, thought the Gen was on fire because of the white-hot gold of that nager.

Then the earth shook and a deafening roar belched dust, rock, bits of shredded wood and oddly, a child's doll, out into the flat apron in front of what had, until that moment, been the mine entrance, below them. They were knocked to the ground, where they lay watching the trees sway and feeling the earth shudder. Granite blocks cracked from the mine rock face, breaking away to tumble down the mountain below them, leaving a wide swath of crushed trees in their wake.

Boy, teeth clenched against the pain in his leg, dragged himself toward Gordy, until he lay flat on the ground, where he was marginally more comfortable, with the weight off his leg. Gordy sat up from where the ground had tossed him, knees pulled to his chin, better to watch the continuing mayhem. After a time when the destruction eased off into the occasional explosion of rock hitting the ground below a cliff, Gordy turned to study Boy. "Well," he said finally, breaking the silence between them, "this has certainly been a day."

Boy couldn't think of any response to this, and so remained silent.

"It's as good a time as any to introduce ourselves properly. What brought me to this mine in time to whisk you out from under a mountain, was hearing you shouting out your name, your clan and your lineage. But you don't know what the words mean, because they are in a different language from either Simelan or Genish." He waited for Boy to say something.

Boy stubbornly glared at him. Waiting.

The Gen continued, as by this time Boy knew he would. "You were speaking in Cherokee. Translating from the Cherokee as we go, your name is Avrom Ten Feathers, clan Blue, of the Quachita Cherokee. Your lineage is through the Merryweather line, born of the original Alauno Light Enclave..."

Boy caught his breath as he realized the shape and weight of the gift his mother had given him. He had a name! His father had never called him anything but 'Boy,' combined with a variety of swear words. Joy welled, taking away the pain of a broken leg, and the terror of having a crazy Gen sitting just out of reach. "I am Avrom...." he whispered.

Very formally the Gen removed his wide brimmed hat, slapping it against his leg to remove a layer of mine dust. "Avrom Ten Feathers, I am Gordy Merryweather, of Three Rivers clan, Wide Plains Mizsip sept. I'm kin to you, through the Merryweather lineage, born of the original Alauno Light Enclave. There are five generations between us, but family is still family." Then the shenning bastard had the nerve to flash a satisfied and amused white grin at him.

Boy (now Avrom), couldn't find any words. He stared down the slope.

Gordy stared down the slope.

After a while the Gen shifted his position. "I'm glad I put my horse upstream from here. He should still be there." Then, without saying anything more got to his feet and walked away. Avrom stared after him, unbelieving. He didn't know if he was relieved or not. This was it? The

Gen was just going? After waiting until the other's steps faded away, he reached back under the tree, pulling at the dead stick hanging from one of the branches. Heavy and long, it would serve as a crutch.

Forcing himself to his feet, he put the stick under his arm and put his weight on it. The wood crumbled under his hand. He bit off a cry as he fell. If Gordy was near he didn't want the Gen to know he was in trouble. He was just getting himself painfully onto his good leg when Gordy returned, leading a saddled horse with a pack mule following along behind. "Where's your camp?" Gordy demanded.

Avrom sighed. He was alive, and about to lose all his stuff. Gens were all thieves. "My camp is downstream." He pointed. There didn't seem to be any choice. Gordy would find it sooner or later.

"Let's get you on the horse, and you can show me." The next thing Gordy had him in the saddle, and he was in so much pain, he was sweating and close to fainting. Distantly he heard the Gen say, "We'll see what we can do for that leg, the sooner the better. You don't want it to heal crooked."

Once they were at Avrom's camp, which Gordy said looked quite comfortable, he helped Avrom onto Avrom's bedroll. Then he knelt beside the broken leg, hand hovering over it, looking into the distance as if he were contemplating something rare and fine. Suddenly one hand was pulling at his ankle and the other pushing. Through the screaming pain Avrom felt a 'click' in the bone. "What did you do!" he howled.

"Set it. Seemed best not to tell you ahead of time. Now…stop flailing those tentacles before you get them in knots," he said irritably. "I've got to focus down."

Too sick to do anything else, Avrom let Gordy have his way. Again the Gen held one hand over the break. After a moment, Avrom felt the most amazing warmth enter his leg, stealing away the pain, leaving him with a fading memory of the previous agony. Then the Gen's hands came up, hovered over his face, and feeling sleepy, and oddly, safe, he closed his eyes. Warmth ran like soft threads through his body. For a time the sensation was mostly in his arms, and then crept down his body, until it seemed to him he was glowing, outlined from the inside out.

Avrom opened his eyes. He felt amazingly comfortable. It was night. He had a blanket over him. There was a fire not far away and the Gen was seated beside it. He was eating something from a tin plate. "You're still here."

"Ayuh," the Gen said, "You're hurt too bad for me to just go off and leave you…"

"That's all right. I can manage," Avrom broke in quickly.

Gordy's attention snapped away from Avrom, fixed on a distant tree or something. The searing, cold, aching void of Attrition paralyzed Avrom, and he slammed hyperconscious.

A moment later, the golden attention swept back over him and the Gen's voice crept into his awareness.

"You can manage? Really?"

Avrom shook his head, wondering what had just happened.

"I've decided to stick around to take care of you. Besides," Gordy added brightly, "that will give us time to teach you the proper way of taking selyn from a donor."

Something in the Gen's voice made the words sound vaguely like a threat. Deciding he'd all the excitement he could stand for one day, Boy pulled the blankets over his head, snuggling down into the warmth. "I am Avrom Two Feathers of the Blue clan," he whispered in Genish. "Of the Quachita Cherokee."

His mother made sure he remembered the message she gave him to carry, but it was because of Gordy he knew he had family…somewhere. He might be welcome into that family, if he didn't have to take a Kill.

What if…maybe… Perhaps…he would go and find out what it was all about?

How hard could it be to find a place called Quachita?

ABOUT THE EDITORS

Karen L. MacLeod met Jacqueline Lichtenberg at a *Star Trek* convention in 1976, reading *House of Zeor* as her introduction to Sime~Gen. Karen's editing credentials go back to 1977, working on various amateur writers' editing projects and freelance editing of various novels for Jacqueline Lichtenberg and Jean Lorrah. Karen has edited several award-winning novels for clients and publishers over the years. Authors D.H. Aire and Donna Fernstrom are among her clients. The Sime~Gen fanzine, A Companion in Zeor, which Karen has edited since its inception, followed in 1978.

Karen has also been the editorial consultant for Sime~Gen Inc. since 1996, working with manuscripts and posting information and novels to the Internet. Karen is also currently the Assistant Webmaster for the domain of simegen.com, where responsibilities include constructing and maintaining web pages, and editor in residence for the domain's World-Crafters Guild School.

Karen is a supporter of many charities and an advocate for therapeutic horseback riding. She began therapeutic horseback riding in 1989 and rode until 2006, owning her own horse for 4 years. Karen was a member of PATH INTERNATIONAL, formerly the North American Riding for the Handicapped Association, among other organizations for the disabled in the United States. Her website can be found here:

http://www.simegen.com/bios/klbio.html

Zoe Farris has been a fan of Sime~Gen since 1974. As Zoe was an avid reader of Sci-Fi and Fantasy novels, the Galaxy Book store in Sydney, Australia ordered in *House of Zeor* for her, and from the first line she was hooked.

In 1997 Zoe discovered Sime~Gen online. Being able to communicate directly with the authors, Jacqueline Lichtenberg and Jean Lorrah as well as other fans gave the series a whole new dimension for her, and she began to write fan fiction in the S~G universe. "The Legend of the Creeping Need," which is one of the stories in this book, was one of the first that she wrote for Sime~Gen and was inspired by something Jean said in an online chat session.

Zoe worked for many years as a Counsellor and helped to write and compile many books, training manuals and booklets in the field of Mental Health. During this time she also ran workshops on how to write a short story, and took part in NanoWriMo each year.

After Zoe commented on the Sime~Gen Facebook page about creating a concordance, Jacqueline asked her if she wanted to make it official. In early 2013 Zoe commenced work on the Sime~Gen Wiki and the Concordance with help from Karen, Jacqueline and Jean. After that, Zoe was asked if she would like to work on this Anthology and was all too willing to be a part of this exciting project.

Zoe is Coordinator for and administrator of the Sime~Gen Group on Facebook. at https://www.facebook.com/groups/SimeGen/. She continues writing her own fiction, as well as writing in the Sime~Gen universe.

ABOUT THE AUTHORS

Mary Lou Mendum — Mary Lou was raised in a house full of overflowing bookshelves and quickly became a voracious reader. After encountering her first S~G book at the public library during high school, she was horrified to discover that future installments would come at intervals measured in years, not days. She sat down at her typewriter to make up the slack and by some five years later, the results were coherent enough to merit publication in the S~G fanzines. She has been playing in the Borderlands S~G roleplaying cooperative since its founding. Besides writing, her hobbies include quilting, horseback riding, and birding.

Donna Fernstrom — Donna has always loved reading, wildlife, and various mystical pursuits, but never thought she had the self-discipline to be a 'real writer.' Growing up in Michigan with frequent trips to the pine woods in the Northern part of the lower peninsula, she developed a love for nature and exploration. Having lived in Wyoming, Colorado, Nebraska, and now in Virginia, only in the past 9 years was she able to finally realize her dream.

When Donna finally set aside the 'rules' and began writing, she began with fan-fiction short stories. Her tales often take a dark turn, exploring worst-case scenarios and struggles to overcome emotional trauma, even when the setting seems idyllic. Sime~Gen was her favorite series, from the first book she read (RenSime), so it's fitting that her first publicly viewable work was fan fiction set in this Book Universe.

Eliza Leahy — Eliza is an Australian writer, singer and artist. She has been described as an "eclectic mix of all that is best in both the modern and the ancient"; but as that is her own description it probably should be taken with a grain of salt. She has been a Sime~Gen fan since her collage days and is now looking forward to introducing her grandchildren to the Sime~Gen universe.

William Long — William was born in Greenwich, Connecticut, spent time in Washington State, and has lived in California for most of his adult life. William has been involved in fandom since the late 1970s;

he started in *Star Trek* fandom and has been involved in other forms as well.

William has been associated with Sime~Gen since the mid-1980s, and has read and re-read many of the books. His favorite book in the series is *Ambrov Keon* because the main character, Risa Teague, seems more real to him.

M. Alexis Pakulak (Lexie) — Lexie was trained in geology but has taught adult classes in creative writing for over two decades. She has been published in a number of magazines and websites, including Freefall, Mensa Canada Communications, and simegen.com. Since 2004, she has been a member of the Borderlands co-op fiction project, using the Internet as a tool of collaborative writing. She lives in Calgary, Alberta, with her husband, Steve, and two cats, thousands of books, and many cubic feet of unfinished handicraft projects

Zoe Farris — Zoe has been a fan of Sime~Gen since *House of Zeor* was first published. Like other fans, Zoe wonders how the Sime~Gen split would affect the lives of people living in her own country, Australia. Zoe has published information pamphlets and booklets as part of her Counselling work, and has written some unpublished non Sime~Gen works, but she prefers to explore life in her favourite Universe of Sime~Gen.

Marjorie Robbins — Marjorie Robbins joined Sime~Gen fandom more than thirty years ago, crafting her own Householding as a vehicle for fan writing. Householding Chanel (http://simegen.com/sgfandom/householding/chanel/) in the Ancient world was a loosely knit group of fans dedicated to serving the Sime~Gen universe in any way they could. Membership was open with restrictions. Fans pledged if they were interested either in roleplaying, writing, or working on simegen.com. They also had to be willing to accept what had been established for Chanel's background for any stories set in or around Chanel.

Marge crafted six stories based on her Householding, under the tutelage of Jacqueline and Jean. Two of those pieces appear in this Anthology, one of which is co-authored with K.L. Schaefer.

In 1987-88, Marge was the head of the Sime~Gen Welcommittee; an initial contact point for new people investigating Sime~Gen fandom, and the novels existing at the time. Her question and answer fanzine, Householding Chanel Inquirer was an outgrowth of Marge's work on the Welcommittee.

http://simegen.com/sgfandom/householding/chanel/hci1.html

D.H. Aire — It seems to have been destiny when D.H. Aire, whose mother was going into major surgery, was given *Channel's Destiny* by a concerned friend. As his mother recuperated, he went to the bookstore and bought every other book in the series he could find.

Decades later at WorldCon in Chicago, Aire met Jacqueline Lichtenberg and Jean Lorrah. When he learned about this anthology he had to write a story for it — and set it at Cahokia Mounds in Collinsville, Illinois, near St. Louis for several reasons. The first sci-fi convention he ever attended was Archon, which is held in Collinsville, and having been to Cahokia Mounds, he thought its history as having been the largest city in North America for going on a thousand years, and having been forgotten, made it an ideal setting for a Sime~Gen story, where our history was just as lost.

D.H. Aire is the author of the Highmage's Plight Series: *Highmage's Plight*, *Merchants and Mages*, *Human Mage*, and *Highmage*. To learn more, visit him at www.dhr2believe.net or follow him on twitter at @ dare2believe1.

Katherine X. Rylien — Katherine has enjoyed Sime~Gen fiction for over 3 decades. Friends she made through the fandom influenced her decision to move to the east coast, where she lives on a riverbank with her partner, Kerwin Schaefer. She's written other short fiction and also 3 unpublished novel manuscripts.

Katherine has also taught martial arts, flown around the midwest at the controls of a small plane, and her most recent interest is target shooting. She works in IT, currently as part of the networking team for the local hospital. Her life is not as exciting as all this makes it sound, but she's having a pretty good time.

R. K. Hageman — Rhonda of Englewood, Colorado first started writing Sime~Gen fiction (as Rhonda K. Marsh) for 'Companion in Zeor' back in 1981. She became a S~G fan in ninth grade after finding *House of Zeor* and *Unto Zeor, Forever* in the library of her junior high school. *House of Zeor* is still her favorite of the whole series. The S~G universe has played an important role in her life and the lives of some of her closest friends, who together form Householding Kelin, founded in 1981 and still going strong. Her story "Vincent of the Gate" was originally written in 1997 but never published; "More Than Meets the Eye" comes from a concept (also dating to the late 1990s) about the impact of changeover and hyperconsciousness on a teen with autism. Tenlee in "More Than Meets the Eye" was named after Tenley Albright, the U.S. Olympic figure skater.

Laurie Pollack — Laurie jokingly describes herself as "living in order to read." In particular she has always loved reading science fiction. A precocious reader, by 9 she was reading short stories by Isaac Asimov. But when in the late 1970's, as a college student, she discovered Sime~Gen, which then consisted of only a few books, she was hooked. Laurie greets with joy every new Sime~Gen book or story.

Laurie has written poetry since she learned to print at age 6. She self-published one book of her poems, "PeaceWalk," in 2006. Since then she has focused on sharing her work electronically on social media and in her blog webpoet1.wordpress.com.

"The Box" is her first Sime~Gen poem and was inspired partly by her belief in the sacredness of all human life despite the differences that may create intolerance. She lives near Philadelphia, PA with her partner of twenty years (and recently, legal spouse) Mary, and two cats who generously allow the humans to share their space.

N. Eileen O'Neill — N. Eileen O'Neill lives on the hazy boundary between dreams and reality. She has been a Sime, and a Gen; anything she writes, she has lived. Sometimes she believes she died years ago, but never realized it, or that she has never existed at all. These thoughts do not distress her. She often wears the face that you would not care to display in public, but which you would feel lost without. More of her work can be found on secretpens.org.

K. L. Schaefer—I've been an amateur writer ever since I was in my teens. Once I discovered fan fiction, I wrote in numerous universes.

It all started with Jacqueline's Sime~Gen novels, which inspired me to write my first story meant for other people to read in the fanzines, where my Frevven stories appeared. Jacqueline invests a lot of her time and energy helping and critiquing her fan writers. I would never have learned how to plot without her. I thought all one had to do was scribble down whatever stuff came to mind. Thanks, Jacqueline!

Now, with the introduction of ebooks, self-publishing is finally available to aspiring writers without tons of money, so I decided to give it my best shot with some of my original stories, and just recently, a full-length SF novel.

I write what I call Anthropological Science Fiction: no hard science, no space ships or galactic empires, and definitely no humans. I prefer to imagine what other sorts of sentient beings on faraway planets might be like, especially ones who reproduce in ways very unlike we do, and then figure out what their societal arrangements might be like as a result.

As for me personally, I live in the Sunny South, not too far from the hurricane-ridden shores of North Carolina, along with my partner, my cat, and a longtime friend.

Contact me at KLSchaefer@suddenlink.net if you'd like to know more about my SF ebooks.

Andrea Alton — Andrea was born and raised on the south side of Chicago. After moving around the country, rather more often than she liked, she returned to Illinois to settle down so far south of Chicago that she is now in a different county. Here, she has achieved a lifelong, and admittedly weird, ambition to reside in an old schoolhouse. One would think that as the daughter of a plumber, she would have paid more attention to how the shower was installed. However, it's a relatively minor inconvenience and is more than made up for by living surrounded by woods.

She graduated from ISU at Normal with a degree in "Special Ed— of the Maladjusted," which might account both for her interest in the Sime~Gen series and the characters she chooses to create. She acknowledges a great debt to Jacqueline Lichtenberg's encouragement, advice, and patience in those early days which resulted in the creation of her first novel, *Demon of Undoing*.

It is with deep enjoyment she has settled down to her computer to write a new story for this latest Sime~Gen publication.

Made in the USA
Las Vegas, NV
11 March 2023

68928932R00163